BOOK SIX IN THE WEST BADEN MURDER SERIES

The Doomsday Clock

PATRICK J. O'BRIAN

PUBLISHED BY FIDELI PUBLISHING INC.

ISBN: 978-1-60414-665-3

DEDICATION

This book is dedicated to my good friend Shane Buis who was taken from us too soon. No one was ever a greater help to me on my West Baden projects than Shane, and these books are better for having been touched by him.

THANKS

Thanks to Brad Wiemer, Barb Caster, Nannette Bell, David Blackford, Korby Sommers, Stephanie Barber, Steve DeLisle, Mike Ritchie, Tim Lee, Rick Shellabarger, Deron Clark, Brian Kidd, and Aaron "Tex" Standridge for their assistance.

Special thanks to Kendrick Shadoan at KLS Digital for creating the cover, handling photography, and doing a great job as always.

Visit www.klsdigital.com

Other novels by Patrick J. O'Brian include:

The Fallen
Reaper: Book One of the West Baden Murders Series
The Brotherhood
Retribution: Book Two of the West Baden Murders Series
Stolen Time
Sins of the Father: Book Three of the West Baden Murders Series
Six Days
Dysfunction
The Sleeping Phoenix
Snowbound: Book Four of the West Baden Murders Series
Sawmill Road
Ghosts of West Baden: Book Five of the West Baden Murders Series
Red Rain
Sin Killer
Hallowed Grounds

Non-fiction projects by Patrick J. O'Brian include:

Risen from the Ashes: The History of the West Baden Springs Hotel
Pluto in the Valley: The History of the French Lick Springs Hotel

Check out the author's other projects at
www.pjobooks.com
or look him up on Facebook.

CHAPTER 1

Todd Parish felt certain he was going to die.

Bobbing up and down on a fishing boat in the middle of October wasn't his idea of fun, but it was his job. He wasn't on a fishing trawler for fame and glory on some television show, though his assignment felt equally dangerous. Working for a billionaire he respected and admired, Parish put his life on the line for more than just a paycheck. Being one of the good guys, he wanted to do his part in hiding a majorly evil force from the world and those who would use it.

Even kill for it.

Named the *Shamrock* because its new owner wanted to pay tribute to his Irish heritage, the 174-foot trawler cut through the worst of seas without falter. Painted black with green accents, the former U.S. Navy vessel cost Henry Flanagan a small fortune four years earlier. Tired of fishing for someone else, the experienced deckhand became a green captain when he purchased the boat from a retiring captain. Though some of the superstitious fishermen thought it bad luck to repaint and rename a ship, Flanagan did just that.

Built in 1945 to serve the U.S. Navy as a fuel oil barge, the *YO-204*, like its *YO-65* class sister ships, served no real purpose to the military after World War II drew to an end. Many of the oiler boats were sunk to create artificial reefs, or used for target practice during military maneuvers. The *YO-204* escaped such a fate by random chance until it was sold in 1976 to a crab boat captain who wanted to replace his old boat. Its holding tanks were converted for storing crab and creating additional engine room, and the boat was christened *Sea Lady* by its new owner. The rest, Flanagan stated, was history.

Normally a bodyguard for his employer's son and stepdaughter, Parish took the special assignment after a sit-down meeting with the man. The terms were clear, extra pay was provided, which he considered hazard pay, and Parish was off to Alaska for the start of cod fishing season. Though he and the two men accompanying him bought a fishing vessel and its captain for the week, their intention wasn't to take anything from the sea, but rather discard a cursed item almost a century old.

Standing on the starboard side of the boat, Parish found himself clinging to the equipment normally used to lure and ensnare unsuspecting crab. Feeling rather seasick, he questioned how much longer his stomach could hold out before he upchucked over the side. Trying to keep his mind from dwelling upon the churning in his stomach, he stared up at the night sky. Instead of clear skies containing stars that winked at him, the night sky cast down angry freezing rain, adding dampness to the already brisk air. Knowing he couldn't have custom ordered more horrendous weather conditions, Parish shuddered momentarily, folding his arms as a small wave sloshed over the side. His gear blocked most of the sea water, but some droplets sneaked through small exposures, causing him to curse under his breath.

Carrying a Glock 22 semi-automatic in his shoulder holster, Parish felt like a polar bear, wearing a thick rugged weather jacket and a stocking cap. He also donned insulated rubber gloves the minute he stepped outside for some fresh air, rather than stinking up the living quarters if he vomited. A fear of the trawler being struck by a rogue wave with him trapped inside replayed through his mind, so he felt safer standing outside. He chalked up his worries to inexperience on the sea.

"You okay?" Mark Teakon asked, startling him as he joined Parish at the side railing.

"I've been better," Parish admitted.

"It's easier if you take something for it."

"Already have," Parish grumbled unhappily.

Teakon, a history professor at Amherst College in Massachusetts, partnered with Parish's employer to dispose of two gemlike cubes. While Teakon's hired gun tagged along, currently below decks, Parish acted as an armed witness to protect the cube onboard from falling into the wrong hands. The *Shamrock* needed to travel to the central most part of the Bering Sea before they tossed it overboard.

More than just a professor, Teakon took on the responsibility of hunting down cursed objects across the globe, making himself an expert on their history through written texts and experience. The death of his wife at the hands of someone possessing a cursed object prompted his research, understanding, and desire to hunt them down, keeping his teaching job as a cover once his new passion consumed him.

"How much longer before we reach the drop area?" Parish inquired.

They had already been at sea over a day.

"Another couple hours and we should be to the deepest waters."

What little bit Parish knew of the Bering Sea included the fact that it was split by an Alaskan and Russian divide. The bottom held shelves of varying depths, so Teakon wanted to find the deepest area possible before discarding the cursed object. While he asked the captain's opinion, it seemed the professor had an area in mind before they ever launched from the Alaskan coast.

Nearing sixty years of age, Teakon stood several inches shorter than Parish with a full beard peppered with brown and gray hairs. His thick head of similarly colored hair was tucked beneath a navy blue stocking cap. Reaching into the pocket of his dark pea coat, which stuck out near the waistline from his protruding belly, Teakon produced a small metallic box slightly larger than a jewelry box for a wedding ring. Constructed of lead to conceal the colorful object inside, the box felt heavy when Teakon handed it to him. Parish hated touching the cubes, having done so only a few times, because he knew what evil their users carried out to reap sinister benefits.

He still found it difficult to believe such tiny objects created so much havoc around the world, quickly handing the box back to the professor. Cursed objects offer their users a specific benefit, always requiring a sacrifice of some sort, which in this case was human life. When Parish took the job of bodyguard to two children, he was warned of danger, though he never expected such a heavy burden. Given several chances to quit or be reassigned, he chose the most dangerous possible assignment, looking at the bigger picture. With a wife and two children of his own, he wanted the world to be a safer place for them, so he put his own life at risk.

As the boat bounced from striking a wave crest, Parish clasped a bundle of nearby ropes attached to a pulley system from fear of tumbling over the side. Cursing himself for volunteering to board a boat, he wished they could have rented a helicopter or small plane and dropped the cube into the tumultuous water. Doing so, however, would have put them all at risk because certain individuals and groups wanted to possess the cubes. Renting one of the few local aircrafts risked drawing attention to their small group, so Teakon opted to lease one of the dozens of fishing trawlers heading to sea. Parish didn't much care for flying, either, so his prospects for comfortable travel appeared bleak either way.

"I can't wait to be off this thing," Parish stated sourly.

Teakon chuckled.

"It's the only way, Todd. Mr. Clouse and I agreed to this location specifically because we knew the cube would churn on the bottom until it fell into a ravine deep enough to keep it forever."

"Nothing's forever," Parish said grimly.

"Yeah, I know," Teakon conceded. "Some scientists believe man crossed the Bering Strait on foot during the last ice age, migrating from Asia to North America. Though we'll never see it, the Earth is constantly shifting and adjusting."

"Dust in the wind, right?"

Teakon nodded.

"Something like that. Are you a religious man, Todd?"

"Yes. I go to church on Sundays and say my prayers."

"Has your experience with these objects changed your perspective?"

"It's affirmed my beliefs," Parish said before another small wave jolted the boat, causing him to tighten his death grip on the ropes. "If there was no heaven and hell, where would such evil objects come from?"

Teakon never found time enough to reply as the distant sound of helicopter rotors pierced the turbulent sloshing of waves against the trawler and the deafening rain around them. Parish immediately suspected the aircraft was closer than the sound indicated, proven correct when he spied red and white lights overhead in the distance.

Greg Slone, a former military man who protected Teakon on the more dangerous assignments, appeared in the doorway from the staging area where deckhands often changed their gear. Dressed for the inclement weather, carrying an automatic weapon like the guns often toted by SWAT team members, he tilted his head toward the sound.

"If that's not the Coast Guard, we're in trouble," Slone stated with his usual stone-faced expression, pulling a pair of binoculars from his gear to examine the helicopter more closely. "Shit."

Teakon turned pale, obviously not expecting to have their transportation discovered, much less invaded, before disposing of the cube. He looked over the side of the boat as though contemplating tossing the encased cube immediately.

"You have to," Parish insisted.

Instead, Teakon looked to Slone for advice.

"Modified civilian chopper," Slone reported. "At least four onboard."

"They have to be searching blindly," Parish reasoned aloud. "How could they know which boat we took?"

"The name on the side is a start if someone blabbed about three guys leasing a boat without a crew."

Either someone in the helicopter knew the boat by name, or the aircraft simply went from boat to boat, hoping to spy Teakon or Slone. Parish might not have been on their radar, but no crew working on the decks and three men dressed for mountain hiking instead of fishing was a dead giveaway.

"We need to get below decks," he said. "Maybe they'll think the crew is sleeping after unloading the equipment."

No equipment remained aboard the deck, only because it was removed before the *Shamrock* ever left the Dutch Harbor. Even so, Teakon didn't appear convinced.

"If I get trapped down there, I can't throw this thing over the side before they snag it."

Teakon looked shaken well beyond any panic threshold Parish recalled witnessing in the man. Like a scared, cornered rat, the professor didn't know which direction to run. Completely out of his element, Teakon didn't move until Slone snagged him by the arm as the helicopter drew dangerously close.

"They know it's us!" he yelled over the howling wind to Parish. "They've already seen the boat's name and they're still coming."

"Ditch the cube!" Parish insisted to Teakon, still seeing indecision in the man's eyes. "Throw it and get to safety. I'm going to get the captain and get ready to abandon ship."

Slone's expression showed that he didn't like any part of Parish's intentions.

"Getting in a raft will make us a big floating target. We need to make a stand."

Teakon didn't look so certain. Reaching into his pocket, he tossed Parish the encased cube.

"Do it," he said before allowing Slone to stow him inside the closest doorway.

Parish held the small box in his hand, staring at it momentarily before ascending the stairs to speak with the captain. Teakon neglected to inform the captain of their real intentions, simply paying him well with money provided through Parish's employer. Assuring the captain they weren't dumping weapons or bodies at sea seemed to ease his conscience. Paying him double the amount he received for a week's worth of fishing also swung him to their side in a hurry. It only took one witness saying Captain Henry Flanagan left the docks without a crew to start a firestorm of rumors.

Barely twisting the handle before bursting through the door, Parish received a stunned look from the captain. Dressed for the warm interior of the cabin, Flanagan wore beige cargo pants and a black turtleneck sweater. Getting ready for a long season of catching crab a week at a time, returning to unload, and crab fishing all over again, the captain had begun growing a beard that appeared a few days old.

"What's wrong?" Flanagan asked quickly.

"We have company."

Looking out the window through the driving rain, the captain discovered the helicopter closing in on the boat's position. Despite the unusual circumstances of their voyage, Flanagan insisted his three visitors learn about the safety and escape measures aboard his vessel. Each of them tried on a survival suit before learning where the two inflatable rafts were stowed and how to deploy them.

"Unfriendly company?" Flanagan inquired with grave concern, letting his boat battle the waves momentarily without his guidance.

"You could say that. We'll probably need to abandon ship."

"You're kidding me, right?" the captain asked with bewilderment. "I'm not leaving a boat that costs five times more than my house."

"They'll kill you and leave you to go down with your ship."

"Boat," Flanagan corrected him, despite the dire circumstances surrounding them. "I didn't sign on for letting my boat sink, or being shot at by pirates."

Thinking fast, Parish tried outsmarting the invaders at their own game. He knew they wanted the cube at all costs, likely unconcerned with human life in the process.

"Can you turn off the power from in here?" he asked the captain a few seconds later when an idea came to him.

"I can shut down the engine and most of the lights."

"And no one else can start it if you take the key, right?" Parish asked, seeing the helicopter approaching the bow, slowing so its crew could scale down to the boat using the ropes that dropped a few seconds later.

"If I have the key, the boat won't work for anyone else," Flanagan assured him.

"Good. Shut everything down that you can and follow me."

Looking at him with uncertain green eyes momentarily, the captain flipped a number of switches that threw the deck and the cabin into darkness. Only a few marker lights and the helicopter's spotlights illuminated the trawler and the rough seas around it. Flanagan took the keys from the ignition console, looking to Parish as a dim glow penetrated the front window.

"I don't like this," he stated.

"It's the best chance we have. If it works, you might not lose your boat in the process. I need you to grab each of us a survival suit and get one of the life rafts ready. Don't inflate it until I tell you to."

"And what are you going to do?"

"Try and keep these fuckers from setting foot on your vessel if I can help it."

Parish followed Flanagan out the cabin door, immediately pulled his semi-automatic from the shoulder holster beneath his coat. Wishing he possessed heavier firepower aboard the trawler, he noticed Slone taking cover below the metal stairs. Slone took aim, as did Parish, waiting for the mercenaries to reveal themselves as armed and dangerous before opening fire. Only when four men dressed in black began descending the ropes, firearms slung around their shoulders, did Parish fire shots that seemed to have little effect on his targets.

He quickly realized they wore body armor, so he aimed for the legs of one man, hitting him somewhere close to the knee. Unable to hear the man's painful yelp, Parish spied a burst of blood emitting from his target, confirming the hit. All four of his enemies descended the ropes with precision speed, hitting the boat deck within seconds. Safely behind the metal stairs and the corner of the cabin, Parish exposed his body just long enough to take a few shots, immediately seeing two of the men targeting Slone.

Automatic gunfire forced Parish to take cover behind the corner as bullets ricocheted off the stairs. Apparently sharing the same idea, Slone took down one of the intruders with a shot to the thigh, providing the injured man's partner time to target him in the process. Slone tried ducking for some nearby pallets, but shots rang out before he left his partial cover behind structural metal beams. Parish watched the man's shoulder flinch awkwardly as a bullet entered and passed through Slone's flesh. Several more followed, burying themselves in the man's chest, finishing him as he slumped to the deck.

Now two angry wounded men, and their two uninjured partners, turned their attention to Parish, whose cover wouldn't suffice once they rounded the cabin and opened fire. He hoped Flanagan was making headway with the survival suits and the inflatable raft. Enclosed on all sides, including the top, the modern escape raft was meant to help survivors battle the cold, summon assistance, and travel under limited power. Most importantly to Parish was the full enclosure, which kept the assault team and helicopter pilot from peering inside.

Doubting the captain had ample time to fulfill his hurried assignment, Parish debated how to buy Flanagan time without getting himself killed when the unexpected happened. Teakon burst out of the metal door below, throwing his hands up as though in surrender. All four mercenaries froze at the sight of the unarmed man who ran to Slone's side, checking his vitals. Parish knew, as did Teakon, that Slone was beyond saving. Teakon gave Parish the subtlest of hopeless looks in the dim lighting, tilting his head toward the back of the boat, before standing and producing a sidearm as he neared the port side of the trawler. Knowing immediately that Teakon meant for him to break for it, and discard the cube if the feat hadn't already been accomplished, Parish stood just long enough to see another innocent man's death.

Teakon took aim at the four men, holding the gun in his right hand as he reached into his pocket and pulled out a small object, holding it over the railing momentarily to tease his adversaries. He allowed them little more than a glance to speculate whether he held the cube or not, before releasing the object. A satisfied grin crossed his face, as though quashing their objective with his efforts, but making his life worthless in the process. He fired two shots that hit nothing solid before all four mercenaries opened fire on him, striking him once or twice before he tumbled over the railing. Parish saw the man's heels swing upward as Teakon fell headfirst off the boat, instantly swallowed up by the rough seas that gladly devoured any victim who came their way.

"Inflate it!" Parish yelled, finding Flanagan in the back of the boat already inside a survival suit.

With a simple push of a button, the enclosed raft inflated itself with an internal pump like some kind of bouncing castle at the county fair. Parish stood guard, watching the corner like a hawk for anyone brazen enough to peer around it. No helmet was going to stop a bullet at such close range and the mercenaries intended to survive so they could spend their blood money. Ignoring the hissing sound behind him, Parish reached back with his left hand until he felt Flanagan close enough for conversation.

"You have a storage hatch right below us, don't you?"

"Yeah," Flanagan replied, apparently unhappy with the realization of Parish's plan. "We'll be fish in a barrel if they search it."

Parish noticed the helicopter had fallen back to a surveillance position to provide better lighting for the mercenaries. Knowing these men wanted the cube at any cost he prayed his diversion was enough to distract them while he put a secondary plan into action.

"Push it in," he said in a hushed voice to the captain, who shoved the life raft over the side without exposing himself to the helicopter's lights.

It took less than ten seconds for Flanagan to pop open the hatch to the empty storage area and the two men to jump inside before the mercenaries rounded the corner. Parish had snagged the survival suit left for him by Flanagan, dragging it down with him out of sight so the mercenaries didn't grow suspicious.

Reeking of long dead fish and their organs used for bait, the hold overwhelmed Parish momentarily, but he quickly grew accustomed to the smell. Feeling like he was imprisoned within a sensory deprivation chamber, Parish discovered smell was about his only useful sense because he couldn't see anything, and all around him metal kept him tucked tightly into place.

Prompted by information relayed to them from the pilot, the men immediately dashed to the opposite side of the boat, seeing the orange inflatable raft bobbing along the waves. Standing nearly eight feet tall, with a zippered top that kept water out in case of listing, the raft also kept anyone from readily seeing inside.

Regretting that he never found ample opportunity to toss the encased cube over the side without being seen, Parish needed only a few seconds on the deck to carry out Teakon's final wish. The tromping of footsteps and rain hitting the metal hatch above made him feel like a refugee in hiding from a death squad, tapping and probing for his presence. Parish couldn't see Flanagan's eyes in the darkness, but he suspected they were either closed in prayer or wide-open with anticipation.

"Check this entire boat," one of the mercenaries barked above them. "If they're in that raft we'll chase it down with the chopper."

"We could just shoot it," another voice said.

"And risk losing the objective? You care to explain that to the man who hired us?"

"You mean the man we've never seen?" the second mercenary grunted.

Both men paused, which concerned Parish gravely. Unable to see a thing in the darkness, he heard both of them shuffle around above him before stepping off the cover. He readied his firearm when they attempted to yank the handles to the hatch, but the handles locked automatically when shut into place. With no locks on the inside, Parish and Flanagan were literally trapped inside the hold until the doors were forced open or Parish shot the locks. One of the first things Parish and Slone had done when they boarded the boat was memorize every square foot of storage and equipment, taking nothing for granted.

Hoping Flanagan didn't make a peep, Parish waited a few agonizing seconds until the mercenaries stopped tugging on the hatch, realizing they weren't getting in very easily.

"Let's check over the rest of the boat," the leader said as thunder rolled in the background.

It took several agonizing minutes, but Parish waited for a sign that the four men were done with their evil deed. He wondered if Teakon's sacrifice gave them the impression the cube was already overboard, curtailing their exhaustive search for the cube or additional human life. He knew at some point they were going to have to check every crevice in the boat, but they risked the life raft getting away because it wasn't traceable by using radar like the trawler. Parish grew more nervous by the minute, trying to steady his nerves for the captain's sake, but Flanagan stood silently beside him in the darkness.

"Is this your grand plan?" Flanagan finally asked just above a whisper with an edgy tone. "To get us shot like dogs down here?"

"Patience," Parish whispered back. "They need to locate the survival raft or risk losing it. They *have* to leave soon."

Being trapped in a storage locker the size of a bedroom closet almost made Parish forget about his seasickness. The turbulent waves didn't seem so bad within a confined space, plus he needed to use his senses to stay alive. He listened attentively for what seemed like five minutes before the four men met just outside the cabin above the two trapped men.

"You two stay here and continue the search of the boat," the leader said. "Starks and I are going to chase down that life raft with the chopper. Remember, we're looking for that cube. Any people you find aren't useful once they give you information."

"Understood."

Parish felt some relief that the two injured men were conducting the local search. He waited until he heard the helicopter leave in the direction of the life raft before grabbing the survival suit at his feet.

"It's about time for us to get out of here," he informed Flanagan. "Where's that other life raft?"

"Right beside this hold. If you fire that gun, they're going to hear it."

"What choice do I have?" Parish said more than asked, feeling the first of the locks by hand before taking aim in the darkness.

He suspected the two gimpy hired guns were below decks, conducting a more thorough search. Waiting until thunder masked his movements, he fired a shot that disabled the first locking mechanism. He located the other lock and fired again within seconds as thunder continued to roll ominously in the distance, hoping noise didn't carry particularly well through the vessel's metal hull.

Climbing out of the hold, Parish quickly donned his survival suit, feeling like a seal out of water, barely able to move. Flanagan wasted no time retrieving the second life raft, monitoring the area around them while Parish pulled the last of the suit over his thick waistline. Intentionally keeping his right arm out of the survival suit's sleeve, Parish vigilantly positioned himself to watch for the two mercenaries while the captain inflated the craft.

"It's ready," he said after half a minute or so. "I'm unzipping one side because we'll have to swim for it once we're in the water."

"Get in and I'll push it over," Parish said, wishing they had thrown it overboard when it was only partially inflated. He spotted several synthetic ropes tied to the raft, serving as tethers so a swimmer could stay in contact with the inflatable vessel even if he couldn't climb aboard. "I'm a certified diver."

Flanagan eyeballed him skeptically, probably due to Parish's husky form.

"Seriously," Parish assured him. "Now get in before you get us both shot."

Climbing inside the orange device, Flanagan positioned himself in a corner of the rectangular craft before Parish muscled it from the deck to the railing. He strained momentarily to clear the railing and direct the life raft away from some rather precarious edged metal along the side of the boat before releasing it. Securing his firearm in its holster, he zipped up his coat before he finished donning the survival suit, including the hood that slipped over his head once he removed his stocking cap and stuffed it inside the suit. Assured that the cube remained in his pants pocket with a quick pat, he leapt over the side, securing one of the life raft's handles as he hit the water with his right hand. Had he missed, he and Flanagan might have drifted apart, becoming additional casualties claimed by the rough seas.

Parish quickly realized the survival suit did not shield him from the elements completely as the biting cold of the sloshing water touched him like sharp fingernails clawing at his skin. Simply meant to slow the hazardous effects of the water, the suits bought the wearer about an hour before hypothermia set in. Bodily functions shut down as the body went into shock, leaving only a corpse inside an orange floating marker for Coast Guard helicopters to find.

Putting such thoughts out of his mind, Parish tugged on the tethered line, willing himself closer to the inflatable craft as it washed further away from the trawler. The rain continued to pour, as though sent along with the mercenaries to prevent him from escaping. Flanagan unzipped the side closest to him, stretching out an arm to help Parish climb inside to safety. After clinging to the base of the unzipped side, Parish kicked to pull himself inside, finally relieved when his entirely body wasn't touching the Bering Sea.

By no means comfortable, the cramped space inside the vessel was dark and cold, but mostly free of water save the droplets the two men brought inside with them. Parish landed against the solidly inflated wall of the craft, watching the *Shamrock* drift further away from them as Flanagan securely zipped the opposite side.

"We're pretty much done in now," the captain bemoaned as he slumped against a different side of the life raft. "We didn't even get a mayday off before leaving."

"We'll be fine," Parish assured him, unzipping his survival suit far enough to reach inside and pull out a small device.

"What's that?"

"A transmitter. The second I activate it, my boss knows to send the Coast Guard after us by tracking its frequency."

"This thing can transmit for help," Flanagan stated sourly. "I was more worried about getting back to my boat."

"You've got insurance, don't you?"

"Yes, but losing a week or two during the crab season is financially disastrous. I've got a crew depending on me to help them feed their families."

"We might still recover her, but we can't transmit for help until our company leaves. If they can track us, they won't hesitate to shoot us and sink every last piece of evidence. Besides, my employer will take care of your losses if we don't find her."

Flanagan's expression softened in the extremely dim lighting just a bit.

"Sorry about your buddies."

"They were colleagues, but they were good colleagues," Parish admitted, learning how admirable Slone and Teakon were during the brief time he spent with them.

He dug into his survival suit, finding the lead box inside a pocket before pulling it out. The box's pointy corner had been digging into his skin the entire time as a painful reminder of the task at hand.

"It's all about this, of all things," Parish lamented, opening the box to reveal a green cube created from an emerald.

Even in darkness it seemed to glow, seeking attention from the outside world. Like a siren, it lured men to its beauty, but it didn't kill them outright. Men killed one another to fuel the evil cube and possess it for their betterment.

"What is it?" Flanagan asked, stunned by its beauty. "Is it like that rock from the *Titanic* movie?"

"No. It's pure evil."

Parish closed the lead box, wondering if he dared throw it to the sea since Teakon led the mercenaries to think it was dropped within a mile of their present location. Even with modern technology, finding a tiny lead box on the bottom of the ocean was like the old adage of finding a needle in a haystack. Torn between the risk of carrying it longer, or daring bring it back to Indiana with him for a later second attempt, Parish decided to let the sea have it as an offering. He unzipped the nearest opening before tossing the encased cube to the water, verifying that nothing stopped the waves from devouring it.

"Why did you do that?" Flanagan asked, dumbfounded that someone would discard what looked like a harmless, beautiful gem to such a fate.

"Because it's my job."

Hoping their life raft quickly became the figurative needle, Parish settled into his spot as comfortably as the elements allowed. The two men needed to wait for the helicopter to come and go once more, if they could even hear it over the weather and rough seas, before transmitting for assistance. Built to endure the choppy waters, the life raft could outlast a human being in the elements, so Parish planned on waiting as long as possible before tripping the transmitter.

Taking a deep breath, he felt some relief that his job was accomplished, though the deaths of Slone and Teakon weighed heavily on his conscience. He wondered how the mercenary crew tracked them down, knowing that any investigation on his part endangered his employer's wishes for secrecy.

Placing his head against the hard rubber base of the inflatable interior, Parish tried to get some rest before summoning the Coast Guard.

CHAPTER 2

Parish officially survived his incident of terror when he and Flanagan were picked up by the Coast Guard. It took a few days, but he returned home to Orange County in Southern Indiana. Originally from the area, Parish felt a rush of relief when his flight arrived in Indianapolis, and overcome with joy when he found his wife and two children at home awaiting his return.

He met with his employer first thing the next morning, giving Paul Clouse details about the trip to Alaska and the outcome. Despite numerous other issues clogging his calendar, Clouse listened attentively to the information, openly disturbed about the deaths of Slone and Teakon. He expressed relief that Parish survived the horrific ordeal, blaming himself for not being more prudent before sending the trio to Alaska. Clouse excused himself from Parish only a few minutes after learning the details of the trip, saying he planned to assist the families with funeral costs.

It wasn't until almost two weeks later, on a Friday, that he requested to sit down with Parish once again. On Halloween of all days, Parish met with Clouse at the man's prized West Baden Springs Hotel in the grand atrium. The two briefly shook hands as Clouse suggested they take their conversation inside one of the available conference rooms along the ground floor.

Nearing forty years in age, Clouse lived a charmed life in the eyes of some, but Parish knew the hardships the man endured from the moment he ever stepped foot inside the one-of-a-kind domed hotel. Rising from part-time architect to the man who owned the building, Clouse lost a number of friends, permanently, living in fear that his family might be targeted by the types of individuals Parish encountered on the trawler.

"You know what day this is," Clouse began when they sat across from one another on the narrow side of the long conference table.

"Halloween, sir."

"And you know about my history with this holiday, so I'm hoping for an uneventful Halloween."

"Yes, sir."

At one time Clouse informed Parish, eventually insisting, that he could call him by his first name, but Parish remained constantly respectful, raised to act accordingly by his parents. Clouse had since given up trying to dissuade his family's bodyguard from changing his ways.

Standing just over six feet, Clouse remained very trim and toned from daily workouts. His full head of brown hair was parted to one side, while a mustache of the same color resided on his upper lip. From looking at him, no one knew he had inherited land and assets totaling in the low billions. A very down to earth boss, Clouse formerly worked as a professional firefighter, so he came from a normal background. Wearing blue jeans, a flannel shirt over his T-shirt, and what appeared to be brown hiking boots, he appeared ready for a walk with his wife along the trails.

"It seems the Coven, or some organization just like them, has an interest in the cubes," Clouse said almost dejectedly. "I'm working on patching our relationship with Julie Knowles after her two partners were killed in Alaska."

The Coven, a group created by Clouse's former arch nemesis, sought to obtain a few of the cursed cubes for their evil purposes. Led by Martin Smith, the group members seemed to disappear after Smith's death less than a year prior. Clouse partnered with Mark Teakon and his associates to ensure the cursed objects stayed out of malicious hands. Julie Knowles served as their local partner in Massachusetts, never working in the field to recover or hide the objects. Her bond with Clouse wasn't very well established, because Clouse often worked with the professor instead.

"We have to reorganize this whole thing, and not just with Julie," Clouse stated. "There's a more worldly force than Smith could ever put together going after these things."

Parish cleared his throat.

"I seem to recall Teakon stating something about Armageddon if the cubes were ever brought together."

Clouse's blue eyes met his with cognitive recognition.

"I can't imagine why anyone would want to literally end the world, but maybe this group has plans to capture all of the cubes. It seems Teakon might have held out on some important information."

"Or maybe he just didn't know the whole story. He seemed awfully trusting of me to dispose of the emerald cube."

"No offense, but it sounds like he was in a pinch."

"None taken, sir."

Clouse rubbed his chin momentarily in thought.

"We need to work with Julie more closely if we're going to discover who these people are and what they want. This is going to take more than a handful of us stumbling around, trying to figure out who's after the cubes."

"A task force, sir?"

"We need a group effort, whatever we call it."

"I'm in, sir. Whatever you need."

Parish realized too late he probably sounded like a suck-up, trying to get in the boss's good graces with his quick response.

"No, Todd. You've done plenty, and you've got a family. I'm not putting you in danger again."

"Sir, you know I'm loyal to this cause, and to you. Keeping these objects from falling in the wrong hands makes my job easier because I know your family is safe."

Clouse forced a grin.

"You know, when I picked you to watch over my kids, I knew you were a good man who was loyal to his own family, Todd. Coming back here and working for your father was noble, because you put your family first."

"You're leaving out the part where I was flat broke, sir," Parish added, drawing a genuine smile from Clouse.

"While that may be true, you had experiences that could have landed you a job with better pay, in far larger places than French Lick. What I'm trying to say is I knew you were a good find on my part, but you've far exceeded my expectations with your loyalty."

"And with all due respect, I want to see this through, Mr. Clouse. I know I can't keep up with the former military types you'll have to hire, but I can represent your interests in the field."

Clouse openly gave the option some thought.

"I'll consider it. My conscience can't take much more strain, Todd. I've lost enough friends to this madness, and I'll be damned if I put the people I employ in harm's way."

"Sir, I'm not exactly a babe in the woods. You've sent me to a dozen schools and seminars, which I considered preparation for retrieving these objects."

Clouse stood.

"Let's take a walk, Todd."

Parish followed his boss out of the conference room, wondering if he was about to get reprimanded or their conversation was getting deeper.

Following Clouse into the rounded atrium, Parish tried to avoid looking up at the six stories of rooms and balconies above him. A mammoth skylight built into the ceiling provided rays of sun that lit the atrium where people sat in plush furniture, played chess at tables along the walls, or sat outside the hotel's bar named after a previous owner. Though Clouse had moved his family out of their sixth floor suite several months prior, memories still flooded Parish's mind of guarding the man's children at the hotel.

"Seven years ago to the day my life changed drastically," Clouse admitted. "My wife was murdered and I found myself the pawn in a game I didn't understand."

Parish simply hung his head, already knowing much of the story from hearsay. Not once had he ever thought of his boss as pompous or pampered. He knew of the ordeals plaguing Paul Clouse from the man's occasional melancholy state and what visitors and friends stated. Parish wasn't around during much of the man's troubles with Martin Smith, but the newspaper articles tried making sense of the murders surrounding the hotel seven years prior.

Making a game effort to report the truth, the newspaper and television reporters lacked inside knowledge about the cursed objects and what motivated the Coven.

"The reason I tell you this, Todd, is because it needs to end. It needs to end now. No one else should have to go through the hell of these past seven years."

"Sir, you still have two of the cubes. Isn't keeping those safe from harm enough?"

"I have one of the cubes and Julie has one," Clouse corrected. "And while she may have the power of tracking the cubes, who's to say any of us are safe from harm? They tracked your group down in Alaska, which means these people know who we are. I say it's time to start hitting back and using my resources."

"That will just put your family at risk again, sir," Parish said with genuine concern, following his employer from the atrium to the hallway that never ended, simply curving around the atrium's outer wall in a full circle.

"I know, which is why I'm going to get a few key people in place and put them under the radar the next few months."

"What about you?"

"I'll disappear, too. If all goes well, I'll have someone in place that Julie Knowles trusts so we can move forward with a search for the cubes."

Parish wasn't sure he agreed with such a bold move for a couple of reasons. One, it put the lives of many good people in jeopardy by searching for the cubes. Two, gathering the cubes seemed to play into the hands of their enemy. If some evil entity truly wanted to gather thirteen cursed objects for the sole purpose of ending the world, putting the cubes in one spot would make their objective easier if they discovered the hiding spot. Obviously, hiding the cursed objects didn't work very well, as Parish learned in Alaska, but at least the emerald cube was out of harm's way. While the cubes remained in the hands of corrupt individuals, lives would certainly be lost to fuel the cursed objects and use their powers, but Parish felt that letting sleeping dogs lie seemed the better course of action for the greater good.

"Don't get me wrong, Todd," Clouse said. "I want out of the cube hunting business once and for all, but I'm the last one who gives a shit about finding them who has the financial backing. I'm flying to Amherst to speak with Julie in person, and I want you to come with me."

"Me, sir? Why, if I may ask?"

"Because Julie doesn't seem to trust you very well after losing Teakon. I need to put her fears to rest if we're going to move forward."

Parish didn't feel particularly happy about the mistrust, but he understood since he and Julie Knowles had never met. He felt like a bargaining chip, though he trusted his employer implicitly not to make him a sacrificial lamb.

"I'm looking to hire a few trusted individuals who can devote their time to finding these objects and hide them away."

"How exactly does one interview for such a job, sir?"

"There is no interview process. The three individuals I have in mind are perfect candidates. I've had Mark scoping out hundreds of candidates since we last dealt with Martin Smith and his people. These three will either say yes or no to the proposition."

Clouse referred to Mark Daniels, his good friend in charge of casino security at the other major hotel he owned just down the road from the dome. A former police officer and detective, Daniels knew of the cursed objects, and more importantly, how to conduct background checks without drawing attention to their cause.

The two men eventually stepped onto the hotel's veranda where rocking chairs allowed guests to stare out at the waning beauty of the sunken garden. A fountain sprayed several streams of water into its own base which would soon be drained and the water supply shut down for winter. Parish leaned on the railing, staring at the green garden momentarily as Clouse relaxed his shoulder against a support beam.

"So, are you up for flying to Massachusetts?" Clouse asked.

Still not fond of flying, Parish didn't let his feelings show.

"When do we depart, sir?"

"Tomorrow morning if that works for you. The sooner the better."

Parish knew Clouse wouldn't keep them away very long. He often did daytrips for business, typically booking commercial flights with little notice, or leasing a local pilot if the flight wasn't more than a state or two away. Somewhat curious about how events were about to unfold, Parish wanted to stay in the loop. He also wanted to assure Julie Knowles he took the necessary measures to dispose of the cube, making the most of Teakon's sacrifice.

"I'll be ready tomorrow whenever you need me, sir."

Clouse nodded with satisfaction.

"Someone will call you with the details."

CHAPTER 3

Glad that Clouse didn't ask him to carry out chauffeur duties when they arrived in Massachusetts and rented a car, Parish simply took in the beautiful New England fall view while his boss drove. Orange leaves often lasted about two weeks around French Lick, never equaling the quantity or quality of what he saw beyond his passenger window. The sun glowed in the early afternoon hour, giving a false impression that the beautiful fall day felt warm and cozy. In truth, Parish and his employer dressed for the weather, Clouse wearing a brown leather jacket that shielded him from the biting wind when they stepped from the passenger jet an hour earlier.

Riding along the downtown area of the quaint college town gave Parish a good view of the brick buildings. Considered a small city with less than 40,000 residents, Amherst provided a quiet setting for students, limited in crime and violence. It also provided a perfect front for Mark Teakon and his associates to conduct their search for cubes touched by the devil himself.

Clouse pulled up to a bookstore along the main drag that appeared to cater toward all readers, rather than the student clientele. With a brick façade painted beige, the store looked inviting with two large picture windows looking in and a hanging sign that read "The Book Nook" in green lettering. It hardly appeared like camouflage for a vault beneath the ground floor that harbored cursed objects and their dirty secrets.

But Parish knew it was exactly that the second he saw it from Clouse's description of his one and only previous visit.

Feeling his stomach tighten as he followed his employer to the door, Parish felt apprehensive, like a police officer about to tell a family member a loved one was dead. Julie Knowles already knew this, but the bodyguard knew he needed to spill details, painful even for him, to satisfy her. Because everyone on Clouse's payroll survived Halloween without any incidents, Parish took this as a good omen heading into the winter months.

A tiny bell rang when Clouse opened the front door, alerting a young woman behind the counter to their presence. She recognized Clouse immediately before casting a skeptical eye toward Parish, who opted to wear a suit rather than dress down for the occasion. He typically donned a suit to alert reporters and curious onlookers to the fact that he was protecting the Clouse family. Like a Secret Service agent, he stood out like a sore thumb, but similarly he carried firearms to protect those he served.

The store looked more like a small-town library than a book store with its old wooden shelves lining the walls, with a few islands centered along the old hardwood floors. Parish heard the floors creak when he stepped onto certain boards, possibly acting as a subtle security measure for the owners. A few reading tables with chairs, all wooden, were off to one side, while a cash register occupied a sturdy counter on the opposite end. Lights hung from the high ceilings above on poles, like classic gymnasium lighting.

Barely older than a college graduate, Julie wore her creamed coffee brown hair out to her shoulders, sporting glasses that made her appear studious. Upon seeing her visitors, she stepped from behind the counter, setting down a rather thick log book of some sort. Rather petite, she gave an aura that indicated she was still someone to be reckoned with in any arena. Parish said nothing as Clouse introduced him, though he nodded courteously when they all went to sit at a large reading table with six chairs surrounding it.

Julie sat closest to Clouse, looking him in the eye when she spoke.

"I'll let you know exactly where our arrangement stands when I hear from Mr. Parish about exactly what happened to my two colleagues."

Parish wondered if Teakon had recruited her from one of his history classes, perhaps mentoring her in more than just history. He quickly put such a tarnished thought behind him, wishing to retain his belief that Teakon was a heroic man of virtue.

"I certainly hope our arrangement hasn't been compromised," Clouse said adamantly. "This was a terrible loss for all of us, but Mark envisioned us starting something that would protect people from these cubes for all time."

Folding her hands, Julie said nothing as she looked to Parish, patiently waiting for him to begin his tale. He tried to give her every detail of the journey, especially focusing on the invasion of the trawler and how Teakon and Slone perished. Living through the ordeal proved no easy feat, but retelling the tale without breaking down was equally difficult. Parish wasn't one to show his emotions while at work, but he struggled to maintain his composure when relaying how Teakon sacrificed himself to ensure Parish had a fighting chance to survive or at least dispose of the cube.

"That sounds like Mark," Julie concurred when Parish finished detailing the events, staring down at his hands before forcing his eyes closed to shut out the dire images.

Her eyes appeared misty, conveying her feelings for the man who mentored her into such a dark and mysterious world. Parish knew saving the planet from destruction and its people from being victims of homicide to power the cubes was no light task. The details of her partnership with Teakon and Slone still eluded the bodyguard, because even Clouse never learned much about the trio. Parish felt especially protective of his boss for that reason, knowing partnerships sometimes ended badly, possibly with betrayal.

"So where do we stand now, Julie?" Clouse dared ask.

"I trust you," she answered, looking to both Clouse and Parish. "Both of you. As much as I want out of this dirty business of hunting down the cubes, it's come to my attention that we have a much graver problem than anyone suspected."

Parish stiffened, already under the impression their dire situation couldn't grow much darker. He hated being on the outside looking in throughout so much of the search. Clouse had hired outside help before with mixed results. Only somewhat effective in obtaining results and the cubes themselves, the method left a gaping hole in the trust department between Clouse and those he already employed who knew the secret.

Hopefully the three that he and Mark Daniels researched were the perfect hybrid of trustworthy and incorruptible personalities required for such a job.

"Hunting down the cubes is risky," Julie stated. "Mark knew this, and you butted heads with him on the subject, Mr. Clouse. While I'm not a fan of hunting them down, it has come to my attention that another group will stop at nothing to own them all. You and I both know that can never happen because of the hazardous implications involved. We've all heard the predictions running rampant about 2012 ending the world as we know it. While that statement may be off, give or take a few years, the end could come in the form of these thirteen cubes."

"You're the expert, Julie," Clouse admitted. "We need you to lead us on this, especially with Mark gone."

"I've been going through Mark's research and conducting my own. There's one cube in particular that concerns me, because it could ruin everything we've worked so hard to prevent."

"What does it do?" Parish inquired, feeling his stomach tighten.

"It apparently allows the user to teleport through time," Julie said, taking a deep breath with a gravely concerned expression. "I received a document stating as much in the mail. Mark had a solid lead about a man involved with this particular cube and bid on the man's effects at an estate auction. Considering how little he paid for it, I don't think anyone else knew about our inside information."

Clouse rubbed his cheeks and chin nervously, realizing the ramifications of such power.

"How do we know it hasn't already altered this continuity as we know it?"

"We don't for certain, but it seems unlikely the cube was ever used, because a group secured it soon after its creation. A group very similar to our own."

"And they publicized their existence in a document?"

"No," Julie said, letting a grin slip for the first time since their meeting began. "This was a letter from one member to another, stating in rather vague terms they were transferring possession of the cube from one member to another for safe keeping. The content infers that they were safeguarding the cube from worldly forces that wanted to own it."

"But thanks to your book, you know who's possessed the cube over the years," Clouse stated with an airy wave of his right hand.

"That's true, but we've hit a dead-end at some point."

Parish knew from Clouse's description that a leather-bound book was created with the cubes, bearing the names of the original owners. Apparently slipped into the original spell or curse with the cubes, the book then became part of the legacy, bearing the name of each new owner of each distinct cube. Teakon always said the writing appeared in the book, not by human hand, but from the devil himself when each cube changed ownership.

"What kind of dead-end?" Parish asked, still somewhat skeptical about the powers of the old book.

"It seems the same individual has possessed the cube for the last forty years or so," Julie informed him. "The problem is the man disappeared immediately after he took possession of the cube."

"He went into hiding?" Clouse asked with a raised eyebrow.

"I don't think so. From what little bit I've gathered, it seemed his identity was probably compromised and wherever his body may be, the cube is probably nearby. This isn't fact, so don't get me wrong, but the trail ends with this man."

Clouse sat pensively a moment, folding his hands. Parish knew from working for the man so long that his employer's mental wheels were churning. When it came to the cursed objects and protecting his family, Paul Clouse always had plans in place.

"There may be a way around this issue," he finally said. "Are we in agreement that this time cube *needs* to be found by us first?"

"Absolutely," Julie replied earnestly.

"I've been conducting background checks on three types of people who may be of use to us in locating and retrieving the cubes," Clouse admitted. "I wasn't going to move forward without your blessing, but I've picked my three people and still need to sit down with them. This is important, because one of them is a psychic who might be able to locate this particular cube if we can get her on the trail."

Julie didn't bother hiding her concern.

"Bringing new people into the fold could be very dangerous."

"I understand that, but you and I alone cannot go hunting down these objects. Nor can we simply sit back and watch them being harvested by this other group. No matter the cost, we need to maintain at least a few of these cursed objects so the endgame can't be reached."

"I trust you've researched your three people?"

"Very much. I'm ready to sit down with them and make sure they're right for this before putting them to work."

"That's fine, but I'd like to have some input and feedback on the situation. You, I can trust, but not three new people all at once. This partnership can't be a one-way street."

"Agreed," Clouse stated. "We need each other more than ever."

"I'll help as best I can from here, but the time cube is our priority."

Clouse gave her a mock grin.

"Then *time* is of the essence. Maybe it's time we talk some more about the details."

***

Parish stepped outside the store to let Clouse discuss the new game plan with Julie. He loved the look of a colorful autumn, finding the weather more suitable to football than sightseeing. Even the local smells were like something out of an antique or candle shop, like burning wood from a fireplace and freshly baked goods from a coffee shop just down the street.

Because he hadn't worn an overcoat, and therefore found no place to stuff his hands, he slipped on black leather gloves to shield them from the cold. Every inch of exposed flesh felt chilled to the bone after his ordeal on the Bering Sea. Spending several hours bobbing in a life raft so close to freezing water changed his physical tolerance to the cold. Maybe his mind subliminally exaggerated the experience, but Parish didn't care to ever see the ocean again.

He felt better knowing Julie believed and trusted him, but he still wasn't thrilled about even more people joining their secretive group. The objects they collected tempted people, especially those weak in morals and mind, to fall prey to their own desires. In a mortal world, such people jumped at the opportunity to prolong their lives, renew their youth, or any number of unspoken benefits.

Taking a stroll down the picturesque street, Parish thought about the incident on the Bering Sea and how the Coast Guard finally pulled him and Flanagan aboard their ship. It didn't take long for their helicopter to track down the man's boat, which miraculously remained afloat after being completely abandoned. Parish didn't care to join the captain when he was reunited with his trawler, but being stuck at the Coast Guard base for hours of interviews made him privy to information.

He spoke with Flanagan only once at length, but the captain informed him the entire ship looked as though burglars had overturned it. Anything that wasn't bolted down was strewn across the floors and decks, while the engine room required some repairs before the boat's engines could be started again.

"Those sons-of-bitches probably did a hundred-thousand dollars in damage to my crab boat," the captain had revealed when they sat on a hall-way bench, each holding a steaming cup of coffee.

"I'll let my boss know. I'm sure he'll compensate you for whatever the insurance doesn't cover."

"That's a relief," Flanagan said sarcastically. "The next time someone offers to buy my services I'm going to respectfully decline."

Thankfully the captain provided very few details to the authorities, which allowed Parish to put a spin on his version of the story. Luckily Parish hadn't given the captain details in the first place, so the man only knew about the events he witnessed. With all other witnesses either dead or gone, he became the primary resource for the investigators. Parish absolutely could not reveal anything about his true purpose for traveling along the Bering Sea. Thankfully, dropping his employer's name bought him a lot of credibility, so his tale about doing some seafaring research narrowly flew. He said he wasn't sure why people invaded the boat, chalking it up to an unusual band of pirates.

Parish wasn't accustomed to dealing with authorities, much less lying to them with cover stories, but he believed Clouse saved him, at least from a frustrating life of obscurity. Assisting the man with his quest to rid to world of its greatest evil felt like the least Parish could do. He rather enjoyed his usual job of keeping watch over the children, but loved the opportunities to travel. He didn't hope for danger, but kept vigilant for the rare occasions when it came his way.

Patiently waiting for his employer, Parish walked to a nearby park bench, taking a seat as he watched a young couple sitting a few benches down from him. Despite the light, steady breeze, he was able to overhear them talking about wedding plans and the young woman finishing her college courses in the spring. He thought about Mark Teakon and how so many students were probably going to miss him on campus, possibly holding vigils to honor him. He knew Julie missed her mentor, and though she didn't say much about Slone and his gruff personality the same surely went for him.

The young couple playfully tapped one another on their noses and kissed like puppies, very brief but without fear of showing their affection, or worrying about who might be observing them. How lucky they are, Parish thought of them, remembering when he dated his wife and felt the same way. Maturity dulled some of the playfulness, but he still felt passionate about wanting to spend the rest of his life with her and watch his children grow into young adults.

He watched the young couple literally put their foreheads together and talk lovingly in whispers. Parish wished his problems could be as simple as theirs. If only they knew how their life issues paled in comparison to the unseen dangers all around them, they might rethink their future together. Such people had it good and never knew it, living obliviously at a young age. Parish thought like them once, but his views on strangers and their motivations differed after meeting some very evil people over the past few years. He wanted the world to become a safe place once again so he could feel comfortable taking his wife and children on vacations and out in public. While he didn't usher them into the house at all times, Parish took measures to keep them safe without revealing the dangers of his job.

He believed in Clouse, and considered himself game for whatever plan the man conceived to keep the cursed objects out of evil hands. At the moment Parish simply wanted to get back to Indiana and slide into his normal routine for a while.

CHAPTER 4

Despite the passing of Halloween, roller coasters and other rides continued to run at the theme park known as Great Realms at the edge of Mason, Ohio. Management decided to get one last weekend out of the season before closing down for winter and beginning construction on the park's new ride. Ground had already been cleared, and the concrete stabilizing pillars placed along the dirt-covered land for a new roller coaster.

Clay Branson didn't much care about the business end of the theme park.

His concerns centered mainly around his new life in Mason and the past he left behind. Just young enough to leave his job as a police officer in Northeastern Indiana and join the Mason Police Department, he loved everything about his new life. Working as a local police officer provided him with a second job as park security during the operating months. It also allowed him to spend time with his fiancée, who happened to be the daughter of the park owners.

Clay didn't move a state away on a whim, or to endear himself to the Trimble family. After he helped alleviate a major threat at the park, he returned to see Casey Trimble several times on dates, knowing he wanted to spend time with her. Though she was nearly ten years his junior, he loved how she handled herself at twenty-five years of age. Bold and daring, she saw through bullshit and admired people who mirrored her good values. Clay shared her values because of his job, and because he hoped to outlast the trouble from his past that haunted him.

Walking along the main drag where half a dozen fountains spouted water into the air, adding to the cool breeze wafting across the park, Clay observed his surroundings. People packed the park, hoping for a few last roller coaster rides or memories with their children before the park went into hibernation. Now in his second season with the park, Clay adapted to the routine rather easily. He was being groomed for the head of security position due to open in another year or two when the man holding the position retired.

Strangely enough, Casey's parents had begun training her for every job in the park when she reached the legal working age. She loved and respected her fellow employees, whether she ran the rides or vended candy from an enclosed stand. He loved her more than words could describe, as much as he loved his first wife and child who were taken from him forever in Japan.

Clay sauntered along the paved walkway, trying to forget his years in the Orient. As a teenager he wanted to escape his overbearing police officer father and the home life he thought was so bad. He learned many things, including some very powerful tactics that his *sensei* taught with traditional means. A master of martial arts and hundreds of weapons, Clay knew how to kill a man with little more than a finger, but such knowledge never clouded his judgment or moral fiber. He trickled the information about his past to Casey through conversation, letting her digest it a piece at a time, fearing he might lose her otherwise.

Though his past wasn't sordid through actions he initiated, Clay had killed men in the name of self-defense. Strangely enough, some of the men he lived and trained with in Japan were the same people who tried to kill him within the span of a year.

Things had quieted down recently, allowing him to proceed with his engagement to Casey and their wedding plans. As he passed a coffee shop along the end of the main strip, Clay detected someone waiting for him around the corner. Casey always liked to try taking him by surprise, making it her little game with him. It never worked, because his heightened sense of his surroundings clued him in about danger and other strong emotions in his vicinity. He wasn't psychic, but his training in Japan opened up his mind in ways he never thought possible.

When he rounded the corner he caught Casey in a hug before she even had time to surprise him. She giggled in response, allowing him to embrace her and plant a quick kiss on her lips. With so many people in the park, he hated looking irresponsible considering he wore the park's police uniform. She typically took her duties more seriously as well, but the end of the season was upon them.

"I can't believe today's our last day," she said, walking with him toward the kiddie area of the park. "What are we going to do with all of our time?"

Clay grinned.

"I can think of some things."

Casey returned a playful, yet slightly naughty look.

Young, vibrant, and intelligent, Casey showed remarkable wisdom for her age. Able to read people and their intentions from a mile away, she trusted Clay implicitly, which he earned by never betraying her trust.

Wearing a park uniform that indicated she was working a vending stand at least part of the day, Casey had let her strawberry blond hair down to her shoulders. She smiled easily, making her face a virtual ray of sunshine in Clay's eyes. Slender and athletic, Casey showed an interest in learning some of the arts Clay had mastered in Japan, but he wasn't ready to take on a student quite yet with so many events consuming their schedules. He wanted her to learn for her own betterment, and to be able to better defend herself, because he wasn't certain the danger from his past was behind him.

"How's your day?" he asked, looking from her to the closest ride in the children's area.

"I've been selling cotton candy and pretzels to hyperactive kids. I need Tylenol in a bad way."

Clay chuckled, taking hold of Casey's hand. They walked along the side, so most patrons weren't going to notice their affection in the wake of their own jubilation.

"When are your parents going to rescue you from unruly children and greasy food?"

"Oh, they imprison me in the front office from time to time because they know I'm happy anywhere. I've been here for the ups and downs, so I'm happy just taking my time and learning everything. There are close to a thousand employees who depend on us to give them a paycheck every two weeks."

"I'm privileged to be one of them," Clay said sincerely with a smile. "Meeting you was the one good thing that happened to me the first day I came to this park."

He referred to the day when he and some friends stopped a terrorist incident at the park, all because someone wanted to end Clay's life in an elaborate plan. That day remained a blur in his memory most of the time, because he hated recalling the specifics. Casey's trust in him, a complete stranger at the time, gave him the means to secure the park and eliminate his adversaries.

"How long is your break?" Clay asked his fiancée.

"I'm the floater today. Only got a few minutes before I head to the candy store."

"More sugar and kids. Should I draw you a hot bath tonight?"

Casey looked up to him lovingly.

"Maybe a nice dinner out will make me feel better."

"That can be arranged," Clay said as they stopped walking. "Maybe we can have something sweet for dessert."

Casey reached around his neck, pulling him in for a long kiss without fear of who might be watching them.

"That's just a preview, stud," she said before turning to head for her next work station.

"I like it," Clay said under his breath.

He continued walking through the park, making his presence known when necessary. A few times he overheard parents telling their children they would have the park officer arrest them if they continued to act unruly. Clay hated people telling children such things, because he didn't want kids living in fear of police officers dragging them away. Ending negative stereotypes about police officers was nearly impossible, so he certainly didn't like it when people contributed to them unwittingly.

Sounds of rides spinning and roaring entered his ears, along with delighted screams from numerous children. So late in the season the costumed mascots didn't walk around receiving hugs or taking pictures with the children, but colors still flooded the kiddie area like a rainbow was shot down by a rocket, raining pieces across the theme park. He heard contemporary pop music playing in the background, though it didn't seem quite as appropriate in the cool fall air as it did during the sweltering summer days when the park was wall to wall people.

During the winter months a skeleton security crew remained at the park while the office personnel worked intermittently. Not until the early months of the following year would human resources begin the hiring process for the next season. Clay expected to work some security during the winter, possibly learning from their security director to bide his time.

Passing through the colorful rides with their lights and localized music and carnival sounds, Clay reached the opposite end of the kiddie area where a wide concrete path led to the waterpark. A train also made a circuit around half of the park, transporting guests to the waterpark or a faux western town where shootouts occurred on the hour between actors. Soon after Clay crossed the tracks that intersected the walkway he looked up to an old wooden fortress covered in ivy with a sign that hung crookedly on its one remaining metal clasp.

A few people passed him, walking the other way, but otherwise he was alone on the concrete path. With the waterpark and western attraction closed for the year, few people found any reason to take the train or walk away from the park's open attractions. Clay's eyes refused to leave the fort, not because it was such a neat vintage attraction, but rather because he sensed something dangerous nearby. Feeling certain he was an intended target, he reached toward his firearm just before the gleam of a gun scope caught his eye from the fortress's top area.

Clay dove for some nearby bushes, hearing the distinct sound of a suppressed firearm from above. He hit the ground, tucking and rolling as he did so, feeling no shooting pain or blood oozing from a fresh wound. Regaining his footing, Clay drew his sidearm as he pressed his back to the building. The shooter likely knew he missed the shot, meaning he would opt to retreat hastily or return to ground level in order to try finishing his assignment.

Listening intently, Clay heard nothing for a few seconds before the rustling of the ivy from within gave the would-be assassin's movements away. Three wooden walls comprised the fort, leaving the fourth area completely open for showmanship purposes when the western town actors wanted to use it. Now entangled in a cat and mouse game, Clay moved along the wall without a sound, keeping his gun in a ready position.

Edging his way toward the open area, Clay continued to listen for movement inside. Uncertain whether his attacker was a traditional assassin or someone trained like himself, he exercised caution. Carrying nothing except his firearm and a metal ASP baton, his arsenal felt a bit lacking without any projectile weapons or blades. Spotting a tree at the end of the wall, he darted forward before the gunman tried shooting him through the wall, diving behind the tree for cover. Peering around the side, he found the man inside the three-walled fortress training a silenced pistol in his direction.

Able to use the tree to block his entire body when he stood upright, Clay heard two shots emerge from the pistol. The tree absorbed both bullets, buying him some time to reach up for a branch before tugging himself upward into a flip that landed him atop the branch. Using his new vantage point, Clay kept his firearm at his side, wanting to know why this man targeted him specifically. Killing the would-be assassin produced an adverse result, so Clay safely peered around the tree, trying to locate the man's knee for a quick disabling shot.

Seeing nothing before him, Clay heard no heavy breathing or running through the tall grass, so he quickly determined the man was close to the tree. In one motion he dropped down, grasping the branch while maintaining his grip on the gun, swinging his legs where he believed the man was hiding on the other side of the tree. Hitting nothing except air, Clay landed on the ground, immediately sensing danger behind him, so he rolled sideways behind the tree once again as two more quieted shots rang out from the man's gun.

He grasped the extendable baton from his gun belt, shook his hand to extend it, and whipped his arm behind him, around the tree, striking something solid and drawing a pained groan. Hurt but not disabled, the man stumbled from behind the tree, still trying to train his gun on Clay, holding the side of his head. Clay continued to circle around the tree, away from the gun until he found an opportunity to swing the baton around the tree again, striking the man's left hand, which dropped the gun after a nerve ending was struck.

Already knowing this man was not trained in the ancient art of *ninjutsu*, Clay pounced like a cat, flooring the man in one move from behind the tree. Holding the end of the baton against the man's throat, Clay made certain no one was walking the nearby path before beginning his interrogation.

"Talk, or this baton can go through your vocal cords, or your carotid artery, with a simple push. Who sent you to kill me?"

"Some Japanese guy," the man gasped, obviously not doubting the threat.

"What Japanese guy?" Clay asked, putting pressure on the baton.

He knew about a dozen men from Japan who weren't happy with him being the star pupil of their class when they carried on an ancient Japanese tradition. Being the only American among them didn't do much for his popularity, but he excelled because he knew of nothing else to focus on at that time.

"Some old Japanese guy met me in San Francisco," the man stammered as Clay applied more pressure with the baton. "He paid me half up front to kill you and your uncle in Muncie."

"Bill?" Clay asked, feeling an emotional spike that emanated from genuine concern. "God help you if you touched him."

"I didn't," the paid assassin replied, trying to squirm away from the baton's force. "The old man said your uncle knew too much and needed to die, but he insisted you go first."

Clay had an idea of who paid the man to kill them both as the pieces fell together in his mind. After two previous attempts on his life by his former fellow students failed, he began to question how they located him and their ulterior motives for trying to kill him. His relationship with Bill had grown a bit more distant after the last attempt on his life, because Bill hid information from him for his benefit. Inquiries about Bill's silence went unanswered to the point that they stopped talking altogether. Clay's move to Ohio simply added to the ease of them not communicating, though Clay very much wanted to confront Bill after this near death experience.

Forcefully flipping the man to his stomach, Clay applied handcuffs to his wrists before radioing his fellow park security officers for backup. He wasn't exactly sure what he wanted to tell them except that the gunman tried to shoot him with a rifle. How the man bypassed any of the gates with a loaded weapon eluded Clay, but he didn't plan on sticking around for the interrogation personally.

After explaining the situation as briefly as possible to authorities, he planned on paying his uncle a visit after a two-hour drive to his hometown.

CHAPTER 5

It wasn't until late Sunday evening when Clay arrived in Muncie, Indiana to find the college town the same as ever. Actually deemed a small city, home to Ball State University, Muncie was all Clay ever knew during his formative childhood years. The son of a city police officer who spent very little time around their home, Clay found alternative methods of entertaining himself during his teenage years, finally forming a bond with a man who worked for his father around the house. After several serious discussions between Clay, his parents, and Ryo Nosagi, it was decided that Clay would travel to Japan for mentoring from Nosagi.

Casey sounded disappointed when he tracked her down inside the theme park before leaving, simply stating a family issue required his attention in Indiana. She knew his father was in poor health, so she gave her blessing, and Clay said nothing to indicate a different reason for leaving. Coming from such a tightknit family, she held out hope that Clay might put aside his differences with his father before it was too late, but he couldn't share her optimism. Too many bad childhood memories kept him from ever truly forgiving the man.

Clay found Bill home by himself when he reached the country home his uncle had purchased soon after landing his job at the local hospital as the head of maintenance. Bill's life became an endless sequence of meetings, phone calls, and overseeing inventory between employees dropping in to ask questions or receive orders. Before Clay moved to Ohio, he changed Bill's life by entering him into the secretive world of *ninjutsu*, teaching him in his customized *dojo*.

"This is unexpected," Bill said when he answered the front door to the four-bedroom home that included an in-ground pool and hot tub before he added a three-car garage and coy pond in the front.

"Is Emily due back soon?"

"She just left for a business trip. Come inside."

Bill stood a few inches taller than Clay, remaining in excellent physical condition for a man in his mid-forties. He dressed casually at home with blue jeans and a flannel shirt to fend off the cooler weather. As he led Clay toward the immaculate, well-furnished living room, Bill looked back at his nephew with deep blue eyes through his eyeglasses. Not one to conform to trends, he still wore his brown hair parted to one side while a thick mustache of the same color covered his upper lip.

"You should've called if you were coming home," Bill said as he dropped into a loveseat.

Clay chose a recliner, unsure of where to start a conversation with his uncle. He needed to know the truth, and rather quickly, if he planned on preventing any further attempts on his life.

"I'm not exactly here for a social visit," Clay said up front.

"Oh?" Bill asked with genuine surprise.

The fire in the fireplace behind him warmed the entire room, completing the Terry Redlin cozy painting feel of the entire property.

"A man tried to kill me at the theme park today."

"Kill you?"

"I'm pretty sure you know where this is going, Bill. It's a repeat of what happened a few years ago, except this guy was paid to single me out. His orders were to end your existence once he finished with me."

Bill took a deep, unsettled breath, cupping his chin and cheeks a bit nervously.

"Care to explain why someone might have a need to kill you?" Clay pressed. "Maybe something you knew that someone couldn't afford to have leaked?"

Reflecting back to the night in question, Bill took a moment to collect himself before speaking.

"When that guy at the park thought he had me all but dead he made a confession, Clay."

"You mean the one you emptied a full magazine into?"

"Yeah, that one. Anyway, he confessed who hired him to carry out the attack against the theme park and your buddies."

Clay cleared his throat emphatically.

"And you couldn't find reason enough to tell me that someone might try and take my life in the future?"

"I didn't think you wanted to hear the truth."

"That the man who taught me everything I know, including the principles I live my life by, wants me dead?"

"How did you know?" Bill asked, unable to look his nephew in the eyes.

"Intuition. I looked at the pieces and nothing seemed to fit. There wasn't a real motive for these guys to come after me, because their type only cares about using their training for profit. It dawned on me that maybe I was being tested, then it occurred to me that I was asked to travel to Japan under false pretenses altogether."

Bill looked to him with grave concern, biting his lower lip.

"There's a lot more to this than you know, Clay. After the incident at the park, I did some pondering too. You and I growing distant is my fault, and it's because I feel a strong sense of guilt for not stepping in sooner."

"How could you have stepped in sooner? You helped save thousands at the park that day."

"That's not what I mean. I should have known better, and I should've stopped your father from sending you to Japan."

Recently Clay's father had taken a turn for the worse regarding his overall health. Slowed by a stroke at age sixty, only two years after retirement, the senior Branson found himself virtually confined to his home. Clay's relationship with his father was always distant, icy at times, so he didn't play the part of the dutiful son and rush home to check on his father, though he did phone regularly. And though he hated to think in a hateful manner, he supposed karma caught up with the old man at long last.

"Did you ever question why your father had a Japanese man doing handiwork around the house?" Bill asked.

"I suppose it crossed my mind, but I wasn't even twenty yet, Bill. A lot of things distracted me back then. What are you trying to tell me?"

Bill hesitated momentarily, looking to the ceiling.

"I wasn't in the picture back then, but I think your father was into something illegal that involved imports and exports. Your *sensei* was part of whatever he was doing, but they put on a front to fool everyone else."

"And you never said anything about this sooner?"

"I never connected the dots until the attack at the park when I found out Nosagi was behind the attempts on your life. After that I did a little research and asked your mother a few things. It didn't take a genius to figure out what your father did back then. Your buddy had some overseas connections he used to import new drugs into our country."

"So all that time I spent on the drug task force, stopping drugs between here, Gary, and Chicago, was in part because of my father's dealings?"

"That's a safe bet, but it's not the worst part."

Clay's face wrinkled in confusion, wondering what could be worse than his own father turning his back on every vow he took when the city swore him in as a police officer. In better economic times, Clay's task force put a stop to the heavy drug trafficking between Muncie and the northern cities. Clay moved to Ohio around the time the police chief disbanded much of his group, mainly due to financial cutbacks and a mayor who didn't much care for public safety.

Bill stood to tend to the fire, using a poker to move the log into a better position to intensify the flame. The fire tamed the dampness choking the fall air, at least inside Bill's house, while providing a warmth that electric and gas heaters imitated poorly.

"At this point I've practically disowned your father," Bill admitted. "Based on my dealings with him back in the day, and talks with your mom, I think your father sent you away for his own benefit."

"Yeah, so I'd be out of his hair."

"No, so you could learn to be an assassin and work for him when you came back."

"What?" Clay asked incredulously.

"Why else would Nosagi whisk you away to Japan, train you to do all of those things, and create this huge façade, Clay? He set you up with the perfect, quintessential life over there only to rip it away from you? *He* murdered your wife and son, Clay. Nosagi has been behind everything that's happened to you since you graduated high school."

Feeling like he was standing in some movie revelation moment where the camera quickly distanced itself from the shocked main character, Clay found himself figuratively slapped in the face.

"I'm sorry, Clay," Bill said compassionately. "I didn't tell you this before because I was afraid that going public with any of it might put you in even more danger. I'm really sorry."

"So am I," Clay muttered, barely able to digest so much negativity at once.

In the matter of one day his life went from walking on air to plummeting toward the earth without a parachute. He knew his life could never be the same, much less normal, until he located Nosagi and dealt with him.

Permanently.

Uncertain whether or not he was capable of killing his former mentor, Clay knew he needed to confront the man. Living the remainder of his life with Casey wasn't an option if he found himself looking over his shoulder every hour of every day.

"I'm going to find him," Clay vowed aloud.

"If I can help in any way, name it."

Clay wasn't certain how he felt about his uncle at the moment. While Bill kept certain truths from him, it seemed his uncle did so with Clay's best interest in mind. The man had always been more like a big brother than an uncle to him, treating him very well when he lived in the Muncie area. Even so, Clay decided he needed to return to his new home to check on Casey and begin his search for Ryo Nosagi.

"I've got to go, Bill."

"Don't leave like this," Bill said just short of pleading. "If you're pissed at me, just tell me."

"I don't know how I feel right now."

Clay stood to walk to the doorway where Bill intercepted him by blocking the door with his arm.

"If you find him, I'll help you any way I can, Clay. I want to make this right between us."

"We'll see," Clay answered neutrally, brushing his uncle's arm aside as he stepped outside to drive home.

Finding Nosagi was probably going to be difficult, and might even require him traveling to Japan. He didn't live in some soap opera where he could conveniently take time off work, or simply pick up another job if he quit the police department. With limited options, Clay needed to make some important decisions concerning his life and his future very quickly.

CHAPTER 6

Russ Greene couldn't believe how the past few months drastically altered his life. His career, retirement plans, and ambitions of putting evildoers behind bars for the United States Marshals Service abruptly came to an end. Luckily for him the occasional exciting fugitive chase, bank robbery cases, and constant battle against drug dealers and their labs ended on his own terms when a more lucrative job offer came his way.

Approached by Paul Clouse in the middle of November, Greene listened to the man's sales pitch about thirteen cursed cubes with skepticism and minimal interest, believing he was flown to Massachusetts as part of some television hoax show. Even when Julie Knowles chimed in with information and some of the history her group endured getting the cubes back, he wasn't convinced. While obituaries of Greg Slone and Mark Teakon backed their story to some extent, making him feel for them, it wasn't until they showed him a cube and the leather-bound book that Greene found himself convinced.

The book's writing revealed Julie as the latest possessor of the cube, but when she handed the cube to Clouse the book scrawled Clouse's name immediately in immaculate handwriting at that very moment. Seeing the writing live and in person, Greene felt certain his eyes grew as big as saucers. He doubted some kind of magic trick was responsible for the ghostly script before him, so it took only a little more description of their personal experiences with the cubes, followed by their impending hunt, to convince him to join their team.

Clouse also revealed to him that the cursed objects were indestructible when he took a hammer to one of them, causing it no damage whatsoever. It seemed Greene had a lot to learn about his new occupation because it dealt with religion and specifically the occult. The notion of Satan himself cursing objects in some sort of pact felt foreign, if not impossible, but Greene felt this new knowledge backed general religious beliefs.

Basically wanting Greene to replace Teakon as the leader of the hunting operation, Clouse offered him far more money than the government could dream of providing. There wasn't a pension per se, and the risk sounded steep, but the reward to someone as morally sound as Greene far outweighed the danger.

Working the private sector never crossed his mind because he loved his job, but the thought of stopping possibly the greatest source of evil in the world intrigued him.

Greene found himself accepting the job the day after the meeting in Massachusetts because there were no attachments to hold him back. It appeared Clouse knew he wasn't married, had no children, and wasn't in a serious relationship at the moment. Clouse also revealed that he knew of Greene's moral fiber through his lack of an arrest record, his unblemished personnel file, his responsible finances, and the fact that he lived tobacco and alcohol free.

"I want someone I can trust, who won't be distracted by vices," Clouse revealed during their conversation.

Greene felt certain the man possessed better means of background checks than the government, but he supposed money provided such assets. Clouse never went into details about his riches, or how he obtained them, but he made it clear he possessed financing enough to conduct a full hunt and retrieval of each cube.

Conducting his own research, Greene learned a few things about Clouse, though sorting fact from myth proved difficult. The media was never fed complete stories, and apparently the local police were shielded from the unbelievable truth as well. Greene used his credentials one last time to conduct the check on his new boss before turning in his badge and firearm to his lieutenant with his immediate resignation. His sudden departure shocked his fellow employees and his lieutenant, but Greene refused to provide any reasons or information, simply stating he took a job in the private sector.

A whirlwind of information swept over him in a short time, including the fact that Clouse wanted to hire two more necessary individuals to complete the team. Greene reviewed the two selections with his employer, agreeing with the picks completely as his faith in Clouse grew. They agreed that Clouse's choice to replace Greg Slone with a new, well-rounded expert in survival and weapons could wait because they needed someone with a specific talent to help them find the suddenly valuable time cube.

Because the cube's owner disappeared decades earlier without a trace, only one realistic option remained for the group to track the cube. While Greene found himself unfamiliar with psychics, and highly skeptical, Clouse assured him the process worked with the correct person using his or her talents. The two discussed the religious ramifications of using a medium in their quest, knowing the Bible plainly stated interactions with such people were taboo.

Now, in the middle of December, Greene found Liz Harper by his side in Schaumburg, a Chicago suburb, looking for their first major clue in the search for the time cube. Though he had yet to see Liz in action with her psychic abilities, her résumé looked impressive. She worked with police agencies in searches for missing persons and those responsible for committing unsolved murders.

Clouse made certain she never touched any of the cubes or the leatherbound book during the interview process. When Greene inquired why, Clouse explained contact with any of the objects involved in the curse might send a flurry of images through her mind about the origins of the cubes and the book. He wanted all of her concentration, and her abilities, focused on finding the most dangerous of the bunch once she accepted the position on their team.

He quickly discovered very little rattled Liz, as though she had seen the same types of gruesome scenes he had as a law enforcement officer. In a manner of speaking he supposed she had through her visions, but visions failed to provide the odors associated with death, or the shock of seeing a corpse waiting around a corner when it wasn't expected. Seeing such things in a third person capacity also removed the element of danger from the equation.

A native Californian, Liz acted down-to-earth for someone with such extraordinary abilities. She dressed like a gypsy at times, wearing dark tops and colorful shawls with dark slacks or long skirts. Today, with snowfall steadily falling around the Chicago area, she sat in the passenger seat of their rental car wearing a winter coat with a shawl of orange and black swirled colors. Her black hair was tied in a bun atop her head, held in place by a scarf as though she were an elderly lady heading out for a BINGO night on the town.

In truth, Liz was several years short of middle-age, choosing to put forth an eccentric appearance to match her talent.

"How do we handle this?" Liz inquired as Greene turned down the street toward the house in question.

"What do you mean?"

"I mean you no longer have a badge and I'm not exactly a poster child for civilian search advocate groups."

"We've been through this already," Greene said with a sigh. "Thomas Ervin, an officer with the Chicago Police Department, disappeared in 1979. Our information tells us he was the last one to possess the time cube, guarding it against those who wanted it for their own purposes. It seems soon after the cube was created, someone from this department has always kept it safe from groups like the Coven that Mr. Clouse dealt with. We're about to visit Trudy, his sister who never married, to see if we can gather any additional information, or you can do your thing."

"That still doesn't explain what you told her."

Greene peered intently out the side of the windshield, searching for the appropriate house number. In the older neighborhood all of the houses ran together, literally a few feet apart from one another with short fences across the front that held mailboxes.

"She believes we're with an advocate group, as you alluded to, dedicated to searching for missing persons. What do you need from her to do your thing? Because I'm just here as a mouthpiece."

"Don't worry about me. I'll get what I need from her and hopefully we can get a lead."

"We need one," Greene grumbled as he pulled in front of the correct house, a residence with metal siding painted yellow that appeared in desperate need of a facelift.

Liz followed Greene to the front door where he knocked, waiting patiently a moment until a thin woman with glasses opened the door and examined them with a hint of mistrust, as though they might be there to eat her.

"Ms. Ervin, I'm Russ Greene, and this is my associate Elizabeth Harper. I spoke with you about our group and possibly starting a search for your brother."

"Come in."

Liz tried giving him a skeptical look, indicating she thought this woman was a complete weirdo, but Greene turned away before Trudy saw him acknowledge anything. While she looked a bit like Adrian from the early *Rocky* movies, Trudy had yet to prove she was anything more than a single hermit surrounded by thousands of strangers.

"I'm not sure how you can help," Trudy said as they followed her inside the well-kept, yet dated residence. "My brother's been gone the better part of thirty years."

"He disappeared without a trace," Greene stated. "We specialize in generating a trail where the police and other agencies have failed through less conventional means."

"This house was his, you know," Trudy said with a hint of sadness in her voice. "When Mom passed away it fell to me."

Greene began to surmise the reasons for her lonely life, having everyone she cared about dying or disappearing in time. From the looks of the house's décor and the dated walls and carpeting, Greene believed Trudy froze herself in a time when her family surrounded her and she knew happiness.

"What can you tell me about the days leading up to your brother's disappearance?" Greene inquired as they all took a seat in the living room.

"Nothing, really. He went to work that week like usual, and he even called me the day before he disappeared."

"Did he seem upset?"

"No. It was an ordinary conversation. Look, I've been over this with the police a dozen times. Don't you know all of this already?"

Greene shifted his position, trying to find some sort of comfort level without a badge and holstered gun to provide authority and backing in his new career.

"I have an idea, but I'm not privy to the police reports, Ms. Ervin. It's important I have an understanding what led up to his disappearance."

"Do you have anything that belonged to your brother?" Liz asked without hesitation or any provocation.

Trudy simply gave her a stunned look in return.

"Maybe an article of clothing or a household item he owned," Liz continued, not fazed one bit.

"How does this help at all?" Trudy questioned.

"Liz can see things that other people don't," Greene explained ambiguously.

"Like a psychic?" Trudy asked excitedly, a mix of bewilderment and glee showing in her face.

Greene felt like he was sitting between padded rooms in a psychiatric ward. Often called upon to deal with unusual individuals during his marshal days, he knew how to exercise patience, but not how to deal with the supernatural element he now hunted.

"Exactly like that," Liz said, picking up on Trudy's intrigue like a relay runner grabbing a baton.

"I've always wondered when they might bring a psychic into the mix," Trudy said elatedly, standing to search for an item.

I'm in hell, Greene thought, figuring he was dealing with this bizarre woman in the slimmest of chances that he might advance his hopeless search. He wasn't a big fan of Liz yet, though that might change in a heartbeat if she proved herself worthy of Clouse's blessing.

Trudy returned a minute or so later carrying a display case full of badges that she set upon her lap as she took a seat. Carefully opening the box, as though it contained ancient, valuable relics, Trudy plucked a silver badge in the shape of a star from its resting place. She looked at it momentarily, openly missing her brother as she stared at one of the few things he left behind in the wake of his disappearance.

"May I?" Liz asked, tentatively reaching for the badge.

Trudy nodded, reluctantly relinquishing custody of the silver star as though it might vanish any moment.

Liz took hold of the badge, barely able to clasp it within her hand before her body jolted slightly and her mind took her to a different place.

CHAPTER 7

When Thomas Ervin took over the responsibility of caring for the most dangerous object in the world, he knew little about its history or the unheralded organization that chose him for the job. He only knew that five Chicago police officers comprised the group, and they monitored his progress on the department for several years before choosing him.

Once he passed several initiation phases, including extensive interviews and trust tests, Ervin was given the cube and told to hide it somewhere safe and tell no one where he placed it.

Ever.

The responsibility fell to him until one of the five died and they began the search for someone new to protect the cube. A heavy commitment fell on Ervin, one that required sacrifices similar to those of a Catholic priest. His life surrounded the defense of that cube, not allowing him to have relationships or stray very far from Chicago because he needed to remain in close proximity of the cursed object.

Continuing to live an everyday life by reporting to work and occasionally heading to taverns with his friends, Ervin checked on the safety of his albatross from time to time. Guarding the most dangerous object in the world while unable to tell anyone about his efforts became somewhat of a burden sometimes, but he understood his silence kept the world safe. He hungered for knowledge about the cube and the sister cubes he merely heard rumblings about from his fellow protectors.

After finishing his afternoon shift Ervin decided to drive around to clear his mind. A night of frustrating calls had left his blood pressure elevated, so he decided to cool off before heading to his dark and empty house for the night. He drove through Chicago en route to Schaumburg, deciding to drive a bit further before reaching his house. For some reason he felt impulsive about checking on the cube, as though it called to him for some reason.

Cursed objects took on a life of their own, as though programmed during their creation to lure weak-willed men and women to them like sirens at sea. In this case the cubes shimmered and glowed when touched, somehow projecting their abilities into the minds of those who held them. Ervin avoided handling the cube after his first few unsettling experiences, or donned gloves when he found a need to touch the square gem. Still in uniform, he already wore leather gloves, along with the leather duty jacket that creaked whenever he shifted in the driver's seat of his 1973 blue Plymouth Roadrunner.

Lucky to not be driving through drifting snow, Ervin felt certain his late November run to the county road where he kept the cube hidden would be the last until springtime. It took nearly twenty minutes to escape the confines of Schaumburg, and another twenty to reach an old bridge he remembered from his childhood. Numerous trips to visit his grandparents on weekends left the haunting vision of the decaying bridge imprinted in his memory. A short bridge constructed atop a stone foundation in the 1940s, the structure's days appeared numbered, so Ervin monitored county contracts and construction projects with great interest in case it was due to be replaced or demolished.

Gone were the street lamps, passing trains, and the criminal element that kept Ervin busy on a daily basis. Only trees, open fields, and the occasional residence created his current scenery, relaxing him a bit despite the frigid temperatures going head-to-head with his car's heater. Ervin eventually found the road that led to the bridge, turning the steering wheel with an open palm, grinning to himself. Visiting the bridge felt like going home again, stirring childhood memories for him each and every time.

Careful to check behind him every few miles to ensure no one followed him, or accidentally stumbled upon him requesting directions, Ervin pulled to the side of the road just short of the bridge. He stepped out of his car, slapped in the face by the biting wind and frigid temperatures. Thankful the blizzard conditions of the previous year weren't back, he walked toward the bridge, hearing the crunch of frozen grass and small rocks beneath his shined work shoes. He wore his regulation hat for the little warmth it provided his head, zipping his jacket a bit higher as he walked.

Thinking he heard the rumble of a car motor in the distance, Ervin stopped in his tracks, spinning to look for headlights. He spied nothing in the distance, no longer hearing anything aside from the wind through the nearby trees. Thinking his head was still swimming with the noises of the city, he grunted to himself before continuing his walk.

When he reached the beginning of the bridge, Ervin carefully stepped down the embankment, avoiding any loose rocks that might send him tumbling like a dislodged boulder. While the bridge itself rested on concrete, the ends were made of decorative rocks that began to loosen over the years as their mortar gave way. From his childhood days, Ervin knew that certain rocks came out with little more than a tap. Once he decided to make this the cube's hiding place, he expedited the process of breaking the seal, memorizing exactly where he placed the cube once he dug out a tiny cove for it.

Most of the rocks were light in color, with a handful in the medium gray range, and a few more that appeared dark gray in daylight or moonlight. Ervin counted the dark rocks from the leftmost edge until he got to the fourteenth one that resided just above his head. Using his height as a vertical marker and the memorized number as the horizontal reference, Ervin worked the dark rock about twice the size of his fist free from its resting place, reaching behind it to find a tiny deer skin pouch he once purchased from a rural flea market. He originally stuffed the cube inside the pouch to keep it from shimmering at him, like a wink from an attractive woman, whenever he laid eyes upon it.

Temptation to alter the course of time enters any rational person's thoughts from time to time, so Ervin didn't want any coercion from an inanimate object. As he pulled the pouch from its resting place for a quick look at the dark blue object, he heard a vehicle approaching slowly from the same direction he traveled. Suspecting the worst out of necessity, he stuffed the pouch into a jacket pocket, believing anyone who put forth the effort to tail him would not rest until they examined the area after murdering him anyway.

For all he knew, someone was above checking on his car, wondering if it was abandoned by the side of the road. He only thought of the worst scenario for self-preservation purposes. Ervin walked a longer way around the side of the bridge before scaling a nearby dirt hill to ground level with the bridge itself. Finding a car parked beside his Roadrunner, he dashed to a nearby large rock and ducked behind it.

Two men stepped from the car, looking very official as though they worked for the federal government. Both wore fedoras and dark suits with heavy overcoats. Ervin suddenly felt positive the two men had followed him by shutting down the headlights to their Ford LTD sedan. They looked like serious characters, especially when they both looked cautiously around as they stepped from the car, one even drawing a firearm without provocation. Ervin felt positive the backseat or trunk was reserved for him, with or without a bullet in his skull.

He now faced two major threats. One, he needed to place the cube in a new hiding place immediately, provided he survived this encounter. Two, if these two men knew about him, and more importantly, the cube, someone likely sold Ervin out to the government or another agency. The only people who supposedly knew about the cube were Ervin and his four fellow police officers.

If he couldn't trust them, he needed to dispose of the cube forever and tell no one about his experiences.

Unless these men did something careless, like distance themselves from their car enough for him to make an escape, Ervin suspected he might be involved in a shootout within minutes. He simply waited and watched as the men exchanged glances before walking in different directions. Wondering momentarily if they were robots, able to communicate without speaking before carrying out their orders, Ervin crouched behind the rock, reaching for his sidearm as one of the men walked in his direction.

Neither man glanced around in search of him, which only reinforced his opinion that his pursuers were androids or aliens, using technology beyond his comprehension. Ervin quickly shook off the notion, figuring the agents developed their plan before stepping from the vehicle. Government spooks or not, they were not allowed to lay hands on the cube, even if it forced the Chicago cop to use deadly force.

It took less than a minute for each man to reach one side of the bridge. The one not holding his firearm pulled out a flashlight, turning it on and shining it down to the bottom. Ervin knew their search was quickly going to reveal he wasn't there, meaning they wouldn't hazard the steep walk to the bottom. He decided he needed to make a run for it, and quickly, if he wanted to avoid a firefight.

Darting from behind the large rock, he cut across the short field to his car, drawing the attention of the two men almost immediately. Closer to the cars than his pursuers, Ervin drew his firearm and fired into the right front tire of their car before jumping into the Roadrunner. Not daring to look ahead, the cube's guardian slid his ready key into the car's ignition, hearing it roar to life before he looked up and noticed the two men drawing down on him, their firearms trained at his front windshield.

"Shit," he muttered, throwing the car into reverse, narrowly missing the LTD behind him as he backed a safe distance down the road before pulling the steering wheel hard to the right.

Not one shot was fired as Ervin slammed his foot on the gas pedal, putting the bridge behind him in a hurry. He breathed a sigh of relief as his mind raced to contemplate the next logical move. Hiding the cube was his priority, and Ervin knew to have contingency plans for virtually every situation, but executing them in the dead of night wasn't a cinch.

After a few miles Ervin began to slow his car, not wanting to draw attention to himself. The last thing he wanted was a documented stop by local law enforcement, or even a random passerby recalling that he spied a speeding Roadrunner in the overnight hours. While spending a few minutes deciding which of his next hiding locations he wanted to use, Ervin glanced behind him, thinking he noticed a glimmer of metal in the unusually intense moonlight. Seeing no headlights, he began thinking his imagination was getting the better of him when he felt his body lurch forward from a rear impact.

Shaking off the initial shock rather quickly, Ervin stomped the gas once again, seeing no headlights behind him. Either the two men were certified in race car pit stops, to change a tire so quickly, or a backup team took over in the pursuit.

Still highly familiar with his surroundings, Ervin pushed the knob for his own headlights, turning them off before he veered into a field. A cat and mouse game ensued with neither vehicle yielding to the darkness, so the young police officer knew only time and fate separated one of the vehicles from hitting a large object that disabled it. Luckily the moonlight lit the field fairly well, and though Ervin probably passed the field hundreds of times over the years he didn't know every square foot of it by any means.

He knew of a large tree near the center of the field, so he drove toward it, hoping to pull off a feat that might get him out of his current predicament. While the bumps and small rocks took a toll on his car, he simply hoped it could outrun the LTD, or at least outlast it. Unwilling to blink for fear he might crash and make himself a sitting duck, Ervin slowed just slightly until he saw the tree atop the next hill. He headed directly toward it, gaining speed despite the protests from his car whenever it struck a dirt mound or rock, lifting it a few inches off the ground.

Figuring he might be sentencing his car to death, Ervin continued pushing its limits, drawing dangerously close to the tree. He waited until he was within ten feet of it, hoping the men behind him were too distracted to see the danger, before swerving hard to the right. Ervin's racing heart virtually jolted within his chest when he heard a horrific crash behind him. The sounds of metal twisting and snapping reached his ears when the heavy engine block collided with the unmoving tree trunk, the speed of the impact alone compressing the car like a squeezed accordion.

Ervin brought his car to a stop, trying to catch his breath from the nerve-wracking ordeal momentarily as he stared in the rearview mirror. Smoke or steam rose from the engine block as the pungent smell of antifreeze was carried his way with the light breeze. The brake lights on the LTD glowed an eerie red, as though the driver's foot might be stuck in position, or his body was crumpled entirely beneath the dash. Still shaking from adrenaline and the experience that brought him closer to death than anything in his entire life, Ervin reached under the seat for a spare revolver he kept with him at all times.

His four fellow protectors told him to *never* tie himself to any situation by firing his issued sidearm outside of his workplace. Science was on the verge of breakthroughs in DNA and forensic technologies, including firearms analysis. They kept up on such technology, often attending seminars and workshops to remain ahead of adversaries who wanted the cube.

Flinging his door open, Ervin decided to provide some fast closure to the situation before someone noticed the scene from the normally quiet road. Already marching with a purpose toward the disabled LTD when his door shut itself on the rebound, Ervin kept the spare firearm clutched in his right hand as he walked. Despite approaching the passenger's side, he saw the driver more clearly, slumped over the wheel, his mouth agape while his fedora hung limply to the opposite side, one edge still pinned between the steering wheel and the man's head.

Drawing closer to the vehicle, Ervin saw only a little bit of the passenger's back because the man appeared pressed against the dash, probably not wearing his seatbelt during the pursuit. Ervin was now within ten feet of the vehicle, raising his firearm to ensure the two men reported nothing to whomever sent them. He hated the idea of killing in cold blood, if the two men weren't already dead, but he understood the importance of keeping the cube safe from evildoers.

Within a second, as though he had played possum the entire time, the passenger sat back in his seat, taking aim at Ervin with a revolver. Ervin found himself unable to pull the trigger before the other man fired at him, but he delivered a fatal shot a split-second after the man's bullet struck his abdomen. Immediately clutching the wound, Ervin staggered forward, seeing that his bullet entered the man's forehead, killing him instantly as wide eyes returned his stare. The driver showed no signs of life in the forms of movement or even breathing, but Ervin fired a bullet into the vehicle, striking the side of the man's head just the same to ensure the two men didn't follow him or summon help.

Blood trickled from his wound as Ervin painfully returned to his Roadrunner, determined to hide the cube before seeking medical assistance. His mind raced for anywhere nearby where he might dump the cube, ensuring its safety, until he could return to it. Driving toward the road, determined to distance himself from the bloodshed behind him, Ervin thought of two possibilities in the form of a pond and a quarry less than a mile from where his grandparents once lived. After his grandfather passed away, his grandmother moved in with the family for a time, but they eventually placed her in a nursing home. Ervin supposed he chose the area to hide the cube because it provided him with an excuse to revisit his childhood from time to time.

He considered the pond a better hiding spot, because it spanned a few football fields in length, often used for swimming or fishing recreationally during the summer months by the owners and their friends. While the cube would certainly be hidden better there, Ervin considered the task of finding it again rather daunting. Besides, the pond remained highly visible from the road and neighboring houses, meaning he couldn't risk getting caught trespassing while trying to retrieve it.

The quarry, however, remained filled with stagnant water all year round. Somewhat deep, at least from what he'd heard, the pit provided direct access to the cube at the bottom through a simple, strategic dive. Ervin knew two of his fellow protectors were certified divers, and if he didn't want to enlist their help by revealing his blunder, he felt certain he could take a crash course in diving.

Now driving toward the quarry, Ervin felt a bit dizzy. He reached for the concealed cube, stuffing it into an inner pocket within his duty jacket. Fighting to stave off the fatigue and blood loss that required his body to rest, he steered off the county road onto a dirt road that went uphill toward a metal gated fence. A construction company occupied the property during Ervin's childhood, but he seemed to recall his grandfather saying they dug for coal or minerals there once.

Uncertain of what entity owned the property, Ervin knew he hadn't seen another person step foot on it in years. Looters and vandals sometimes broke in for a look, so obviously someone monitored the area because a new lock always appeared on the mesh wire fence at the end of the dirt road.

Ervin cut the lock with a pair of bolt cutters he kept in his truck for just such occasions before returning to his car, feeling drained of all energy. He needed to conduct his business and leave the property to avoid the risk of passing out and being found by the keeper of the grounds. More importantly, he needed to ditch the cube, so he drove a few donuts along the dirt-covered grounds to make it look as though teenagers were driving recklessly on the property, then steered directly toward the quarry where the ground was solid enough to avoid leaving tire tracks.

Nothing really blocked the entrance to the quarry, because the fence that once surrounded the property fell into disrepair years prior, and the watery pit actually resided a little more than twenty feet below the edge of the property. Ervin simply needed to drive to the edge of the property, step from his car, and drop the cube into the dark water below. Instead, he succumbed to the gunshot wound, feeling his head swirl before it fell back against the seat while his foot remained pressed against the accelerator.

Brief sounds entered his ears during his semi-conscious state, including glass cracking and shattering, along with water gushing nearby. He awoke once to find himself surrounded by complete darkness with freezing water up to his chest, still seated inside the Roadrunner. Wanting nothing more than to fight his way out of the dire predicament, Ervin felt his body betray him, lethargic and exhausted to the point that he barely felt the deadly chill of the water. He tried the door, finding the water pressure holding it in place against his diminished attempts to escape. Knowing an air pocket would remain in place for hours, possibly days, within the car, Ervin drifted into a permanent, peaceful slumber with false hope.

CHAPTER 8

Clay Branson continued to work part-time at the theme park, despite the season ending. All year round the property required security forces to keep trespassers away, because people wanted to sneak peeks at the coming year's new ride being constructed, or simply walk the grounds without crowds around. Clay could appreciate that sentiment, hating the hot summer days where he felt like an ant amongst millions of other ants, simply trying to plow his way through the wall of people.

The fact that Nosagi wanted him dead continued to plague him, though he didn't spend every minute of every day consumed with revenge or worry, especially around his fiancée. He hated keeping secrets from her, but telling her about Nosagi endangered her if Clay confronted his former master and failed.

Clay had other worries as his father's health declined, though he still refused to return home. He remained angry at his uncle for keeping secrets and nearly getting him killed, but mainly for keeping secrets.

Dressed for the cooler weather, Clay walked along the main drag where people first entered the theme park, trying the door to every restaurant and gift shop as he headed toward the rides. Quiet and abandoned for the winter, the rides often stood against the elements without coverings while their trains were taken to the maintenance shops for an overhaul. Mechanics and security guards occupied the park during the winter months until directors and managers returned in early spring.

No snow fell from the sky in the greater Cincinnati area, but the wind chilled to the bone. Clay hated doing foot patrols, but he couldn't inspect every inch of the property on a four-wheeler, or in one of the marked park police vehicles. Shivering slightly, Clay moved to the end of the main drag toward the mammoth observation tower. During the season two elevators took guests to the top where they could gaze across the entire park, well above all of the rides and games. Several coin-operated telescopes were fixed along the security railing for better views of whatever guests wanted to see.

Clay simply stared upward, unable to see the telescopes from the ground, though he recalled several romantic encounters with Casey atop the tower after park hours.

His radio crackled momentarily before the voice of a fellow Mason police officer who worked security at the park called for him.

"Clay, I've got some people here at the employee gate who want to talk to you."

"Did they say who they were?" Clay asked, possessing no clue about who might want to speak with him.

"No, but they want me to tell you they have information about some guy named Nosagi," the officer asked more than stated.

Curiosity and a bit of shock caused him to stiffen when he heard the words.

"Please send them to our office, Cal," Clay replied after a few seconds.

Apprehensive, yet chomping at the bit to hear news of his former mentor, Clay fought the urge to powerwalk or run toward the security building. Hidden behind the high fences that separated the patrons from the inner workings, the security office sat apart from the other management facilities.

His instincts told him anyone wanting to kill him probably wouldn't stop at one of the main gates to announce their presence, but Clay wondered if anyone who knew about Nosagi could be on his side of the law. He crossed the median, circumventing the five large fountains normally surrounded by a large pool of water. Fenced in to keep guests away from the water, the fountains changed colors at night thanks to waterproof lights at their bases during the summer.

When he reached the office, Clay used his staff identification card to let himself in with a swipe through the electronic reader. He paced the floor a few minutes until Cal Unger brought a husky man in a suit and another man dressed in casual attire. The second man introduced himself as Paul Clouse, and the man who looked like a bodyguard as his associate Todd Parish.

Once Unger left, Clay offered the men seats in a nearby conference room where he sat across the table from them for observational and self-preservation purposes.

"How can I help you?" he asked, directing his question toward Clouse.

"I'm here to offer you a job," Clouse answered without hesitation. "There's no sense beating around the bush because I need your skill set to retrieve something important."

"What does this have to do with Nosagi?"

"Your former teacher has possession of the object I need."

Clay found himself somewhat confused because of the vague statements coming his way. The last thing he expected when he woke up and worked out that morning was a job offer and the chance to find his former mentor, but it sounded like both opportunities landed at his door.

"It sounds like I need to hear this from the beginning," he finally said.

Clouse spent nearly half an hour telling him a tale of how a friend betrayed his trust, all in the name of obtaining a red cube that gave the possessor back his or her youth if used regularly. He went on to tell about meeting Mark Teakon, and how the professor showed him that the red cube was only the beginning. By the time talk of a leather-bound book came up, Clay felt highly skeptical of the entire saga. Clouse proved he knew quite a bit about Nosagi and the man's plan to train assassins and use them for his own benefit.

"How exactly did I land on your radar?" Clay asked the question that was skimmed over during Clouse's talk.

"The terrorist incident was very public news," Clouse answered. "It didn't take much beyond a traditional background check to learn about your time in Japan, and the other terrorist incident in your hometown. The rest of the story just fell into place."

Clay rubbed his chin, still a bit skeptical about the man before him and the story he brought with him.

"So I'm to believe my former *sensei* possesses a cursed object in addition to heading up a criminal organization?" Clay questioned once Clouse finished, though he already knew the latter statement held true.

"He's isolated himself on an island just off the coast of South America," Clouse stated, unwavering in his composure. "The locals thought it was cursed before he arrived, and now they warn everyone to stay clear of the island."

"Why is that?"

"Because everyone who steps foot on the island dies, Mr. Branson. I know Nosagi possesses a cube that allows him to turn dead or inanimate objects into creatures that carry out his bidding. For every person he murders, he gains a new servant unable to question orders or be anything but loyal to his every command."

"This just seems a bit farfetched to me," Clay said hesitantly. "You're asking me to give up my life here to track down some cube and my former teacher who may or may not be where you say he is."

Clouse provided a weak grin.

"I understand your skepticism. At first I was the same way, which is why I brought you proof of Nosagi's whereabouts."

Clouse nodded to Parish, who opened a briefcase and pulled out a thin stack of photographs showing habitation on the island in the form of a lodge or retreat of some sort. In one of them, Clay could make out a man of Oriental descent relaxing on a lounge chair of some sort, surrounded by henchmen that looked unusually proportioned. Considering the image was taken from above, and so far away, Clay questioned the details, wondering if the photograph was some sort of hoax.

Any doubts were erased when he saw the next photograph, quite possibly taken from a boat anchored offshore. Clay saw what appeared to be the same man strolling along the sand near the water's edge. He stared downward, providing no clear look at his face, but the next few images showed him lifting his head to stare out to sea, providing a perfect look at his features. Though aged almost fifteen years, the man was indeed the instructor who misled Clay, murdered members of his family, and failed in turning him into the assassin he dreamed of leasing out for murders and thefts.

"This is no easy undertaking," Clouse said, seeing Clay's face flush with anger. "Just to get to Nosagi you'll have to literally fight off the army he's amassed over the past year."

"Why hole up on an island?" Clay asked no one in particular.

"He still has communication set up with his employees. If he learns that my group is aware of his possession of the cube, he'll certainly send someone after us. It's a perfect way for him to conduct business while staying off the radar."

"How did he come into possession of this cursed object?" Clay asked, though he still couldn't believe he was inquiring about something that sounded like it came from an original movie on the Science Fiction Channel.

Clouse tapped his fingers on the conference table a moment, looking to a list from his briefcase.

"Does the name Quinton Shelby Lucas sound familiar?"

"No."

"We think Nosagi assassinated him personally for some reason, probably stumbling upon the cube at the man's estate. The cubes tend to make their presence known when there's a chance someone new is willing to use them."

Clay gave a quizzical look, though he refused to inquire further. Only one thing consumed his mind at the moment.

Nosagi.

"I need to make some arrangements at work, but I want you to take me to this island."

"I'm not asking you to simply do this one job for me," Clouse said. "There are thirteen of these things, and I'm assembling a team to help me track them down before the wrong people find them."

"I have a good thing going here," Clay stated. "With Nosagi gone, I can finally live without looking over my shoulder. If I survive this confrontation, I'll bring you back your cube, but that's all I can promise at this point."

"I pay well," Clouse added. "Well enough for you to quit your job, help me with this, and continue your internship toward the security director's position."

Clay mentally admitted the man did thorough homework, though he still wasn't sold on the supernatural aspect of the job.

Clouse seemed to sense he wasn't going to budge on his stand regarding the one-time partnership to retrieve the cube, drawing a deep, patient breath.

"Fair enough," he said. "I'll take you to Nosagi, but you'll be accompanied by Todd here. Consider the job a trial basis, and once you see what I've told you is entirely true, we'll have a position waiting for you whenever you choose to join us."

"I work better alone," Clay said, looking toward Parish. "Other people will slow me down and endanger us all."

"Believe me, I don't plan on getting off the boat once we're there," Parish assured him with a serious look and tone.

"In that case," Clay said, "I have someone I want to bring along as well to make sure everyone is adequately represented."

Clouse smiled, but it faded quickly.

"Sounds like we have a deal. Make your arrangements and let me know when you're ready to head south."

"Soon," Clay assured him. "You're the small miracle I was waiting for, but I hope you don't harbor secrets like Nosagi, or it'll be you that I come after next."

"After what I've been through, I don't fear much," Clouse replied evenly. "I also have no reason to lie to people who think as I do. We're willing to risk our lives to keep the world safe from these *objects*, and I believe you'll come to think as we do."

"We'll see about that. I'm just glad my passport is in order. With luck, I won't need my affairs in order."

Clouse stood for them all to shake hands briefly.

"With luck, we'll all be standing here in a few weeks thankful to be alive."

All of them knew that failure on Clay's part might create a trickle effect that put Nosagi on the path of each and every one of Clouse's employees until he felt satisfied he was no longer a target. Clouse understood a toll needed to be paid for him to gather all of the cubes, but he hoped to avoid the steep price of human life whenever possible.

CHAPTER 9

"So what did you see?" Trudy asked with a hopeful gleam in her eyes.

"Nothing," Liz lied perfectly, not displaying any signs that she was still shaken by the events that entered her mind from the past. "I thought I had something there for a second, but it was a false triggering."

"Do you want to try a different badge?" Trudy offered, holding up the case with eyes that pleaded for Liz to make another attempt.

Liz honestly wanted to get out of the house immediately to jot down what she saw during the vision, but she wasn't about to arouse suspicion by doing so. She touched another badge, then another, truly getting no further results the second, third, or fourth time around. She finally shook her head negatively, prompting Trudy to stare despondently toward the floor.

"I'm sorry."

"It's okay. I guess I was just hoping for answers after all these years."

"We're not done searching just because Liz couldn't get something," Greene said, taking the pressure off his colleague. "There are other ways to find Tom. Somewhere, someone knows something."

Trudy looked up, on the verge of tears.

"I hope so. The one thing I have left is the hope that one day he'll walk through that door. Everyone says there's always hope until they find him, well, you know."

Greene nodded understandingly.

"I've seen crazier things happen."

It took a few minutes to settle Trudy down and guarantee her they would inform her of any findings before Greene and Liz left the house. Liz felt absolutely terrible for hiding her incredible new discovery from Trudy, but her reasons for doing so eased her guilty conscience. She knew danger followed their investigation wherever it went, and they were probably about to begin a paper trail that led to the quarry where Thomas Ervin met his end.

Snow continued to spit from the sky, landing on Liz as Greene opened the passenger side door for her. She buckled her seatbelt as Greene slid into the opposite seat, placing the key in the ignition before looking her way with an expectant look.

"You saw something, didn't you?"

"I saw quite a bit actually. Can we just get out of here?"

As Greene drove them toward some of the main roads, Liz informed him of what she saw during the vision. When she finished, Greene stared out the windshield at the snow splattering against the warm glass, pensively breathing.

"We need to find that quarry without calling attention to ourselves," he said at last. "If we go poking around, that's dangerous for everyone involved."

"The library," Liz suggested. "We look up some county geography without asking anyone or using the internet and we find out where there was a quarry, or we look for businesses that went under just south of Chicago."

"That could take some time."

"It beats having men with guns come after us or Trudy."

Liz hated the thought of placing Trudy in danger. Greene told her to assume everything they did was being monitored, because another group was simply waiting to swipe the cubes from them the minute they surfaced. The time cube, in the wrong hands, could simply end their existence at any point in time if their adversaries gained control of it.

Greene programmed their GPS to search for nearby libraries, coming up with several branches in Chicago and a few south of the city.

"The larger branches are more likely to have good resources," Greene stated.

"But the county libraries take more pride in their history," Liz countered. "I worked at a library for three years."

Perusing the options, Liz finally found one near the area she believed Tom Ervin drove to on the night he died. She would know from some of the landmarks when they neared the library, so she chose the Naperville Public Library.

"This one," she said, touching the screen to indicate where she wanted Greene to drive them. "If we're lucky, I'll recognize something along the way."

"A lot can change in thirty years."

"I know. It was dark and there weren't many landmarks, but if we find that bridge, I think I can navigate us to the quarry. And if we get to the library first, so be it."

Greene didn't appear as assured as Liz felt. She knew roads changed, and the occasional new building was erected, but she doubted the rural landscape changed drastically over the course of the past three decades. A strange feeling that they were being tailed kept nagging at her thoughts. If Clouse possessed the resources to conduct elaborate background checks on people and learn their traits, certainly other people and organizations were capable of doing the same thing.

Through the side window she observed the landscape transition from the cold industrial setting of factories and old brick houses to winding country roads and trees bare for the winter. Christmas was less than two weeks away, with a strong possibility it might be snowy white, unlike holidays from her childhood. No loving husband or boyfriend awaited her with open arms, or any children who stared eagerly beneath the tree for a wrapped surprise. Twice Liz had opened herself up fully for a relationship that appeared to be sailing toward marriage, but twice she found herself disappointed.

At times her gift felt like a curse, so she kept quiet about it for the longest time until recurring visions virtually forced her to aid the police in the search for a missing seven-year-old who was kidnapped. That particular story ended happily, with the boy returned to his parents, though most cases Liz assisted on didn't give families the conclusion they prayed would come. Liz hoped closure was enough for them, but she never kept in touch with families once they were given final word of their loved ones. She found the ordeal painful enough without trying to create bonds that served as painful reminders of those she couldn't help.

"We're here," Greene said after what seemed like only minutes because Liz had drifted off to sleep, the flurries outside putting her under their hypnotic spell.

The brisk air refreshed her when she opened the car door, like a bucket of water to the face. She followed Greene up the sidewalk, walking through the door as he opened it for her. Beneath his gruff exterior, including the thick beard and brown eyes that often narrowed, like those of a predatory animal seeking prey, Greene acted the part of a gentleman. She wondered if he felt somewhat helpless with the federal government behind him, though she suspected he didn't encounter the bottom of the criminal barrel in Nashville, Tennessee.

She felt safe with him, not in the romantic sense of *The Bodyguard*, but rather the professional detachment Kevin Costner's character showed initially. Greene appeared capable in every facet, which explained why Clouse chose him to head up their team, but something about his personality remained vacant.

One instant of physical contact might reveal his entire past to her, but Liz didn't want to know intimate details about her colleague. It was better, she decided, to let nature take its course and see if he spoke more about his background.

"Where to?" Greene asked once they found themselves inside the comfort and warmth of the public library.

"I'm going to see if they have a local or state publication area. You might want to try periodicals and check out defunct construction companies from the 70s."

Greene nodded before beginning his search for old newspapers, which Liz hoped might be loaded onto microfiche for ease and timesavings. She found the library indeed kept an Illinois Room loaded with books new and old that covered local and state events. Picking out several hardcover books that showed promise, she leafed through them for pictures or information about local quarries. Strangely, her vision failed to show her a single road sign, or any markings along the property where Thomas Ervin took his final breaths.

She wondered if they might have better luck simply driving around the county roads until she found a familiar landmark. Daylight disappeared around suppertime in the afternoon, which meant their window of opportunity was dwindling. The gray, gloomy skies permeated the library's interior, trying to down her mood and make her listless. Liz refused to give in, knowing she was so close to finding Thomas Ervin and bringing closure to his sister. She understood the score, meaning Trudy couldn't know any information until the cube was recovered. Many more lives were at stake if secrecy wasn't maintained until the blue square was in safe hands.

Receiving an answer to her query was as simple as asking a local what construction company once housed its operation atop a hill with a nearby quarry, but Liz understood that any paper trail or witnesses to their search could lead the wrong people back to them.

Or the cube.

She continued flipping through the pages of a county history book that covered buildings, outbuildings, and historical sites that had come and gone over the decades. Deciphering the age of any building during the course of a vision never proved easy, so she started at the turn of the Twentieth Century to avoid missing any useful information in case the building she saw replaced an older structure.

A strange sense that someone was watching her crept into her mind. Looking up, she saw the perpetual gloom outside, but she felt a presence behind her. Placing her hands over the book pages, she turned to look both ways behind her seat, finding no one in the room with her. No one stood at the framed entrance looking in, but she still sensed something, or someone, nearby with ill intent.

She wondered if the unseen, virtually unknown enemy might have contracted someone like her to give them an insider's advantage. Fighting the urge to find Greene, Liz cursed herself for acting like a scared schoolgirl as she turned the pages briskly. A shadow to her right caused her to look to the doorway as a librarian stood there with a friendly smile.

"Finding everything okay?"

"I think so," Liz answered as positively as she could muster.

"If you need anything, just let us know."

"Thank you."

Liz decided the book was written, or at least published on a local level. Someone invested a lot of time into the research of information and collection of photographs for the hardcover book. She looked through the images covering the first few decades, figuring a construction business in the county wasn't likely passed down through several generations. Based on the area's appearance in her vision, it was plausible the business opened and closed within a year or two.

Growing impatient and feeling on edge from the thought of being observed, Liz fought to keep her concentration on the pages, flipping through the 1940s and 1950s rather quickly. A strange sense that she was drawing near an answer caused her to examine each page a bit more thoroughly, even reading instead of skimming the text.

When Liz reached the year 1964 in the book, she found a familiar building pictured atop a hill listed as Clausen Excavation, which probably meant they bid out contracts for construction, or possibly dug for minerals where the quarry later existed. She now knew the location existed in the southern part of DuPage County, and amazingly the address was listed in a column right beside the photograph.

Pulling a scrap piece of paper from her handbag, Liz jotted down some information despite immediately committing the address to memory.

She closed the book with both hands, causing a clapping sound before she returned it to the shelf, disobeying library rules about not re-shelving books. She intentionally placed it far away from its original position, going through the trouble of turning the flat side toward her as she hid it behind a row of tall books. If anyone tried tracing her tracks, they weren't going to have an easy time of it.

As Liz left the room to find Greene, he walked the floor rather briskly toward her, a disconcerted look etched across his face.

"What's the matter?" she asked.

"We need to leave. *Now.*"

Liz was about to ask for elaboration when he took her by the wrist and led her toward the exit. She spied two men in dark suits exiting a black sedan through the door's glass just before Greene pulled her against a nearby wall, motioning for her to keep quiet with a finger to his lips. Concealed behind some shelving, they observed the two men walking through the entrance from a side view. Only when the men passed the front desk did Greene take Liz by the hand and dart out the entrance with her in tow.

"They could be looking for an overdue book repeat offender," Liz suggested jokingly as she opened the passenger side door.

"Fat chance," Greene retorted. "I've seen enough government spooks to know their kind."

Liz thought the men looked eerily like the mysterious men who chased Thomas Ervin through the very county where she now found herself teamed with Greene. They didn't wear fedoras, but they shared the same shrewd, dark eyes.

"They were packing guns," Greene informed her.

"How do you know that?"

"I'm trained to notice details, Liz. If I missed a suspect with a gun in my former life, he might shoot me in the back later."

He started the car, trying to back out of the parking lot undetected, but the two men burst through the front door at the moment the rental car hit the open road. Greene muttered a curse word under his breath before gunning the accelerator to put some distance between them and their new stalkers.

"These guys remind me a lot of the men who were after Tom Ervin," she confessed.

"That's not a good thing, considering how he ended up."

Greene took some corners rather hard, trying to remove them from the sight of their pursuers. Liz kept looking over her shoulder, seeing the black car quite a distance behind during the first few turns. It took a sharp right turn away from the business district for Greene to lose them as he parked the car behind a large dirt hill beside a vacant lot.

"Why would they risk coming after us in the open like that?" she questioned.

Not even breathing heavily for having narrowly escaped torture or death, Greene maintained his professional composure, again affirming why Clouse chose him over dozens of candidates to lead the search.

"That's awfully brazen," Greene admitted. "Whoever controls this particular cube literally controls the destiny for billions of people over time. And I struck out in the periodical section. I was standing to stretch my legs when I saw them pull up outside."

Liz gave him a cagy grin.

"I didn't strike out. In fact, I know exactly where to find the remains of Mr. Ervin."

"That's good news," Greene said, smiling for the first time the entire day. "Now we have to tread carefully."

Liz considered telling him about the feeling she was psychically being spied upon, but she wasn't certain she believed it herself. While it explained how the men were suddenly acutely aware of their location, she felt Greene was still put off by her abilities. The idea of her gift acting as a figurative modem, sending and receiving information, had never crossed her mind. While she didn't want to place their objective in jeopardy, Liz needed more proof before spilling the beans about her theory.

Right now she simply wanted to get Clouse the information and let him create a strategy for retrieving the most dangerous object in the world.

CHAPTER 10

Harlan Samuel Stone found himself working in the offices of the FBI in Albuquerque, New Mexico. Somewhat new to the Bureau, Stone found the job to his liking, though he wanted a transfer to his home state of Texas in the next few years.

Like many people born south of the Mason-Dixon Line, Stone was given two names that rolled off his mother's tongue whenever he did something wrong as a child. He couldn't count the number of times he heard "Harlan Samuel!" during his childhood. By his teenage years Stone grew to hate the sound of both names, so he tried whenever possible to have friends and schoolmates call him by his last name or the ever-popular "Stoney" nickname.

No longer in the Hoover days, agents enjoyed a more casual atmosphere at work. Though much of the work was white collar in nature, Stone found it a welcome change from patrol duties in Houston. Sitting at his desk, perusing a case file regarding an abduction that crossed state borders between Arizona and New Mexico, Stone fought the urge to prop his feet atop the desk for more comfortable reading. Civilians worked in the office, and both suspects and witnesses crossed the FBI offices, so he dared not visibly relax.

At home it wasn't uncommon for him to kick back on the front porch and watch the world pass him by. In the county he saw more activity from wildlife than people and traffic, which suited him just fine.

"Still daydreaming that we'll get assigned to that case?" Dom Givens asked, seated at the desk across from Stone.

"Why does the SAC hate us so much?" Stone asked, putting on his glasses with his free hand to see his colleague more clearly.

Stone referred to Bryson Elliot, the Special Agent in Charge of their field office.

"What you mean to ask is why does he hate *you* so much? I got nothin' in it."

Givens was a black man born and raised in California who volunteered for an assignment in New Mexico because his wife's family resided in Santa Fe. He and Stone got along very well, often working cases together, but Stone openly disliked the SAC, which meant he and Givens shared joint punishment.

Stone tossed the file atop the desk in disgust, wanting to investigate more than his desk and the nearest restroom. After a stint of tedious surveillance duty on a man suspected of aiding his brother-in-law with hacking a local government website, Stone found himself in possession of a list of potential terrorism suspects. Ordinarily the assignment might be invigorating, but he quickly discovered different lists were assigned to each team and his suspects were the least threatening, and least likely to be affiliated with terrorists.

He currently hated life.

"Where did you get that file anyway?" Givens asked.

"I lifted it off of Harrison's desk. I feel like one of those people who have to read fiction to escape their humdrum lives."

"Your life will be a lot more exciting in the unemployment line, Harlan Samuel."

Stone gave a sharp-edged grin.

"I'll keep that in mind, Dom. What kind of respectable mother names her son Dom anyway? I've been meaning to call your mom and ask her. It sounds like you should be doing hits for the mob."

Givens shook his index finger at Stone. The two often chided one another over their personal lives to relieve work tension.

"Oh, so you think I should be a Tyrell, or maybe a Jermaine? Something a little more urban, like maybe Darnell that says I just missed the cut for the NBA? You know Dom is short for Dominic, right?"

"I'm well aware as you've told me a dozen times or better. It just never gets old getting a rise out of you."

"You ain't seen a rise out of me, Harlan Samuel."

"I never should have told you my middle name."

Givens grinned mischievously.

"Your dear mother did the honors when she told me all about your upbringing."

"She's getting coal for Mother's Day."

Stone picked up the file, walking it back to his fellow agent's desk where it belonged. It burned him that the SAC disliked him because he didn't hide the fact that he was a proud Texan currently stuck one state away. When he started with the branch, Stone put the other agents to shame with his tenacity and fearless attitude. He didn't care what parts of town he entered, or what prominent citizens he needed to interrogate to solve a case. Things only got better when the powers that be paired him with Givens, thinking the two were destined to mix like oil and water. And while a complete stranger might think they hated one another to the core sometimes, they actually enjoyed working as a team.

"You are such a racist," Givens joked when Stone returned to his desk.

"How can you say that? You're the one renaming yourself. Besides, I've eaten what your wife calls barbeque and said nothing derogatory about it."

"You Texans and your food," Givens said, shaking his head.

"We do it right over there. I can't help that you yuppies from California only eat nuts and berries."

"There you go again, Stoney. You just see me as Trivette to your Walker."

"Hey, Trivette was smart."

"And I'm not?"

Stone threw up his hands.

"I wasn't saying that! I'm just saying give the man some credit."

One of the female agents walked past the duo, giving them a quizzical stare.

"Don't you two have anything better to do than insult one another's heritage?"

"Actually, we're about due to violate some poor schmuck's civil rights because Lord Elliot deems it necessary," Stone answered.

He was about to make another comment sure to land him in hot water with the SAC when the phone atop his desk rang. Based on the ring, he knew the call was from within the building, and not from an outsider. Scooping it from the receiver, he wondered if Elliot was spying on him with hopes of accumulating enough dirt to fire him.

"Stone."

"Harlan, it's Sandy. Can you come to my desk, hon?"

"Sure," he replied to Elliot's secretary, wondering if he was about to be terminated after all.

Unlike Elliot, Sandy Newberry was a joy to be around on a daily basis. She had worked under two previous administrators, admitting to Stone that Elliot displayed the most temperamental personality of the three. She gave Stone insight about the reasons Elliot probably didn't like him, but none of it eased the tension because Stone wasn't about to change to appease his boss.

Despite his comment a moment earlier, Stone wasn't doing any fieldwork because of the late afternoon hour. He planned on heading home to see his wife soon because Elliot never gave him meaningful work that inspired him to work long hours. Stone played along, not wishing to lose his job, though he wished he could wriggle out from beneath the SAC's thumb long enough to get a transfer to his home state.

Elliot enjoyed tormenting him too much for that to happen anytime soon.

"What was the call about?" Givens questioned.

"Sandy had something for me. Maybe Bryson took an early retirement."

"The boy needs to."

Stone gave a halfhearted smile as he stood, ready to face whatever new punishment the SAC wanted to hand him.

Wearing dress slacks with a starched white shirt, Stone resembled the old-school FBI most agents fought to abolish. On this day he wore a tie bearing the Texas state flag in its bold red, white, and blue colors wrapped several times around the accessory. He wore a western style belt, since buckles were frowned upon at the workplace, though he did opt to wear shined black cowboy boots instead of shoes.

"It's no wonder he hates me," Stone said under his breath as he walked down the hallway, the clopping sound of his boots preceding him as he entered the SAC's office.

Relieved to see Elliot's door shut, and the lights off, Stone gave Sandy a smile as he placed both arms on her desk and leaned forward slightly.

"How's my favorite cowboy?" she asked in a slightly more cheerful tone than usual, indicating she indeed had good news.

"I reckon I'm doing fine," he said, intentionally letting his drawl slip.

He fought to suppress his accent and language on a daily basis because he couldn't be taken seriously as a federal agent if he spoke words like "y'all" and "cattywompus" on a regular basis. Only Sandy and his wife saw Stone's natural demeanor because he felt comfortable around them.

"What's the news, darlin'?" Stone asked.

"You're going to Washington."

"Washington?" Stone retorted, taken aback. "What the hell for?"

"I don't know. The Deputy Director wants to meet with you personally."

Stone waited for the punch line, or someone to call him to let him off the hook from whatever prank they were pulling. No agent in the field met with the Director or Deputy Director, or anyone higher than their SAC for that matter. Considering the unremarkable nature of his career lately, Stone couldn't fathom why anyone with clout would want to meet with him. Anyone with dreams and ambitions at work the past few months had avoided him like the plague.

"You're serious?" he finally asked, raising an eyebrow while doing his best to give a penetrating stare.

"Yes," Sandy said with a chuckle. "You're on the eight o'clock flight from Albuquerque International to Washington National."

He felt certain his jaw dropped, giving him the dumbfounded look he felt through and through.

"What? Tonight?"

"Can't keep the Deputy Director waiting, Stoney. He wants to meet with you immediately."

Stone looked to his watch, realizing he might need to use his credentials just to ensure he made the flight. Just over three hours to go home, pack, change, and make it through the airport security checkpoints didn't seem feasible, but he sensed urgency enough to make it happen.

"Here's your flight information," Sandy said, handing him a packet.

He leafed through the paperwork as though it might be a hoax, or part of some delusional dream, finding it completely authentic.

"Thanks," he said, starting to walk away almost absentmindedly.

"Don't forget us little people when you get your office with a view."

"Yeah, right," Stone said with a laugh as he picked up his pace, ready to see what new chapter awaited him.

***

Amazed he didn't have to catch a connecting flight, Stone decided the Deputy Director truly wanted to see him right away. He read two newspapers during the flight, tried to sleep, and even watched the in-flight movie just to pass the time, hoping to keep his nervous jitters at bay. Barely able to remember running home to pack, Stone felt as though a hurricane carried him through packing a small suitcase, quickly explaining the surprise to his wife, and finally to the airport where he used his credentials to bypass several levels of security so he could travel armed.

Stone soon discovered the small airliner was nearly filled to capacity, explaining why it never landed until reaching Washington D.C. Most of the people were dressed for business, obviously part of the Washington crowd. Based on observations alone, he figured at least two Congressmen were flying with him, talking with their aides during much of the flight.

Thanks to a phone call from Sandy, Stone found a rental car waiting for him at the airport. While his travels never took him to the nation's capital, Stone followed directions well, so he soon found his way to the hotel where he was booked, which also happened to be where the Deputy Director requested to meet him.

Bright, dazzling lights weren't new to the federal agent, but Stone found himself swelling with pride just stepping foot in Washington. To think, dozens of United States Presidents lived and served there, monuments and treasures were housed within the sacred city, and even the tragic events of 9/11 had touched the city with the icy finger of death. It was almost immediately after the terrorist attacks that the FBI went from chasing white-collar criminals to battling terrorism and tracking down spies.

Somewhat disappointed that Alan Stewart didn't request a meeting at FBI Headquarters, Stone figured the man had his reasons, particularly since the time change meant the midnight hour had come and gone a few hours prior.

He found himself wondering what kind of FBI leader summoned a typical everyday agent for a late night meeting outside of official offices, though he tried to avoid dwelling on the topic.

Even the adrenaline from anticipating the meeting failed to keep fatigue from setting in as Stone pulled into the hotel parking lot. He received a parking voucher, parked the rental in the nearby parking lot, then walked toward the hotel with a purpose. Sixteen stories loomed above him, but Stone observed an outdoor pool, closed for the winter, adjacent to an interior lounge housing a pool, sauna, and hot tub. A few signs indicated the hotel restaurant, which included a bar, remained open for another hour. It looked high dollar to Stone, but for some reason he expected he might find his answers waiting inside.

Instead of entering the restaurant, Stone walked through the one remaining unlocked door toward the front desk to check in. He decided to test the waters, wanting to spy the Deputy Director before Stewart laid eyes on him. Besides, he didn't want to act anxious, even if the anticipation was eating him from within. His armpits felt damp and sticky from both excitement and nervousness, considering Stone had never been summoned by anyone higher than his direct supervisors before.

A few minutes later he pocketed two keycards to his room before turning around to find a man wearing a suit standing behind him. While the Bureau had changed significantly over the past few decades, he felt certain the man wasn't seasoned enough to hold an administrative position in the organization.

"Please follow me, Agent Stone," the man said immediately with no introduction.

Still carrying his small suitcase, Stone followed the stranger into the restaurant, directly over to the bar. The man ducked into a segregated room momentarily before emerging to wave Stone into the same area. He let Stone pass, standing erectly at the door like a security agent, so Stone set the suitcase at his feet before entering the room with a single covered table.

A well-dressed man with salt and pepper hair stood to shake hands with Stone, a very wide smile crossing his lips.

"Agent Stone, Alan Stewart," he said, introducing himself.

"Deputy Director," Stone replied respectfully. "It's good to meet you."

"Have a seat," Stewart offered. "Would you like a drink?"

Stone gave him a skeptical look, wondering if business hours were truly over considering the apparent urgency of the meeting.

"You're off the clock," the Deputy Director stated.

"In that case I'll take a draft beer."

"I had you pegged for more of a scotch man," Stewart stated before calling out their drink order to the bartender just outside the isolated room.

"Only when things aren't going so well," Stone replied.

The agent escorting Stewart brought in their drinks momentarily. Stone only took a swig when the Deputy Director raised his glass, feeling like he might explode from curiosity.

"I have a new job title for you, if you're willing to accept it," Stewart said, cutting to the chase before taking another healthy drink from the glass.

Stone took a deep breath, trying to find the right words to speak.

"I know, you're wondering why you of all people," Stewart stated for him.

"You read my mind."

"It's not just one reason, Harlan. You've had ambitions since you were a teenager that still haven't materialized. First and foremost, you joined the Houston Police Department hoping to make your way into the Texas Rangers someday. In order to bolster your résumé, you worked your way into the Bureau so you could gain experience in investigations. Do I paint a reasonably accurate picture so far?"

"You're not too far off," Stone replied, not thrilled about having his failed ambitions laid out before him.

"Freshly married, you just turned thirty-six, and you have a supervisor who isn't thrilled about your aggressive tactics or your stand on your home state because he favors the Oklahoma Sooners. You want action, but Elliot holds you back because of some weak grudge. Your record is impeccable, you possess a bachelor's degree in law enforcement from Texas State University, and you dress like us old-timers. I see you left your boots behind in lieu of shined shoes, which I hope you didn't do on my account."

Stone gave a sheepish grin, hating how right the man was about every detail. Stewart possessed ideal intelligence about Stone, as though he'd taken a personal interest in him for quite some time.

"You don't need to hide who you are around me," Stewart said with a dismissive wave of his hand. "There's no need to hide your accent or dress differently for my sake. I want to offer you an assignment that will take you off the grid and put you working directly under me. You'll be a rogue agent of sorts, watching highly dangerous individuals for the sake of national security. That is, assuming of course, that you're interested in hearing about this position."

"You have my attention, sir. But this sounds like more surveillance."

"It's not just monitoring their activities, Harlan. These people are after lethal weapons of mass destruction and they're Americans, just like us. I'm asking you to put a stop to domestic terrorism by any means. There's no need for me to butter you up, but you're an expert marksman, you speak Spanish well enough, and you've studied both jujitsu and tae kwon do, so I know you can take care of yourself. Are you up for some action?"

Stone didn't like the vague nature of his assignment, but he supposed he could sort out the details later. Working directly under the Deputy Director promised a lot of clout for his future with the Bureau, and anywhere else he chose to seek employment.

"You do this, and do it well, and I'll see what we can do about getting you in with the Rangers, if that's what you still want."

Taking a hearty swig from the beer, Stone looked Stewart in the eye with subtle delight that came from ascension to better places.

"I'm in, sir."

"Good," Stewart said, leaning back with a smile. "I hope your passport is in order, because you're going to South America in the very near future."

Stone tilted his head in curiosity, wondering just how far his new position was going to take him in both position and geographical locations.

CHAPTER 11

Todd Parish decided he liked being on a fishing trawler better than bobbing and weaving on the Pacific Ocean west of Peru. While Clouse had arranged reasonable travel conditions that kept Parish, Clay Branson, and Bill Branson out of the public eye, Parish still felt certain they were being followed.

One positive aspect was that Clouse decided to wait until after the Christmas holiday to send the trio on this particular mission. Nosagi wasn't going anywhere, and another pressing matter regarding a different cube came to Clouse's attention. It seemed the other situation required assistance from lawyers, and some research into property rights before a plan was formed.

Strangely enough, the current mission lacked thorough planning, only because no one ever laid eyes on the island and survived. Satellite images and distant photographs provided very little intelligence about the nature of Nosagi's defense. Parish hated being outnumbered, feeling that the Bransons brought a different agenda with them, though Bill didn't seem thrilled about giving up a weekend to assist in the effort. His nephew kept saying something about Bill owing him, though Parish knew none of the details.

After Clouse's personal pilot flew them to South America in a private jet, the gear was unloaded without much inspection by local officials. They seemed more interested in the money tossed their way to help unload the disguised gear and place it on the boat the group rented. Each of the three men dressed the part, acting as though they were fishing at some company's expense, but the gear was not fishing poles, lures, and bait. Instead, a variety of weapons and equipment remained inside the packs until the boat was at sea.

Not a large boat by any means, the fishing vessel fought the ocean surface the entire way, occasionally feeling like a toy being pushed back by the choppy waves. More than half an hour passed before anyone even spoke, creating even more tension between the three men who felt unhappy about the trip for various reasons. Parish busied himself by pulling his familiar AR-15 from a footlocker, checking it for damage while making certain the spare magazines were all present. Bill steered the boat toward their designated location, using a small GPS mounted beside the steering wheel to guide him.

"I'm still not happy with you dragging me along on this," Bill said heatedly to his nephew, as though the statement required some built up courage on his part. "When I offered my assistance, I didn't think you'd honestly drag me this close to your mentor. You're damn lucky I have a passport."

"And you're damn lucky I'm alive after what you pulled," Clay retorted, seated on an overturned crate as he inspected some gear. "I could've ended this a long time ago if you had said something."

Parish tried not to listen, but with only three of them on a medium-sized fishing boat he found it hard to ignore conversation.

"The locals call this place *la isla de la muerte*, Clay," Bill said, his voice trembling with concern. "Do you know what that means?"

"The island of the dead," Parish stated, casually inspecting his Glock sidearm. "I heard some fishermen saying to avoid the area before we left."

"I *know* what it means," Bill said with open frustration, shooting Parish a testy look as his nephew said nothing, simply checking over his own array of bladed weapons. "I just want to know why we're doing this, or why we couldn't just leave well enough alone."

"You didn't tell him?" Parish asked Clay, concerned that Bill really had no idea what he was motoring toward.

Clay looked up without so much as a grin.

"You mean your ghost tale about cursed objects and zombies running around the island? Of course not."

"What is he talking about?" Bill asked Clay, who simply shrugged both of his companions off, focusing on his weapons instead.

"It's a little hard to explain," Parish began, "but my group is chasing after thirteen cursed objects that individually do a lot of harm, but together might bring about the end of the world."

"I've heard of cursed objects," Bill replied, flushing red in his face before turning his attention to his nephew. "And you failed to bring this up, Clay?"

"The way you failed to mention my mentor is secretly the leader of an assassination guild?" Clay fired back, standing to get face to face with his uncle.

Parish spotted something in the distance, feeling certain they were approaching their target island.

"I hate to break up this family squabble, but I think we're within range."

All three men stood silently a moment, staring toward the small island with limited greenery, some natural rock structures, and possibly some sand near the water. It hardly looked like paradise, but the island didn't show obvious signs of peril or death. Only the sloshing of small waves licking the boat and the purring of the boat's motor broke the silence momentarily until Bill broke the silence.

"What exactly is the plan?"

"I'm going alone to confront Nosagi. If I survive, I'm bringing Mr. Parish here a souvenir to take home to his boss."

"Are you sure you want to go alone?" Parish questioned. "I'm not sure you're comprehending the serious nature of what you're going to find on that island."

Clay shook his head negatively.

"Regardless of what I find on that island, it's going to be made from organic material. I think I can take care of anything organic with this."

Holding up a modified, razor-sharp *katana* with a slightly shortened blade, Clay slid it into its sheath before packing the sword and other weapons into a small pack he then placed on his back for easy transit. Parish observed him putting on a modified gun belt that holstered a semi-automatic Glock 17 on each side. What little glimpse Parish got caused him to believe the guns were modified to house larger, more deadly rounds. Perhaps Clay worried about more than just reanimated corpses after all.

"Sure you don't want any backup?" Parish asked.

"I'm sure. If I'm successful, I'll shoot up a flare to let you know. Give me an hour, and if you haven't gotten a sign, you two better get out of here."

Parish hated the idea of standing by, but he knew what kind of culture Clay and his former mentor lived and breathed. A common man posed little threat to those trained in the ancient art of assassination. He wondered how Clay entered such a life as an American, but he figured he and Bill had plenty of time to discuss matters once Clay departed for the island.

With each passing second the boat drew closer to the island, which now had a background of dark, ominous clouds. Distant thunder rolled, adding to the trepidation of the moment, each of the men now having some understanding of the danger ahead.

"This should be good," Clay said quietly when the boat was within swimming distance of the island.

Despite the choppy water and hidden dangers on land, Clay made certain his weapons were securely attached to his modified backpack and gun belt before diving in without another word.

"Is he always like that?" Parish asked Bill.

"He's a bit embittered lately. A lot of that is my fault."

"My employer seemed to think he's the best man for the job, even if Clay doesn't."

"Oh, he's good alright. I just hope he's aware of the danger his former mentor poses. The man has tried to kill him twice now."

"Let's hope the third time isn't a charm."

***

In a move to conserve energy, Clay only paddled when the tide carried him toward the shore because each time it returned the water erased some of his progress. Truth be told, he didn't want to believe a legion of the undead awaited him ashore, but the battle with Nosagi was certain to take a toll on his body. Any additional surprises required expending energy before the life and death struggle, so he decided to let the tide work for him.

His thoughts drifted to Casey momentarily, and how he longed to see her again. Clay quickly put his emotions to bed, knowing they sapped his focus like a leech. Confronting Nosagi and surviving the encounter required every ounce of his concentration and mental sharpness he could muster.

While the ground froze solid close to Cincinnati, Clay found the water approaching the island warm like a soothing outdoor bath. He sensed grave danger once the tide washed him closer to the shore, his feet touching the jagged rocky bottom for the first time since leaping from the boat. Wearing athletic shoes that were a new hybrid for water and land, often used by triathlon competitors, Clay avoided scrapes or cuts along his feet. Had he chosen to don the traditional clothing he wore in Japan, like the ninja footwear known as the *ikitabi*, his chances of being battered and bruised would have gone up significantly.

He hoped nothing happened to his uncle, or Parish, because he felt completely responsible. If the choice were his, he would have come alone to confront Nosagi, but Clouse wasn't going to provide him with the location unless he brought Parish.

A bargain was a bargain.

Wearing a form of durable hiking shorts, along with a tank top, Clay remained comfortable, though he felt like he was betraying some of the traditions he learned in the Orient. He supposed his mentor had long since abandoned some of those same principles, so he didn't dwell on his thoughts. He hoped his clothing might dry out before he confronted Nosagi, but he wasn't wasting one precious second standing on the beach. About twenty feet of bleached sand awaited Clay, scrunching beneath his feet as he walked toward the thicket of trees awaiting him. The rocks, as it turned out, were a small mountain of sorts beyond the wooded area on the opposite end of the island.

And while the island wasn't very large, the wooded area ahead showed Clay no visible end. He trudged across the remainder of the beach, entering a labyrinth of trees, vines, and various shrubs that failed to make room for any kind of manmade trail. Clay was almost certain the intelligence was entirely false, or they picked the wrong island to land upon when he spied activity ahead.

Oh, crap, Clay thought as numerous figures appeared from behind trees and large rocks. He quickly assessed the situation, memorizing the position of each human figure while conducting a head count. Clay found eleven figures from left to right, none of them still among the living based on the level of decay on each body. Each of the reanimated dead stared at him with blank, glassy eyes, silent as they stood in place, as though awaiting a command. Tattered clothing dripped from each of the male zombies, a few of them holding firearms while the rest gripped rocks or heavy sticks.

"Guess they weren't lying," Clay said to himself, reaching behind him to pull his sword from its scabbard with deliberation.

Utilizing a different strategy than usual, since the undead couldn't be killed, Clay needed to blind his adversaries so they couldn't attack in mass, or track him. Beyond that, he needed to disable them, which might require a bit more analysis and experimentation. Clay scooped up several rocks from the sand as he picked up his pace, jogging toward the leftmost adversaries partially obscured by the vegetation. The second from the left wielded an automatic weapon of some sort, so Clay flung the rocks toward its eye sockets, hitting the mark just enough to throw the military uniformed zombie's head back. Already at a full sprint, Clay ignored the undead flanking his left and right, charging instead toward the armed threat in the center. His *katana* found its mark, severing the head and both hands in one swift motion as the body parts and rifle fell to the ground.

Checking for booby-traps in the woods while being pursued, even for someone with Clay's skill set and sense of danger, wasn't a wise move. He decided to stand his ground at the edge of the woods, using limited cover to engage the small army that had already begun closing on his position with the disabling of their first member. The headless, handless body still squirmed and moved on the ground, determined to the last to assault Clay in some fashion. Ignoring it, Clay beheaded the body to his left, then another one to his right before they could strike him with blunt weapons.

The familiar sound of a gun clacking reached his ears, so Clay dove into the brush for cover, able to see one of the other animated dead pointing another automatic weapon in his direction. Bullets sprayed the shrubs where Clay initially ducked for cover, but he continued to move into the woods like a snake keeping contact with the ground. Only able to obey simple commands, the undead minion continued firing in exactly the same spot until the magazine ran empty a few seconds later. Clay emerged from the woods like a charging predator from the African safari, cutting down more of the enslaved men who weren't at peace. Heads, hands, and the occasional foot landed atop the beach with minimal red splatters, since the lifeblood belonging to the mindless slaves stopped flowing weeks and months prior.

Like a whirlwind, Clay spun, sliced, and observed with uncannily trained diligence as his body stayed in motion. He noticed one of the remaining undead gripping a sidearm, raising it to take aim as Clay downed one of his fellow zombies with a precision slice of the neck using the *katana*. All of the undead minions moved stiffly, as though simply commanded to defend the interior of the woods from which they emerged. An ordinary man, even a soldier, could easily be outnumbered and murdered by the mob while carrying standard firearms. Explosives, or a sword for that matter, changed the odds considerably.

Seeing the gun aimed in his direction, Clay grabbed a headless corpse before it collapsed, using it as a shield to absorb the bullets. He could have thrown a weapon to blind or disable the armed dead man, but Clay knew once the bullets were spent, he needed only expend enough energy to chop off potentially harmful body parts before proceeding into the woods.

Ironically, the corpse appeared to have been shot or stabbed in the chest, one eye now drooping from its socket. His once beige dress pants were torn and tattered below the knees, while his white dress shirt indicated previous struggles because of the brown and green stains permanently etched within its fabric. The dead man's skin, now a pallid greenish color from its original olive shade, showed minimal signs of decay, as though the animated dead's regular movement kept it from falling apart. The collective made no sounds, like the moaning and groaning zombies make in horror movies, which caused Clay to believe Nosagi somehow instructed them on exactly how to behave and defend the island when he took control of them.

Clay threw the bullet-riddled body to the ground before using his sword to continue mowing through the legion of the undead. It took less than a minute for him to leave a trail of body parts in his wake before he stood on the beach, observing his work to ensure no stragglers remained. Convinced none of the former human beings were left standing, Clay prepared to enter the woods when the sound of plant life being trampled reached his eardrums. Holding his *katana* before him, Clay looked at the second defense wave reaching the edge of the woods, far more dangerous than the first because it wasn't made of flesh and blood.

"Shit," he muttered, seeing more undead and nearly a dozen tribal statues ready to pulverize him.

CHAPTER 12

It took a good five minutes before Parish or Bill looked at one another or spoke. They busied themselves with cleaning weapons or checking gauges on the boat. Both worried about the outcome on the island for different reasons. Perhaps those reasons kept them from speaking cordially, or Bill simply remained upset for being dragged along on a highly dangerous trip. From what Parish learned, Bill possessed no military or police background, and his engineering degree helped little on an uncharted island.

"This whole cursed object issue," Bill finally said, sauntering toward Parish who continued to inspect his AR-15. "Is it the real deal, or were you just trying to exaggerate the danger to get Clay onboard?"

By now Parish had changed clothes, wearing a black flak vest over a black shirt and tech pants that provided plenty of pockets. Several knives and other assorted weapons were stuffed into the vest and Parish's gun belt. He also kept an additional survival knife strapped to his leg with a Velcro sheath. Staying vigilant in case anything followed Clay from the island, or Clay didn't come back at all, Parish continued preparing for the worst possible scenario.

"It's not my story to sell," Parish answered without looking up from his gun. "But if it makes you feel better, I've seen the objects up close and personal."

"What do they do?"

"They cause men to kill one another for personal gain. There are thirteen of them, and each one does something different."

Bill put his hands up to his head in frustration.

"This is all too much. It's bad enough Clay's mentor wants him dead and then I find out he's mixed up in cursed objects? This can't be happening."

"Take it easy," Parish said, putting forth some compassion. "Clay is going to take care of Nosagi, get the cube, and the world will be a little safer."

"And that's why you're putting together a weapons depot over there?"

Parish grinned.

"What can I say? I like my guns."

Standing, Parish looked to the island, seeing the blue-green water move toward the island before returning. The boat, now anchored, continued to bob gently as the dark clouds in the background appeared to be moving beyond the island instead of heading their way.

"How much trouble could my nephew be in?"

"It's hard telling," Parish answered. "We're not sure how long Nosagi has been holed up on the island, or *why* for that matter."

"How the hell does he get supplies?"

"He must have transportation, but we never spotted any planes or boats in our images."

Parish wondered how many tourists had traveled to the island, only to find a nasty surprise awaiting them. Surely search parties went looking for the missing tourists and locals, only to find themselves victims of Nosagi's traps.

Gunfire suddenly erupted, shattering any preemptive thoughts that might have been forming in Parish's mind. He scooped up nearby high-power binoculars, observing Clay's progress on the island as he emerged from a thicket of shrubs, tearing into what appeared to be human forms standing stiffly on the beach. No one with any sense of tactics simply stood in place with a blunt weapon, Parish deduced, until he saw the group act collectively, trying to bring Clay down by converging upon him.

"Should we do something?" Bill asked, peering through a second set of binoculars.

"I think he's got it handled."

"It's my fault he's in this predicament."

"Sounds like he would have come after Nosagi regardless of when he found out the truth," Parish said calmly, observing Clay cut down the undead as though they were store mannequins.

A different splashing sound than the water lapping the boat reached Parish's ears, distracting him from the beach battle. He held the binoculars at his chest, scanning the water for any kind of intrusion, wondering if something from the island detected their presence. Few dangerous ocean creatures resided near the island, and Parish doubted any sharks or large sea dwellers were going to attack a recreational boat. He leaned over the rear of the boat, looking for anything foreign in the water. The boat wasn't close enough to shore for him to see the seabed, but Parish saw some ripples coming around the back of the boat, as though something in the water took time enough to observe them.

"What is it?" Bill asked.

"I'm not sure, but I don't think we're alone."

Parish started to reach for the AR-15 to provide some firepower against whatever object was large enough to create wave-like ripples if it showed itself. He failed to make it before a large anaconda with numerous injuries to its exterior surfaced along the boat's aft end. Mesmerized by the grand scale of the serpent, Parish continued to slowly reach his right arm toward the rifle, studying the exterior of the serpent.

Probably twenty feet in length, the snake slithered in a swimming motion along the water's surface, but Parish noticed something not quite right.

"Holy shit," Bill muttered, catching a glimpse of the reptile for the first time.

"It's not alive," Parish said, taking notice of the pale skin and multiple wounds along the scales and flesh. "It's reanimated just like the hoard Clay is facing."

Not only was the exterior flesh damaged, but several gaping holes appeared a few feet behind the head, near the halfway mark, and closer to the tail. Such wounds in any organism were fatal, confirming Parish's statements. His firearms weren't going to kill something already dead, though bullets might rip apart the snake's long frame enough that it fell apart when it tried to attack them.

"It can't get us up here, can it?" Bill asked, backing away from the railing.

"Don't be so sure," Parish answered, touching the AR-15's cool metal as the head of the snake launched from the water directly toward him.

He tried to retreat from the surprising attack, but the decaying mouth of the snake, without the restrictions that living muscles and tendons brought about, snagged him by the head and shoulders. Without time to react, Parish found himself pulled into the water as the snake immediately tried to wrap itself around his torso. The same freedom that didn't restrict its mouth from opening prevented it from truly constricting around him, though it held his right arm in place so he couldn't swim very well using conventional strokes.

Apparently content just to sink to the bottom and drown Parish, the reanimated anaconda didn't readjust its position until Parish wriggled his arm free from the loose grip. Considering he barely took a breath before the sneak attack, Parish fought and kicked his way toward the surface, reaching it seconds later. He gasped for a breath of fresh air, finding Bill scrambling for a weapon or method to combat their adversary. Unfortunately for Parish his efforts to survive allowed the deceased guardian to reposition its body for a different sort of attack.

Parish felt additional weight on his legs as he fought to stay near the surface, grasping for the boat's rear railing. He clutched the railing at the very second he lost the ability to kick because pressure surrounded his legs, immobilizing them rather effectively.

"Find something sharp," Parish stammered before the snake yanked him underwater once more.

The pressure that started around his legs now moved up to his waistline, and Parish realized he was being swallowed by the anaconda. He knew under ordinary circumstances the pressure of the animal's muscles crushed ingested prey, suffocating it if necessary before digestion began. In this case, however, the muscles fit like a stretched sock, effective enough to swallow him easily, but incapable of constricting or putting crushing force on him.

Parish fought to reach the water's surface once more, but after a few decisive gulps, the snake swallowed him whole. He felt his captor swimming toward the sea floor, apparently making a second effort at drowning him. Parish fought against the skin, testing how much play the dead tissue provided him for movement.

Suddenly the anaconda changed directions and swam toward the surface, allowing him a breath through one of the three gaping wounds along the skin when it rose above the water. Trying not to panic, Parish thought of only one reason the snake might choose to surface over attempting to drown him.

It wanted to ensnare Bill Branson and get a double kill for its efforts.

***

Though Bill might have looked like a panicked mouse trying to escape being a serpent's lunch, his experiences with danger and near death helped him keep his wits about him. He searched the boat for weapons other than firearms, or something to help him trap the reanimated beast. He quickly located a machete used for cutting tangled lines or burdensome dock moorings, scooping it up before returning to the boat's aft section.

Several seconds passed without any sign of Parish or the anaconda, including any kind of splashing or bubbles from beneath. Bill almost wrote off his traveling companion when the snake surfaced in search of something.

Him.

Half of the snake was bloated, indicating it had swallowed something. At first Bill figured Parish was a goner, either drowned or suffocated by the snake's tissues conforming to his body and leaving no air pockets to breathe. A few seconds later, however, Bill felt his heart race at the fact he wasn't necessarily alone in his struggle against the undead creature just yet.

Bill could barely see Parish's face through one of the gaping wounds along the snake's body, trying to breathe before the animal dove below the surface again. The outline of Parish's fingertips along the snake's loosely fitting skin showed as ten bumps and a bit of his palm pushing against the skin to keep it from suffocating him further. He attempted to speak through the hole as the anaconda spotted Bill before advancing toward the boat, its tail end swishing back and forth in the water. It swam almost as easily as a water moccasin, somehow retaining its instincts for pursuit and devouring prey.

"Grab something-"

The snake dove beneath the surface, swimming under the boat, which cut off Parish's message. Apparently looking to surprise Bill, or find the easiest way to snatch him from the safety of the boat, the anaconda surfaced along the port side.

"Cut its head off," Parish managed to state before the serpent took him beneath the water again.

Bill stared at the machete in his hand momentarily, seeing a problem with Parish's suggestion, in that Parish remained close to the serpent's head instead of sliding further into the lengthy form. He couldn't say that he blamed him, considering one of the few holes from which to breathe was located directly behind the head with those formerly beady eyes that now appeared glazed with a blue film.

"Come get some," Bill muttered angrily, locking eyes with the island's guardian.

Unaware of the dangerous machete in Bill's right hand, or unconcerned, the undead serpent lunged toward the back of the boat, opening its mouth widely in an attempt to snag Bill. Ducking while he backed away simultaneously, Bill lost his balance, falling to the deck as the bladed weapon fell beside him. Fortunate the machete didn't cost him any fingers, Bill stayed low, grabbing the weapon as he prepared for another round with the beast. He chose to stand in the center of the deck where he was best able to spot his attacker and parry if necessary.

He felt perspiration dripping down his forehead and cheeks as his eyeglasses began fogging up to the point that he could barely see. Holding the machete defensively in front of him, Bill listened for sounds, focusing with the one sense as Clay taught him about when they were still on good terms. Valuing the lessons Clay gave him with instruction on weapons and mental awareness alike, Bill could never devote himself to the warrior's code like his nephew. Clay spent four years in Japan living and breathing the old rituals of the samurai and ninja, continuing to practice to this day on a daily basis.

When the snake appeared for its next attack, Bill raised the machete, prepared to chop off its head, or slash it in the mouth to cut the cheeks and weaken the jaw mechanism. About to bring the figurative hammer down on the serpent's jawline, Bill saw the beast open its mouth for another attack. At the top of its throat Bill spied black hair surrounding a bald spot that could only belong to Parish. Bill delayed his attack long enough that the anaconda snapped at him, barely missing his leg. If he found himself caught by the dead reptile, Bill imagined he would be swallowed, crammed into the lengthy belly as he compressed an already miserable Parish toward the tail.

Bill decided if the creature made the mistake of revealing its hind end to him, he would chop it off and provide Parish an alternate escape route. For the moment, however, he simply needed to survive the attacks to keep Parish's hopes for escape alive.

CHAPTER 13

Clay found one redeeming fact with the emergence of his latest adversaries from the wooded area. If they were roaming through the vegetation, it seemed unlikely traps and snares awaited him within the shaded areas, so he trudged forward to confront them in the available cover.

Uncertain whether the tribal statues before him were native to the island, or something Nosagi brought with him, Clay knew his swords were practically useless against their carved stone forms. Barely sapped of energy from the first round, he suspected the second wave wasn't going to be so easy. None of the zombies held firearms this time, but every one of them grasped blunt or bladed weapons. Clay stole a glance at the statues, which looked harmless with their awkwardly wide mouths, oval-shaped heads, and lightly detailed chests and arms. They barely possessed true legs, most of them lumbering behind the zombies, indicating they were by no means agile.

Hoping this might indeed be the last wave, Clay started for the zombies before half of them even began raising their knives, swords, and thick branches toward him. Immediately beheading the first, he adeptly sliced diagonally through the chest of the next one, rending it useless as the two pieces fell to the ground along with an arm victimized by the *katana*. He tore through several more undead bodies, laying them to waste as the statues drew closer, beginning to surround him so he couldn't simply run into the woods.

Finding a semi-circle around him, his options were to fight or retreat to the ocean behind him. If Clay chose to, he figured he could dodge and weave through the small army, but he didn't want to discover more enemies in the woods with this group behind him. He also didn't want them to turn their attention to his uncle and Parish, who were probably growing bored with guard duty on the boat.

The entire experience felt surreal to him, like being on the set of some fantasy adventure movie. Such things couldn't be real, despite what Clouse had said about the cubes and their mystical powers. Clay now understood the depth of Nosagi's evil, fueling a controlled rage inside him to reach his former mentor and bring his reign of terror crashing down.

A few straggler zombies waited behind the line of statues, some of which were the size of an average man, while a few stood almost eight feet tall. Clay slipped his sword into its scabbard along his back, reaching to his sides where he drew the two Glock pistols and began firing into the faces and necks of the first two statues, hoping those were weak points. One of the statues disintegrated, crumbling to the ground in a heap of broken pebbles. The other continued marching toward him, but he jumped to kick it just above the torso, sending it back into a small boulder that caused it to lose balance. Falling to its back, the statue also crumbled into loose mortar and rock shards.

Figuring a lead pipe might be his best weapon against the unnatural monsters, Clay needed to settle for the available objects nearby, or his firearms. The statues tried to surround him, but their plodding steps kept them from making a solid perimeter. Holding a Glock in each hand, Clay fired at two more of the statues, using more ammunition this time before they crumbled to the ground. Two of them staggered toward him simultaneously, raising their club and spear respectively to smash him into paste if they found their mark. Waiting until the last possible second, Clay rolled out of the way, watching the two statues bring their weapons down upon one another. Both shattered almost immediately, their pieces tumbling into small rock piles along the beach. The tide would eventually take them home to the bottom of the sea, but Clay still had four more statues and five zombies to eliminate before moving into the woods.

A frontal roll put him past the statues, allowing him to holster the guns and cut through two more zombies with his *katana*. Deep down he knew the tissue and flesh his sword cut through were once living human beings. Strangely enough, some of them died trying to put an end to Nosagi's rule over the island. Clay's blade beheaded yet another zombie dressed in battle fatigues that probably worked as a solider for hire or served in a military group.

Another zombie raised a club of some sort against him, but Clay sliced cleanly through the forearm, dropping it and the weapon to the ground. In the return motion, he severed the head, rendering the body useless as a defense mechanism. He barely detected the motion of a statue behind him until the shadow loomed over him and the heavy footsteps caused the ground beneath his feet to tremble like an earthquake tremor.

He sidestepped a clubbing blow from the statue's stone axe, intentionally backing toward the last remaining zombie, a woman dressed in the remains of a skirt and blouse. Obviously a tourist who chose the wrong destination with her group, her glossy, cold eyes stared at Clay ravenously, wanting to bite, claw, or assault him with her large knife to inflict damage. When Clay felt the earth shake beneath his feet a second time, he dodged the blow from behind, watching the stone axe crush the zombie beneath its unforgiving weight. Little more than a puddle of dark blood and strips of flesh emerged from the weapon before it was pulled from the ground. The human tissue mixed with the sand, creating a colorful decoration of natural colors, spelled the end of the zombie adversaries.

More importantly, Clay used the precious seconds to draw the Glocks because four statues remained to end his existence. While they weren't nimble, the statues only needed to graze Clay to strike a killing blow or set him up for certain death with a secondary hit. He walked backwards toward the wooded area, firing his guns at one of the statues, using six bullets total to crumble its aged form to the sandy beach.

Out of bullets in one gun, he decided to exchange both magazines for the full ones at his side. Clay quickly ejected both magazines to the ground, dodging a stone mace in the process as two of the taller statues closed in on his location. The one busied itself retrieving its mace from the sand as the two both swung their weapons toward Clay. He rolled away from the danger as their weapons collided with one another, shattering instantly. Both statues lost parts of their arms in the process, which failed to deter them from focusing on Clay. All four stony figures directed their focus on him as he finished inserting both fresh magazines. Questioning whether three-dozen rounds were enough to down all four statues, Clay took aim at the first one's neck, trying to separate the head from the torso. The feat required only six bullets before the head plopped to the ground and the body crashed beside it in dozens of pieces.

Three statues remained as adrenaline pumped through every fiber of Clay's body. Dodging a swing from the closest piece of living art, Clay felt a bit friskier, delivering a sidekick to the abdomen area hoping to save some ammunition. Such a kick to the sternum of a human being shattered the bone, incapacitating or killing the recipient. This blow did little to weaken the stability of the statue, and in return Clay received a curious tilt of the head from the unusually disproportioned figure.

Strange, Clay thought, that any of the reanimated objects contained any traces of personality. He wondered if Nosagi was able to program them like robots or train them like attack dogs with various traits. Living isolated on an island, the man probably had nothing except time on his hands to play with his new toys.

As one of the other statues took a swing at him, Clay avoided the blow by closing the distance between them, leaping toward the chest of the tribal statue to launch himself toward one of the other two. He kicked a different statue this time with significantly different results. The statue itself looked down to its chest, its wide oval mouth seemingly registering surprise as a large crack began around the nipple line. Quickly spreading across the chest and down to the rocky stomach, the crack caused the dismantling of the statue as it broke into two pieces that landed atop a fallen counterpart in a shattered heap.

Clay took aim at the closer of the two remaining statues, firing both guns simultaneously into its head and neck, trying to take it down. The head broke away from the neck, falling to the ground almost immediately, but the statue continued toward him, toting a dangerous sword made of solid rock. It took a giant swing downward, allowing Clay to evasively roll to his right before shooting it in the knee, crippling it by dropping it to its remaining knee. Instead of wasting ammunition in an attempt to break it apart, Clay shot out the other knee to immobilize the statue while he dealt with its partner.

Refusing to give up, the statue pulled itself forward using the sword as a cane of sorts to drag its body along. Clay ignored it, methodically shooting into every body part of the one remaining whole statue. It flinched as though feeling each bullet penetrate its natural armor, holding a short spear it wanted to aim at Clay. Weakened by stress cracks in various areas, the statue survived one kicked from him as it missed with a swinging spear. Clay dodged a downward swing of the spear, which the statue used like a sword, before kicking upward into its lower chest. Stopping in its tracks as though making a horrific discovery, the statue looked down at its compromised torso before crumbling into smaller stones.

Dropping his guns to the sand momentarily, Clay picked up a black rock the size of a softball and hurled it at the struggling legless statue with his left arm. The stone hit the statue in the shoulder blade, starting a crack that resounded throughout its body until it literally fell into dust that mingled with the beach sand. Giving a brief sigh under his breath, Clay took up his Glock firearms, stuffing them into their holsters before trudging toward the trees.

He stiffened at the sound of screeches from some form of primates ringing through the trees toward his direction.

"Damn it."

***

After several short bursts of breathing when the anaconda surfaced, Parish decided he couldn't wait for Bill to assist him. For some reason, the undead serpent seemed to employ a game plan that kept it from getting chopped up while securing its prisoner. Based on the way it chose to surface repeatedly, the snake obviously had ideas of attacking Bill Branson.

Trying to communicate with Bill cost him valuable seconds he could have spent attempting to free himself from the belly of the deceased creature. Parish tested the elasticity of the skin restraining him, realizing his arms and legs were able to move slowly beneath the weight of the thick skin. Between the water gushing inside and the natural deterioration of the intestinal track, Parish felt slime all around him, penetrating his clothing while further slowing the ability to feel around his surroundings.

When the snake surfaced again to stab at Bill with its mouth, Parish sucked in a deep breath as his right hand slid close to his waistline. The serpent's skin pressed Parish's hand against his own body, making it difficult to reach the survival knife strapped to his right leg. The two smaller knives sheathed within his survival vest were fine for minor cutting or close-up combat, but they weren't heavy enough to filet the anaconda's skin to facilitate his escape.

Reaching the knife proved difficult as the snake thrashed around, constantly trying to reposition its head to attack Bill or find a better attack zone around the boat. Even as his hand neared the survival knife Parish worried about how to unsheathe it without cutting himself initially or when he turned it into the decayed flesh of the serpent.

Constant pressure from the thick flesh and the water surrounding the anaconda left Parish feeling as though g-forces were compressing his own hand against his body. This time the serpent remained beneath the surface a longer period of time, as though realizing it needed to incapacitate its first victim before pursuing another. Parish knew he had about thirty seconds before his body began screaming for air, so he doubled his efforts to free the survival knife.

When the pressure seemed to intensify, Parish questioned whether the undead creature was taking him deeper, or possibly out to sea. Grunting to himself, he slid his hand down his stomach, then along his waistline, before using his elbow to shove out the skin surrounding him just enough for his hand to find the knife handle.

Clutching it like the lifeline is was, Parish pulled the edged weapon from the sheath before finding it incredibly difficult to turn the blade to an effective position. He could feel the serpent kicking toward a destination with renewed effort, pitting itself against Parish's resourcefulness. Clearing the sheath at last, the knife's tip found its way into the soft, slick skin of the anaconda, piercing the inner and outer layers almost simultaneously. Water immediately gushed through the slit, leaving Parish fewer tiny pockets of precious air from which to breathe.

He wasted absolutely no time in running the sharp edge of the knife upward through the skin, creating a hotdog bun effect that provided him a nice opening from which he could escape. Parish barely remembered to take a deep breath before thrusting himself through the large gash to the saltwater freedom awaiting him.

Surrounded by darkness and water, Parish required several seconds to regain his senses because the surface wasn't even visible. Mentally cursing to himself, he began kicking toward the surface, praying enough air remained within his lungs for him to complete the journey. He worried that he might be too far from the island, or the boat, to help either Branson. Too far out and he might be washed out to sea with little hope of reaching any form of safety.

His thoughts quickly returned to the dilemma at hand when he spied daylight above him and something brushed against his leg. Parish immediately knew the anaconda wasn't giving up on sending him to the bottom of the Atlantic, but his lungs were burning too badly to combat the island's guardian until he drew a breath of fresh air.

Feeling a tug at his leg from the snake trying to wrap itself around him, despite the gash lining most of its side, Parish kicked his feet desperately toward the surface. He kept the survival knife clutched in his right hand in case the serpent made a frontal attack. Parish was on the verge of sucking in water because his body demanded he breathe, unconcerned with what gas or fluid entered his lungs.

At the same instant the anaconda wrapped around his leg to tug him down to the bottom, Parish felt the sweet relief of fresh air. His face broke the rolling liquid plane just long enough for him to take a breath before his adversary pulled him under. Without so much as a glimpse of his surroundings, Parish found himself encumbered by darkness once again. He pulled his leg upward, dragging the insistent serpent with it as he tried remaining close to the surface.

Parish jabbed at his attacker with the knife, striking it several times in the face before catching the knife inside its mouth. He pulled the blade toward him, ripping the upper portion of the snake's head down the middle, effectively ceasing its ability to grasp anything with its mouth or small teeth. Able to wriggle his leg free, Parish surged toward the surface again, thrilled when the sun and warm air greeted him. He wildly twisted his body, looking for anything that resembled land or a boat, finding both directly to his right. Wasting less than a second, Parish began swimming toward the boat where he saw Bill Branson frantically scanning the water for him or the anaconda.

"Bill!" he called out, wanting his only salvation to know his location before the snake attacked him again.

Between the wind and choppy water, Parish's cries for help went unheard as he felt something rub his left leg. Knowing the serpent wanted to wrap itself around parts of his body for another assault, Parish began swimming toward the boat with determination.

Almost twenty strokes toward his destination, Parish felt a tug at his leg, but he shrugged it off, determined to reach solid footing before making a stand. By now Bill had spotted him, desperately searching for a weapon or some sort of pole to help Parish aboard the boat. Still a good forty yards from the boat, Parish felt his body betraying him as each stroke felt a bit heavier than the last.

Having the anaconda tug at his leg like a needy child certainly didn't help matters, but he dug down for some reserve energy. Each foot closer to the anchored boat drove Parish that much harder, especially with the tide giving him a gentle push from behind. He felt especially fortunate the damage to the snake kept it from grabbing him tightly enough to pull him too far under the surface for him to recover.

His arms felt like they were each carrying weight bands, growing heavier with each stroke, but refused to give up after surviving the snake's deadly attacks and the incident on the fishing trawler in October. In the back of his mind, Parish grew concerned that Clay might not outlast whatever awaited him on the island, which in turn endangered the two men awaiting his return at sea.

Parish finally neared the boat as the serpent repeatedly tried to wrap around his leg and pull him beneath the surface. Bill reached down for him without assistance from an oar, pole, or anything else. Parish missed clasping his hand the first time as the anaconda pulled him down, likely reminding Bill of several scenes from the *Jaws* movies. He heard Clay's uncle calling his name from beneath the surface, so he kicked his way upward, immediately reaching his hand upward in desperation. When he felt Bill clasp his hand and wrist between both of his hands, Parish tried helping however he could, relieved that true safety was inches away.

Trying to land his feet against the boat to help lessen the burden of his weight for Bill, Parish felt his already waterlogged boots barely getting any traction against the smooth side. Now a stationary target, Parish found his own body being used as a rope in a tug of war between Bill and the serpent. He pushed against the boat and upward with his one free leg, trying to tip the battle in Bill's favor.

Bill braced himself against the inside of the boat, pulling with every bit of strength he possessed until both Parish and the anaconda tumbled into the boat with him. A "holy shit" moment occurred between all three parties as Bill and Parish exchanged stupefied looks and the serpent simply looked between them with glassy eyes at the sides of its split head. Parish tried standing to attack the creature with his survival knife, but he slipped on the wet deck, falling directly on his hindquarters.

As he scrambled to regain his footing, Parish found his feet slipping in some kind of liquid oozing from the anaconda, causing him to fall repeatedly like a comical cartoon character. Before he was able to stand on his own, Bill had grabbed the nearby machete and crossed the deck with purpose before swinging the weapon downward. The move lodged the machete in the wooden surface, but not before severing the head of the anaconda, essentially rendering it useless. For good measure, Bill pried the weapon loose to repeat his swing several times over, leaving the serpent in half a dozen pieces before hurling them over the side of the boat with a disgusted expression. Parish helped throw the last few meaty chunks into the sea, watching them slowly sink to the bottom as he breathed a sigh of relief.

"Thank you."

"You're welcome," Bill replied, visibly shaken by the bizarre experience. "We need to check on Clay."

Scooping up some binoculars, Bill looked toward the island, seeing nothing except the carnage left behind by his nephew.

"We'll just be in his way," Parish stated, continuing to drip water onto the deck.

"I know," Bill said with quiet resolve. "We'd probably get killed or taken hostage, which would complicate things."

It took nearly every trick in the book for Parish to survive one adversary, so he couldn't imagine confronting numerous undead people and creatures. Both he and Bill were virtually panting from the deadly confrontation, and Parish felt absolutely drained of energy and fighting spirit. He questioned Clay's chances of survival, envisioning Bill reluctantly steering the boat away from the island when the one-hour timeline expired.

Just the same, Parish picked up the other set of binoculars to observe Clay's progress, hoping against all odds his gut instinct proved incorrect.

CHAPTER 14

Unsure of what to expect, Clay kept his *katana* drawn at his side. Based on the lack of sound from the human zombies, he wondered if the primate sounds were from living or dead beings. Considering Nosagi's ability to manipulate and train those around him, Clay wasn't going to be surprised by whatever he saw.

Leaving the beach behind, Clay trudged into the woods to find several small monkeys hopping in the trees above. Snarling, they appeared bent on attacking him, and the glaze in their eyes indicated someone beat him to ending their lives. The first jumped to a tree just in front of him, about fifteen feet above Clay. It landed on a branch, stared at him less than a second, and leapt toward him bearing its teeth with intentions of sinking them into his throat.

Able to slice a baseball into two perfectly equal halves with his sword, when thrown by a professional pitcher, Clay easily timed the speed and trajectory of the attacking primate. What felt like a touch of overkill under ordinary circumstances proved necessary as he basically let the undead animal cut itself in half from head to toe. Clay needed only flick the sword to the correct angle as the monkey's momentum sent it through the blade.

The other two waited mere seconds before initiating an attack on him, but Clay beheaded one as it jumped to the ground, using it as a launching pad to propel itself toward him. Its larger partner jumped down from a branch, ducking and rolling his first swing of the *katana*. Clay wondered if the captive undead creatures learned from the deaths of their colleagues and other observations during training or battles.

Whatever it learned the first time around didn't help when it attacked again, charging at Clay. It ducked and rolled similarly to Clay's defensive movements against the statues, making a fatal mistake by duplicating the direction and landing spot it chose the first time around. One clean swing through the waistline cut the primate in half, but before the two pieces even began their descent toward the earth Clay provided a vertical cut with the sword that turned two pieces into four.

Barely taking a breath after the latest wave of attackers, Clay continued walking deeper into the woods, which were hardly as dense as they looked from a distance. He saw a clearing ahead, almost immediately, that indicated what little civilization the island offered awaited him momentarily.

His heartbeat doubled the instant he spied a man knelt down in a small dirt circle on the far end of the clearing. For some reason the clearing housed only a few deteriorating stone structures in the center, which might have been altars that outlasted the elements over the years.

As the storm clouds drifted away, a sunbeam hit the center of the clearing with perfect timing. Clay observed the gray-haired man from a distance as he meditated from the kneeling position. Immediately sensing a ruse, since no one with hearing could have missed the commotion on the beach, Clay cautiously stepped forward. His heightened senses detected danger, though strangely enough it wasn't from the man he assumed was his mentor less than a football field's distance from him.

From the corner of his eye Clay spied someone else entering the fray to his left. As though sent at the perfect moment to answer his question, a flawless figure, dressed completely in formfitting white stood before him. Armed as well as Clay, and with similar weaponry, the woman possessed full locks of blond hair and an expression that indicated she knew how to use blades.

"I didn't realize Nosagi needed a bodyguard," Clay said, fishing for information, hoping to find a way around another obstacle.

"He doesn't," the woman replied in a self-assured voice, though she didn't strike him as the mercenary for hire type.

"Then maybe you should step aside and let me do what needs to be done."

"I don't think so. Like it or not, I have a partnership with your former mentor, so I can't let anything happen to him."

Clay twirled the *katana's* handle in his right hand momentarily.

"You realize this may not end well for you."

"I'll take my chances. Nosagi trained me, and I suspect you're a little rusty, if not fatigued from your exercise on the beach."

The man across the clearing stood at last, walking into the opposite side of the woods without so much as looking behind him. Clay started in his direction, but the woman drew her own sword, moving his way with foreboding steps. Deciding he needed to solve one problem at a time, Clay drew a deep breath, meditating momentarily without carrying out any *kuji-in*. To a ninja, the *kuji-in* were hand signals used to draw focus or a particular state of mind necessary to carry out a particular task.

He had spent some time on the boat drawing his focus before swimming to shore and dispatching the numerous guardians. Making a costly mistake after coming this far wasn't in his plans, but he desperately wanted to know if the man who just left the area was indeed his former mentor.

Taking a risk, Clay sprinted past the woman, counting on his senses to alert him to any danger approaching from behind. If she was truly trained by Nosagi, she knew how to use any number of throwing weapons. She would also possess excellent conditioning, much like Clay, who now counted on his to get him across the clearing.

Instead of hurling weapons at him, she took chase, using a shorter route to cut him off before he entered the woods on the opposite side. Clay engaged her as their swords crossed, discovering she knew her techniques exceptionally well. Considering their craft relied more upon finesse and cunning than brute strength Clay needed to consider her a worthy adversary until he learned otherwise.

Clay crossed his blade with hers momentarily until he found a defensive position, his back facing the direction he wanted to travel.

"I don't know what he's paying you, but it can't be worth risking your life for him."

"He's not paying me at all," the woman said before taking a deliberate cut at Clay's head which he blocked with his blade.

"Then he's lied to you. He does that exceptionally well."

She took several shots at him with her blade, which Clay deflected. He wanted to know details about her relationship with Nosagi, but time was running out to catch his former mentor if it was indeed Nosagi who fled, and not some kind of body double.

Backing away from her to provide adequate spacing, Clay pulled a silver sphere the size of a gumball from a storage pouch along his waistline. Within a split-second Clay pulled the device and threw it against the ground where a vertical plume of yellowish smoke flowed skyward. Typically used to create distractions, smoke bombs provided ninjas an escape from their enemies. With only one true direction he wanted to travel, Clay simply needed to provide a head start, rather than escape altogether.

By the time the smoke reached its full capacity, Clay was already covered by the trees. He quickly scanned the area, seeing gigantic rocks to his left and more trees and brush to his right. Directly ahead he spied water, and bobbing at a crudely constructed dock he noticed a pleasure boat fully capable of sailing the ocean tides.

He saw the same man undoing the moorings, readying the boat for a quick escape. The Nosagi Clay once knew never ran from a fight, but he also thought the man was upstanding and truthful. He almost yelled to distract the man momentarily, but he quickly decided against it. He couldn't afford to let the woman know his location, if she didn't already, and he wanted an opportunity to take at least one shot at Nosagi.

Clay sheathed his sword with practiced ease, into the pack behind him. From another pouch along his cloth belt, he pulled out two *shuriken* stars, throwing them simultaneously at the man undoing the line. Having little doubt the man was his former mentor, or an evil minion at the very least, Clay watched the four-sided blades spin through the air until the man drew a sword from his side, deflecting one while torqueing his body to dodge the other completely.

Nosagi, Clay thought, seeing the man's face for the first time. Though aged almost fifteen years, the face looked much like he last saw it. Gray hair had replaced much of the black, leaving it peppered, but Clay knew not to believe the man's advanced age made him any less dangerous.

The brown eyes narrowed with disdain when they locked with Clay's blue eyes, registering the indisputable fact that he recognized his former pupil. He stepped into the boat with an eerie calmness, as though leaving for vacation in the Bahamas rather than eluding a battle that might take his life. His eyes flickered, in less than a blink, beyond Clay's left shoulder indicating something closing in on his former protégé. A smug grin crossed his face before he eased the boat away from the wooden dock.

Ordinarily Clay might have taken more time to note some details about the direction of Nosagi's departure but he knew the mysterious woman was behind him. Clay stopped running only to duck in the same instant as two metal spears about six inches in length flew over him. He remembered Nosagi teaching him the same offensive technique years prior, rather satisfied the man hadn't taught new tricks to his recent students.

After several assassination attempts on his life, Clay knew he either had to reason with this woman or kill her. With Casey in his life, Clay could hardly afford to look over his shoulder on a daily basis and live a normal life. Both Clay and the woman in white stopped running on the beach beside the dock, drawing their blades once more as the sound of a boat motor grew more distant.

"This isn't necessary," Clay said, circling her with his *katana* held defensively before him.

"You talk too much," the woman replied, attacking him with her blade, Clay easily deflecting it the first few passes.

She read his defense, swinging low instead which threw him off-balance. He blocked the low swing, leaving his torso and arms for attack, which allowed her to graze his shoulder with a quick adjustment of her sword. Clay blocked the backstroke, ignoring the stinging sensation that accompanied the fresh cut. Taking to the offensive, Clay swung his *katana* in several different directions, one stroke after another, keeping his adversary in a defensive position until he managed to position his blade beneath hers, knocking it upward and out of her hands. Her grip had loosened ever so slightly because the tip of his sword drew dangerously close to her fingers during the last exchange.

Finding an opportunity to end the conflict if the woman's skills weren't on par with his, Clay thrust the blade's tip toward her face. Keeping her palms flat, she caught the sword between her hands, preventing Clay from striking the killing blow. Placing both hands on the hilt for better strength and leverage distribution, Clay pushed the blade toward her, but she backed away, keeping them at the same pace until the *katana* struck a tropical tree behind her as she ducked away from the blade.

Leaving the sword momentarily, Clay engaged her in hand-to-hand combat as she deflected several of his punches and kicks until he landed a glancing blow alongside her face. Stunned only a second at best, she managed to avoid a square punch aimed for her sternum as she did a backflip that might make most professional gymnasts green with envy. Determined to find a way to disable or kill her so he could pursue Nosagi, Clay prepared to draw another weapon from his pack when she launched a smoke bomb of her own, disappearing from sight behind the cloud of manmade smoke.

Clay might have missed her altogether except his sharp hearing detected the brief and subdued sound of a splash near the dock. He started toward the unsafe looking structure, stopping in his tracks when a Jet Ski emerged from beneath the wooden planks, taking off in the same direction Nosagi chose to travel. It seemed they had formed a contingency plan to meet up in case the island's guardians failed to eliminate Clay.

Grunting angrily to himself, Clay sprinted through the clearing once more, not slowing a bit until he reached the opposite end of the beach. He ran into the water until it reached his waist, slowing his progress to a crawl. From there he dove into the sea, battling the current as he swam toward the boat ahead of him, praying a chance to catch Nosagi presented itself.

He knew better than to swim directly against the current, so Clay took an angle that approached a corner of the boat so the gentle waves didn't constantly bat him backwards. As he drew nearer the vessel, concern grew in his mind because he didn't see Parish or his uncle. Though he doubted Nosagi dared take the time to harm either of them, Clay's former mentor obviously harbored little concern when he sent people to assassinate Clay and eliminated the police officer's friends and family in the past.

When he finally threw an arm over the boat and began pulling himself aboard, Clay found his uncle seated on the deck with his back against the rail, trying to catch his breath. Several small chunks of what looked like a giant chopped up eel dotted the deck near his feet.

"What happened here?"

"Giant undead anaconda," Bill answered. "Turns out the guy who hired you wasn't lying."

"That's an understatement. Where's Parish?"

As though on cue, Parish emerged from the housing quarters with a few firearms and a second machete in his arms.

"Good to see you made it back," he said upon seeing Clay, setting down the array of weaponry. "How did you make out?"

"We need to head that way," Clay said, pointing the direction. "Nosagi has an assistant and they both took off toward the mainland."

Bill scrambled to his feet, taking the helm as he quickly gave the boat full power and steered in the indicated direction.

"Assistant, huh?" Parish asked, taking Clay's side as they both stared ahead, hoping to catch Nosagi for different reasons.

"He'll say whatever it takes to land a capable apprentice. I'm sure he's fed her worse lies than he told me years ago."

Clay's anger stemmed from more than just the four years he spent overseas. His own father let him fall victim to a lie, for the betterment of a drug empire, no less. The law and Clay's own moral code kept him from seeking revenge on a family member, especially since his father was dying, so he focused his attention on Nosagi.

Evidence of Nosagi's sociopathic nature lay strewn across the island behind Clay in the form of over a dozen human beings the man killed just to build his own enslaved army. Clay wasn't sure if their boat could catch Nosagi and the mysterious woman, but if they didn't, the chances of finding him again were slim at best. Already well behind his former mentor, Clay felt certain his only hope of finding them would be if they landed in a major port. Realistically, the dock the trio launched from was about the only official landing for fishermen and commercial vehicles that could be reached from the island on a standard tank of fuel.

He doubted Nosagi was foolish enough to show his face in the villages, knowing Clay or other entities might be tracking him. And a few hours later the group would come to realize Nosagi and the woman vanished without a trace.

CHAPTER 15

From his front row seat in a four-seat 1969 Cessna, Harlan Stone had seen virtually everything from a distance. Using high-powered binoculars, Stone observed the anaconda attack, and Clay Branson surviving a hoard of strange-acting humans and mobile statues. He wished he could have recorded the entire incident from start to finish, but maintaining a healthy distance from the scene to keep his involvement secret was his highest priority.

Managing to use his credentials at the airport in order to learn where Branson and his friends were heading, Stone quickly booked a flight to South America. Stewart arranged for both boat and air travel in the meantime, instructing Stone to follow the group wherever they went. He also made certain the agent knew to remain unseen.

With the nearest cell phone tower possibly a hundred miles away, Stone used a satellite phone to call his employer as the pilot began circling the island with every living being now heading for the mainland. The pilot, a local man who commonly rented his plane and piloting skills to Americans, spoke decent enough English for Stone to communicate.

"Keep circling," he said, making a stirring motion with his finger to illustrate his wishes.

Stone pulled out a digital camera as his satellite phone tried to make contact with Stewart. Snapping some pictures with a telephoto lens, Stone knew there would never be detail or clarity enough to explain what he actually saw, but the numerous bodies lying on the beach told a story of their own.

Although the freelance pilot said absolutely nothing, as though completely oblivious to what he had witnessed, Stone had little doubt the man saw the same exact scenario without the benefit of binoculars. No stranger to assisting the FBI and CIA, the man likely knew talking about many of the stings and surveillance missions he piloted would end badly for him.

Stone managed to snap about four shots before his supervisor answered his cell phone.

"Stewart."

"Boss, you're not going to believe what I just witnessed."

"Where did Branson go? That's what I need to know first and foremost."

"He came out to this island a few hours from the mainland. I'm not even sure you're going to believe what happened when he got here."

"Try me."

Stone took a few more pictures as he cupped the phone between his ear and shoulder, trying to avoid missing some prime images.

"He fought off these people, but they weren't exactly normal."

"Not normal? How so?"

"Well, they looked like they were in a trance, or under direction from something. Almost like zombies."

"Interesting," Stewart replied without the slightest hint of growing interest in his voice.

"And these stone statues were walking toward him, but he shot most of them and took them down. It was the most uncanny thing I've ever seen."

Stone tried to maintain his composure, but he still couldn't believe his own eyes and mind to accurately recount the bizarre scenario. He felt like a kid peeking through a wall and seeing some monumental event only the adults were supposed to know about.

"Where is Branson now?" Stewart asked, unfazed by the information.

"He met up with the other two men and took chase after another boat."

"Follow him."

"What about the other vessel?"

"Don't worry about it. Just keep tabs on Branson and don't let him make you."

Not wanting to question his boss, or endanger his new position, Stone hated to ask questions of Stewart, but the man's behavior struck him as odd.

"Sir, I basically just watched him cut down fourteen or so people and you're acting like it's an everyday occurrence."

"There are two problems, Agent Stone. One, those probably weren't people as you and I would classify people. I'll explain that when you get back. And two, you're far, far away from our jurisdiction, so you are to simply follow him and report back to me. Is that understood?"

"Yes, sir."

Stone severed the connection before having the pilot circle the island four more times, closer with each pass, as the agent snapped more pictures of the carnage below. He wondered what business Branson had with the two people on the opposite end of the island and why they took off individually. He also questioned Alan Stewart's motives for having him conduct this unorthodox surveillance and giving him partial answers to his inquiries.

Catching up with any vessels traveling along the water wasn't going to be difficult for the small plane. Stone needed to assess the situation and make certain he guessed where Branson's party was going to land so he could beat them to their destination. Making a landing at the airport would take up precious minutes, even before Stone drove his rental vehicle to the dock to locate Branson once more.

Based on the way things ended on the island, however, he doubted the subject of his observations was about to do anything noteworthy.

Only time would tell.

CHAPTER 16

All of January and half of February passed with no luck for Russ Greene on the cube hunting front. After the Bransons and Parish lost Nosagi in South America, the deceitful Japanese native disappeared from sight with his new apprentice. The entire group knew it might be mere weeks or months before numerous people disappeared from a particular geographical area again, leading them straight to him.

In the meantime, Julie Knowles conducted some research that led her to believe another cube was being used for financial gain, particularly during prime sporting events. It seemed a certain man was winning rather big on a consistent basis at the horse tracks particularly, and the name mentioned in a newspaper article matched the one etched in Julie's cursed ledger.

Greene worked with Julie, attempting to locate the lucky better whose known total winnings netted at least twenty million dollars. Their search reached a dead-end rather quickly when they discovered he abandoned his modest house in Missouri after the newspaper article publicized his good fortune.

"Lucky my ass," Greene said of the man's attributing his winnings to good fortune.

Though he placed bets all over the country, the man seemed to have a penchant for the Kentucky Derby each May. Finding him wasn't going to be easy, considering he could live anywhere and simply pay for everything from food to living quarters with cash. He didn't have a cell phone on record and hadn't used a credit card since the article went public. Greene credited the man for knowing how to live off the grid, but he needed to find him soon, and with good reason.

Not one to place all of his eggs in one basket, Greene developed a plan with Julie's assistance too elaborate to set into place at the last minute. He planned on continuing to track the man known as Lincoln Daine through every means possible while asking Clouse for financial assistance to execute his plan. Although Greene no longer possessed federal powers to do much on his own, he maintained several excellent contacts and knew a plethora of ways in the private sector to track individuals. He found himself working more like a private investigator without his credentials, but serving a greater good made the sacrifice worthwhile.

The only other front requiring his attention was the time cube outside of Chicago. Clouse worked in secret to find what individual or entity owned the land. Greene's instincts told him to put a small army on the grounds before they even acquired the land to protect the cube, but Clouse and Julie felt it wiser to simply stay as far away from the property as possible. Clouse also ordered his attorneys to put feelers out on dozens of properties in the greater Chicago area to create a smokescreen in case someone monitored their activities.

Greene doubted there was any "in case" about it. He felt certain every hotel employee confirmed to do more than sweep floors, wait tables, and work a hotel desk was under observation of some sort from a separate group.

With the onset of a harsh winter in upper Illinois, Greene doubted anyone was going to easily access the filled in area where Thomas Ervin and his car had rested for the better part of three decades. Clouse had sent one of his employees on a fieldtrip to the property in secret for a detailed report about the property's condition, because any public actions taken through lawyers endangered the harvesting of the time cube. Little had changed about the property over the years, except that the quarry was now filled in with dirt, likely for safety reasons.

Greene felt compelled to assume the cube was still inside or near the car through gut instinct. If the world had indeed been altered by someone's use of the time cube, Greene supposed he would have no knowledge of an altered time continuum because life as he formerly knew it would be erased worldwide.

Implications from the cube's use were mindboggling, so he tried to avoid dwelling upon such thoughts for very long. Instead, he focused on obtaining the other cubes and making the world a safer place.

Liz returned to California temporarily, mainly to get enough belongings for a move to Indiana. Greene considered it important for the team to remain within close proximity because he never knew what information might come their way suddenly. Clay Branson returned to Ohio, his future with the group still unclear because his sole motivation to align himself with them disappeared with Nosagi and his new apprentice. Julie remained closer to the East Coast because her secure facility housed the cubes the group captured. Right now the number remained staggeringly low because of the fiasco in Alaska and the complete failure when it came to landing any new cubes.

Sitting in his apartment, because a permanent house made him easier to find, Greene stared out the window at the outskirts of Bloomington. The adjacent parking lot and several trees provided a bland late morning view, but Greene intended to unpack only what he needed and move again soon. He refused to house near the campus of Indiana University, preferring quick access to county roads and highways. Plans of housing the group together, once the team was comprised, ran through his mind. Being in charge of a one-of-a-kind unit provided him with numerous challenges, sometimes making him question whether or not he was capable of completing such a daunting task for Clouse.

Growing up in the farmland of Montgomery County in Tennessee, Greene dreamed of escaping and working in the big city. His uncle worked as a deputy, which inspired him to look to law enforcement for a career that guaranteed an escape from plowing fields and harvesting corn and other crops. He remembered the man visiting their farm, laying his gun belt across the table after a long day's work to join the family for summer sometimes. As a boy, Greene thought the sight of his uncle in uniform, toting a firearm, was like something out of the movies. He paid his dues, struggling through four years of college in the Nashville area after high school, driven by his lifelong dream.

He could have gained experience with a local police department instead of attending college, but Greene wanted to understand the outside world. Besides, he didn't want to linger around his home area, especially as a deputy who garnered no respect from the public. He aspired to work somewhere where the world was indeed his playground and he wouldn't feel confined.

Not every night was devoted to homework and studying, but Greene stayed the course and finished his four years with a respectable GPA and an understanding of social behavior away from the farm. He worked in Arizona and Oregon a few years before finally returning home to Tennessee, discontented with the lifestyle outside of his home state. Working in Nashville, a city filled with iconic outward appearances, taught him that not everyone in the Music City was charming both inside and out.

And then came Paul Clouse with a job offer that took him to an even darker place.

Greene peered at a nearby calendar, realizing just over a month remained before the Sunland Derby took place in New Mexico. His elaborate plan required a number of calculated guesses to prove correct, along with a little luck. Even if the initial phase of the plan went according to his projections, the latter part could fail utterly and cost Clouse a lot of money. While Clouse had openly stated money was no object when hunting the cubes, he tended to prefer sure bets to a longshot. This plan fell somewhere in the middle.

Before calling his employer for a blank check, Greene decided to make a different kind of call. He hated dragging any of his former colleagues into the mess he now called a career, but the federal government possessed better resources for finding missing people and criminals than any local agencies or freelancers like himself.

Scooping the cordless phone from its charger, he decided to use a landline rather than a cell phone, again erring on the side of caution. Unsure whether his former colleague would help him, or if Daine could even be found, Greene suspected his next call was to his employer asking for some financing after he provided a convincing narrative.

***

In a complete departure from his normal afternoon, Chase Dalton found himself seated at his desk in Estes Kefauver Federal Building. The building housed numerous courts, along with the United States Marshals Service, which currently employed him. Working in downtown Nashville came with some perks, but Dalton liked the nightlife and the Music City's atmosphere more than anything.

Not a conformist by nature, he hated wearing a tie and slacks to work on a daily basis, but until Casual Friday made a comeback he saw no alternative. With his sport coat draped over the chair behind him, Dalton typed a report into his computer regarding a prisoner transport that went wrong for local authorities. The prisoner escaped custody, but Dalton and another marshal found him within hours by visiting the man's usual haunts. He felt certain the paperwork was going to take longer than the search itself, but Dalton needed to know details if any aspect of the case ever appeared in a courtroom.

"You meeting us at Miss Kitty's later?" one of his colleagues asked on his way through the office, referring to a downtown tavern.

"Maybe," Dalton answered neutrally. "Depends on what the girlfriend wants to do."

His fellow marshal made the sound of a whip snapping while giving a smirk as he exited the office.

Dalton rolled his eyes, returning his attention to the report, which neared completion.

For almost the first time that week the clouds gave way to some rays of sun, providing a bit of warmth and a glimmer of the spring season to come. Dalton's back felt warm from the natural light piercing the window behind him as he typed, wondering how soon he could change into regular clothes for the evening.

It took another five minutes for him to read over the report and finally officially enter it into his departmental database. His lieutenant had mentioned several other assignments that needed attention, though not urgently, so Dalton thought about checking into those when his phone rang.

"United States Marshals Office," he answered officially. "Deputy Marshal Dalton speaking."

"You sound like you're ready for the weekend," a familiar voice replied.

"Russ? That you, you sly dog?"

"The one and only."

"I *am* ready for the weekend. What has you calling from Hawaii, or wherever you moved to?"

"I wish," Greene scoffed. "You wouldn't trade me jobs for anything if you knew what I was doing."

Dalton always wondered exactly why his former partner did leave the marshals service. Everyone knew it was a private sector job, but the man never gave one single hint about exactly what the job entailed. Even Secret Service agents were able to talk about what they did, even if they refused to provide details.

What could possibly be so secret that Greene took a vow of silence regarding his new career?

"So where are you calling from?" Dalton asked.

"Indiana at the moment."

"How are you supposed to protect the president from there?"

Greene chuckled.

"He's here to speak about his new corn-based weapon of mass destruction."

"Incredible stuff. I'd like an autograph sometime."

"I'll see what I can do," Greene replied, unable to stifle a brief laugh.

Dalton remembered why he and Russ Greene worked so well together. Both grew up with something missing in their lives. Greene longed for the city as a teenager, feeling more enslaved every season he worked with his parents on their farm. Dalton lost both of his parents at the age of ten in a tragic car crash. He finished out the remainder of his formative years in West Virginia living with his grandparents. Given all of the love and support a boy could ever want from his grandparents, Dalton longed for an escape to something bigger and better, often entertaining himself with police dramas and true crime books.

During his college internship at a local police department, Dalton forged a friendship with a veteran West Virginia state trooper. The man, who became a surrogate uncle of sorts to him, recommended joining the FBI or the U.S. Marshals as a job that could take him away from the state that haunted him with memories of his parents. Though the trooper eventually retired, Dalton kept in close touch with him over the years, thankful for the man's advice and understanding.

Perhaps Dalton saw some of the trooper's traits in Greene, including unequalled work ethic and a certain stubborn nature that could only come from someone who no longer accepted denial. No matter how many rules and regulations slowed Greene, the man obtained results time after time by circumventing the red tape.

"I'm actually calling for a favor," Greene said, returning Dalton to the present from memory lane.

"I should have known there was a reason I'm just now hearing from you after *months* of silence."

"It's been a busy couple of months. I'm trying to track down a missing person, Chase."

Dalton tapped a pen atop his desk momentarily, wondering why his former colleague couldn't track such a person himself.

"Missing person, eh?"

"I've tapped out my resources on this end. You're my last resort before I have to make a big play I'd prefer not to."

"Am I allowed to ask questions?"

"The less you know the better."

Dalton sighed.

"Is he even a real missing person?"

"He is, but he might be voluntarily out of sight because he's done some bad things."

"Fine," Dalton said, figuring he owed Greene at least one favor from their days of working together. "What's the name?"

"Lincoln Daine."

Greene spelled the last name, since the spelling wasn't common.

"You going to rescue me from government work one of these days, big shot?"

"I could probably use someone with your qualifications. There's no turning back once you agree to this job though."

Dalton grunted to himself, waiting for the computer to come up with information about Daine. Short of opening an investigation, Dalton could only search basic information about Daine as a person of interest. Missing persons were typically dealt with by state police or the FBI as the marshals focused on fugitives, prisoner transportation, and court security. They occasionally worked in asset forfeiture or bank robberies when the FBI was busy with homeland security, but Dalton seldom witnessed much excitement.

Before he could contemplate Greene's casual offer, Dalton's computer screen blinked, displaying some basic information about Daine.

"He looks squeaky clean, Russ. It gives an address."

"Old news. He's on the lam. Does it give any relatives or contacts?"

"No. No criminal record means we don't have his network, but you already know that. What are you really wanting, old friend?"

"I need to find him. The man has a track record of winning big at races and disappearing."

"And you think he has a little help on the side?"

"Something like that, yes. He's careful not to use credit cards or a registered cell phone."

"Then why call me at all?"

"Just hoping for a longshot. Also, he uses a bookie in the Nashville area sometimes."

"How does that help?"

"He bets on football and basketball every so often, and he has to be present."

Dalton grumbled audibly.

"Give me the name and I'll visit the guy if I find time."

Greene provided the name and location of the bookie, not certain himself if Daine ever used the same betting source twice. He seemed excessively cautious about covering his tracks, as though he knew his habits might get him discovered by someone wanting the cube.

"I owe you," Greene said.

"I know. And I have a feeling I'm going to regret doing this."

CHAPTER 17

It took Dalton only two days to report back to Greene that the bookie had evidently moved to a new location. Though he felt confident he could track the man down, Dalton said he probably needed another few days to a week.

Unwilling to let fate decide his chances of success, Greene went to Clouse with his plan, asking for some heavy financial assistance and permission to use or hire a few people for a few months. His plan involved getting a horse, with longshot odds, to the Kentucky Derby in May. Any number of hurdles stood before him, but once Clouse gave a green light on the financial end, Greene needed only buy into an existing horse already on the cusp of being Derby material and get it to Louisville by hook or crook.

To ensure all parties involved were represented, Greene accepted Matt Teakon for the sake of Julie Knowles, and a man by the name of Craig Jennings on Clouse's behalf. Matt Teakon had worked with Julie and his uncle, Mark Teakon, on several dangerous encounters before Clouse formed an alliance with their group, so the younger Teakon was very much trusted by Julie.

Jennings worked under Clouse at the West Baden Springs Hotel and French Lick Springs Resort as the head of security. While Jennings did not oversee the casino security, he often kept busy during the tourism season at both hotels. Events like vintage baseball, hot air balloon rides, golf tournaments, train rides on the Monon, weddings, and concerts kept Jennings occupied.

"I feel ridiculous," Craig Jennings said, standing front and center before the track at Sunland Park Racetrack & Casino in New Mexico.

Formerly a shop teacher before Clouse hired him to head up security at the hotels, Jennings lived in the country and disliked big city life. It wasn't uncommon for him to wear cowboy boots to church or even jump in and sing with the gospel band occasionally, but he didn't feel comfortable at the moment.

"Suck it up," Matt Teakon replied. "I'm a fish out of water, too, you know."

Both men wore black slacks, black cowboy boots, and black leather blazers along with black cowboy hats. Only Teakon's red dress shirt and gold bolo tie provided contrast on his part, while Jennings wore a bolo with a large turquoise stone centered in silver over his white shirt. Neither spoke with a New Mexico drawl, and neither felt confident acting their parts, much less speaking differently, so Greene told them they were posing as investors who had brought their business to New Mexico a year ago.

Jennings wished his employer had come down personally to play the part, but he knew Clouse was needed elsewhere much of the time. At least Clouse once owned a horse or two and liked wearing boots.

"Hell, the only reason they picked me for this was because they needed someone who knew the situation," Jennings complained, keeping his voice low as a preliminary heat of horses stampeded around the track.

"There aren't many of us, with good reason."

It took Greene some time to train both men what to do during their time in New Mexico, because he never planned to travel with them. He had other matters to attend to in Illinois, so he arranged for Jennings to pose as a co-owner of a horse named Desert Phantom, a three-year-old chestnut colt. The horse had performed well enough in other races that if it placed in the Sunland Derby it stood an excellent chance of being invited to the Kentucky Derby. While Teakon possessed almost expert knowledge of horses from growing up in the Midwest, he didn't feel comfortable or qualified to act as a racehorse trainer. In turn, Greene asked him to pose as Jennings' ranch manager, which worked out perfectly since the horse already resided at the original owner's ranch. No one would ever ask to see Jennings' ranch that in fact did not exist.

Greene discovered that Margaret Stough had exhausted most of her funds just getting Phantom into several key races. Between training, travel expenses, and the entry fees, she could not afford to enter him in the Sunland Derby, one of the most important prep races for the Kentucky Derby. Greene fronted Jennings the money to pose as someone interested in a benefactor position with the horse, basically taking a co-ownership position through the racing season to give Phantom a chance at the most prestigious race in the world.

Margaret wasn't anxious to accept a partner, but she needed the financial assistance after several banks turned her down and other owners shot her lowball offers for the colt. Now eighty-five, she didn't get around very well so she liked the idea of Jennings being the front man for the horse when the media came around. He promised her he could handle the responsibility, a lump forming in his throat during their entire conversation.

Now committed to his double life, Jennings watched as the results from the last race were posted on the electronic scoreboard. He dreaded the thought of his new colt failing miserably during the final race for numerous reasons. Strangely, he felt an attachment to Phantom, and to Margaret, even after being affiliated with both for less than three weeks. It turned out the trainer was about the best choice possible because he only worked with a few horses, and devoted much of his time to Margaret's colt. Not that Jennings truly possessed control over who trained the horse, but he felt certain changing trainers would lead to certain disaster.

It didn't take a racehorse expert to understand only a fool tinkered with something that didn't require fixing.

Jennings also found himself adapting to Mark Teakon's nephew, who apparently assisted the Massachusetts group in hunting the cubes from time to time. He already knew details about the cursed objects that made him an immediate fit with both groups. Close to six feet in height, Teakon possessed brown hair and a full goatee that encircled his lips. A divorcee who recently left a civilian job at a military research facility, Teakon gave up good pay and security for the betterment of the planet. Capable of working with his hands and understanding a wide array of machinery, Teakon seemed to know a little bit about every topic he and Jennings discussed. He often advised Jennings on the way of horses and ranch life, encouraging him to at least understand ranch life so the workers respected him a little bit.

Returning his attention to his attire, Jennings abided by Margaret's wishes for him to dress like a gentleman from New Mexico with some class. He grew out his beard, finding a greater mix of gray with his normal brown hair this time. With little more than a fringe of hair left atop his head, he actually felt somewhat thankful the assignment required him to wear a Stetson.

Feeling a bit more tense as the race drew nearer, Jennings found his stomach in knots all morning long, partly from hoping his ruse worked, but also because he wanted to win the race and potentially put another cube in safe haven. Only a handful of Paul Clouse's friends and employees knew about the dangerous objects, though Jennings woke up most mornings wishing he had never accidentally stumbled into a convoluted plan to use one of them at the cost of a dozen or so lives. Fortunately the plan didn't reach its lethal conclusion, though a number of people died in the process. From time to time Jennings woke suddenly in the middle of night, his bed sheets soaked with sweat after reliving the horror in his dreams.

"You okay?" Teakon asked, breaking Jennings' trance.

"Fine. Just nervous about the race is all."

Surrounded by thousands of people wanting to watch the race, despite the cool, windy weather, the two men passed the time by reading the program or watching the other races. They didn't bother mingling with the nearby people, since most of them were simply spectators and not fellow owners. In the past few weeks they learned that March nights in New Mexico were below freezing and it took until lunchtime for the temperatures to swing to sixty or seventy degrees.

Jennings hadn't asked Teakon much about his uncle's life, and even less about the man's death in the Bering Sea. Considering Teakon volunteered little information about either situation, and seemed short whenever either topic was brought up, Jennings only asked a few questions before giving up completely.

Trust wasn't easy between the two men because they represented different factions searching for the same thing. No one was really certain Clouse and Julie trusted one another, but they worked together for the sake of Mark Teakon. Jennings knew Clouse surrendered the cubes to the deceased college professor, affirming his belief in his employer's intentions. He wanted to believe the cubes were being cast out of society's reach one at a time, never to be seen again, but nagging feelings otherwise haunted him.

"It's too bad Margaret couldn't come," Teakon said, making small talk at this point.

Her nerves, more than her health, kept her from attending the race. Despite investing so much money into Phantom and bringing him to this race, she let Jennings confront the press, assuring him she would make the trip to Louisville if their horse was invited.

Two more preliminary races started and finished before Jennings and Teakon watched Desert Phantom being led by one of the stable hands, his jockey already in the saddle. Jennings knew little about the jockey, Johnny Gomez, except that Margaret placed complete faith in him. The man had lost his last two racing gigs to more seasoned riders, but Margaret loved the way he handled horses, often reading their desires. He seemed to have a knack for keeping them safely in the middle of the pack once a race started, only letting them put on a burst of speed when he felt they were ready for a charge but not in danger of petering out.

Jennings had the option of standing almost anywhere along the track, on the upper balcony where the VIP tent was located, or inside the casino. A far cry from Churchill Downs where the stands towered above and around the oval racetrack, this track provided what appeared to be a pen between the casino and the racetrack itself, complete with solid white fencing as tall as most men but easy to see through. The announcer who called the races reported that an estimated nineteen thousand people showed up to watch the day's events and place wagers.

The casino, honoring local heritage, was painted burnt orange, red clay, and turquoise on the exterior, giving it a strident appearance that visitors found difficult to miss. Jennings turned to admire the décor before returning his attention to the impending race, knowing his horse needed to finish at least fourth to accumulate enough earnings to make the big dance.

Wins at the Silver Deputy Stakes and the Grey Stakes the year prior provided him with enough earnings to come this far, but he needed nearly another $100,000 to be one of the twenty horses eligible to run in Kentucky. His last race ended badly when he placed second to last on a different New Mexico track. Margaret's financial troubles apparently led to subpar travel conditions and a lapse in training when she couldn't afford trainer Jeff

Slaton's services for a few weeks. He cut her some slack and stayed with the horse whenever possible, but he took some paying jobs that kept him away from the ranch more often.

"If he doesn't place at least third, all of this is down the drain," Jennings muttered, knowing the winner earned $400,000, second place $176,000, and third place $96,000.

All three positions were enough to take the group east, but only Phantom could decide his own fate. Jennings sucked in a deep breath as the horses were led to the starting gate. In this race only a dozen horses ran, and there wasn't quite so much spectacle, like the promenade or jockey group photograph as there was in Kentucky. Jennings hoped, prayed even, that he was going to see Churchill Downs from the inside. While it wasn't a childhood dream by any means, he thought bringing a racehorse to the track would certainly be a lifetime accomplishment. His primary motivation stemmed from wanting to find another cube and keep it from doing anyone else harm.

"This is it," Teakon said before drawing a deep, calming breath. "In two minutes we'll know if we just wasted two weeks of our lives."

Jennings couldn't bring himself to utter a reply, simply content to watch the horses being loaded one at a time into the starting gate. Phantom drew the third door from the gate, which historically speaking wasn't bad luck. Being on the outside meant a horse needed to make up more ground and work its way toward the inner rail, which often drained any reserves the horses might need during the final turn. Drawing the innermost slot sometimes pinned an aggressive horse against the railing as it struggled to keep up with the pack. Most horses needed only a little bumping and kicking to break their routine and demoralize them to the point that they fell back and refused to run hard.

One of the horses refused to settle in the gate easily, detaining the race start momentarily. It finally entered the gate, led by one of the track workers dressed from head to toe in green coveralls and a baseball cap. Phantom was loaded next without a hitch, leaving only two more horses before the race began along the dirt track.

Although he wasn't Catholic, Jennings made a sign of the cross as he watched the final horse being loaded, knowing the race start was mere seconds away. When the bell rang to signal the race start, Jennings found himself startled because his eyes were locked on the third stall, hoping Phantom could beat eleven other horses and take first place. Admonishing himself for being a bit greedy, Jennings knew enough purse money to take them to Louisville would suffice, but he wanted Margaret to fare well.

Every gate opened, releasing the twelve horses in Phantom's heat. They all emerged cleanly, remaining in a tight pack until two horses dropped back around the first turn. Jennings virtually pressed against the white fence for a look at the track, finding it difficult to see much along the same level as the horses, with dust floating behind the field. Suddenly the VIP tent above sounded like a much better idea, though several monitors provided an excellent view as a video camera followed the leaders.

Every sense felt heightened as Jennings tried to follow the race on the monitor once the horses ran along the back straightaway. Listening to the announcer give a play-by-play was about the only way to keep track of the positions at this point.

Teakon shook his arm and pumped his fist with excitement.

"Hear that? He's moving up the pack!"

Jennings tried listening intently but the man spoke like an auctioneer, rattling off names and positions. On the monitor, he spotted Phantom's blue saddle blanket with the embroidered number three centered in the pack. His eyes locked on the colt, watching it run steadily with five other horses centered between two leaders and the stragglers. The thunderous clop of four dozen hooves had diminished to a distant echo after the horses made the first turn, but Jennings found new sounds in the form of betters and spectators all around him cheering for their picks.

By the end of the opposite straightaway Phantom began moving toward the front of the central pack, but Jennings knew Gomez was battling to hold the horse back. In a mere two weeks Jennings learned the horse had incredible spirit, but the jockey's job was to ensure the colt's determination didn't outlast his body. It wasn't until the pack rounded the last turn that Gomez finally let Phantom surge forward. He began fist pumping as he saw Phantom begin to leave the pack behind him, on pace to catch the two leaders by the finish line.

"Come on," Jennings muttered as Teakon clutched his arm harder this time from the sheer excitement both of them felt.

Phantom overtook the entire center pack, assuring a third place finish at worst if nothing disastrous happened. Jennings rather hoped Gomez didn't push him harder for first place after seeing broken legs and other injuries on televised horseraces. The thought of Phantom suffering such an injury, which in turn required immediate euthanizing, entered his mind for the briefest of seconds. Margaret's dreams would be crushed in an instant, the chance to find the cube in Louisville would die on the dirt track, and evil would indeed triumph.

Jennings watched the horse battle forward during the final stretch, suddenly contending for first place without Gomez even using the whip in his right hand. Obviously Gomez felt content with third place, or sensed the horse didn't want to slow, so he just let Phantom run his own race.

"He's going to do it," Teakon said, putting a fist up to his mouth as his brown eyes stared down the track.

Phantom overtook the second place horse with less than fifty yards to the finish line, creating a frenzied crowd. Jennings started jumping up and down in place a bit when he saw Phantom chase down the leader with less than twenty yards to go. He couldn't imagine what momentum the group would carry with them to Kentucky if Phantom finished first, but he soon discovered it wasn't meant to be. Phantom came within a nose of catching the first place horse, just short of a photo finish, easily securing second place.

Jennings and Teakon exchanged mixed looks of excitement and grave concern after seeing the finish. They were indeed heading to Louisville without much fanfare, which suited their secretive task of locating a certain gambler and the cube he used for financial gain after murdering someone each time.

Based on the reception Clay received at the island west of South America and Parish's experience on the Bering Sea, they anticipated they might not be the only ones heading to the Kentucky Derby.

CHAPTER 18

Paul Clouse learned to keep secrets well over the years, even from his own family. His parents knew little of his ordeals, and now in their retirement years, they needed to be content and happy instead of worried about him. While his self-appointed position as the guardian of cursed cubes put them in danger a few times, he shielded them from the majority of the truth on a regular basis.

When he told his wife, Jane, of his plan to recover the time cube himself, she thought he was losing his mind, but he told her he was going to disappear in a few days and use some unorthodox methods of travel to avoid detection. Feeling certain his every move was being watched by a certain entity that may or may not have been the Coven he dealt with previously, Clouse played it smart regarding the time cube.

Not only did he have his people look into numerous properties around the Chicago area to create a figurative smokescreen, but he also kept the property Liz located under wraps by using a different lawyer, from Chicago, to inquire about the property. Under orders to keep his mouth shut to everyone, including his secretary, wife, and office partners, the lawyer found the property was owned by an investor who failed to do anything useful with it in a decade.

Clouse discreetly had the lawyer approach the man as a contractor who wanted an area for storage. Though the land was nearly impassible from the vegetation growing around it, and the main building showing signs of wear from neglect, the property still seemed passable for storage or light construction work. Names were signed along the dotted lines shortly after the new year and Clouse let none of his people step foot near the property. He figured the best way to keep his secret safe was to let his adversaries follow him and his people while they conducted everyday business.

Not until early April, when the ink on the property thoroughly dried and the weather took away the bitter ice and snow from Northern Illinois did he finally decide to act.

It took more willpower than Clouse expected to leave his property in the middle of the night without kissing his wife and children goodbye. He drove to the train station in Indianapolis, buying a ticket for Massachusetts, which indicated he was sneaking off to see Julie Knowles. Clouse rather hoped anyone observing his actions believed he was carrying on an affair with the young woman. Whatever his followers thought of such a trip didn't much matter to him so long as they believed he was indeed traveling east. In truth, he bought a train ticket from an individual to Chicago discreetly, rather than purchase it at the sales window.

By morning light he stepped from the train, rented a car and drove it to a busy hotel in downtown Chicago. He didn't formally check in because he wanted no paper trail of his travels. Aiming to simply lose any tenacious followers, Clouse hailed a cab from the hotel's courtesy phone, asking for the driver to meet him around back. From there Clouse met with the attorney who purchased the property for him, asking the man to personally drive him to the property, hoping his actions were enough to provide him with privacy for the next day or two.

"You sure you don't want me to stay?" the lawyer asked when Clouse stepped from the car, leaving the door open to converse momentarily.

"I'll be fine. You did get me everything I asked for, right?"

"Of course."

Clouse paid the man handsomely for both legal and errand boy services. His demands certainly weren't outlandish, though the attorney likely found them highly specific.

"I'm just worried about you being out here all alone. How will I know when to come get you?"

Clouse looked up at the partially cloudy morning sky. Puffy white clouds with hints of gray glided across the blue background, gently propelled by an early April breeze. Stubborn hills of snow remained on the grounds, the air cool enough that Clouse opted to wear a fall jacket with a thermal layer. He wore three layers of shirts beneath the jacket, and some insulating legwear beneath his blue jeans. Some snacks, a winter cap and two pairs of gloves were tucked into the pack he brought. He learned on the fire department to always keep an extra pair of gloves handy at all times.

"Come and get me tomorrow morning around this time."

"You're sure?" his attorney asked, his eyebrows arched as though he questioned his best client's rationale.

If not his sanity.

"Positive. See you tomorrow."

Clouse shut the door, watching and listening carefully as the man drove his Lexus down the hill, away from the old construction hub. He wanted to know the sounds of a vehicle approaching, though Clouse supposed he lacked adequate hiding spots if anyone decided to visit him. His pack also carried his cell phone, though he removed the battery from the back before leaving his mansion. Knowing the government or other entities might trace him through the phone communicating with cell phone towers, he decided to bring it for an emergency situation only.

Quickly surveying the property and the equipment left by a rental company through the attorney's orders, Clouse found everything in order. While he trusted his team, Clouse couldn't take the chance of someone else finding the most important of the cubes and using it to his or her advantage. He supposed Greene or Liz could have already unearthed the time cube, but they obviously hadn't, which only raised their stock in his eyes.

Clouse spent almost half an hour climbing down to the spot where the quarry once rested dangerously below the construction headquarters. Several young saplings took residence where water once pooled near the steep natural wall. A few shrubs dotted the dirt wall, which looked almost directly vertical from below. Behind him, a farmer's field stood barren with the previous fall's stalks still clinging to the ground, dead and tan. Because the former quarry belonged on the land Clouse purchased, a small access path stemmed from the main road heading up the hill. The construction company had left an excavator and some hand tools there for Clouse to use, per the attorney's orders.

With limited experience in construction equipment, Clouse carefully positioned the excavator until he got the hang of using the articulating arm. Saying he mastered the machine would have been a gross overstatement of his abilities, but he found himself digging in the quarry area within an hour. All the while he felt more than slightly disturbed about intruding upon a grave. Knowing Thomas Ervin believed in the same principles, and wanted to keep the cube safe from evildoers, drove Clouse onward.

Working up a sweat in no time, Clouse removed the trees, shrubs, and several large rocks before getting to his true purpose. He dug almost twenty feet before he found a need to locate the 3D imaging metal detector the rental company left on the trailer. Not the easiest tool in the world to use, the detector finally provided a range of colors across the screen for Clouse to decipher any objects below him and their depth. The detector promised a range of sixty meters below the ground, though Clouse figured that was under ideal conditions.

He found himself surrounded by virtually the opposite scenario thirty years after Thomas Ervin disappeared.

Despite nature's barricades, Clouse discovered that much of his already dug hole was directly over a large object, which he imagined was a Ford LTD. Ladders stood with the remaining construction equipment when he felt the need to climb down, but more digging needed to be done before he planned on shoveling his way into the vintage car.

Wiping the sweat from his brow, Clouse took a moment to observe the area surrounding him. Very isolated from the city, this wooded area provided the sort of peace and serenity he once found at the West Baden Springs Hotel on the team that helped restore the building. After years of living and working in Bloomington, near the Indiana University campus, he loved traveling an hour south to work at the dome. Unfortunately the job, and the building itself in some ways, led to the darkest days of his life after his first wife was murdered.

Clouse found his name centered in the investigation, eventually cleared thanks to help from a man he now considered a close friend. Angie's murder, and the subsequent events, took him down some dark roads as he discovered the Coven and at the heart of the group, a man he considered a benefactor, friend, and mentor. While that man now lay six feet deep with a slab of concrete covering his charred remains, Clouse carried on his war against the cubes and those who intended to use them for personal gain.

He suffered terrible losses over the years, similar to mounting casualties during times of war. His first wife, his best friend, the family dog, and countless friends and acquaintances did nothing to deserve death. Their only "crime" was affiliation with Paul Clouse, and for that many of them were taken from him too soon. Much of this happened before Clouse even knew the extent or power of the cubes, and subsequently dedicated much of his life to harvesting them for safekeeping.

Hanging his head momentarily, Clouse prayed he wouldn't lose more. A man of religious convictions, he wanted to believe the Lord above was watching over him and approving of his methods. He treasured the friends and family left around him, and he conducted such costly work to maintain their safety.

"Back to work," he muttered as he climbed into the excavator's cab, ready to dig another ten feet before breaking out the shovels.

He spent another twenty minutes trying to fine-tune the digging above where the detector showed the car's location. From there, he created a jagged, staggered side, almost like crude stairs, so the ladder wasn't his only method of entry or exiting the now thirty foot deep hole. Finally the metal teeth at the end of the articulating arm struck something more solid than dirt with a clunk that was unmistakably metal. Clouse breathed a sigh of relief, feeling sorrow simultaneously because he knew he was going to be the first person to lay eyes on Thomas Ervin in decades.

Using the arm to carefully dig a trench around the car, about four feet further down, Clouse worked until the LTD's slightly raised hind end was free. For some reason the car came to rest at an angle, probably due to a large rock or another object dropped into the quarry. Clouse could examine the bottom of the car to find out definitively, but he didn't much care about conducting a forensic analysis.

Jumping from the excavator's cab, he positioned the ladder down one of the more vertical sides of the large hole. He also took a braided rope the rental company provided, tying it to the excavator's arm before throwing the opposite end down the embankment. Being stuck in a hole during a frigid spring evening didn't sound particularly good for his health, so he wanted multiple exits in place. Carrying a shovel with him, he finally descended the ladder until he reached the secondary level just above the car. Assured the rope was in place, he jumped down to the car, taking a moment to admire the courage Ervin put forth in defending the cursed object. Desecrating one's grave wasn't something Clouse took lightly, especially since he and Ervin were kindred spirits.

Positive he wasn't going to like what he found regarding the body's condition, Clouse warily dug around the driver's side door to free more of the sediment from his path. A layer of silt continued to cling to the car's shell from its time underwater, preventing a good look inside. He refused to wipe off the windows for a peek, though doing so would have given him an immediate view of the body's condition. Showing restraint, he spent about fifteen minutes shoveling dirt to the side until he freed the door enough to open it.

Unsure of exactly when the quarry was filled in with dirt, Clouse found two things very interesting about the LTD. One, the door actually opened despite some rust to the body and the uncoated metal hinges. The second and possibly more amazing find was an absolute lack of dirt and mud inside the vehicle.

No water remained inside the vehicle as the years slowly evaporated it into the surrounding dirt particles. Clouse could only assume the dirt dumped into the quarry to fill it turned to mud immediately upon impact with the water, keeping it from breaking the car's rear and side glass. The intact car preserved the terrible odor associated with death, coupled with the mustiness and rot accumulated from the car itself.

Groaning as he covered his mouth and nose with his forearm, Clouse coughed a few times when the permeating smell reached his throat and lungs. He suddenly wished he hadn't overlooked requesting a form of self-contained breathing apparatus like he once used as a firefighter.

Stepping to the inner portion of the door, Clouse finally looked inside the car, immediately seeing a skeleton positioned in the driver's seat. The lower jaw was dropped, giving the impression Ervin's bones spied something ghastly in front of the car. Clouse knew without tendons and muscle tissue, the bone simply fell out of place over the years. No muscle remained and the bones looked surprisingly clean despite their surroundings. While the bones showed only minor yellowing, Clouse discovered most of Ervin's clothing was deteriorated. Nothing stopped water scavengers, then earthworms, from getting their fill over three decades.

About the only thing left was Ervin's duty jacket, and even it remained tattered. Fighting off the urge to vomit from the cocktail of odors entering his nostrils, Clouse dared reach inside the car to probe the jacket with one hand, searching for the inside pocket that housed the cube according to Liz's vision. He found no pocket, but only because the material inside had succumbed to the elements, likely letting the cube fall to a different position.

"Oh, great," Clouse grumbled as he searched around the body for the object.

After searching between the bony legs, around the seat, and just to the right of the body, he finally spied a glimmer from the passenger's side floorboard. The cubes wanted to be noticed, so some unsuspecting soul might use them, and this dark blue cube glistened at him where no light entered to illuminate it.

At him.

Clouse never mistook the purpose of the cubes, or the fact that they knew how to toy with human emotions. Considering himself immune to their charms, he treated them like an abusive parent might an insolent child.

No longer did the protective pouch cover its nature, but it never escaped Thomas Ervin's watchful eye. Clouse reached over the man's remains, careful not to disturb the bones as he plucked the cube from the far corner. He pocketed the evil object, wishing cursed objects could be destroyed, but indestructibility was somehow woven into the original curse ceremony.

Taking a final look into the car, Clouse prayed for Tom Ervin that the man found peace in the afterlife. He shut the car door slowly with his mood deeply somber, wishing things hadn't ended so badly for the devoted cop and protector of mankind.

Clouse decided to leave the area alone and report the discovery of the body to the authorities. Trudy, the man's only surviving relative, deserved the truth after so many years of Ervin's disappearance remaining a mystery. Of course Clouse needed to sugarcoat certain parts of the discovery to avoid talking about his true reasons for using excavation equipment. He suspected a few members of the Chicago Police Department might want to have a talk with him regarding the cube. They would have to use careful wording when probing to see if he found the blue object, and Clouse suspected he might be forthcoming with the entire truth.

A number of variables needed to occur before such a conversation ever took place.

Now barely lunchtime, Clouse locked up the equipment and set everything back where he found it for the rental company to retrieve. He needed to remain hidden until morning with the cube, hoping no one figured out his plan or came to get him. So long as he left the cell phone separate from its battery and remained indoors, his chances remained good to excellent.

His major dilemma became where to hide the cube once he left Illinois. Dumping it into an ocean no longer seemed practical, leaving him to wonder if he might have been smarter to leave it in Thomas Ervin's care. Fortunately nothing pressing awaited him in the near future, giving Clouse time enough to ponder alternative areas in which to hide the cursed object.

Clouse gave the equipment and the partially buried car one last glance before heading up the access road. He planned to rough it overnight in the old building overhead, likely haunted by dreams of Thomas Ervin in life and death. Like the Chicago police officer, Clouse now felt the overwhelming responsibility of guarding the cube looming over him like a dark cloud with unforeseen consequences.

CHAPTER 19

When Chase Dalton finally tracked down the bookie he believed his friend was searching for, he waited until Saturday before venturing into the man's lair. Calling it a place of business, apartment, or living space felt too generous to the marshal. Basically a closet in the back of a convenience store, the room provided both the privacy and secrecy the bookie needed to conduct business. His friend at the front counter only let people through who knew the right thing to say, and fortunately for Dalton an informant provided him with both the location and information.

He dressed much like he might during the week because betters came in all shapes and sizes. A sport coat covered the firearm at his side, and Dalton's credentials remained safely tucked inside a pocket. Walking down a street that appeared far different than most people envisioned when they thought of Nashville, Dalton felt his sport coat flap when the gusty breeze struck it. Strangely, the street appeared mostly deserted with people emerging from one door just long enough to duck into another.

Dalton immediately regarded the store as a dive fit for roaches and vermin with only half of the overhead lights working and a perpetual stench that resembled body odor. Shelves and racks weren't fully stocked, and most of the food items had packaging that looked faded or damaged. He didn't look around very long because the clerk eyed him suspiciously the second he stepped through the front door. The deputy marshal approached the counter with a sense of purpose, deciding not to waste additional time.

"Remember the Titans," he stated the password, which related to the Tennessee Titans football team.

Though the man continued providing a suspicious stare, he let Dalton walk around the counter toward the back room. He gave three knocks with his knuckles in a rhythmic pattern before opening the door, indicating with an open hand for Dalton to enter.

Seated behind a small wooden desk in an otherwise empty room, a haggard man with weathered skin and pale blue eyes barely looked in his direction before focusing his attention on a spreadsheet with numerous columns. Disheveled thinning gray hair covered the man's head and he reeked of stale cigarette smoke. His hands trembled slightly as he jotted something on the spreadsheet, a cell phone held against his right ear by his bony shoulder.

He murmured a name that sounded like a racing horse because it was three words in length before jotting down a number and someone's last name on the paper. Only when he confirmed the name and amount did he end the phone call and look up to Dalton a second time.

"And how can I help you?"

"By telling me about one of your clients named Lincoln Daine."

"Who's asking?"

"Someone who owes a friend a huge favor. I just need to know the last time you heard from him and I leave your place of business alone."

Dalton moved his sport coat aside just enough to display the firearm and the badge he attached to his belt.

"Fucking great," the man sighed.

"Daine," Dalton urged, poking his finger onto the spreadsheet.

"It's been months," the bookie answered without shifting his eyes away from the marshal. "The guy moves around constantly."

"But he always comes back. Certainly a man of your caliber, with such lucrative clients, has the means to reach his clients when something good comes along."

The bookie shook his head.

"Daine comes in when he wants to. He knows the score, and the state of Tennessee isn't usually the place to win big."

Dalton wasn't convinced, so he put forth an expression to indicate he wasn't leaving without at least a little cooperation from the bookie. He didn't envision the man keeping a Rolodex of clients in a penthouse office downtown so he needed information here and now.

Getting a bit more serious, Dalton made a fist before slamming it down on the table where the bookie sat. While his actions failed to frighten the man into talking, the sudden sound of gunfire behind the deputy marshal drew a shocked expression from the bookie as Dalton reached for his sidearm.

Putting his right arm behind him with an open hand, Dalton indicated for the bookie to stay put as he drew his officially issued firearm. He figured someone was conducting a robbery on the store, though he couldn't imagine why anyone would bother knocking off such a rundown business. Holding his firearm at his side, the marshal cautiously turned the doorknob, opening the door just enough for a peek into the cluttered store. He barely put his face to the opening when the butt of a shotgun rammed through the opening, striking him in the forehead.

Dalton fell to the floor in a heap, still semiconscious from the blow. He heard some sounds, but everything reaching his ears sounded garbled while his vision was blurred and fading fast. Between the two senses he was able to determine the man with the shotgun taking aim at the bookie, the bookie pleading for his life, and the sound of the shotgun being fired that caused Dalton's ears to begin ringing more than before.

The bookie's lifeless body fell to the ground beside the marshal, his eyes wide open with a death stare. His chest was red and bloodied from the shotgun pellets, chunks of flesh and clothing dangling with the fresh, dripping blood. Dalton saw the man's killer kneel beside the fresh corpse, pulling something from his own pocket that he touched to the bookie's blood before uttering some words.

"I wish to take the form of this man," is what it sounded like he said, but the statement made no sense to the marshal.

Dalton fumbled for his gun, now unable to find it beside him, as the gunman turned his attention to him. Certain this was the end of his life, but uncertain why, the marshal watched the man reach toward him with whatever object he used to touch the bookie's blood.

***

When Dalton awoke from the unconscious state he fell into at the convenience store he found his ears ringing, his vision still a bit fuzzy, and his head aching as though he'd suffered a concussion from the shotgun blow. Amazed to be alive after the bizarre events that transpired inside the convenience store, Dalton blinked what seemed like a thousand times before his eyes finally stayed open to take in the room around him.

He couldn't recall if he regained consciousness at any point, so Dalton wondered how far removed he was from Tennessee, if at all, and if the day was still Saturday. Feeling somewhat groggy, as though drugs were used to maintain his helpless state, the deputy marshal struggled against his bonds. The familiar clanking of handcuffs reached his ears when he realized his hands were bound together in addition to being bonded with a separate chain to the solid metal chair where he sat.

His feet were also shackled to the chair, which reminded him of a throne because the back sat as tall as most people. Its comfortable padding provided little relief to Dalton as the metal frame refused to budge, even against his considerable strength. At least his eyes finally began to take in the scenery around him, even if he couldn't get up for a closer look.

Otherwise devoid of furniture, the room felt cool and humid with its solid slab floor, indicating Dalton was probably being held on a ground floor. He only knew it wasn't a basement because of the window just behind him to the left. Some dark red drapes that looked decades old from their pattern covered part of the window, allowing some daylight inside. Dalton thought it was a late afternoon sun based on the reddish glare, though he found his eyes equally drawn to the cobwebs and dust clinging to the old curtains.

The walls were covered with vintage Victorian wallpaper consisting of gold and red patterns that complimented the drapes. Above him, intricate engravings showed through the gray shade of the ceiling tiles, causing Dalton to wonder if he was trapped inside an old mansion or the dressing room of a closed down performance theater. No sign of electricity came from the light bulb over him or beneath the door behind him when he strained his neck to look.

Completely helpless, Dalton couldn't even budge the chair once he braced his feet against the ground, much less knock it over. Stripped of his firearm, keys, and any other loose articles, Dalton possessed nothing useful to expedite his escape. The thought of the bookie being blown away in front of him crossed his mind, making him wonder why he was spared at all.

Another ten minutes passed as Dalton cleared his head and found his vision growing better with each passing second. When the door finally opened behind him, Dalton expected to be executed swiftly, or dragged from the room for use as a bargaining chip in some kind of ransom scheme.

Instead, he came face-to-face with himself.

Himself.

"What do you think?" the stranger who looked like him asked, the voice exactly like Dalton's own.

Speechless, Dalton felt certain he was in one of the *Terminator* movies about to be executed and replaced by some machine or clone.

"Before I begin asking you questions that you will answer, I'm going to explain the situation to you," the stranger said, kneeling down in front of Dalton. "You're here because of your friend Greene, and I need him to think that I'm you."

Dalton said nothing, his mind racing for answers. Having his friend's name thrown in the mix only confused him further. What the hell had Greene gotten himself into in the private sector?

"I barely even know Greene," Dalton lied, drawing a smile from his twin self, which gave him the creeps.

"That's not true, and I'm banking on the fact that Greene will offer you a job in your time of need. See, you're about to leave your job with the government and ask your old friend for a job."

Dalton scowled, knowing he was about to be pried open like a can of sardines for information. Though he hated the idea of bringing harm to Greene in any way, he wished to keep all of his body parts intact, hoping for an escape attempt at some point.

"I want to know everything," the mystery man said ominously, leaning forward until their faces were inches apart. "Every detail about your work with Greene, every drink you two shared in a bar. If I'm going to live your life I need to know about your personal life, especially pertaining to Russ Greene."

"How are you even capable of this?"

"Forgive my bad manners. I intended to explain this in detail before starting the interrogation."

Dalton said nothing, just waiting for some answers.

"This little object," the man said, holding up a cube the color of a tangerine, "gives me the ability to look and sound just like whomever I choose."

Sitting back with a stonewalled expression, Dalton said nothing, immediately disbelieving whatever this identical stranger said.

"It's not a genie, however, Mr. Dalton. It requires a sacrifice each time I want to use it, and your buddy is hunting down these cubes and everyone who possesses one. It's only a matter of time before he and I meet face-to-face, and I want it to be on *my* terms."

"What the hell are you going to do?" Dalton asked, his concern escalating for his former colleague.

"I'm going to kill him, of course. Or rather *you're* going to kill him."

"Bastard!" Dalton shouted, trying to buck the restraints that held him in place against the sturdy chair.

"Don't worry. He won't die right away. I need to earn his trust, and for that I need your assistance. Only then can I find out where he's hiding the rest of these delightful little cubes so my organization can take what's truly our birthright."

Dalton still couldn't believe a single word entering his ears, but the proof stood directly before him. How else could the man look and sound identical to him? Even the best technology created by the government showed telltale flaws in the field.

"You're insane," he muttered anyway, trying to provoke a response.

"No, I'm not. It's only too bad your friend didn't trust you enough to bring you with him, or you'd know the truth."

Reaching for a leather handbag behind him, the man drew a pad of paper, a pen, and lastly a knife that appeared surgical in nature, setting each to his right side in order. With the dark, narrowing eyes of a serpent he looked directly at Dalton.

"Shall we begin?"

CHAPTER 20

During the last week of April a number of important items required Russ Greene's attention. He chose to stay in the sixth floor of the West Baden Springs Hotel with his employer's blessing simply to plan for the Kentucky Derby and several other pressing issues.

Liz finally made a permanent move from California to Indiana, based on his recommendation. After proving her worth with the Thomas Ervin saga, Greene spoke with Clouse about bringing the entire team closer in proximity. Clay Branson, still a rogue by comparison, remained in Mason, Ohio without much commitment to the cause. Greene suspected the man might disavow the group completely once he relocated and settled the score with his former mentor.

Putting aside his feelings toward Branson, Greene opted to speak with Clouse about the most important of the cubes privately. His employer traveled to the hotel, meeting him at Ballard's Bar in the grand atrium of the resort around lunchtime. Though the bar was not entirely secluded, both men felt safe in the hotel because the likelihood of someone listening to their conversation or observing them seemed remote. After all, Clouse owned the hotel, and therefore all of the security cameras, personnel, and establishments within it.

"Where do we stand with our overall objectives?" Clouse asked once the two men shook hands and sat at a table with bottles of beer before them.

"We stand to lose or gain a lot in the next two weeks," Greene answered. "Right now we still possess enough of the cubes to ensure the world is safe."

"Have you done any further research?" Clouse asked before taking a swig of beer.

"Enough to know that you are labeled as the possessor of one of the cubes," Greene answered without fear of retaliation from his boss.

He didn't much care what Clouse thought of his opinion at this point, grasping the notion that their quest far exceeded the worth of either man.

"For now it stays in my possession," Clouse answered firmly. "It's safe."

"Safe from whom? There are people who would kill in the blink of an eye to possess that thing. They would gladly abduct your family and fillet them in front of you until you surrendered it."

"Point taken," Clouse said calmly. "And so long as no one except you and Julie know that I possess it, I shouldn't have much to worry about."

"Oh?" Greene asked, sitting back to create some distance from his employer. "And what if you were to use the cube? Maybe take a trip back in time and save your first wife? Or your best buddy from high school?"

Clouse barely raised an eyebrow as his glare relayed his opinion on the matter.

"I didn't bring you into the fold to serve as my backup conscience, Russ. While I appreciate everything you and the team have done thus far, that cube stays with me until we can guarantee it doesn't fall into the wrong hands."

"That's the problem with cursed objects. They never go away."

Both men took a drink from their beers, trying to calculate what the other was thinking.

"I simply didn't appreciate being left out of the loop," Greene stated for the record.

"That's understandable, Russ. But you've got to understand that a game changer like the time cube isn't something I can just toss into a local safe and forget about. Believe me, if I had plans to do something about the past, it would already be done. I've suffered a lot of losses the past ten years, but it's brought me to this point where I can actually do something good that affects, if not saves, billions of lives."

Greene understood Clouse's point, knowing that meant the book linked to all thirteen cubes became equally essential from a protection standpoint. For the past few months a thirst for knowledge about the cubes ate at Greene from the inside, not because he sought their power, but because he knew great leaders understood their enemy.

"I doubt this is the last time we'll be having a conversation about that cube," he informed Clouse.

"I certainly hope not, and I'm very open to ideas about keeping it safe well beyond our years."

"Tom Ervin certainly did a good job," Greene said with a sharp edge to his tone.

Clouse caught the meaning, though he masked his feelings about the thought of sacrificing himself in a dark and lonely grave with the cube.

"No disrespect, boss, but when you said you wanted me to keep the cubes safe from everyone because you trusted me implicitly, I thought you meant *everyone*."

"I thought I did, but for now this is the exception to the rule."

Thumbing his beer bottle momentarily, Clouse looked more at ease about the situation, understanding Greene's perspective.

"Aside from questioning my moral fiber, what else is on your mind, Russ?"

"I want to let Liz get more involved."

"More involved?"

"Until now we've been operating on conjecture, a handful of documents, some research Mark Teakon conducted, and a book that may or may not be our ally. I want her to handle some of these objects and see if she can tell us where they came from, and maybe something more about them."

Clouse held his beer, stared at it momentarily in thought, and finally put it down to look Greene in the eye.

"That can be a dangerous game, especially if what she said is remotely true about someone tapping into her thoughts. We don't know if the other side has someone with equal or greater ability than hers."

"We also don't know if the other side possesses three-quarters of the cubes, preparing to murder us in our sleep so they can carry out their plan."

"I leave it up to you," Clouse said, holding up both hands. "Just know there are significant risks if the other side gains an understanding of things. Right now we have a strategic advantage because we possess the book. If they find out about it, a lot more people will die."

Greene nodded.

"We already know they're watching our every move, which is why we can't safely dispose of the cubes. Maybe it's time to start learning who our enemy truly is."

"How so?"

"We set up stings all the time when I worked for the government," Greene said with a cagy smile. "Maybe we can lure someone into a trap and get them to talk."

"If the other side can play dirty, I don't see a problem with that."

Clouse held up his bottle and Greene tapped it with his. Aside from the recent sneaky stint, Greene liked and respected his employer wholeheartedly.

***

Near the end of the conversation with Clouse, Greene received a call from Chase Dalton in which his former colleague asked to meet with him in person.

"It's urgent," Dalton said in a hushed voice, as though someone nearby might be eavesdropping.

Greene offered to travel to Tennessee, but Dalton countered, saying he could make it to Indiana by nightfall. Deciding it wasn't any big deal, Greene provided his friend with the name and address of the hotel. He then made arrangements with Dan Duncan, the hotel manager, to put Dalton up for the night before returning to some paperwork to pass the time.

During the day he made plans for the Kentucky Derby, along with potential ideas to dispose of the remaining cubes where no one could find them. He felt a lot more pressure doing his current job than he ever experienced working for the government. While some of the names written in Julie's book let him know who possessed the cursed objects, in some cases he found absolutely no information about the people through his research. Searching for people seemed much easier with government computers, informants, and anonymous tips.

Uncertain whether or not his friend would call or simply show up, Greene remained inside the hotel most of the day. He left once to buy a deep-dish pizza down the street at one of the local pizzerias, choosing to escape the hotel walls in lieu of the fine dining along the ground floor.

The sun began setting around the time Greene stepped onto the hotel's veranda, admiring the serenity around him, wishing more moments in his life could feel so care free. Much of the day he found his mind wandering to what kind of trouble Dalton stepped into that required a face-to-face talk with him. Dalton was never one to deviate too far from the rulebook at work, and he never dabbled in illicit activities outside of work.

Greene's stomach grumbled because lunch at the pizza joint was almost eight hours behind him. He decided to hold out in order to show his friend some good hospitality in the French Lick area when Dalton arrived.

Some of his planning on the hotel's sixth floor put him in contact with Liz a few different times. Both were currently staying there for different reasons. Liz had yet to find an apartment or house locally, which Dalton attributed to her being a picky California girl. Greene simply needed to remain close to most of his team, and West Baden provided a solid base of operations.

Paul Clouse and his family once lived in the sixth floor suite of the hotel because it provided them safe haven from the public and anyone wanting to harm them. More than once people had tried using Clouse's family as leverage against him to obtain one of the cursed cubes, which forced his retreat into the hotel. While the hotel itself initiated many of the problems in Clouse's life, he felt the public setting provided protection, and the isolated sixth floor made it easy for his bodyguards and hotel security to protect his family.

Because none of the hotel's two-hundred-forty-six rooms took up space on the ground floor, each of the other five floors housed over fifty rooms each. Much of the top floor's space was transformed into a suite sectioned off from the other rooms initially. When Clouse moved his family there, the entire floor was transformed into a penthouse of sorts, complete with workout facility, dining areas, special guest rooms, and office space. While its rounded hallways comprised a massive amount of square footage, the segmented areas made it feasible that Greene and Liz might not spy one another during the course of a single day.

Looking out to the sunken garden, Greene paced the veranda's tile surface momentarily before taking a seat on one of the white rocking chairs placed behind the railing. Often sure to keep busy every second of the day, Greene found the sensation of simple relaxation rather foreign. Even now he wanted to look anxiously over his shoulder, feeling certain someone was spying on him or preparing to assault him in search of the cubes.

He sometimes wondered who Clouse's alternate choice for his job might have been. None of the people Clouse researched were revealed to one another, but Greene felt certain he, Liz, and Clay Branson were the man's top picks with good reason.

When Greene decided to stroll around the back of the hotel, he noticed the bulbs in the Victorian green lamp posts coming to life, illuminating the brick drive and the garden area. He saw a couple about to take a carriage ride, one of the many perks about staying at the hotel. Between the stables, two major golf courses, the spas, the casino, and a theme park just over half an hour away, people found numerous reasons to spend the night.

Spying headlights approaching as he walked along the driveway, Greene stepped aside to look at the vehicle. Because it wasn't quite dark outside yet, he was able to see inside the government-issued sedan, noticing his friend Chase Dalton. For some reason Dalton didn't even look around, much less notice Greene right beside him. He continued to drive toward the parking lot, so Greene chose to follow on foot. Thinking his buddy might have suffered from fatigue during the long drive from Tennessee, Greene decided to lend a hand and carry some luggage.

He passed the valet area, which Dalton had also bypassed, heading directly to the regular parking lot. Following the sidewalk up to the parking area, he found Dalton unloading a suitcase from the trunk of the sedan, wearing slacks and a dress shirt minus the tie. He appeared tired, but not haggard as he set the suitcase on the ground to shut the trunk.

"Want some help with that?" Greene asked.

"No, I'm good," Dalton said in a tone that indicated he didn't know who was speaking to him, possibly thinking a valet was searching for an easy tip.

When he did finally turn around, he noticed Greene standing there and stuck out his hand after a few seconds. They shook hands, which Greene considered a new concept only because they were always so casual around the office. Of course he hadn't seen Dalton in months and their relationship was no longer based on their occupations.

"Good to see you, Russ."

"Likewise, Chase. You drove right past me back there."

"Sorry about that. I'm just so tuckered out after this drive I wasn't even looking."

Greene noticed his friend only brought a small suitcase, doubting Dalton planned on staying long.

"Traveling light, I see."

"Yeah," Dalton answered with a weak smile. "This all came unexpectedly. Boy, have I got a tale to tell you."

"You can tell me over dinner because I'm starved. What sounds good?"

"What do you have here?" Dalton asked. "On second thought, anything sounds good as long as it goes with beer."

Greene thumbed toward the hotel.

"There's a bar inside that serves a couple dishes."

***

Greene waited until his friend settled into his room and changed clothes before meeting him at Ballard's Bar. Part of the bar sat just inside the atrium with traditional barstools and a television usually tuned to sports of some kind. The outer portion was located inside the atrium itself and provided nearly two-dozen seats for guests to sample some of the spirits or get a bite to eat. Little more than appetizers rounded out the menu, but it was decent food and usually served quickly.

"So what's this big story of yours?" Greene inquired. "You had me half scared to death when you called."

"I don't even know where to begin," Dalton said, shaking his head.

In detail, the man weaved a story that captivated Greene during the entire telling.

Dalton relayed how he was ambushed at the convenience store, kidnapped, and brought face to face with himself in a musty old room. The entire telling took nearly twenty minutes, during which onion rings and potato skins came and grew cold because neither man touched them. As Greene heard that one of the cubes was responsible for his friend's peril, he felt partially responsible, swelling with the notion he needed to retrieve that cursed object at any cost.

"How the hell did you get out of there?" he finally asked, knowing the details leading up to confinement in a smelly room.

"That's the tricky part," Dalton confessed, finally munching on an onion ring. "The guy had some henchmen watching over me because he wanted to use me for information to infiltrate our department."

Greene didn't take offense to the implication he still worked for the government because he hadn't been gone terribly long.

"It was just like in the movies. When they let me go to the bathroom I overpowered one of them and got his gun. After that I just made a run for it and called you when I got far enough away from their hideout."

Unsure of what to say because the last portion of his friend's testimony seemed rather brief, while the rest was filled with details, Greene simply tipped his beer bottle to his lips. As though on cue, Liz crossed the atrium, taking notice of their conversation. She appeared unsure of whether or not to join them, so he waved her over before making proper introductions.

"Liz assists me in my new job," Greene added as she took a seat at the table.

Despite Dalton telling him one of the cubes was responsible for his current predicament, Greene didn't reveal his new line of work. He felt an obligation to explain the truth to his former colleague, yet he didn't want Dalton placed in additional danger.

"Are you ever going to tell me exactly what you left a perfectly good government job for?"

Liz gave Greene a smirk, as though daring him to speak the truth.

An awkward silence encompassed the table momentarily until Dalton spoke.

"I'm sorry to bring all this trouble up here, Russ. I was hoping maybe you'd be able to help me get to the bottom of this issue with the guy looking identical to me."

"Well, there's a lot to be said about plastic surgery these days."

"And sound like me, too?"

Greene looked away uncomfortably, not wanting to speak on the subject with Liz present. He wasn't certain he ever wanted to speak to anyone outside of his current group about what he did for a living again. His earlier meeting with Clouse only compounded the issues already swirling through his mind.

"Maybe we should talk more about this in the morning," he finally suggested. "We're probably a little too amped up to keep talking business."

Dalton nodded.

"I appreciate everything you've done for me, Russ. I just didn't know where else to turn because no one else would believe me."

"Well, that's quite a story you've got, old friend," Greene said neutrally. "I won't be far, Chase. Get some rest and we'll talk some more in the morning."

Dalton stood, giving Greene a friendly nod before finally shaking hands with Liz. From the corner of his eye Greene noticed Liz tense the briefest of moments when physical contact was made. She didn't flinch like Dalton's skin was cold, or from static electricity. No, Greene decided immediately, Liz *saw* something beyond the physical world.

She played down the minimal change in behavior immediately, and Dalton seemed none the wiser about any indiscretion on her part.

Greene watched as Dalton gave them a quick wave before heading toward one of the large doorways to find an elevator. He waited until the man disappeared from sight before looking to Liz with anticipation that she met with a knowing gaze. Greene found it uncanny how they already knew one another so well that he didn't even have to speak to receive the answer he needed.

"That isn't your friend," she said evenly, though her words came with a hint of sadness. "What he spoke wasn't entirely untrue, but it was from your friend's perspective, and he was the perpetrator."

Somehow Greene sensed the truth, even before Liz uttered the words. The Chase Dalton he knew wasn't forgetful or impersonal. Had he not been informed, however, Greene might have eventually bought into the ruse.

"Is Chase…?"

Greene couldn't finish the sentence, already feeling the heavy burden of befriending anyone because friends easily became targets.

"He's alive so far as I could tell," Liz answered. "This man, whoever he is, possesses one of the cubes."

Greene reasoned that the man wanted inside information through joining Clouse's team, using the connection between Dalton and Greene as the means. His mind, working like an analytical computer at times, couldn't help but wonder if there was a connection between this imposter and Lincoln Daine. After all, Dalton went looking for Daine as a favor to his former colleague. Thinking beyond the surface layer, Greene wondered if he had spoken to the real Dalton at all, and perhaps this man was Daine, or an accomplice.

Either way he needed to act and act soon.

"Act casual and walk with me to the garden," Greene asked of Liz, who complied without hesitation.

The two walked across the atrium, finding themselves outside a few minutes later, away from snooping eyes and ears.

"What else did you see beyond what he told me? And how did you know what he told me anyway?"

"I could sense what he told you in the vision. He's keeping your friend prisoner down there in case he stumbles and needs information. There are armed men at the location."

"Anything else? Could you see the cube?"

"Yes. He held it in front of your friend, telling him everything about it. I think Chase is in grave danger."

"That goes without saying."

Greene knew the imposter would never reveal everything to Dalton unless he planned to dispose of him soon after.

"Your friend found the bookie, but the whole thing was a trap," Liz said, trying to remember details from the lightning flash of information. "It was in a convenience store, and the way they took him seemed well-organized as though they planned it in advance."

Suspecting the link between Daine and this imposter might now lead to a larger organization, Greene wondered how to proceed. He wasn't willing to gamble with Dalton's life, but he needed to ensure the villainous group learned nothing about his intentions or his people.

"Do you know where they're holding Dalton?"

"By sight," Liz answered. "I could guide you there when we get close. It looked like downtown Nashville, but not the better part."

Greene had some general ideas of ideal hiding spots. He didn't want to rely upon Liz to direct him, because he hated putting her in any kind of danger.

"What are you going to do?" Liz asked, her concern showing over the glowering look crossing his face.

"What needs to be done," he answered simply. "Thank you, Liz. I'm going to recommend you get a good night's rest because we may be heading south in the morning."

Greene hoped to discover his friend's location through other means, but that required the execution of a quickly assembled plan.

CHAPTER 21

Due to a stroke of luck Greene altered his plan slightly, putting it into action just after midnight.

Liz knew this because he called her less than half an hour after their talk outside the hotel. He told her to pack lightly for an overnight trip to Nashville with Todd Parish. While Parish wasn't technically part of their group, he often came in handy for last minute assignments. He brought a rental car by the hotel close to one in the morning and picked up Liz for an overnight drive to Tennessee.

She now found herself in the passenger's seat beside Parish, waiting for something that Parish had yet to divulge. Looking to the sky Liz discovered a nearly cloudless blue above her before looking down to the dashboard clock.

8:13 a.m.

"Not to sound like a broken record, but exactly what are we waiting for?" she inquired.

Parish parked about one block away from the building she identified as the old theatre where the real Dalton was being held. In a neglected portion of the downtown area, away from newer construction, taverns, and neon lights, the theatre looked like an oversized house with faded red and gold paint. The roof showed major wear as a few large areas no longer contained shingles, and some of the windows contained holes the size of baseballs and small rocks. Signs on the front door and a few of the lower level windows indicated the place was condemned, and likely up for demolition. Parish simply grunted when they drove by slowly the first time, possibly thinking the signs were forgeries.

"We're waiting for someone else to show up," Parish answered. "I'm just here for backup purposes."

"Is it Clay Branson?"

Parish looked at her as though slightly surprised and impressed at her intuition.

"How did you dupe him into helping out again?" Liz wondered aloud.

"*I* didn't do anything. There's only one thing that man wants, and Russ offered it to him."

Liz scoffed at the notion.

"I don't recall us locating Nosagi for him a second time."

"No, but if Russ is correct, we're facing off with a criminal element, and not just individuals. It stands to reason that Nosagi might be part of that clan."

"Something tells me Clay was fed less than the entire truth, which means my fearless leader will have to answer for it later."

Parish grinned slightly.

"That's *his* problem. If our part goes well here, he might not have much to worry about. We need Dalton back before he can proceed with his plan at the hotel."

Liz immediately grew concerned.

"And who's backing him up if you're here?"

"No one so far as I know. He's a big boy who can take care of himself."

Hoping Greene didn't do anything rash, Liz wondered exactly what he planned to do with the imposter. From her vision she knew the imposter was dangerous and just as analytical as her team leader. The one thing he lacked, however, was compassion because he showed about as much remorse for murdering the convenience store clerk as some people displayed after swatting a mosquito.

Leaving the car turned off for obvious reasons, Parish rolled down the window only to have someone pop up from below a few seconds later, startling both he and Liz. Parish actually gave a little yelp until he discovered their visitor was none other than the man they expected.

"That wasn't necessary," Parish berated Clay.

"But it was fun," Clay replied while Parish caught his breath and Liz chuckled at the husky bodyguard's demeanor.

"Bet you're fun at horror movies," she commented.

"I've *lived* horror movies, thank you."

Parish looked feverishly around both sides and behind him.

"What the hell did you drive?"

"I'm two blocks down," Clay answered. "I didn't think it was a smart idea to look like we're having a block party outside the place."

Parish scowled at the implication he parked too close to the theatre.

"Anything changed?" Clay asked.

"We haven't seen a thing."

"Then they're all inside, which makes it a bit difficult, especially in broad daylight."

"Greene wants this to be completely non-lethal, too. We don't need any police looking for us, even if we are doing the right thing."

Clay soured a bit.

"He says it's the right thing, and he says he'll get me Nosagi, but I'm probably better off hunting him down myself. And what is it with everyone assuming I'm some kind of murderous bastard because of my particular skill set?"

"Weren't your kind paid assassins back in the day? And didn't your *sensei* train most of your clan to maim and kill?"

"Touché."

"Boys, can we get to the business at hand so we can head home?" Liz interjected.

Clay looked to the theatre nearly ten seconds, analyzing it.

"Give me five minutes and I should have Greene's buddy out of there."

For the first time Liz noticed he was dressed primarily in black with a holstered sidearm on his left side. A few weapon handles emerged from around his shoulders, indicating he brought several bladed weapons and possibly more interesting goodies with him.

"What do you want from me?" Parish asked Clay, wanting to be part of the action after driving nearly six hours south.

"Stay here and watch her. I'll handle this."

"Excuse me?" Liz asked defensively, but Clay was already across the street, making a stealthy approach to the theatre.

She folded her arms unhappily.

"You men are all alike."

"Yeah," Parish replied without much empathy, watching Clay until he disappeared behind some overgrown shrubs. "We're insufferable."

***

Clay started by walking from the side of the theatre to the rear, listening intently at each window. He only heard the sound of distant voices at a window near the rear, where he guessed the old dressing room might be located. Because human beings, even paid underlings, were social creatures, he figured most of the men guarding Dalton were gathered in one area, content to check on the prisoner every so often or conduct rounds.

The nature of the building limited the number of windows, particularly along the auditorium and stage areas within. Clay decided to search for access to the basement, figuring the building would have such an area due to its age. Overgrown shrubs and untended grass made it nearly impossible to search anything directly against the building, but he finally found one small window that disclosed a basement indeed existed. Unsure of exactly what purpose the window served, Clay realized it was too small to serve as emergency egress and not attractive enough to add to the building's décor.

Suspecting no direct access existed from outside the building, like some old farm house with a stairwell leading down to the cellar, Clay decided to try the window. He needed the element of surprise, so barging through a door, or trying to scale a wall to the second floor meant taking a huge risk.

Hardly anyone ever guarded a basement.

Placing his body between the shrubs and the small window, Clay made certain he wasn't visible from any first or second story windows before using the blade of a throwing knife to work on the old window's weakened metal clasp lock. It took mere seconds before the lock gave way, which implied the previous owners relied upon some form of security device they disabled before surrendering the premises. Unfortunately the window tilted inside, so Clay forced its hinges beyond their capacity, breaking their thin metal before pulling the window outside and discarding it. He now needed to work quickly due to the minimal chance someone spotted the glass missing through the thick shrubbery.

With the difficult part out of the way, Clay removed the small utility pack from his back, placing it to one side of the window before peering inside. Just enough light entered behind him to illuminate the concrete floor almost eight feet below. Aside from an old wooden chair no furnishings showed themselves, so Clay clutched his pack and slid his body through the narrow opening. He barely fit, letting his feet enter first, followed by his legs and torso as he clutched the window's frame with conditioned fingers.

Once inside, his feet silently hit the floor as he scooped up his weapons pack and slung it around his back once more. As both a police officer and an unwittingly trained assassin, he had dealt with fellow killers and the worst of criminals in the past. Along the way a few Special Forces types had crossed his path and Clay handled them just fine as well. He suspected these were probably locally hired guns, though he knew not to underestimate them. Despite his training and abilities, Clay could be taken down by a well-placed blade or bullet.

Discovering the basement was immense, probably the full length and width of the building above, Clay wasted little time looking around except to find a route upstairs. A few tattered costumes remained along one rack, probably ravaged by moths overs the years, appearing rather faded.

When Clay discovered the stairwell, he struggled to see details in the low lighting. He tested the old, creaky wood with one foot, finding it both noisy and in slight disrepair. Finding a way around using the stairs directly, he placed his feet on the large boards to either side of the stairs, which supported the stairwell, and began ascending toward the door above. He avoided using the hand railings altogether, compensating with his practiced balance to steady himself with posture and foot strength.

One major disadvantage about not having many windows along the theatre walls was the inability to assess his location. Clay suspected he wasn't near the room where he overheard conversation based on his proximity to the access window. More than likely the basement stairs led to the backstage area, which only made sense. If so, he expected to find an area engulfed with darkness, but there was only one way to know.

He turned the knob, pushing the door into whatever room awaited him, indeed finding darkness ahead. A squeaking noise accompanied the door's movement, so Clay quickly leapt into the room ahead, discovering it was one side of the main stage. Looking around, he found no one waiting for him as voices carried from a nearby room. Suspecting the men might do routine patrols, or check on their prisoner, Clay drew a *kusari-fundo* from his pack for defense. Basically a chain with two weighted ends, the weapon provided non-lethal means of subduing an adversary without creating a commotion. Entirely customized by Clay, the two weighted ends actually served as handles capable of containing the short chain when pushed together to comprise one longer handle.

Clay left the handle intact, ready to pull the ends apart in a split-second if need be. He silently walked toward the conversation, wishing to know how many potential enemies awaited him. Brushing past some levers and old backdrops lining a wall, he spied into one of the old dressing rooms, finding three men playing cards around an end table layered in dust. Seeing no sense in attacking them if he could simply sneak Dalton out of the building, he continued his search through the ground floor, finding only empty rooms until he came upon a set of stairs leading upward.

He ascended them, only to discover they made both a creaking and a clopping noise simultaneously, prompting someone above him to speak.

"About time you came to relieve me."

The voice came from around a banister and the speaker remained out of view until a person drew near the top stair. Clay debated whether to make a hasty retreat or continue onward toward an inevitable confrontation. His major concern stemmed from the other three hired guns overhearing a struggle, but they were practically halfway across the large building.

Clay decided to confront the lone guard in the hope of freeing Dalton the easy way.

He decided to flatten his profile against the wall of the stairwell, hoping the guard might get antsy and look over the side. It took mere seconds for the man to grumble and mutter something under his breath before stomping a few steps away from his post to look over the banister. Listening intently to the footsteps, Clay determined his adversary planned to simply look over the edge because the steps sounded linear.

Already set, Clay pulled apart the two handles and purposefully threw the center of the chain upward in practically one motion. Timing the henchman's arrival perfectly, Clay watched the U-shaped end of the chain seat itself around the man's neck. Originally intending to pull the man down to his level, Clay changed plans when the man immediately began to squirm before the chain was able to grow taut against the nape of his neck. Instead, Clay let his own weight tug the man's head against the solid wooden banister, stunning him momentarily as the chain released its hold.

Quick as a cat, Clay ascended the stairs, jumping the banister's railing like a cowboy jumping a fence. The man had barely grunted when his head hit the wood, but he was about to shout for help after regaining his wits. Clay delivered a form of sidekick that connected with the man's abdomen, both knocking him back and deflating any chance of audibly signaling his buddies.

Still holding the *kusari-fundo* like a coiled snake in his left hand, Clay unraveled enough of it to swing the short section of chain at the man's head, knocking him to the ground with a gash to his left temple. Only when Clay dropped down and wrapped the chain around the man's neck to subdue him and quickly render him unconscious through oxygen deprivation did he take time to truly examine the thug to understand the nature of the men guarding Dalton.

Dressed in dark slacks with Italian loafers, the man wore a pastel purple shirt with the sleeves rolled up to his elbows. A silk tie of purple and glistening gold trim gave Clay the impression these weren't common gang members, but rather up and coming mafia types. He suspected these men were soldiers trying to make their way to a higher rank in whatever family employed them. The sidearm tucked into the man's belt along his back never became a factor, but Clay pulled it out and discarded it just the same.

The struggle lasted mere seconds before the well-dressed man gurgled for air one last time before going completely limp. His arms fell by his side, and Clay laid him on the hard wooden floor after ensuring he wasn't dead or dying. Years often passed between actual life and death combat for Clay, and though he maintained his skills, he knew a fine line existed between incapacitating someone and killing them.

Standing, Clay found three closed doors surrounding him. He was about to reach for the first knob when he heard a commotion coming his way like a herd of buffalo. Shouts of panic and anger reached his ears, meaning somehow the other three men were alerted to his presence. How mattered little, because now Dalton's rescue became that much harder.

"Crap," Clay muttered, looking around for the best area to make a stand.

CHAPTER 22

With only seconds to decide how best to defend himself and combat three armed men, Clay dragged the unconscious sentry close to the banister. Wanting all eyes to immediately shift to their fallen comrade, he flipped the switch for the hallway light, creating near darkness except for a thin morning light piercing the maroon curtains in the only hallway window.

Clutching the chained weapon between his hands, Clay pressed his body flat against the floor along the banister, waiting for the three henchmen to draw closer. He assumed an unconscious position in case he was spotted, just to further confuse them. In seconds they reached the second story, clambering for better positions to examine their fallen colleague as they made nervous comments. If they were able to see in the nearly completely darkened hallway, none of them made mention of Clay. It took a few valuable seconds for any of them to consider that the darkness around them and their buddy's condition wasn't a natural occurrence.

By then it was too late.

Despite all three men already having their weapons drawn, Clay closed his eyes after hiding beside the banister to adapt them to the darkness, simply relying upon sound. When he sprung from his position, Clay struck the man farthest to his left, sending him tumbling down the staircase. He used the chain casing for the strike, leaving the chain itself free for him to swing and wrap around the second man's gun hand. Once the chain was knotted into position, Clay yanked it upward, removing the gun from play before he kicked the man in the sternum. Clay barely took time to watch the man's back strike the solid wall behind him before turning his full attention to the last henchman.

Hearing the grunt followed by the thud of the second man, Clay assumed a gun was already trained on him even before he glanced at the last of the trio. Luckily during the last kick Clay hadn't stood idly by, choosing rather to swing the chain simultaneously in the direction of the last henchman. Taking his best guess at where the man's gun was pointed, Clay aimed the chain, learning within a second's time he came close enough.

Grazing the man's hand just hard enough to deflect it before the trigger could be squeezed, a battle tested Clay wasted no time or movement. Pouncing like a cat toward the mentally stunned henchman, he pinned the gun against the man's chest before hitting some nerves that loosened his grip on the firearm. From there Clay plucked the sidearm away from the hired gun, which left him vulnerable momentarily as he slid it down the hallway floor.

A bit more feisty and intelligent than the other two, the third man rammed his head against Clay's to cause separation. Clay stumbled back a few steps, feeling pain something like an ice-cream headache as the man lunged at his jaw with a fist. Though he sidestepped the first swing, Clay couldn't avoid getting socked in the stomach with the opposite fist. Luckily his abdominal muscles didn't have much give, so the blow barely registered.

Clay grasped one handle from his chained weapon before swinging it across the man's jaw, breaking it just beneath the chin. He waited less than a second before clipping the side of his adversary's temple with the hard casing. The man simply grunted, tough as nails, so Clay raised a knee to his sternum, forcing every bit of remaining air from his lungs.

Despite the setback, the henchman clasped Clay's shirt in two places, hurling him against the wall with a thud. Another knee to the chest caused him to lurch forward, however, allowing Clay to throw the chain around his neck and draw it tight. While he preferred a quicker method of subduing this subpar sentry like his buddies, Clay felt thankful for the opportunity to simply end their skirmish.

Within a few seconds Clay had chased the remaining oxygen supply from the man's lungs through careful manipulation of the chain. Assured the man was simply unconscious and still breathing with a look at rise and fall of the chest, Clay made certain the other two mafia types weren't moving before entering the room containing Chase Dalton.

"Based on the ruckus can I assume you're here to save me?" the government employee asked.

"You can, and your buddy Greene is ultimately to thank," Clay answered as he undid the restraints binding Dalton to the chair using his personal handcuff key.

Dalton's face displayed signs of being beaten with a swollen lower lip and bruising on his right cheek. Clay didn't bother asking if the mafia wannabe goons roughed him up, because he suspected he already knew the answer. One of the man's brown eyes carried a purple hue all around it while a thin gash was prominent along the top of Dalton's scalp because his ordinarily shaved head was grown out to stubble after the rough few days since his abduction.

Shaking his numb hands loose, Dalton rubbed the reddened areas where the restraints had dug into his skin. It required a minute for the marshal to get circulation in his legs from sitting so long, but he finally stood under his own power before following Clay out of the room.

"Some handiwork," he noted as they passed the four unconscious forms along the upstairs floor.

Clay said nothing as he led the man out the front door and down the street to where Parish and Liz remained vigilant from their vehicle.

"That was a little longer than five minutes," Parish chided, keeping a straight face.

"It beats you shooting up the place, or getting in my way."

"Boys," Liz interjected sternly, reminding them of the bigger picture.

"They'll get you to safety," Clay said when Dalton offered a handshake as thanks.

Clay shook his hand, but his mind was already motoring ahead toward his next move. He wanted to know Nosagi's location more than anything else, and he was promised that and more information once Dalton was rescued. He didn't care who Greene needed to torture for details, or how he went about it, so long as the information was obtained.

Before walking away, he observed Parish pulling out his phone and sending a text message of some sort. He could only assume the man was informing Greene that their operation went successfully.

Clay hoped to hear his own good news in the near future.

***

In the overnight hours Greene decided to make some changes. He started by shaving his beard, leaving his face completely clear of hair. The lack of sleep left his eyes a bit puffy and red when he looked into the mirror. Accustomed to long nights from his government work, between stakeouts and surprise raids on criminals, Greene kept his body fueled with coffee and energy drinks. When he did take a catnap his cell phone remained by his side at full volume to ensure he didn't miss any messages or calls.

Just before nine that morning, Greene finally received a text message from Parish that their mission was accomplished and Dalton safely with them. Standing in the sunken garden, Greene looked around at the plant life beginning to turn green with the warmer weather. Less than a month prior he might have seen his breath in the early morning hours, but just a week away from the Kentucky Derby and another potential opportunity at securing one of the cubes, a warm breeze brushed against his bare forearms.

He walked inside, calling up to the pretender's room, acting as casual as humanly possible given the circumstances. Stating that he found some answers to the man's problems, he asked to meet him in the basement, which contained the larger conference rooms within the hotel. He then asked Dan Duncan, the hotel's manager, to assist Craig Jennings in a thorough search of the false Dalton's room.

"Gladly," Duncan answered from behind his office desk before standing to march toward the security director's office.

Jennings happened to be in town for a few days despite the Kentucky Derby occupying much of his time recently. With Louisville only an hour away, Jennings found time to conduct research at the hotel when he wasn't with his horse's training staff. Acting the part of the owner, he left Teakon to monitor the staff and manage the day-to-day affairs in Kentucky where Phantom was currently residing.

Both Duncan and Jennings had participated in the cursed object game long enough to know what needed doing. They were up to speed on the situation with Dalton and the imposter, which solidified their understanding of the urgency to find the cube. If the man escaped he could literally assume the identity of the first person he made contact with and murdered.

A few minutes later Greene took a seat in one of the comfy leather chairs surrounding a small oval conference table. Although the smallest of the conference rooms in the basement, containing only a dozen seats, this particular room contained the most technological equipment, often used by Clouse to hold staff meetings and sometimes secretive meetings. Because the nature of the latter meetings required nothing spoken to leave the room, it was often swept for listening devices, and the walls and ceiling were redone with soundproof materials once Clouse began his quest to collect all of the cubes.

Greene waited less than five minutes before the imposter who stole his former colleague's identity walked in with a wide smile, apparently anticipating an offer to join the team or at least learn some answers about his unsuspecting enemies.

Strangely enough, Greene expected the exact same thing from this encounter.

"What's up?" the stranger asked, looking around the conference room as though it suddenly occurred to him that the isolated room was an unusual place for a personal discussion.

"Have a seat," Greene offered, waving his arm toward one of the comfortable chairs.

Remaining calm while the imposter reluctantly walked toward a chair, Greene held up a remote control to press a button that activated the metal bars that secured the conference room doors. Clouse had them installed to ensure meetings remained private, but the room doubled as a panic room of sorts. A far cry from the security of Fort Knox, the room offered limited protection until authorities were summoned or an alternate escape route presented itself.

"What's that about?" the man asked with a stunned look after hearing the metal bars lock into place.

"A form of security," Greene answered, standing as he pulled a silenced pistol from the back of his belt. "This room was built so no sound could escape. I suggest you answer my questions honestly, or you'll be on the receiving end of as many bullets as it requires."

The man sucked in a deep, cautious breath, refusing to break character just yet.

"Russ, we've known one another for years," he said with a look of grave concern. "Why are you doing this?"

Without moving more than a few inches, Greene fired a bullet into the man's right knee, drawing a pained cry immediately. The man clutched his knee as he leaned forward, coming just short of tumbling to the floor in a crumpled heap. He continued to moan and groan in agony, finally shooting a hateful glare in Greene's direction.

"I don't even care to know your name," Greene said. "Yet."

"If I tell you anything they won't let me leave these grounds alive."

"I doubt that," Greene said with a suspicious smirk. "Your group can't be that well-connected."

"We're far more expansive than you could ever imagine. The incident last October was just the first phase of things to come."

Now Greene's suspicions were proven true. A collective of rich, connected individuals seeking the cubes for themselves put his people and his employer in grave danger. He needed to know what people comprised the roster of such a group or he'd spend an eternity trying to locate them individually. He wasn't sure if they possessed any of the cursed objects, and if they didn't, their names would not appear in the manifest.

"I need to know everything," he demanded evenly.

"You can't let me live any more than they can. Just shoot me now and be done with it."

Greene took aim at the imposter's other knee and fired a round that connected with flesh and bone. Again the man screamed in agony, clutching the new injury before looking to the door as though thinking of escape or some kind of impending rescue.

"Regardless of my plans for you, this can go rather quickly or be painfully dragged out," Greene stated grimly, still not visualizing the endgame of his plan beyond this interrogation.

He knew leaving an exact clone, in appearance anyway, of his good friend wasn't a good idea if he located the cube. And if this individual used the cube to alter his identity again he might prove impossible to find. Greene decided he needed to extract any possible information in his present situation or risk staying a step or two behind the coalition trying to undermine everything he struggled to preserve.

"You don't deserve to live," he admitted to the stranger, "and it's dangerous for me to allow you to. After all, you've killed countless people for your own benefit."

"Then stop beating around the fucking bush and execute me because I'm not telling you anything," the man sneered.

"Why?" Greene asked before pausing. "Why would you stick up for people who only do harm to others? You don't have any desire for redemption?"

"Redemption?" the stranger laughed through the pain. "If you knew the things I've done, the events I've conspired in, you'd know there's no such thing."

Having no experience in psychology, and painfully aware that his interrogation skills from his marshal days didn't apply, Greene saw few options remaining. He could continue to search for a shred of human decency in this imposter or simply apply various forms of torture until answers spilled forth. With the carpet a complete loss and no one hearing the disturbance as of yet, Greene found no reason to deviate from his original plan.

His cell phone vibrated at his side, indicating a call or text message was being received. Plucking it from his side, Greene found a new message awaiting him from Craig Jennings.

Found it.

"It seems my colleagues have found your cube."

"Good for you," the man replied without any real emotion. "Now kill me or get me some medical attention."

Greene shook his head.

"You're not getting off that easily. Tell me more about this group of yours or the next bullet finds its way into your nut sack."

The man's eyes shifted uneasily toward his genitalia, obviously weighing over how much pain he wanted to withstand before his death or release. Short-term pain before death might be tolerable, but complete loss of a man's genitals, followed by years of life without sex if he survived, likely gave him something to consider.

Considering Greene's reputation didn't peg him as a murderous type, the imposter probably figured his chance of survival as reasonable. If the collective who sought the cubes truly did their homework they would know the former government man went by the book. His work history got him noticed by Clouse, but Greene's attitude changed when he was put in charge of saving the world on a regular basis.

Before he could continue pressing the threat of immorally neutering the man, Greene's cell phone buzzed with a new text message from Jennings.

Come out here. Dan can watch him.

Stepping outside the conference room momentarily after he unlocked the door, Greene found both Jennings and Dan Duncan waiting in the hallway. He slapped his gun into the hotel manager's hand, looking Duncan in the eyes.

"He shouldn't be able to walk, but if he tries just shoot him in the leg again."

Duncan nodded with approval.

While he wasn't cut out for adventurous work like some of Clouse's employees, Duncan understood the mission statement because cursed objects nearly cost him his life twice. None too tall, he possessed a potbelly his sport coats concealed fairly well. His sand-colored hair showed some graying in the temples much like the flecks of gray that appeared more prominent in his mustache over time.

"What's wrong?" Greene asked Jennings as Duncan slipped inside the conference room before someone noticed their impromptu gathering.

Jennings let a grin slip.

"We found some interesting things in his room that might give you some inside knowledge about our friend in there. I left them up there if you care to have a gander."

"Let's take a walk," Greene said, adjusting his tie and dress shirt before they went upstairs, assured no blood droplets stained his clothes from the interrogation.

CHAPTER 23

A pair of black cowboy boots clopped against the wooden floor of the old theatre as Stone stepped inside the back entrance where Clay Branson and Chase Dalton had departed just minutes earlier. Confident he would locate Branson with minimal effort soon enough, the FBI agent surveyed the ground level, finding several pieces of information including the abducted man's name and some contact information pinned to a board that he pocketed. Deciding the building had been chosen because of its abandoned nature, Stone headed upstairs where he heard minimal commotion. He put aside his main objective by simply taking time to enter the building instead of following Branson. Out of professional curiosity, Stone wanted to know what kind of death and destruction his target left in his wake this time.

With his hand atop his firearm, prepared to draw the instant he spied danger, Stone slowly ascended the stairs to discover one of the four downed henchmen coming to, fumbling for the cell phone inside his sport coat. By the time he regained his senses enough to see the FBI agent reaching the second floor, Stone kicked the man in the head hard enough to render him unconscious again.

"Stay down, son," Stone said, reaching for his own cell phone to touch base with his agency benefactor.

He placed his boot heel on the next man in line to make sure he wasn't going to regain consciousness, while watching over the rest of the hallway area. All four were still breathing, but it didn't look as though they'd be leaving the premises anytime soon. Moving on, Stone took in the musty smell of the theatre, seeing dust linger in the wake of a sunbeam emitting through a set of dingy curtains. Beyond the dust he noticed a heavy chair with handcuffs still drooping from the arms, and the agent began to piece together exactly why Branson traveled to Tennessee.

Feeling a step behind the Ohio cop and two steps behind the man who directed his actions, Stone wanted some truthful answers. Branson's actions didn't mirror those of an evil man, rescuing a federal marshal from local thugs, or traveling to a different continent to disable a few dozen living dead. Stewart fed him information only as it became necessary, but he did tell Stone the undead were a menace created by the man Branson was tracking.

What disturbed Stone most was the fact that no one else was after this man, or that Stewart sat on such information like a mother hen waiting for the right governmental eggs to hatch. Stewart simply told him the information, and the Oriental suspect, were not their agency's problem. Stone began to question the man's integrity and loyalty, which in turn led him to question his own. Above everything else, Stone wanted answers, which meant continuing to follow orders and document his actions, even if those actions incriminated him down the line.

When the time came, Stone planned to choose his allegiance accordingly, hoping his choice benefitted his career, but only if he remained on the right side of the law.

He crouched down, looking for any further clues along the floor. Finding nothing of use, Stone plucked his cell phone from his side, deciding to call Stewart to report his findings and see if the Deputy Director fed him any new information.

"Stewart," his boss said after one ring.

"Branson just rescued someone from this old theatre in downtown Nashville," Stone reported, returning to the hallway.

"So he's working with them," Stewart muttered just above a whisper.

"With who?"

"Nothing for you to worry about."

Strange, Stone thought, that Stewart wanted no additional information or details, almost as though he knew about the abduction of Dalton and the possibility of a rescue attempt. The feeling he was being used always resided in the back of the agent's mind, but now he felt like an absolute pawn in some kind of grander scheme.

Though he wasn't the most ethical agent in FBI history, Stone thought more highly of his abilities than to serve as someone's lapdog.

"Where is Branson now?" Stewart inquired as Stone walked along the hallway, kicking one of the henchmen in the head as he regained consciousness, losing it just as quickly.

"Heading back to Ohio," Stone lied, simply assuming the man would return to the same area as always.

Branson lived a very open life, working for the local police department and the theme park security force where it appeared he was being groomed to take over. During the course of his time around the theme park Stone had learned some interesting things by talking to some of the locals.

He sauntered down the stairwell, remaining vigilant as he cupped the phone to his ear, heading for the rear exit.

"I'm heading back to Ohio unless there's something else you need done," Stone said once he stepped into the overgrown lot behind the building.

"Just keep up the good work, Harlan. I've got an important meeting today and things may be looking up for both of us very soon."

Stone heard background noise from Stewart's end, guessing the man might be walking through an airport. Sounds of garbled voices and an announcement being made over an intercom reached his ears. He sometimes wished he could tail Stewart to discover what business the Deputy Director conducted on a daily basis.

When he reached his most recent rental car, Stone slid inside the driver's seat. Before he started the ignition he looked to his right where several yellowing newspapers sat atop the seat. Spending so much time in Mason, Ohio left him with time on his hands while Clay Branson worked shifts at the theme park or patrolled in the city. By happenstance Stone stumbled upon some information during a noontime lunch when two park employees discussed an FBI agent who visited Great Realms and helped avert a terrorist takeover. Upon further digging, Stone learned that Jack Turpin, the FBI agent in question, spoke with Clay Branson during the day of the major incident.

Rumor had it that Turpin offered Branson a position within the FBI, which one theme park employee believed was a "rogue agent" position in the Los Angeles branch of the Bureau. At the time Alan Stewart was the assistant director of the branch, and apparently Branson turned down the offer to stay in Mason. Now it seemed someone else was courting the cop for his unique services, but that didn't explain Stewart's continued interest in the man.

The obvious solution to Stone's new dilemma was to find Turpin, a colleague within the Bureau, and inquire innocently about the theme park incident. Turpin, a fellow Texan who worked with the Houston Police Department before joining the Bureau, would certainly speak freely about their home state and share work stories.

Picking up the top newspaper, Stone sighed from frustration because learning the truth never proved an easy task. His ideal solution wasn't feasible because Turpin retired from the FBI that past November only to fall victim to a fatal car accident in January at the age of fifty-five. And while the reported account made the accident seem completely legitimate, Stone doubted a man with Turpin's knowledge, experience, and good health was involved in a one-vehicle accident without some kind of external factor being discovered.

Putting the newspaper down, Stone decided to continue his dual investigation carefully or risk winding up in some mysterious "accident" down the road.

Starting the car, Stone picked up the phone to call his wife. He hadn't spoken to her since the previous day and he needed a reassuring voice before moving forward with some potentially life-altering decisions.

***

"Who the fuck is this guy?" Greene asked, palming a handful of various licenses and ID badges from numerous states and companies.

"I thought you might want to see this before you proceeded," Jennings said. "With some of this information you might be able to piece together some of his movements."

"It'll take weeks or months to get what we need, Craig," Greene grumbled. "We need to know something so we don't walk into the Derby blindly next week."

Greene tossed the laminated identifications atop the unmade bed, thinking he might try retrieving some fingerprints or DNA from them. If the cursed object allowed the imposter to completely impersonate people, he was going to know exactly what identities the man had assumed. If his own

DNA or fingerprints were left behind, Greene could figure out the imposter's identity and use the information against him, which required days or weeks. However, the effort would link him to other key figures that impeded Greene's mission to obtain and dispose of the cubes.

Lit by natural daylight from the glass door panels facing into the atrium, the luxury room looked immaculate other than the bed being used overnight. Majestic and clean, all of the rooms were held to high standards in Clouse's hotel, but Greene was going to ensure this room wasn't touched by the staff until he retrieved everything he needed.

"Here's this," Jennings said, handing him a yellow cube that gleamed a momentary wink at Greene when it touched his hand. "We found it tucked between the matresses."

Ignoring the cursed object's beauty and charms, Greene stuffed the cube into his right pocket, imagining the countless lives that might be saved once he locked it away.

"We need to collect his belongings," he informed Jennings. "Everything. And use latex gloves so we don't get our prints on anything."

Jennings nodded.

"You still have friends who can do that stuff?"

"I gave up a government job, but I still have connections. Given the importance of knowing what this guy knows, I'll find a way to identify him."

"The methodical torture method isn't going so well?"

Greene returned a sly grin.

"It's just getting started."

"Probably for the best if I don't ask any questions?"

"Probably."

Jennings stuffed his hands into his pockets, continuing to glance around the room, including the open suitcase sitting atop a chair in the corner.

"This guy probably has ties to Lincoln Daine, doesn't he?"

"It would explain why he intercepted my buddy in Nashville. If that's the case, they're both part of the larger group he alluded to, which might include Clay's mentor."

"If they're obsessed with getting all of the cubes they have to be planning to combine them. That can't be a good thing."

Greene only knew of rumors about what might occur when the cubes came together. Mark Teakon's research was considerably incomplete, which worried him greatly. Most of the man's findings stemmed from discovered letters, diary pages, and a few personal interviews that often came second-hand at best. None of the accounts painted a remotely optimistic picture about the end result if the cubes were brought together.

Only one true way to discover the truth occurred to Greene and it meant traveling back to when the cubes were created or originally conceived by the group that possessed them first. Unwilling to use the time cube, which Clouse kept hidden anyway, he figured Liz might be able to envision the crucial events if she came in contact with one of the cubes. Using the time cube was immoral and dangerous, but asking Liz to subject her mind to one of the gravest events of all time wasn't easy to ask.

Greene knew there might come a time when he needed to ask Liz for that sacrifice, but he prayed for another solution to present itself first.

"Can you get everything together and store it on the sixth floor?" he asked of Jennings.

"Sure. I'll get it handled."

"Thanks."

Greene headed out the door, prepared to continue the interrogation until he learned about the dangers still lurking, waiting for his team at every turn.

And possibly the Kentucky Derby.

With a chance to secure a majority of the cubes at his fingertips, Greene wasn't about to take any chances. Now on the verge of breaking open the major secrets that eluded him, Greene wanted to shut down the syndicate opposing him and guarantee world safety. He didn't like the idea of conducting an illegal interview at the hotel, but moving the imposter opened an entirely new set of problems.

He needed to wrap up the interrogation soon since Dalton was coming back from Tennessee with Liz and Parish. Curiosity ate away at his mind when he wondered what kind of havoc the imposter wreaked upon Dalton's career and personal life. Either way, Greene planned on knowing all kinds of answers within a few hours.

CHAPTER 24

Greene returned to the conference room only to find a bizarre scene awaiting him. Standing beside the door Duncan continued to hold the loaned firearm, but the imposter was lying face down on the ground beside the chair where he initially sat.

Without speaking, Greene simply looked to the hotel manager who gave a helpless shrug as he returned the gun by slapping it into Greene's palm.

"He just fell over," Duncan said without empathy. "Probably faking."

"Thanks, Dan," Greene said as the manager let himself out.

Taking a slow walk toward the downed villain, Greene held the pistol in a ready position near his waistline. He didn't hold it defensively, but rather in a spot where he could hold it over the imposter while he spoke his mind.

"If you're going to play games and pull this shit there's no reason for me to prolong double tapping you in the head right now."

Very little blood pooled on the floor beside the imposter because Greene made certain not to fire at major arteries or blood vessels when he shot the man's knees. After momentary thoughts of kicking the man, Greene simply fired a silenced shot into the floor, bringing a flinch from the man in response.

"Feel free to get back in the chair."

"I can't," the man moaned, beginning to stir as he propped his upper body on his elbows, struggling to move along the carpet.

"Then you can just sit there because I'm not touching you, but you're going to answer my questions."

"Just shoot me and be done with it."

"It's not going to be that easy. Obviously there's no sense appealing to your morality so this will just be long and painful. And since I'm not very experienced in torture it'll just take all the longer."

The man shot him a detestable glance the likes of which Greene never saw from the real Chase Dalton.

"Do your worst then."

"I don't have to," Greene confessed. "I've got your fingerprints and DNA from the items you left upstairs. Even if the fingerprints aren't your own, I'm positive the DNA is still yours, which means I'll soon know who you are and I'll know about everyone in your life."

"And what? You'll go after my family? You don't have balls enough for that."

"Try me. And what do you have to gain protecting people who want to destroy the world for personal gain anyway? You're not going to be around to see any of it."

"I have plenty of incentive because you don't have a clue what you're dealing with. You've been two steps behind this entire time."

"But I've got *you*, don't I?"

Greene turned for the door, prepared to get to work by obtaining the man's DNA from the samples Jennings removed from the room. He didn't particularly like the idea of submitting the fingerprints in case he somehow implicated Dalton in something illegal that the imposter might have carried out.

"They aren't your friends," he said, turning around to address the imposter one last time. "And if history is any indicator, they won't have your back once you're incarcerated or dead."

"It beats selling out to tree-hugging pussies like you."

Greene gave a sly smirk.

"We'll see."

***

Nearly six hours later Greene had sent the DNA samples to an FBI contact out of Indianapolis for comparison to a national database. He wasn't expecting a miracle, knowing even a rush on the sample meant weeks or months of waiting. Even so, he needed to explore every avenue to discover the imposter's true identity and trace the man's steps backwards to establish his contacts and family.

Keeping the prisoner under wraps proved moderately difficult considering business as usual allowed several corporations to hold meetings in the other conference rooms. Duncan and Jennings took turns monitoring the imposter, who wasn't very mobile with a bullet in each leg, while Greene collected, stored, and shipped the DNA samples. In the meantime men and women dressed in business attire wandered through the hallways, unaware of the grave situation occurring mere feet from their meetings.

Greene made very little progress during the interrogation, often being belittled or called names by the man who possessed the information he required. Walking a fine line between incapacitating the man and inflicting pain kept him from drawing additional blood. Unfortunately the mental aspect of torture put him no closer to the truth, so he found himself walking out of the room more often than he cared to.

On this return trip, however, he walked into a scene he never expected after making certain the hallway was clear before opening the door.

While Dan Duncan stood beside the door, the imposter was lying face down beside the conference table, arms sprawled outward. He looked as though he wanted to move, to be anywhere except the position he was frozen in atop the carpeted floor. Unable to even turn his head to look at Greene, the imposter found a handful of new issues to overcome if he wanted his inevitable death or freedom.

Stripped down from head to toe, except for his underwear, the man was lying helplessly along the floor with numerous thin needles protruding from his skin. To someone with lesser knowledge it might appear he was literally pinned to the floor, but Greene immediately saw the source of the needles and understood why the man was incapable of movement.

"Having fun?" he asked Clay Branson, who knelt beside the man, examining the needles and their placement.

"Get him off me!" the man demanded. "I'll tell you whatever you want to know!"

Greene sauntered over to the imposter.

"Why the change of heart? I thought you were a stone, incapable of being broken."

Seeing Branson at the hotel came as a surprise, but Greene decided to play along with it since his unwilling guest was in genuine distress.

"What seems to be the problem?"

"I can't feel my legs! I can't feel anything!"

Branson leaned over to needlessly speak softly to the prisoner.

"You're not going to feel it when I cut off your balls either. After that, it's on to your toes, one at a time."

"Can I talk to you for a minute before you get to cutting our friend apart?" Greene asked more casually than he felt.

"Sure."

Greene gave Duncan a nod that he could take off, and the hotel manager gladly did just that. Branson followed Greene into the hallway once Duncan left, leaving the hapless imposter screaming inside. Thankful no one else heard the cries while the door remained open a few seconds, Greene couldn't help but like Branson's style.

"Dare I ask why you're here?"

"To get results. Your people let the word slip about this guy and I figured I'm not getting a better chance to learn where my former mentor is holed up."

"Feel free, but there's a lot more at stake here. Can I count on your help until I'm finished with him?"

"The needles pull right out. Once I warm him up you won't need a thing."

"I'll take that as a no," Greene said, opening the door to the conference room.

"We can take turns," Branson counteroffered.

"What exactly did you do to him?" Greene asked, blocking the doorway with his arm.

"Nerves in the human body are a tricky thing. They can take away all feeling or inflict a lot of pain when pierced just right."

Greene couldn't help but draw a grin as he allowed Branson to walk in first.

Their prisoner grunted and groaned, struggling to move, now stripped of his free will and command over his own body. Though Greene couldn't grasp his associate's knowledge and control over nerve endings, he felt somewhat assured they were about to receive solid answers because the imposter showed true panic for the first time.

"Get these things out of me! I'll tell you anything you want!"

Branson made no effort to hurry to the man's side, letting the psychological impact burrow just a bit further.

"Doesn't deprivation of the senses usually take longer to kick in?" Greene asked Branson rather casually.

"Usually. Part of my training was to build immunity to having none of my senses available. Then you get pretenders like this guy who need every advantage to make their way in the world."

Reaching down, he tinkered with one of the thin needles ever so slightly, causing a yelp from their prisoner.

"Anything you want," he pleaded once more.

"You know what we want," Greene said. "I need names and places of people who possess the other cubes."

"Particularly Nosagi," Branson chimed in. "Have you heard that name?"

"That's about the only name I *have* heard," the man confessed, looking between his two interrogators. "I talked to him a week ago and I'm supposed to meet with one of his representatives in a few days."

"When and where?"

"I wrote it down. It's in my luggage somewhere."

Greene confirmed the information with a discreet nod.

"What was the meeting about?" he pressed.

"Something about getting the cubes and their owners together. I think they were going to shoot me an offer for mine."

Or just shoot him Greene thought with a major concern in mind. He wondered how anyone other than his own group knew about the imposter or his cursed object. Until a few days ago this man was off their radar and Greene still hadn't learned his identity though it dawned on him he might find out from Julie Knowles through Clouse the name of this man without confirmation from DNA or fingerprint testing. He chastised himself for not thinking of such a solution earlier, but the day hadn't exactly been normal.

For some reason Clouse didn't like Greene having direct contact with Julie more than necessary. To Greene it felt like an us-versus-them team effort between the people who had survived horrific experiences with the cubes and those he hired to combat and eliminate the greater threat.

"I need the information for that meeting," Branson stated, looking to Greene.

"You'll get it. I need to know for certain if there are more of these people associated with him."

"There aren't," the imposter answered emphatically. "They said they tracked me through some kind of psychic or something."

Greene felt figuratively stabbed through the heart. Liz had proven herself invaluable to the cause over the months, but if the enemy employed a psychic of their own, and he or she was somehow more effective, then Liz's fears of being mentally invaded might prove true. Even worse, if she was accidentally providing information through mental wavelengths, the entire team was in jeopardy.

A year prior he might have thought his mind was coming unraveled at the thought of psychic powers and their various abilities. Liz proved him wrong almost immediately, but he relied upon her experiences to guide him through the rest of the psychic world.

"Why didn't they just kill you?" Greene inquired of his prisoner, still thinking something about the man's answers felt misleading.

"They knew they couldn't find me because I kept changing identities. They said their psychic saw my phone number in a vision and I could either sell them the cube and live or they would hunt me down. The whole reason I kidnapped your buddy was because I wanted your resources to check on these people."

"If you were posing as Chase you could've looked all of that up yourself."

"I don't have his training. I needed you for that."

"I'm not sure I believe that. You probably tortured him and asked him some questions in Tennessee."

"I roughed him up, but he wouldn't sell you out. That's why I came here in disguise. I've answered your questions, so can you let me up now please?"

"No. Did these other cube holders say why they wanted your cube?"

"*No.* The conversation wasn't exactly friendly."

"And you just agreed to a meeting based on a phone conversation?" Branson asked curiously, though Greene knew he was itching to see the information about the meeting.

"They mailed me a severed hand."

Greene looked to Branson, wondering if the hand in question might be from an island located in South America. For all he knew, the statement, or the imposter's entire testimony, might be one big lie.

"If you were counting on me to get you information, why did you have goons guarding him in Tennessee? Why didn't you just kill him like you apparently do with everyone else in your path?"

Instead of answering, the imposter struggled against his bonds and the nerve-deadening pins that pierced his skin, grunting and groaning.

"I guess someone isn't ready to tell the truth yet," Greene stated before turning his attention to Branson. "Ready for a look at that note about the meeting?"

"Sure."

Greene felt a bit foolish for assuming the man would break so easily. He knew the man had masterminded Dalton's abduction with some kind of inside information, but the slip about a psychic worried him. Extremely few people knew about the cubes, and even fewer knew about Clouse and his team created to hunt them. Only those people, with ill intent, possessed motive to infiltrate the small group and learn its secrets.

He didn't feel very reassured about extracting answers from the man after evaluating the current state of affairs. Branson didn't seem the least bit deterred by the turn of events or the possibility that the stated meeting might not even be a true, scheduled event.

"Don't sweat it," Branson said evenly. "He's going to crack eventually, even if it takes a little more prodding on our part."

Greene wasn't sure exactly what his uncommitted ally meant, but he hoped the prophetic words came true.

CHAPTER 25

"**M**other fucker," Greene muttered when they went through the imposter's belongings and discovered everything that the man said was apparently a lie.

Even the slip of paper with a date and time turned out to be some kind of meeting or appointment that had already occurred.

"I'm about to go medieval on his ass," Branson said sourly.

"I'm running out of reasons to stop you. We need answers without calling a lot of attention to ourselves. This hotel is still my boss's place of business."

Standing on the furthest floor from the basement, Greene realized he needed to take an elevator down immediately. Because Parish, Liz, and the real Dalton were on their way to the hotel he wanted to clear up any unfinished business beforehand.

With the man paralyzed by Branson's needles there was no need to leave someone in the room to guard him. Greene stood silently beside Branson during the elevator ride until the doors opened on the first floor. Because they took the passenger elevator and not the service elevator the first floor was the final descending stop.

When the door opened Greene stepped toward the basement access door but Branson lingered momentarily, staring at something he spied through the large doorway into the hotel atrium.

"What's wrong?" Greene asked, stopping midstride.

"Nothing. I'll catch up with you in a minute."

Taking only a few seconds to stare into the atrium, Greene saw about half a dozen guests milling around as the morning sun illuminated the round area through the glass atop the dome. He also noticed a blonde wearing sports clothing that hugged her athletic figure crossing the atrium toward the opposite entryway.

Branson appeared fixated on her above all else, which Greene found strange considering he was in a phenomenal situation with his impending marriage and he was the one more intent on interrogating their suspect.

Grunting to himself, Greene walked to the metal door that pushed open, allowing him access to the basement after walking down some carpeted stairs. He bypassed a few of the conference rooms, finding one filled to capacity with some investment group before reaching the locked room where he left the imposter.

Strangely the room was no longer locked and the door appeared ajar a few inches, splintered wood marring the side where the lock and doorknob once worked to keep it shut.

"Fuck."

Reaching beneath the back of his sport coat, Greene drew his firearm after a quick glance revealed no one else occupied the surrounding hallway. Holding the gun in a ready position he kicked the door gently with his right foot, allowing it to swing open slowly, but silently.

Only the muffled voices of the group a few doors down provided any noise along the basement. Greene felt unnerved as he peered around both sides of the doorway, seeing no one inside except his prisoner lying in the center of the floor with a weapon of some sort sticking out of his back. Assured no danger lurked inside the room, he stepped forward to examine the body, noticing a short sword of some kind went completely through the chest of the imposter, still standing erect because the pointed end remained embedded in the floor.

Kneeling beside the body, Greene realized the man never had a chance with the paralyzing needles throughout his body and two disabled legs to boot. He felt like an accomplice to murder even though he didn't stab the man through the heart and run like a thief in the night.

A small pool of blood surrounded the wound along the back, soaking into the imposter's shirt as the man lay lifeless. He imagined the carpet was absorbing the blood on the opposite side, but Clouse could seal off the room and have everything repaired. Greene wondered whether to call the police or simply dump the body because the man looked identical to his friend. That particular decision could wait as Greene refused to be mesmerized by the strange homicide.

The wound looked clean, very professional in nature and Greene suddenly understood what Branson might have thought he spotted in the atrium. He also learned some truths the man now revealed in death that he hadn't spoken in life. Either he was in cahoots with the organization competing for the cubes and they ensured his silence through murder or they really were tracking him. Greene doubted the latter scenario, suspecting the man worked for the group and figured he could infiltrate Clouse's fold by getting close to Greene and learning all of his secrets.

He wondered if the imposter simply followed Dalton until the time to strike arrived or if the villainous bunch knew about Lincoln Daine as well. If so, he might find the Kentucky Derby far more dangerous than he originally anticipated, having to watch for so many adversaries.

For now he simply needed to provide Branson with some backup and make sure the conference room remained secure. With cell phone numbers for both Duncan and Jennings he decided to call the hotel manager, hoping Duncan knew how to fix the door jamb without hiring it done and hiding the body.

As he pushed to dial the man's cell phone number, Greene felt reasonably assured the businessman grew up working for a living before he made his money. He found it strange that a millionaire like Duncan felt content running the daily affairs of a grand hotel, but he supposed many people held a fascination for the West Baden Springs Hotel.

"Duncan," the manager answered momentarily.

"Dan, I need you to come downstairs and secure the conference room."

"Again?" Duncan bellyached.

"Yeah, and that's not the worst of it," Greene said as he walked briskly toward the stairwell. "Our prisoner is no longer alive."

"You *killed* him?" Duncan asked in a hushed voice as though he might be near eavesdroppers.

"No, but someone didn't want him talking to us."

Greene opened the metal exit door, securing it behind him as best he could before darting up the stairs toward the ground level.

"So you *let* someone kill him? I'm trying to run a business here and I don't need you conducting guerrilla warfare tactics down there."

Feeling certain he would smack the hotel manager if he was present, Greene didn't have time for questions about his methods.

"You have a bigger problem in that the assassin might still be on the grounds."

"Fantastic," Duncan replied sourly. "What do you need me to do?"

"Quit bellyaching and get down here, would you? We're on the same team."

"If you say so. I'll get it handled."

Ending the call and clipping his phone along his belt, Greene pushed through the door on the ground floor, taking his best guess where Branson might have traveled during the past few minutes. The parking lot felt like his best hunch, so Greene headed toward the exit doors nearest the valet stand.

*****

While Greene continued toward the basement, Clay followed the blonde he spied in the atrium toward the exit she chose. He remembered her from the island, feeling confident she hadn't spotted him, though she acted wary of her surroundings as though suspicious he might be somewhere nearby.

Occasionally she glanced behind her, but Clay made certain to follow her from a distance, his mind already contemplating the possibilities of how to confront her. As she passed the concierge desk and a bellhop station he saw guests milling about. He knew guests were certainly outside waiting for a shuttle bus to the casino and valets often stood at their outdoor station during favorable weather.

He envisioned a public scene where he tried to confront her and she jumped in the car to escape. From there he would certainly jump atop the car without the benefit of weapons and attempt to subdue her. Disadvantaged because she possessed weapons and a one-ton rental car, Clay would inevitably be shaken from the moving vehicle at best. Experience told him a rental or a stolen car awaited her in the parking lot, so when she exited the double sliding glass doors, he remained inside and veered right to find Craig Jennings' office.

Without knocking he threw the door open, drawing wide eyes from Jennings who shifted in his seat to see who dared barge into his office. His fingers remained poised above his computer keyboard, his expression not particularly endearing once he recognized his visitor.

"I need a view of the parking lot from your security camera," Clay said without hesitation.

"What?"

"Parking lot. Now. This is an emergency."

Jennings typed in a command through his keyboard with heavy fingers, pulling up a view of multiple cameras throughout the hotel's interior and parking lot. With minimal movement of his mouse and a few typed commands Jennings narrowed the screen of twelve images to only two cameras that displayed the parking lot.

Clay's eyes feverishly searched the screen as he made his way around the desk for a better view. He spotted the woman making her way toward the edge of the lot, taking a precautionary glance behind her.

"Those cameras can zoom in, right?"

"Sure," Jennings answered. "What do you need?"

"I need the license plate of whatever car she gets into."

Clay watched with Jennings just long enough to see her enter into a silver Toyota as though she had just finished lunch with a friend instead of murdering someone. He didn't need to see the body downstairs to know why she came to the hotel and what she'd done. Confronting her in the parking lot wasn't wise because he wasn't armed and so many witnesses meant police intervention within minutes.

The moment he verified the car's make and model Clay darted from the office and ran down the hallway toward the lobby entrance, almost knocking over a meandering guest in the process. He reached the door, peering outside without opening it to see if his adversary chose to leave through the main brick road entrance or the side entrance often used by service vehicles.

He watched the car drive down the lesser used side entrance, wondering if she meant to head to Louisville instead of Indianapolis. Granted, smaller airports existed in between either city, but Clay figured she was flying commercial somewhere, possibly even out of the country. Instead of making a scene he bet on a hunch that such a new rental car was equipped with some sort of GPS tracking from the manufacturer or the rental company. While his job provided him the means to contact various companies and check on the license plate he knew a federal agent possessed better means.

Without investigative status on his department, Clay had no rational explanation why he would request a vehicle be tracked. His come and go status lately hadn't left him in the department's good graces, so he decided not to rock the boat until he was ready to assume the security helm at the theme park.

A few minutes later he found Greene in the atrium speaking with the real Chase Dalton. Both seemed pleased to see Clay had returned with no injuries.

"Your head of security helped me get the plate number," Clay informed Greene. "I need to track it down, especially if it's a rental car heading to the airport."

Greene grimaced a bit.

"I've about extended all of my favors. It won't be easy."

Clay immediately regretted not jumping on the car and taking his chances.

"The imposter didn't wreck my career, so I'll give the office a call," Dalton offered. "Even if we can't track the car directly, we'll know where it's going."

"And that's all I need," Clay said, his heart racing in anticipation of drawing closer to his former mentor.

CHAPTER 26

By Friday Craig Jennings and Matt Teakon started their third morning in Louisville, though only their second with the horse from New Mexico. Trainer Jeff Slaton wanted Desert Phantom's comfort level transitioned perfectly from the rugged terrain and hot weather to bluegrass and comfortable air.

Jennings felt a chill in the morning air, just after dawn, when he and Teakon leaned on the track railing to watch their horse run like dutiful owners. Truth be told, they felt less like owners than security guards, vigilant at every turn for the man known as Lincoln Daine. Greene bet on a longshot that the man was going to target the race, which seemed plausible with so many opportunities to accomplish his goal.

Security at the track was excellent, with state troopers and local police officers standing by around the clock. Security cameras provided additional comfort for most owners and trainers, but Jennings saw far too many random people sauntering around the grounds. The press was allowed inside in limited numbers, but every team seemed to have numerous trainers and assistants walking around with the certified special laminated badges hung around their necks.

"Seems like everyone around here has a badge," Jennings said, thumbing his own.

Today he wore a pair of old brown cowboy boots, blue jeans, and a work shirt, along with a straw cowboy hat, which he tilted back for a better view of the track. Teakon dressed similarly, opting for his black hat as he watched Johnny Gomez start along the backstretch to see how Phantom performed on the dirt surface on his second day. When Gomez reached a designated mark along the track Teakon started a stopwatch to time the horse, hoping for moderate improvement over the previous day's mark.

"We didn't really expect Daine to show up early anyway," Teakon noted. "We're here on the off chance he's infiltrated someone's team."

"Doesn't sound like he's a natural horse person, so that seems doubtful."

"You just called the kettle black."

"I never said *I* was a natural horse person, did I?"

Jennings watched his own breath in the chilly morning air, figuring the sun would end such a phenomenon when it peeked above the horizon momentarily. Morning workouts ran smoothly, one assigned horse after another, the jockeys often scrambling to find the next of their multiple horses they were riding over the weekend. After the running of the Kentucky Oaks finished later that day Jennings figured his visual list of suspects would be cut in half because only the jockeys and a few owners needed to stick around.

He heard the click of the stopwatch as Phantom thundered past, his hooves clopping and kicking up dirt, barely visible in the low lighting.

"Better," Teakon said when he looked at the time. "I find myself wanting this horse to win for Margaret's sake, but not at the expense of someone's life."

"That's why we're here, remember?"

"Of course I do. It just sucks that we have to go through the motions when we could be looking for this Daine guy."

Jennings knew their objective was secondary because Greene and Liz were around the grounds as well, unrestricted as they mingled with everyone from owners to police officers. Greene expected to make friends easily with his background as a marshal, posing as security for Jennings and Margaret. Liz, on the other hand, remained by his side pretending to be Jennings' longtime girlfriend. For the assignment Jennings had removed his wedding band and convinced his wife to stay home for her own good. He felt bad quashing her enthusiasm about going to the Derby, but he explained it was related to his job and not entirely safe.

So far as she knew he headed up the hotel security force because he never revealed the rare occasions he hunted down cubes with Clouse's team.

He felt terrible for making excuses when he went on "business trips" but Jennings knew the risk and he wasn't putting her in harm's way.

At first she questioned how a high school shop teacher received an offer for a job doing security, much less leading the force, when he possessed no law enforcement experience. Jennings tried to tell her his military experience gave him an edge and that Clouse felt bad about the experience that accidentally brought Jennings onto his property and nearly caused his death. In truth, Clouse felt hiring the man and giving him a good paycheck beat leaving the lingering chance that Jennings might sue him, and they both knew it.

Truth be told, Jennings actually enjoyed the unspoken half of his job, feeling somewhat like a secret agent out of a movie or a comic book. He experienced events both rewarding and sorrowful that the average person couldn't fathom seeing during a lifetime. Knowing what the cursed cubes could do firsthand, and how they corrupted men, he harbored no regrets about hunting them down and making the world a safer place.

"You okay?" Teakon asked as Jennings watched their jockey ride Phantom to a nearby exit, dismounting as one of the stable hands took the reins.

"I'm good," Jennings replied, reaching into his shirt pocket for a canister of dip.

He popped the top, snagging a pinch between his forefinger and thumb from the canister before inserting it between his bottom lip and gums. As he shook any fine tobacco fragments from his finger he caught Teakon giving him a disapproving look.

"You know the Mexicans aren't going to respect you any more for doing that."

"I'm just trying to fit in, Matt. I don't know horses like you do, and our staff thinks I'm a worthless blob who just buys other people's horses to make a quick buck."

"Well, give them some credit. They're judging based on what they see of us."

"You know, I quit this stuff years ago, but I just want them to think I'm an everyday guy so we can get some help from them."

Teakon gave him a cagy smirk.

"I've already got their trust, so just leave it to me, oh rich and powerful snobby horse owner."

Jennings shook his head dejectedly, knowing he couldn't fit in, and somewhat glad their ruse was likely up after the impending weekend, regardless of the outcome. He spit brown tobacco juice with precision aim at the nearby dirt, a little upset that the experience of his habit hadn't ever entirely left him.

Both men reluctantly left the railing, understanding the need to return to their true assignment, though hating to leave the fairytale behind. Jennings turned his head to spit toward the edge of the track, catching the beauty of the infield as the morning sun began to illuminate some of the awe-striking grounds around them. Manicured to perfection, the lawn would have to endure dozens of racing teams trampling on it over the weekend as they took center stage on the winner's circle.

A newspaper photographer approached the pair, asking if he might get a picture of the owner leading the horse back to the barn for a photo opportunity. Sheer willpower kept Jennings from stiffening like a board at the thought of taking hold of the reins. He knew the Hispanic stable hands already lacked respect for him and he pictured this going badly in two possible ways. One, he added fuel to the fire by figuratively pushing them aside to fuel his own ego in their eyes. Two, he took the reins and horse pulled away from him, or worse, Phantom reared on his hind legs and thrashed as though a gunshot had rang out and frightened him.

He was still fishing for excuses when Teakon nodded positively to the reporter and guided him toward the reins.

"This is good public relations," he whispered.

"If the horse doesn't kill me."

Jennings felt certain he saw a narrowing of Rodrigo's eyes and a thin smirk when he took the reins from Margaret's stable hand, as though the experienced horseman somehow knew one of Jennings' two fears was about to reach fruition. He tried to act naturally when he took the reins, knowing he wasn't a complete stranger to Phantom.

He was more like the divorced father who saw the young horse on weekends and the occasional holiday.

By no means an ordinary horse in any sense of the word, Phantom knew the people he liked and those he did not, and Jennings had never truly tested the strength of their bond. With internal trepidation he took the leather reins and calmly gave a gentle tug, waiting for the horse to either fling him into the air or follow obediently.

On several occasions he had rubbed Phantom's head or spoken to the horse, but never had Jennings attempted to lead him anywhere or expect that he could. He envisioned a scene where the horse whipped his head to one side, sending his pretend owner through the air like some cartoon character who landed with a mushroomed orange explosion fifty feet away in the infield. Of course all of this was greatly exaggerated within his mind and turned out to be completely unsubstantiated when Phantom obeyed the gentle tug of the reins and followed him toward the stable he temporarily called home.

Much to his surprise, the horse even gave him a friendly nudge along his spine that startled Jennings. Luckily the cameras failed to catch his surprise, allowing him to retain his calm demeanor publically.

A few minutes later the photo opportunity concluded and the employees took the racehorse aside for a thorough bath before stalling him. Jennings and Teakon watched from a short distance, finding another fence to lean upon as their eyes occasionally drifted in search of shady individuals. So far neither had come across anyone they thought looked peculiar, lacing their minds with doubts about finding Daine before he struck. They really didn't know what the man looked like, and Daine choosing the Derby to make a small fortune in the first place began to seem doubtful.

"How does it feel to be such an underdog story?" Teakon finally asked to break the tension of their assignment, considering they were fifty-one to one odds almost from the beginning.

"It makes me nervous. I worry that Greene is wrong about this guy showing up this weekend, but I worry even more that he will. At heart I'm still a shop teacher, not a cop or some vigilante. What if we can't stop this guy?"

"We can only do our best. For a shop teacher you're not doing too badly around the horse."

Jennings grinned slightly.

"I don't know much about horses. You can show 'em, you can race 'em, and in a pinch you can eat 'em. That's about the extent of my knowledge."

Teakon couldn't help but chuckle.

"I'm sure everyone else down here takes your philosophy to heart."

Taking one last look around, Jennings decided their time might be better spent away from the racehorse, looking for potential suspects. He motioned for Teakon to follow him, knowing either way his part in the charade concluded the following afternoon.

***

It turned out the mysterious lady indeed headed to Louisville, but not to flee the crime scene or return to Nosagi. Quite the opposite, she settled in near Churchill Downs, spending her time surveying the grounds and preparing for the same exact mission Greene and his people were planning to execute.

Obtaining the cursed cube from Lincoln Daine.

Any doubts Clay harbored that this woman was sinister were erased with the death of the imposter and her trek to Louisville. She, and any associates who might remain hidden from view, possessed a tremendous threat to Greene and his people. While Clay might not have eagerly jumped on board with Clouse's group he understood and believed in their quest. Because of that, he needed to eliminate any threat that might bring harm to the group.

After feeling assured the mysterious blonde wasn't leaving the area anytime soon, Clay used some stealth to borrow a master keycard from one of the cleaning ladies in the hotel directly across from Nosagi's apprentice. He observed her until he was satisfied about her habits, deciding against his better judgment to approach her first. It wasn't in his nature to simply assassinate people without first knowing they truly deserved death. In this case he might have confronted her in any number of vacated areas but he wanted to learn what he could about his former mentor first.

Against every natural instinct, Clay casually walked into the hotel lobby, spotting her seated in the bar beyond the front desk. She often chose a seat that gave her a view of the racing grounds and the front lobby. He assumed she remained vigilant for Lincoln Daine, because Clay would use the same tactic if he wasn't tailing someone else at the moment.

In a public place she might be able to murder an average person without calling attention to herself, but Clay knew the tricks of the trade, even creating a few of his own over the years.

Dressed in khaki pants and a short sleeved button-up shirt that screamed tourist, he crossed the lobby and entered the bar, immediately drawing her attention. Acting far too casually upon spying him, she recognized him and Clay knew it, which made his direct approach that much easier. She continued to act aloof and calm until the moment he pulled up a chair, only then shooting him a stare that questioned his brazen nature.

"That was some interesting handiwork in French Lick," he said while sitting, wondering if she possessed the will to murder innocent people as well.

"I thought it was West Baden," she answered smoothly, her eyes looking toward the entrance instead of him. "You're way out of your league tailing me here."

"I don't think so. If Nosagi didn't teach you adequately you won't last two minutes against me."

Despite his words, Clay knew better, considering her his equal instead of underestimating her.

She finally made eye contact, revealing a sinister grin amplified by the glossy red lipstick she wore. Her low-cut beige dress revealed the tops of her breasts, and Clay fought to avoiding looking down because he knew this woman was a praying mantis, just waiting for a male to show weakness before slaying him. A small, matching purse sat atop the table, causing Clay to wonder what goodies she harbored inside. He wasn't completely weaponless, carrying a few small knives with him and a *shuriken* star in his breast pocket.

"Oh, he told me all about you," she revealed. "How he tricked you into joining the fold because you were noble to a fault."

"Did he tell you how he murdered my wife and son?"

She looked him directly in the eyes without blinking or faltering.

"Yes," she said so matter-of-factly that he knew this woman's veins ran cold with the same ice water that fueled Nosagi. "He also told me you ran back to America like the pathetic coward you are."

Clay refused to let her words intimidate or infuriate him. So far his probe for information brought him more than he expected, so he decided to let her continue speaking.

"And how did you become his prized student?"

"He recruited me after one of his students attempted to rape me and I killed him. See, I wasn't as hard to turn as you because I was tired of the world stomping me into the ground."

"Poor you," Clay said sarcastically. "Becoming a professional criminal and assassin is a long ways off from staking your claim in the world."

"You wouldn't understand, coming from a loving home, never living on the streets wondering where your next meal might come from, or if you could find somewhere to stay out of the cold."

While his right hand gripped the knife in his pocket Clay gave her a cold stare. The bar conversation around them hadn't changed in the least, meaning no one took notice of their discussion. The televisions in the background drowned out most of the chatter taking place, though this woman surely drew several pairs of eyes due to her striking appearance.

"You seem to have done well for yourself," Clay evaluated aloud.

"I'll be doing better once I eliminate you from this assignment."

"You can still walk away from this, and from *him*. It's only a matter of time before I find him and kill him and whoever stands in my way."

"The man did you a favor and you want to kill him?"

"He murdered my family."

"Technically he didn't," she reiterated a partial truth. "You can't tell me you were too naïve not to know exactly what kind of techniques he was teaching you and how they were used in the field."

"He told me he upheld a centuries-old tradition by teaching us those methods. I read the history and I understood why ninja clans existed."

"Nosagi never lied to you. Your father sent you over there for a reason. He saw the potential in you to deviate from the law because you were a troublemaker. You let both of your father figures down."

"Neither of them were father figures in the real sense, and you know that. I hardly came from a *loving* home as you describe it."

"It was your own fault for not embracing what they provided for you. When I kill you, your failure will come full circle, won't it?"

Clay smirked.

"I can see there's no changing your mind, so when and where are we doing this?"

"There's a hospitality area on the second floor of this hotel. I suggest we make use of it after it closes tonight."

"I'm not too fond of security cameras. How about the tennis courts behind the hotel?"

"Too bad you're so shy, but that works for me."

The irony of how inhospitable the sporting area would be when the two brandished weapons later that evening was lost on Clay because he only thought of drawing one step closer to Nosagi and destroying his former *sensei.*

"I'll see you this evening," he said before standing, leaving the bar with his senses attuned to his surroundings in case the woman tried any form of stealthy attack.

She did not, and Clay knew his death meant failure, if not annihilation, for Greene and his team on race day.

CHAPTER 27

While he hoped Greene and the group might have located Lincoln Daine by that evening, Clay learned otherwise when he spied Craig Jennings taking a break from the search. Standing high in the seats within Churchill Downs, Clay saw the man looking out to the infield, his body language indicating disappointment and frustration.

Clay exited the grounds as easily as he had slipped inside, using both his stealth and experience in police techniques to avoid security measures. Destiny awaited him a short jog away at the hotel where he planned on confronting Nosagi's latest follower. He saw little point in reasoning with her now that he knew her heart was contaminated. Killing her served little purpose other than sending a message to Nosagi and protecting the group intending to find Lincoln Daine for all the right reasons.

Determined, yet not led by blind fury, Clay reached the tennis courts minutes after the sun set, leaving only artificial lighting to guide him. He carried numerous weapons which he picked up from a hiding spot shortly after exiting the racing grounds. His pack contained bladed weapons, some blunt weaponry meant to conceal additional damage dealers, and several throwing stars and blades.

He waited less than a minute before she emerged from the darkness, wearing the same black garb as him, meant to conceal their identity and their movements under the cover of darkness. They stood on opposite ends of the tennis court, within a makeshift fighting cage made of mesh wire, only a net separating them.

Clay drew his sword and scabbard from his side, prepared to set them beside him as he engaged in the ritual known as *kuji-in*. A time-honored tradition, the *kuji-in* served as the strength of the warrior, evoking various powers in the person who summoned them to enhance the senses or physical traits of the recipient. As he prepared to bow respectfully to his adversary, another tradition Clay was taught, he noticed she made no movement to carry out the ritual, or show him respect.

"I'm not into traditions," she said almost haughtily. "You can delay the inevitable if you want to, or we can get this over with."

Unfortunately traditions were drilled into him by Nosagi, but Clay knew they were one of the few truths the man taught him. Either the man personally grew tired of traditions himself or he picked students who wanted everything here and now like the new generation. Or perhaps the student pool wasn't quite so plentiful for a man who lived on the run from authorities and cursed object hunters alike.

Clay slowly drew his customized *katana* from its scabbard, letting the covering hit the tennis court with little more than a hushed clank.

"Since I'll be dead momentarily you wouldn't mind revealing where our master is, would you?" he inquired.

In reply she gave a cagy grin that he read through her eyes since the black mask covered the rest of her beautiful face.

"Either way he'll find you."

Before Clay decided on any further words to speak she charged him, leaping over the net as he blocked the swing of her sword with his own, immediately falling into a defensive stance. Though he understood Nosagi taught many of his students similarly, Clay didn't want to assume this mystery woman didn't bring something new to the table.

They crossed swords several more times, each deflecting the other's offensive attacks until Clay performed a backflip over the tennis net to distance himself momentarily while he thought of a new strategy. Putting an end to any further interference, the woman sliced the net cleanly with her sword before attacking Clay, keeping him from deciding on any long-term offensive maneuvers.

Darting toward the nearby mesh wire fence, Clay leaped just high enough to gain a step along the fence and propel himself into a backflip as the woman chased him, narrowly missing his feet with her sword when he initiated the move. Landing on his feet, Clay crouched down, taking a swipe at her feet with his own sword. She jumped to dodge the first pass of the sword but Clay's expert handling of the weapon allowed him to flip the blade for a backhanded swing as expertly as a cheerleader twirls a baton. In one fluid motion the sword acted as an extension of his forearm on the backswing, but his target had already floated backwards, landing on her hands like a gymnast, still clutching the sword as she followed through with a backflip of her own.

Clay gave chase, swinging twice more before she was on her feet and deflecting his attacks. Luckily no one had spotted their activity yet, despite all of the area hotels weathering one of their busiest nights of the year. Even more fortunate was the fact no one opted to play tennis in the courtyard, leaving them to conduct their deadly business in private.

Already deciding the mystery woman was seasoned enough to hold her own in combat, Clay continued to test her abilities, seeing nothing from her that threatened his existence just yet. Luckily the tennis courts provided nowhere to run or hide, providing a contest based on skill and experience without trickery.

As though reading Clay's thoughts, the woman dropped a smoke bomb on the ground, creating a plume of gray smoke that concealed her movements. Often used as a tool for escape or repositioning, smoke bombs provided means for survival or a cheap advantage. Clay suspected she wanted to use immoral means to end his life, so he backed away from the temporary distraction instead of charging toward it.

He quickly realized she had jumped along one side of the fence, looming above him. With one hand clutching her sword and the other clinging to the mesh wire like a fly on a wall, she leapt toward him after shifting the sword to both hands. Clay blocked the powerful strike with his own sword, losing it in the process as it bounced several feet away atop the green court.

Without hesitation the woman went for the kill, lunging her sword directly at him, forcing Clay to duck before bobbing and weaving a few more times while the razor sharp blade missed his cranium by inches. He wanted to reach behind him for a replacement weapon but time didn't permit if he wanted to keep his head attached to his neck.

Clay now knew she was excessively aggressive, not patient enough to wait for a true kill shot. She might have finished a common security guard or lesser military man with her tactics, but Clay was neither of those. He rolled back, reaching into his small pack concurrently to pull out a light wooden cane in the process. Relatively harmless in appearance, the cane was a custom weapon Clay liked to employ, slightly less than two feet in length.

The woman made two cuts with the sword toward Clay's torso the second his momentum stopped. He blocked both death blows consecutively with the customized baton, backing off just slightly to pull it open, revealing a chain hiding within. Quickly twirling one end of the chain, he threw it as his adversary attempted to launch another attack at him, catching the sword in the links before pulling it from her grasp. Irritated, but far from finished, she pulled two wooden canes from her side, pressing upward on levers that produced short blades, like small sickles, atop the shafts. Known as a *kusari-gama*, the cane was much like Clay's weapon in that it concealed yet another weapon.

She swung both bladed canes down upon Clay, forcing him to use the chain for defensive purposes momentarily. The blades were only about half a foot in length, but plenty long and sharp enough to end his existence if they struck any number of crucial spots on his body. After a few blocks of the blades Clay rolled to his right, sending one end of the chain like a lightning bolt toward the woman's left leg, tripping her when he tugged it close to his body without hesitation.

Having no weapon prepared to throw, or a blade of his own readily in hand, he decided to make a bold move and step forward. Still on her back, the woman slashed at him with the *kusari-gama*, allowing him to use the opposite end of the chain to ensnare it before it cut into his knee like a prize bullfighter might use a whip. Taking another step forward, he anticipated that she might try and strike even lower, but his chain was quicker, wrapping the weapon tightly and leaving her weapons useless within her hands.

He attempted to carry out a handstand to relocate behind her for a finishing blow but she scurried out of the way before he completed the move, abandoning her weapons in the process.

Clay landed close enough to his discarded sword that he picked it up, turning just in time to block an attack from a short sword the woman had pulled from a small pack on her back. He knew she was trained exceptionally well by Nosagi, and being female presented no hindrances to her assaults or defense. He wondered which of them was going to find an opening first to finish the other, still determined to survive if only to find his former mentor.

***

Harlan Stone entered the hotel where the mystery woman was staying, under orders to examine her room. Because Stewart wanted him to keep a low profile, Stone gave up his usual duds for a Hawaiian shirt, khaki shorts, and leather sandals. He also wore a floppy straw hat and sunglasses, sure to carry a drink with him as he entered the lobby, giving the appearance he was returning from a nearby party of some sort.

He detested entering the building unarmed, and hated acting the part of a drunken tourist almost as much.

Noticing only one hostess occupying the desk at the late hour, he decided to try the easiest approach first. Stewart had provided him with a few gadgets that left him feeling like a secret agent, including a small device that read swipe card readers. Able to copy data from a card, the little machine also possessed the capability of inserting an attached card into a machine and accessing any local database. In this case, Stone hoped it would snatch all of the available room number passwords, or at least obtain a master code of some sort. Simply inserting the card into a room lock might eventually crack a simple numeric code, but Stone couldn't risk being seen loitering in a hallway.

A pretty girl in her early twenties manned the front desk, but Stone decided flirting wasn't the best method if he wanted access to the card reader sitting beside her computer terminal. He didn't have time, and the agent was fully capable of weaving a lie on the spur of the moment when necessary.

"Can I get a few towels?" he asked, heavily leaning on the desk while purposely slurring his speech.

"Certainly," the young woman answered hesitantly, veiling a concerned look while openly buying his façade as a lush.

She walked back to a room, providing him enough time to insert the false card into the reader, letting the miniature computer begin its penetration of their software. With the room only a few feet behind her the hostess returned in less than ten seconds, which didn't provide Stone with much assurance his device completed its scan.

"There you are," she said, setting the towels beside him as he swayed slightly, carrying on with the inebriated act, praying she didn't look down to her computer terminal.

He decided to keep her eyes focused on him by engaging her in conversation momentarily.

"There is one *hell* of a party out there," he said slowly, basing his actions on how his college buddies back in Texas acted back in the day.

"That's nice, sir," she said, trying to deflect her attention away from him.

No one else approached the desk, so any and all stalling fell to him.

"You know my wife didn't come because of her allergies?" he asked. "Who does that? Skips the Kentucky Derby because of allergies?"

The hostess shrugged, and Stone could tell she was growing uncomfortable, so he decided to try a different approach before security sauntered their way. Hotels were certain to have extra security with the biggest event of the year in town. Stone hoped the person watching the cameras wasn't very attentive, or found something better to do than watch him hack their computer system.

"Can I get one more towel?" he asked her nicely, indicating he was ready to leave her alone if she complied.

He staggered a bit against the counter until she turned her back, immediately reaching for his device and hiding it between the two towels atop the counter. She returned and he nodded thanks before walking unsteadily toward the elevators. With numerous people coming and going, he simply walked into the first available car with a family of four, asking them to push the fourth floor for him. The elevators required a room key, but Stone didn't want to pull out the strange spy gadget in front of anyone, so he let them use their key.

When the doors slid open a few seconds later he stepped onto the fourth floor, counting the windows from one end of the floor to the other once he determined the correct side. From spying outside and watching Clay Branson's movements he knew the correct room when facing it. Now he simply mirrored his technique, knowing which direction he stared from in the various spots where he conducted a stakeout.

Finding what he felt certain was the correct room, he inserted the modified card rather than knocking. He knew the room's occupant was busy confronting Clay Branson outside, and knocking only made him look suspicious to any neighbors or security cameras. Covering his actions with his body the best he could, Stone waited only a few seconds before the device transmitted the numeric code to the attached swipe card and the door lock mechanism turned green.

"Presto," he said, opening the door as he slipped inside.

The curtains were drawn and the bed was made as though the room was awaiting a new occupant. Stone pulled a pair of latex gloves from his right pocket, snapping them over his hands before he touched anything. Amazingly, the bathroom held nothing of interest as the soaps and shampoo bottles remained sealed. Only a small handbag occupied one side of the bed when he scoured the room for evidence of life. He knelt beside it, painfully aware of the fact this woman was trained much like Branson. And while Stone didn't know exactly where the two received their training, or what purpose it ultimately served, he respected their skills, knowing both were secretive and deadly.

Checking to make certain his latex gloves were free of tears, he kept his distance while unzipping the travel bag with an outstretched arm. No booby-traps sprung upward, so he grew a bit more brazen and looked inside. Finding clothing on top, he carefully peeled back the items, discovering a cell phone and numerous identifications underneath.

He decided to call his boss before making any moves, uncertain of exactly what Stewart wanted done with the find.

At this point Stone wasn't feeling very trusting of the Deputy Director because the man refused to provide him with any details while the agent risked his life simply tracking Clay Branson. Granted, the man led a boring life while in Ohio, but Stone knew something was gravely awry when the man battled hordes of undead and locked swords with a woman trained in the deadly arts.

Thanks to some other electronic devices he overheard their conversation that morning, which left him ample time to set up a video recorder pointed toward the tennis courts. He didn't expect great clarity in the dark through a mesh wire fence, but Stone simply wanted to know how the skirmish ended.

Regardless of the outcome he planned on spending a few days in Texas while Branson was either laid to rest or returned to Ohio. Stone didn't really have an opinion of the man because observation alone didn't really speak to the man's character, good or bad.

"Stewart," he heard the Deputy Director say over the phone momentarily.

"I'm in your mystery woman's room. She travels light."

"Does she have a name?"

"Try a dozen or so."

A pause crossed the line momentarily.

"Collect everything and send it to me."

Stone wasn't one to question orders, but he felt rather unethical simply stealing a person's belongings without legal backing.

"Don't I need a warrant? Or something? This isn't exactly legal."

"I will *make* it legal."

Stone knew the words meant for him to carry out the order or find himself unemployed, or dusting an FBI records room somewhere in Alaska. He shut down his phone, suddenly disliking the idea of lingering in the room. Taking up the bag, he exited the room hastily, wondering how the battle in the courtyard was taking shape.

CHAPTER 28

By the time thunder grumbled in the skies above, the thunderstorm was already upon the greater Louisville area. Clay didn't have time to analyze the weather, or the impact upon the running of the Kentucky Derby the next day, because his life depended on his full concentration of the ongoing battle in the tennis courts.

Both combatants were back to using swords, using what few openings presented themselves to swing at limbs. Thus far Clay and the mysterious woman had both evaded major damage from weaponry, but as she swung her sword at Clay's feet he leapt over it, taking a quick cut at her neck which she ducked before their swords clashed again. While their weapons remained intermingled Clay kicked the side of her knee before using her thigh to launch himself into a backflip, creating some space.

She barely registered any pain from the blow because she had moved her knee just enough to lessen the impact. And she swung the sword while he was in midair, but he blocked the attack with his own sword, landing on his feet as she took another sweeping swing that caught the top of his thighs. As the black material split apart, Clay's legs looked as though someone had painted the upper portion of his thighs with a red paintbrush stroke. Perfectly symmetrical, and ordinarily a painful sting, they went ignored as Clay continued to move, tossing his sword behind him before carrying out three consecutive backflips toward the discarded weapon and a mesh wire wall.

Clay noticed during the rotation on his third backflip that the woman wasn't going to allow him to land and scoop up his weapon as he planned. In less than a split-second he conceived a plan to catch her sword's blade with his palms when she struck it toward his face, but he abandoned the notion just as quickly for a riskier gamble.

Hesitating ever so slightly, he waited for the blade to slice downward, aimed for his back while he was still in mid-flip. Relying completely on instinct and past practice, because his head faced the opposite direction, Clay used his feet to clasp the blade and yank it upward in one motion.

Ordinarily the move might have failed utterly, but Nosagi trained Clay to stop a blade between his palms and certainly taught this woman Clay's usual defensive tactics. She was playing right into his habits until he switched up his defensive move at the last second, thwarting whatever chain of moves she planned to use against him.

Now the sword flew above both of them, ripe for the taking. The woman glanced upward to time its descent, providing Clay an opportunity to kick her in the chest, connecting lightly enough that she stumbled a few feet back. He grabbed the sword from the air, sweeping the blade toward her neck, but she recovered enough to anticipate the move, rolling to her left.

Carrying out a sequence of moves, slashes and stabs that all missed because she backed away and evaded them, Clay refused to grow frustrated, keeping his focus on the battle. Strength didn't win these contests, but rather skill, agility, and mental toughness. Basically unarmed, and running out of room as her back drew closer to a fence, the woman threw another smoke bomb on the ground close to Clay, disorienting him momentarily while she scrambled for a new offensive position.

Heavy rain cut loose after the concocted distraction hit the ground, drenching Clay almost immediately. Despite the smoke bomb and raindrops pelting him from above, he kept a clear mind, sensing she might make an attempt to snag his discarded sword rather than draw a new weapon from her arsenal. Considering his back was now turned to his own sword, the move seemed logical, and a sense of immediate danger equivalent to flashing red lights and a blaring siren in his mind warned him of unseen peril.

Based on where his sword landed, he knew she couldn't have leapt at him from atop the fence, so he plunged his current sword behind him, along his right side, knowing how a right-handed person like herself would attempt to slice diagonally through his shoulder blade. Lessening the chance of a blade potentially cutting through him, Clay backed up as he thrust the sword behind him, feeling it plunge into something solid.

All at once he felt the pressure on the sword change as the weight of something tilted the blade slightly. An audible gasp behind him indicated he struck home with the weapon, carving into the mystery woman's intestines to the point that only immediate medical attention might save her.

Retracting the blade as he turned around to face her, Clay discovered his hunch proved accurate. Had he guessed incorrectly on any number of fronts it might be him bleeding profusely as his blood mixed with the rainwater standing atop the green tennis courts. She clutched her wound after dropping Clay's sword to the ground with a muffled clanking sound. Feeling little emotion about mortally wounding the student of his sworn enemy, Clay watched her slump to her knees as the rain continued to soak him. Both combatants understood their skirmish had reached a conclusion as the thunder rolled in the distance.

As the woman took in deeper and deeper breaths, her body trying to compensate for the lack of blood and her heart pumping faster, Clay wondered where her life had taken such a bad turn. She removed the mask portion of her *shinobi shōzoku* as her arm felt limp to her side, still clutching the covering.

"Finish it," she muttered, blood still streaming from the fresh wound onto the already wet tennis court.

"Where is he?" Clay inquired first, removing his own mask, feeling raindrops run freely down his face and into the curves of his lips.

His hair pressed flat against his scalp as though molded into place. The cloth from his outfit stuck to his skin like adhesive, feeling unusually chilly as the rain brought a cold front with it.

Adrenaline kept his battle wounds from bothering him just yet, but the time was coming when his nerves would break like a dam and let the pain come flooding inside.

"You won't find him," she answered plainly, no ambition left within her to lie or deceive Clay at this point.

"I will find him one way or another."

"If you do, it will be on *his* terms. Your new group is on a collision course with death itself. They're in over their heads, and even you can't save them."

She made it clear that Nosagi was part of a larger faction and not just living in isolation as some kind of marked man. Clay knew some difficult choices lay ahead of him, not only about his former mentor, but the fate of the world if Nosagi united his cursed cube with a dozen others. Greene was a hardened veteran agent of the federal government, but still a novice when it came to taking lives or understanding that the world around him contained a spiritual element very few people ever witnessed, much less understood.

Now coughing up blood, Nosagi's pupil wasn't long for the living world. She fell forward, assuming a position on all fours, still leaking blood from the wound and choking on the red fluid rising from within.

Unwilling to take a chance that this woman knew one of the dozens of tricks to induce herself into a coma and slow her heart rate to only a few beats a minute to stave off death, Clay raised the sword above his head. He waited only a few seconds before letting the blade cut through the rain and her neck, severing the head which bounced once atop the ground before coming to rest.

Clay felt no better, despite eliminating a major enemy, because a greater evil revealed itself, proving Greene completely right. Wanting nothing more than to return to Ohio and spend time with his fiancée, Clay felt obligated to stay in Louisville and ensure his allies completed their task. He knew all roads led to the cursed cubes, and from the cubes to the men responsible for endangering Greene's team.

And eventually those corrupt individuals led to Nosagi.

Clenching his fist, Clay set to picking up the discarded weapons quickly, trying to leave the scene looking like the brutal homicide of a Jane Doe. The rain helped wash away any potential DNA left behind, so he only concerned himself with loose weapons and the mask to the mystery woman's *shinobi shōzoku*. He didn't want investigators making any connections between her and the traditions he spent years learning.

At least not yet.

Knowing exactly where the woman stayed, Clay briefly considered sneaking into the hotel and seeing what information her room contained. He decided against the move, making Greene's people his priority and deciding this woman wasn't about to leave her real name lying around, much less information about Nosagi. Despite her strong front, the blonde knew she might not leave their battle alive, her thoughts mirroring Clay's concerns.

Utterly soaked, Clay trudged across the tennis courts, feeling fatigue and pain setting in as the adrenaline faded. He forced his mind to stay focused, checking the area around him for any potential witnesses, finding none. Only as he exited the mesh wire surroundings did he notice a man in the distance stumbling toward a dark sedan of some kind. The man took no notice of Clay, but the Ohio law enforcer recognized something about this individual, even in the dark and from a distance.

His gait.

Perhaps serving as a police officer, or the fact that he lived in constant paranoia since discovering Nosagi was corrupt heightened Clay's powers of observation, but he recognized this man simply by the way he walked. Despite the attempt to disguise his mannerisms, this man couldn't fool Clay because he had appeared in the police officer's daily routine several times over the past few months. Strangely, Clay remembered him from the theme park, the grocery store with Casey, and now a state away in Kentucky.

Retaining enough energy and mental stability to confront the man, Clay decided to put others before his personal vendetta, his instincts telling him this man wasn't an agent of Nosagi like the woman. Though he doubted the rugged man was entirely ethical and pure, Clay decided the inevitable confrontation could wait.

He studied the man momentarily, trying to avoid giving himself away in case a glance came his way. Clay carried on through the diminished downpour, hoping for a successful Kentucky Derby in more ways than one.

CHAPTER 29

By morning only a few clouds lingered over the Louisville sky, but the dirt track was reduced to mud, no matter how many times tractors dragged the surface. Mugginess lingered in the air as Craig Jennings paced in front of his horse's stall, still refusing to accept a true ownership role. Instead he felt helpless because he was forced to play the part while trying to track down a known murderer who possessed a deadly, corrupting force.

He and Matt Teakon were both dressed similarly to what they wore in New Mexico at the qualifying race. Wearing the black leather blazer again had already left him with sweaty armpits and an undershirt clinging to his chest. Fulfilling the wishes of the horse's true owner was the least of his worries as media coverage and the impending preliminary races left the stable area buzzing like a beehive.

Spying cameras from every major television network and several local affiliates, Jennings felt butterflies in his stomach because he knew Margaret Stough was going to make him the front man for the ownership team. He understood the role, knew what to say, and suspected he would legitimately be excited about seeing the horse run again, but felt guilty because he wasn't able to truly assist in the search for Daine.

"You're not helping matters," Teakon informed him, leaning his shoulder rather casually against a wooden post.

"And you're acting a bit nonchalant considering what we're here for."

Teakon withdrew from the post, leaning in once he ensured no one was within earshot in either direction.

"We're here to run a race and act the part of ownership first, search for the bad guy second. Greene and Liz and that theme park cop guy are handling that part of it. We just need to act naturally and not smother the horse. We're a fifty-one to one shot to win this thing, so if there's a payday to be made it's with Phantom."

"I'm still not happy about it. And the theme park guy isn't your average cop."

Jennings started to reach for the canister of tobacco residing in his white button-up shirt's front pocket but Teakon caught his arm.

"Cameras. Everywhere."

Jennings groaned aloud. Clasping the plastic canister fully within his palm, he transferred it to one of the blazer's slip pockets where it would remain out of sight and hopefully out of his mind.

"I told you it was a bad idea to start that again. The hired help doesn't notice anything we do."

"It's a little late for the lecture. My wife is going to kill me if she finds out."

"You haven't told her?"

"She nagged me to quit the first time, so there's no way I'll have a chew around the house."

Teakon chuckled.

"Sounds like you're heading for trouble."

"I'm just kind of nervous with all of this around me," Jennings admitted.

"You have a right to be. No one in their right mind expects you to come all the way from New Mexico and be a natural."

When Teakon spoke the words "New Mexico" he held his fingers up as quotation marks to reinforce their assignment's true nature.

"Come on," Teakon encouraged, leading the way away from the stables as they walked toward the track.

Both wore special passes encased within plastic coverings around their necks for the local police and state troopers working security to see. No one questioned them, regardless of where they went, because they looked the part of horse owners, or at least someone who belonged behind the scenes.

Smells of horse manure faded, replaced by the scent of freshly cut flowers as the two men neared the outer rail. The majesty of Churchill Downs reached a new level as color splashed the grounds like a Thomas Kinkade painting. Certainly no stranger to weddings and funerals, Jennings had never laid eyes upon a collection of flowers that compared to the arrangements throughout the infield and surrounding the outbuildings. As people began filling the seats, the men wearing suits and the women donning dresses and a multitude of hats, the figurative rainbow grew more intense.

Only hardcore fans struck out this early in the morning because the real race didn't take place until late afternoon. Threats of a morning popup thunderstorm kept some spectators away, or at least closer to cover until the races began. The atmosphere, even in the morning light, felt overwhelming to Jennings. Only people like his true employer ever graced Millionaires Row atop the stands, and one needed some luck just to secure a regular seat and sip a mint julep.

Fiddling with his bolo tie, Jennings watched a few horses gallop past the rail some distance away as riders were forced to use the turf area inside the muddy track for morning runs. Tractors continued to tow using various components, trying to stir and flatten the mud with management hoping the track might dry out before the races began.

Acting as casually as possible, he turned around to look at the people around him, wondering if one of them had murder on his mind. Jennings knew any attack or murder within the grounds wouldn't go undetected for long, or possibly at all. Between security personnel and video cameras the notion seemed impossible, which made him wonder if Daine might kill someone before entering the grounds and put the cube's power to use once he came in contact with the horse.

Each cursed object's use varied from its siblings, and no one in his group knew exactly how this one worked. They assumed it worked by touching the intended recipient and passing the enhanced life force from the sacrificial victim, which required Daine to step foot within the most secure area of Churchill Downs. Greene knew this, so he and Liz planned to hover around the stables most of the day, looking for clues. Jennings had no idea where Clay Branson fit into the plan since he audibly committed just the night before.

Local news stations reported a murder down the road outside of a hotel, but the victim was a Jane Doe and police weren't revealing many details. Because of the secrecy on their part, the story quickly tapered off when coverage migrated to the famous horse track. What little backstory Jennings knew about Branson allowed him to surmise that Branson might have removed one adversary from the dangerous path Greene's group was treading. His review of the security footage at the hotel furthered his knowledge of Branson's personal quest, but he personally liked their chances of stopping Daine with the cop around.

"There aren't even any guarantees this will work," Teakon said, trying to reassure him. "This guy might bypass the Derby for something different."

"There aren't that many sports that offer this kind of payday, Matt. You're talking about one team versus another, or a boxer against one opponent. To pick the winner in a race, with so many variables, with so many betters lost in the shuffle, Daine could clean up. Besides, he hasn't struck in a very long time."

Teakon knew better than anyone except Julie Knowles that Daine wasn't lying in a ditch dead somewhere or the cursed ledger would have recorded a new owner for the cube. It made perfect sense for Daine to visit the Derby if only a laminated badge gained people access to the stables.

Both men knew their chances of being a true help to the team rested between slim and none, but their fictionalized roles brought Greene, Liz, and Clay Branson to the dance.

***

Liz acted the part of a horse owner's love interest, stroking the horse's long nose with her right hand after removing a white glove. While some might have thought she was acting dainty, she actually needed skin-to-skin contact with Phantom if any valuable information was available. Nothing happened, so she removed her hand, still smiling at the horse because he was a majestic creature.

"Nothing?" Greene asked beside her, playing his role as an unarmed bodyguard rather well, standing stiffly while wearing a gray suit with a peach-colored tie.

"No. Thankfully."

For her part, Liz wore a yellow sundress and a large white floppy hat adorned with a yellow ribbon. Small flowers of white, blue, and yellow were attached to the ribbon to the right side of the hat's front. A blue rose was pinned just over her left breast atop the dress, a touch she thought of while researching Derby attire online. She also opted to wear shoes with low heels, mainly for the sake of comfort throughout the day, and *not* because she planned on getting involved in any foot chases.

Concern grew throughout the group as minutes and hours passed with no results. Now close to noon, Liz and Greene had only come across Jennings and Teakon once because the two were caught up with interviews and paperwork. She felt bad for them because they spent much of their week in Louisville, going through the motions of ownership because Margaret Stough didn't arrive until Friday afternoon.

Then again, Liz thought, how many people experienced the behind-the-scenes atmosphere of the Kentucky Derby in person? She suspected the travel and worries over the horses racked the nerves of most owners and trainers, especially when the positioning draw took place the Wednesday prior to the Derby.

She felt some relief that she didn't have to fake being the horseman's girlfriend to the extent of giving him a hug or speaking at length. Liz harbored no resentment toward Jennings, but her experience as an actress was limited to a high school play, despite being a California girl. The less she needed to act a part, the better.

"What are we going to do now?" she asked Greene, who appeared on the verge of a meltdown.

Sweat appeared around the collar of his dress shirt, and the veins along his neck were thick and bulging from frustration.

"We can't linger around the horse," he answered, knowing Daine would abort his quest if he sensed people were looking for him, or authorities surrounded the area. "These passes let us roam around just about anywhere, so I suggest we take advantage of them."

Liz pulled out the most recent picture of Lincoln Daine that Chase Dalton was able to provide when Greene called him. Considering Daine had fallen off the radar the past few years, and hadn't been charged by any police agency of a crime, the picture appeared to be something Dalton obtained through unconventional means. He might have used a local police agency to contact the man's remaining family to ask for a photograph because the image appeared to be part of a larger family photo. Distorted and a bit fuzzy, it wasn't much help, but Greene appreciated his friend's effort.

Daine wore his brown hair in a ponytail back then, a five o'clock shadow covering his face. Reports of his more recent appearance stated he'd cleaned up and wore his hair more conventionally short, which basically reduced the photograph's usefulness significantly.

"Why couldn't Chase get a driver's license photo?" Liz inquired as they walked away from the stables.

"Because you need to open an investigation or an inquiry for something like that. It raises a lot of red flags and there will be bigger favors to ask of Chase in the future."

"Because getting this cube from Daine is secondary?"

"No, because I have you and that rogue cop here to help me, so I shouldn't even need the photo. I hope."

Liz looked around, realizing Clay Branson was supposed to be somewhere inside the facility but she hadn't seen him all morning.

"Are you sure he's here?"

"I left a pass for him at the front office," Greene said, leading the way toward the track where several trainers were being interviewed on camera. "There isn't a whole lot more I can do at this point."

They brushed past a few stable hands that looked like authentic horsemen with weathered straw hats and dirty blue jeans. A gate and security guards temporarily kept them from crossing into public view where the stable area met the track and its abundant seating. Liz instinctively checked to make certain her white gloves were snug atop her hands because she didn't want to accidentally touch random people and see aspects of their lives at the risk of blowing her cover.

Her gift didn't always work consistently, or when she wanted it to, but it seemed to present itself when necessary. As though guided by a higher power that wanted her to see certain events unfold, her visions seemed paced. Liz knew her mind couldn't take a flashflood of scenarios in a short amount of time, and she hated seeing the past of anyone she knew personally.

Therefore she avoided touching Greene like his body hosted some sort of world-ending bacteria.

Perhaps the circumstances of their working relationship clouded her judgment, especially since she'd never experienced true adventure before, but Liz rather liked Greene. He was athletic, sure of himself, and fueled by a desire to do right by the world and its inhabitants. None of the cases she assisted police with provided very much excitement because everything she saw or touched was very much removed from the crimes in question.

Greene still carried himself like a government official, often dressing in suits and walking with a rigid swagger. Liz couldn't help but feel safe around him, though it wasn't the emotional stability like a husband provided, or a physical form of protection from a habitually jealous boyfriend. She simply felt unequivocally secure having him near, but felt certain some deep, dark secret from his past might rush forward if they made physical contact.

"What's wrong?" he asked when she balked at walking into the courtyard that preceded the main track area.

An area absolutely packed with spectators and officials.

"Nothing. It's occurred to me that if Daine is going to access the horse he needs to get into the stable area. What if we're looking at this wrong and he's not just sneaking in here sometime today?"

Greene sensed she might be dodging the entire truth from the look on his face. He was trained, after all, to read the way people answered questions while observing their body language.

"Either way, we've come this far, so let's finish the ruse."

Truth be told, Liz wasn't sure she fit in with the well-dressed people standing around the race track. Sure, most of them were fakers, pretending they were rich and civilized for one day, probably returning to their day jobs come Monday morning. Liz envied them in a way, because she had no job beckoning her. Her days were spent searching out evil while putting herself at risk because Paul Clouse presented an offer that took her away from California and the so-called occupation she held there.

"Have I told you that you look great?" Greene asked, possibly sensing her reservations about stepping into public view.

"You're just saying that."

"No," he said emphatically, presenting one of his rare grins. "You look stunning, and if we weren't on duty I'd ask you to dinner at one of these fine Louisville restaurants."

Liz thought the offer sounded sincere, but Greene was known to prod and motivate his colleagues just short of manipulation. Her childhood left her with little self-confidence because she wasn't particularly athletic, wasn't confident speaking around groups, and did well in school, but never achieved the grades that brought scholarships her way. Her parents were supportive enough, but they worked constantly to put food on the table. They never aspired to work their way into the Hollywood scene as actors or writers. Their move to California from Iowa as young adults stemmed from a desire to see lights other than the flashing stoplight in the center of their hometown.

Her parents were simply stuck in a rut, unable to make a sound living or move somewhere else. In turn, Liz fell into their situation, trying to use her ability for good, but only alienating herself from society all the more while struggling to make a living with two or three jobs. With her father deceased from prostate cancer nearly two years now, and her mother's health deteriorating from constant work, Liz accepted Paul Clouse's offer to truly do good for people and to assist her struggling mother.

She remembered the fun times with her father when he took her on walks through the park, throwing a Frisbee on the beach, or fishing off the pier. Liz always considered the fun times she spent with her father rather simple, but as an adult she realized they were also affordable. She never knew they were poor growing up, and she didn't really care because her parents always stayed close to their only child.

Most people saw her and judged her immediately, using words, often hurtful adjectives, to describe her. Greene never addressed her negatively, or made light of her ability, even though she sensed he wasn't sure about its purity. Always inquisitive, he asked legitimate questions about her visions, instead of acting juvenile like some of the police officers she worked with in her home state.

Now he waited patiently for her at the threshold of a public domain she really didn't want to enter, but Liz knew he wouldn't stray far from her once they entered the courtyard. Because of their respective roles Greene couldn't hook his arm through hers and prove his words true, so Liz simply accepted the confidence boost and entered the courtyard for hundreds of people to see.

In the distance, dark clouds closed in from the west as the wind picked up slightly, threatening to ensure the race wasn't going to take place in dry, sunny conditions. Liz expected little else, considering the normal luck of their group.

CHAPTER 30

arlan Stone might have felt bad about neglecting orders from his direct Bureau supervisor if not for the fact he questioned the man's intentions for him. Granted, his behavior toward the criminal element was far from angelic, but it was the criminal element after all. Stone didn't regard regular people with equal disdain, nor did he care to engage in activities that placed innocent people in jeopardy.

As he drove along the rural roads of Harris County, outside of Houston, Texas, Stone pondered exactly why Stewart asked him to monitor Clay Branson. At first Stone figured Branson was a dirty cop involved in some major criminal activity. The incident on the island, followed by the sword fight in the parking lot left him thinking otherwise. Branson showed no inclination toward illegal activity whenever he returned to Ohio, and his other activities certainly couldn't be defined as criminal.

Unfortunately Stewart wasn't very forthcoming with explanations of the bizarre events Stone witnessed. The apparent uprising of undead on the South American island, particularly, wasn't satisfactorily explained when Stone made inquiries. Stewart tried to say something to the effect of innocent people being brainwashed and Clay Branson cutting them down mercilessly, but what Stone viewed was *not* murder. The fact that statues and animals had also attacked the man indicated some rather dark forces were at work on that island.

In his experience he classified Branson's actions as self-defense.

Looking down to some scribbled notes in the passenger's seat, the agent figured he was close to his destination, finding a two-story faux brick house about half a mile down the road. Practically brand new, the house wasn't within sight of neighboring homes in any direction. A white picket fence literally crossed the front yard, hedging the mailbox on either side. Stone checked the address against the sheet of paper, verifying that he had arrived at the address of Jack Turpin's widow.

Deciding to avoid falling off the radar completely, Stone requested the weekend off from his direct supervisor to return to his home state. He threw in the statement that Clay Branson had returned to Ohio, a lie that served to accomplish his goal. And though he certainly planned on spending some time with family over the next few days, Stone decided to take advantage of the opportunity to learn something about his predecessor.

After his flight landed in Houston, Stone turned off his phone and disconnected the battery to ensure he left no digital trail. Though he required a rental car to make the rest of the journey, he put the tab on his own credit card, ensuring no one possessed the legal right to track him later.

He pulled into the finished driveway, wondering if Jack Turpin had spent the last of his savings on a house he barely called his own before his untimely death.

A garage that looked more like a workshop occupied the backyard, the rolling door open as sounds of heavy moving emerged. Stone approached the open door cautiously, hoping his information wasn't misleading. He hated the thought of making the trek into rural Harris County only to discover new ownership at the house.

"Hello?" he called upon reaching the large opening, seeing stacks of cardboard boxes inside, along with tools hung along the walls and a large table saw.

"Can I help you?" an attractive woman with black hair in her early forties asked as she maneuvered around the boxes to lay eyes upon her visitor.

She wore old blue jeans and a faded top appropriate for cleaning out a garage during a slow weekend.

Stone quickly removed the black cowboy hat from atop his head, holding it near his waistline respectfully. The woman looked him up and down, from his shined boots to the red and gray striped tie atop his white shirt. He decided he wanted to look the part of an FBI agent, even if his business here was personal.

The woman appeared stunned after staring at him momentarily, a curious look crossing her face.

"Are you with the Bureau?" she finally asked.

"Yes, ma'am."

Caught off-guard by her question, Stone failed to properly introduce himself, somewhat elated that he seemed to have found the right person.

"Oh, I'm sorry," he said, offering his hand. "Special Agent Harlan Stone."

She shook his hand, though her expression turned a bit wary.

"Kristina Turpin. I thought I was done with the Bureau after my husband died, but then they came around and asked even more questions this past winter."

"I'm here on more of a personal level," Stone confessed.

"Oh?" she asked, wiping her hands with a towel.

"It just recently came to my attention that I'm the man who took your husband's spot in the Bureau."

"His spot?" she questioned with raised eyebrows.

Stone decided to tread carefully, unsure of what Jack Turpin told his wife, or exactly when the couple met.

"When he worked in Los Angeles, Jack was part of a special division. If you don't mind me asking, when did the two of you meet?"

Kristina smiled.

"Let's head to the house so I can get us some tea."

"That sounds wonderful, ma'am."

"Please, call me Kris," she said, leading the way toward the front of the house where an open front porch awaited them.

Stone waited patiently while the widow stepped inside to make them some iced tea. When she returned the agent gladly accepted the tall glass from her, taking a seat on one of the two padded rocking chairs just outside the front door, placing his hat atop one knee. Though it wasn't protected by a screen, or otherwise enclosed, the porch provided shade in the form of a small awning. The concrete floor ensured the elements couldn't weather the surface or leave mold and mildew during any season. Stone had a feeling the house was custom built very recently for Turpin and his wife to enjoy after his retirement.

"Did you know my husband?" Kristina asked once she occupied the other seat.

"No. I just recently learned about him on an assignment."

"Jack was special," she revealed with affection. "He was an absolute gentleman who didn't speak unless he needed to."

Stone simply nodded before taking a sip of the tea.

"You remind me of him a little bit," she confessed. "He always wore his boots and spoke with a slow, thoughtful drawl."

Grinning, Stone thought of how much he fought to suppress his own accent, particularly when he traveled outside of his home state.

"We met when he came back to Houston for his father's funeral of all places," Kristina revealed. "I worked with his mother for a few years before she retired and she prodded him to date me. Jack wasn't keen on the idea after three previous marriages, so he tried to put me off by saying long distance relationships didn't work and he traveled all the time."

She took a sip from her own tea.

"I hate to bore you with the details, Agent Stone."

"You're not boring me at all, Mrs. Turpin."

"But I'm sure you're not here to listen to past romances."

"It's okay. Really. I'm still somewhat of a newlywed myself."

Kristina gave a smile of approval before continuing.

"I think Jack's mother continued to meddle because he finally dated me whenever he came back to Texas. We hit it off, but he was always secretive about his work, like he did something other than what I've always pictured FBI agents doing."

The irony wasn't wasted on Stone, who realized his recent activities were nowhere close to what he expected when he applied to the agency.

"Jack was a loving husband, but he always seemed to have a void in his life. He once told me he worked out of Los Angeles because the travel allowed him to search for his son. I don't think he liked the work, but he seemed determined to find his boy before he retired."

"Did he?"

"No. He found some decent leads in the Chicago area, but his son was adopted and grew up under a different name. Jack's first wife was murdered while he was overseas and his son was already in the foster system when he returned home. It sounded like someone adopted him quickly, which explains why Jack could never get him back, or find much information. But I think he was hurt that his son never looked for his natural parents."

"Maybe he did," Stone suggested. "The system doesn't make it easy to obtain information either way."

"Jack eventually let go of his dream and decided to retire, but he made it sound like retiring might be, well, dangerous."

"Dangerous?"

"I'm not sure that's the right word for it," Kristina said, taking another sip of tea. "Financially we were fine, even after beginning construction on the house, so I wasn't sure why he was concerned."

Stone began wondering if working as a rogue agent wasn't equivalent to being a made man in the mafia. Most people in that profession died as a result of their profession, sometimes by the hands of their own people if they tried to leave the criminal lifestyle.

"Do you have any idea what might have worried him? You're doing his job now, right? I mean I know you make enemies in your line of work, but I didn't think they dared come after FBI agents."

Stone decided not to shatter the illusion that standard criminals might have brought harm to her husband.

"That's really what I wanted to ask you about, Mrs. Turpin. Jack was only retired a few months before his accident. Had his behavior changed at all before his death?"

"Not really. Like I said, Jack was quiet about everything. If something was bothering him, he didn't always show it."

"And he never told you anything about the nature of his work?"

"No. Nothing specific about the cases he worked."

"Do you know for a fact that he worked cases?"

Kristina looked at him curiously.

"Jack never mentioned specifics, but he always implied he worked cases. Is that not what *you* do?"

"So far it's not what I do," Stone confessed. "Did any of Jack's old colleagues come to his funeral services?"

"Not really. Jack said he was recruited into the Bureau after his police and military days were over. He made it sound like he worked special cases and didn't really have too many colleagues."

"What about a man named Alan Stewart? Did he attend the services?"

Kristina shook her head negatively.

"No, but he did call. And he sent flowers. He said it was the least he could do."

Stone questioned how his boss knew about a retiree's death from so far away, especially considering the brief time Turpin spent with the Bureau.

Staring at her glass momentarily, the widow seemed to struggle to ask her next question because the answer might shatter her current beliefs.

"You think his car accident was no accident, don't you?"

Crafting his reply carefully, Stone knew this woman was his only hope of digging up the truth, and so far she hadn't provided any earthshattering information. Going to the local police, or questioning whoever performed the analysis of Turpin's vehicle was sure to raise some red flags, so Stone placed his hopes in the widow's answers.

He decided to answer her question with a question.

"They said Jack fell asleep at the wheel. Had you ever known him to do anything like that? Did he have health problems?"

"No," she answered, her voice a bit more despondent. "He was in phenomenal health for his age. And the few times he drank he certainly never drove. The medical examiner asked me about a thousand questions because I don't think he could find a reason for Jack hitting a tree the way he did."

"And he was pronounced dead at the scene?"

Kristina nodded solemnly.

"I have some concerns about my new position," Stone said slowly. "The less I tell you, the better, but if someone brought harm to your husband I *will* find them."

Stone told the absolute truth, because if he discovered someone within his organization targeted Turpin he would bring them to justice out of self-preservation. He had an idea that Stewart was using the rogue agent program to serve his own means, but Stone still didn't know why or how deep the potential corruption reached. He ran an incredible risk if he tried to investigate the situation himself.

"How do I reach you?" Kristina asked.

"You don't," Stone said vehemently. "I took great lengths to make certain no one knew I came here. If you were to contact me it might put us both in danger. Until I find some answers it's best we don't speak again."

Her expression grew rather grave.

"I didn't mean to worry you like this."

"Well you have, so it's a little bit late to apologize now."

"Again, sorry. Please don't go to anyone else with what I've told you. At this point I'm not sure who to trust, especially around here. Maybe this will all turn out to be nothing."

Stone wasn't particularly good at being reassuring, but he didn't want word of his visit to reach beyond the yard where he currently sat.

"I'm sorry to bring this to your doorstep, but you should be safe if you don't mention this to anyone."

"And what about you?" Kristina asked with open concern.

"I have to take my chances, but I can take care of myself."

Stone set the nearly empty glass of tea atop the porch railing and replaced his hat, hoping to make a quick exit. He only had a few days away from work to see his parents and contemplate the reasonable doubt regarding Jack Turpin's allegedly accidental death.

"Thanks for your time," he said, nodding as he touched the brim of his hat. "And for the tea."

"You're welcome. Just promise me you'll eventually let me know what you find out."

"When the smoke clears you'll be the first to know," he said with a grin.

Sauntering toward the rental car, Stone wondered if he was becoming soft, and if Jack Turpin had experienced a similar transition before someone likely staged his murder to look like an accident.

CHAPTER 31

Craig Jennings found it hard to concentrate on the task before him as reporters descended upon all of the horse owners and trainers like locusts. While the sounds of buzzing wings didn't enter his ears, their words certainly bounced around in his head and he knew more about horse racing than he ever cared to know.

As he walked from the horse stalls to the nearest bathroom he wondered how Lincoln Daine could ever *possibly* get close enough to Phantom to use the cursed object. Between the stationed state troopers and the press, it wasn't easy to go anywhere without a pass around one's neck. Most of the horses weren't accustomed to strangers, nor were they very receptive to being touched by anyone except their handlers. Some trainers hardly ever made physical contact with their horses, often leaving it to handlers or stable hands.

Jennings took notice that Jeff Slaton, Phantom's trainer, and the stable hands didn't stray far from the racehorse. During his morning run and the bath that followed, the men were always within sight of the stall. They occasionally fielded questions from fans or the press, or took turns getting a bite to eat, but someone was always nearby.

Stepping into the restroom area, Jennings found two urinals and two stalls, so he stepped up to a urinal and conducted his business, feeling certain he had the restroom to himself. Sidestepping the pressure of searching for Daine and avoiding the media felt good, and he certainly couldn't wait for the day to end so his life could return to normal.

Normal for him certainly wasn't the standard, but at least he landed in a comfort zone while working at the West Baden Springs Hotel.

After pulling up his zipper Jennings checked his watch, seeing the minute hand closing in on five o'clock. Already a preliminary race had been run on the soggy turf, meaning the time for Phantom to run drew ever closer.

Jennings quickly washed his hands, hearing the sound of everything he did reverberate in the restroom because it was so open, with solid walls on all sides. He dabbed some cold water on his face, looking up to the mirror to see the gray uniform of a state trooper standing almost directly behind him. Complete with the matching campaign hat with the flat brim that many troopers and military sergeants wore, the man stared directly into the mirror, studying something. The trooper hadn't made a move for the stall or one of the urinals, and he certainly could have used the second sink to wash his hands.

Startled a bit, Jennings turned to speak to the trooper but Teakon walked through the doorway first, giving the trooper a nod before addressing Jennings.

"You shouldn't run off like that, Craig. One of the ESPN reporters wants a word with you."

"I already did an interview with them," Jennings groaned, starting toward the door as he shook the remainder of the water from his clean hands.

Margaret was due to arrive any minute with her son, so Jennings wanted all of the interviews and showmanship finished quickly. She absolutely wanted to see Phantom before he ran, and stand in the grandstand during the race. Jennings had made all of her wishes a priority because he cared about the grandmotherly woman and wished her the best of luck with her prize racehorse. He just hoped any success on Phantom's part came via natural means.

Following Teakon back to the stall, Jennings suddenly contemplated why the state trooper stood so silently behind him in the restroom. The man never stated his business, if he indeed needed anything from the pretend horse owner. Jennings decided he was just overthinking the situation after so many hours of observation as security chief at the hotel. Shrugging to himself, he decided more pressing issues required his attention.

***

Lincoln Daine found it necessary to modify his original plan. He had spent the better part of the last year creating and modifying his Kentucky Derby heist while winning bets in lesser sports as means of support. He mentally prepared himself for the security presence, over one hundred thousand people in attendance, and the need to get close to whatever horse was the long shot after placing a major bet.

Two issues still plagued him so late in the afternoon. He hadn't been to the windows to place a bet, but only because he hadn't used his cursed cube on Desert Phantom quite yet. He originally planned to murder someone and take their life essence outside of Churchill Downs, but he decided to arrive early and scout the grounds and activities first. Dressed as a Kentucky State Trooper, he moved about freely without anyone questioning him. Somewhat surprised at his luck, he already possessed a cover story ready if a real trooper questioned him. He knew many of them came from all across the state to work security, so he had a fairly remote post and assignment ready to tell them in reply.

The uniform came from a trooper he deemed the right size and build almost seven months prior who lived outside of Lexington. Daine studied the single man's habits before breaking into his house one day when the trooper reported to work. The lack of household pets and a security alarm made for an easy entry without detection, and within ten minutes Daine possessed the items he needed, complete with hat and name badge. He truly hoped the real Mike Stephens wasn't assigned to the Derby, and even if he was, the chances of the trooper working around the stables seemed remote. The younger troopers were assigned more menial duties like traffic control and standing near the entrance gates.

He had thoughts of strangling the southwestern cowboy standing at the sink because a gunshot would create too much noise, but Daine couldn't afford a lasting struggle either. While the looks of the man dressed in black indicated wealth, Daine stood close enough to him to smell his cologne, which didn't smell like a designer brand. After years of socializing with people on both ends of the financial spectrum, Daine analyzed people by smell, attire, and posture almost instantly.

Taking a thoughtful breath, he tapped the knife folded in the pocket of the stolen pants, thinking he needed a weaker victim as he left the restroom. Selecting a victim and killing him or her wasn't the main problem because he needed somewhere to stash the body where it wouldn't be found for at least an hour or two following the primary race.

By then he planned to be driving through Ohio or Indiana to a new destination with a sizeable check. Daine needed somewhere quiet and secluded, not because he feared being discovered, but rather to avoid losing money to his recurring gambling habit. If not for that weakness he might have retired from the vicious cycle of taking human life to earn money a year ago.

He didn't especially like murdering people for personal gain, but putting his gambling habit to rest felt impossible. Perhaps the earthy-brown cube in his other pocket pushed him toward the card tables and slot machines because it could never be satiated. Daine didn't understand how an inanimate object could possess will or thoughts, but he knew the cube wasn't just a passive device, waiting listlessly for someone to use it.

Walking along the stables, Daine noticed people practically everywhere. And though no particular area housed a mob, it seemed owners, trainers, and reporters stood along every corner. He desperately needed to find someone isolated from the crowd and a seldom-traveled location in which to store a body. Forcing himself to watch rigidly while studying everyone around him, Daine acted the part well, having observed other police personnel throughout the day and watching video from the previous year's Derby.

Most of the police working security remained near what he assumed were assigned areas, so he dared not kick up dirt in the same locations too many times. Daine decided to walk around the stable buildings, along their sides that faced fencing and walls, hoping to locate a straggler who might be heading to a restroom or one of the lesser populated beverage and food areas.

Much of the ground consisted of packed dirt, sometimes atop concrete surfaces, and new, smooth blacktop occupied the areas closer to the gates for loading and unloading of livestock. For some reason the dirt around the stables didn't look nearly as milky as the track, but Daine wasn't taking in the sights. He watched every person within his peripheral vision to see where they were heading and if they might be an easy mark. He wanted the cube charged and ready for the second phase of his plan. The race was over an hour away, but the jockeys and owners took the horses out of the stalls well before that to parade them along the dirt track's straightaway toward the gates to be loaded for the Walkover.

Beginning to walk with urgency, Daine scoured the stall areas for *any* straggler far enough away from the noise of reporters and the security of other people milling around the stables. He felt like a lion, hunting for a gazelle separated from its pack, or injured to the point that it couldn't run very far. He passed a few stalls that weren't being used in one of the rear buildings before spying his quarry slowly shuffling toward a marked restroom area less than fifty feet from the last stable quarters.

"You'll do," Daine said under his breath, watching an older gentleman hobbling on a cane toward the bathroom with a hunched back.

He entertained visions of placing an "Out of Order" sign on the door once he finished the dirty business of murdering the old man to keep people from entering the restroom stall. The custodial closets usually weren't far from the restrooms, often seated in a small space between the men's and women's doorways.

Daine continued to study the old man, who shuffled along at a snail's pace, wearing new clothes, as though this might be his one and only Kentucky Derby. He might have been an owner's grandfather, or perhaps a ceremonial guest from one of the past Churchill Downs events, but Daine intended to make this the man's last appearance on the grounds. As the man finally slipped into the restroom, Daine trailed him to the door, planning to carry out what needed to be done before covering up his crime.

If all went according to plan, he would leave Churchill Downs with millions in just over an hour.

CHAPTER 32

By the time the procession for the Walkover lined up, Craig Jennings wanted to hang his head in failure, but he still had a part to play. Absolutely left in the dark because he'd been isolated from everyone in his camp, including Teakon, the pretend horse owner joined trainer Jeff Slaton and Manny Garcia. Garcia was the primary stable hand who spent the most time around Desert Phantom at the stall. Much like a colorful parade, trainers and some of the ownership camp walked counterclockwise around the track from the stables with their respective horses in front of the thousands in attendance. For some horses it was unnerving because many had never been in front of such a huge crowd and heard thunderous applause.

Jennings knew the Walkover was a cakewalk compared to the race itself when the jockeys and horses required every ounce of concentration.

Teakon had left his side to escort Margaret Stough and her son to the prime seats reserved for their entire party since they were owners. Eventually Jennings would join them to watch the race, unable to imagine how that moment was going to feel. Intuition told him either Daine succeeded in using the cube on the horse, or the killer decided to skip the race for some reason. Not hearing from Greene bothered him immensely, and no one had seen or heard from Clay Branson all day.

"You ready for this?" Slaton asked as they fell in line for the prestigious parade.

"As I'll ever be," Jennings answered.

Under ordinary circumstances owners spent their day hobnobbing with socialites, placing bets, and drinking mint juleps or other various spirits. Because Slaton had recently pulled a muscle in his back he wasn't able to provide jockey Johnny Gomez with the traditional leg up when he mounted Phantom. Jennings volunteered, particularly since horse owners from the New Mexico area preferred to be hands-on in training and races whenever possible. Following such traditions kept Margaret happy, and Jennings felt morally obligated to abide by her wishes since she allowed Clouse and his people to enter the horse ownership aspect of her life.

"When do we meet up with Johnny?" Jennings inquired as the group slowly walked onto the track.

He looked across the crowded infield, spying the famous twin spires atop the grandstand roof. Sounds of the crowd reached their ears whenever the spectators seated there spied local favorites or some of the better known horses and trainers.

"He's with the other jockeys getting the traditional photo," Slaton replied. "We'll meet with him for final instructions shortly."

Jennings tried to take in the whirlwind of activity around him, still concerned about his overall objective lying in ruins like a train wreck. The not knowing pained him because on two previous occasions he had nearly fallen victim to the murderous ways of corrupted men possessing the cursed cubes.

Deciding he was powerless to do anything at this point, Jennings simply accepted his role, surrounded by overcast skies and a far weaker breeze than the morning brought. His black boots immediately took on a thin layer of dirt and mud as he found it slightly difficult to walk. While the track didn't have standing water, the muddy surface felt like quicksand, ready to plant him in the ground.

Numerous reporters walked in stride with trainers, asking each of them questions relating to their horse, or in some cases, their thoughts on their horse's chances of winning the Derby. Jennings fell back when an NBC analyst questioned Slaton about the trip from New Mexico and Phantom's up and down finishes the past year. Slaton handled the inquiry like a pro, furthering Jennings' assessment that the trainer knew his way around a racetrack, no matter how big the stakes.

Positive he was within view of the camera, Jennings really didn't have any other choice. Besides, it wasn't as though he led a secret life like the evil men who possessed the cubes, using disguises and manipulation as they made their way through life. Jennings simply stared straight ahead or looked at the chestnut colt walking in front of him, happy to let Slaton talk on national television.

When the reporter finally moved to the next interesting story behind them in line, Jennings glanced at the crowd, seeing lots of white and colorful dots, each representing a suit, hat, or dress of some kind. By this time there wasn't a vacant seat in Churchill Downs and a buzz of electricity ran through the crowd in anticipation of the annual race.

The procession ended when the groups entered a tunnel leading to the paddock area and walked their horses into tiny stalls. The stalls looked more like divider walls with decorative wooden backings and the name and number of each horse above its respective staging area. On Wednesday Jennings and Teakon had sat in a room with every other owner and trainer to learn which starting position they would receive through luck of the draw, or in some cases, bad luck of the draw. The team drew the number eight slot from a field of twenty, which Slaton informed them wasn't too bad. While no position proved overwhelmingly better for horses placing, Jennings knew the starting gates along the two ends were often recipes for disaster.

Shortly after reaching the temporary stalls the command for riders up was given and Jennings provided his jockey a leg up before breaking off to meet his group in the stands. His pass got him past security as the call to the post was trumpeted from across the dirt track. A friendly state trooper cleared a path for him at the entryway to the seating and pointed out the appropriate direction after Jennings provided the seat numbers. When he spotted Teakon, the two exchanged uneasy glances before Jennings stepped forward to give Margaret a reassuring hug and her son a handshake.

"It's the moment of truth," he said gently, giving her a genuine smile because he wanted her to own a champion thoroughbred. He then turned to Teakon on his other side. "No word at all?"

"Nothing," the man answered with a shrug.

"You both look so handsome," Margaret said, unaware of the turmoil both men felt regarding her horse.

Both uttered sheepish thanks, wondering how many people took notice of their black duds and cowboy hats. Jennings hadn't been in the seating area long enough to know how many other owners surrounded them but for Margaret's sake he was going to hoot and holler like a high school sports parent when the race started.

He heard an announcement being made about local sponsorship and the track management before the announcer asked everyone to rise for the sentimental singing of "My Old Kentucky Home" as a university band played the song. Teakon handed him a program that contained the song lyrics, so Jennings joined the thousands around him in song momentarily, realizing the song was one of loss, which he knew something about. As he belted out some off-key lyrics, Jennings noticed the horses beginning to amble toward the starting gate, and a knot formed in his stomach.

The breeze picked up as a floral smell crossed Jennings' nose once more, just as the sun broke temporarily through the clouds above.

"I'm so scared," Margaret confessed as the first of the horses were loaded into the gates.

"Me too," Jennings replied, though his fears stemmed from knowing a murderous bastard might still be on the loose.

Jennings suddenly wished he would have remembered binoculars, but a screen across from their seats provided a view of the action. Wasting little time, race officials ushered the horses into the green metal gates, closing them within the small area until all eighteen horses still entered in the contest were loaded. Two horses had been withdrawn for various health concerns over the past twenty-four hours, making the field smaller and the betting more interesting.

Barely two seconds passed after the last horse was loaded on the far end of the rail before the starting bell rang and the gates flew open with a thunderous gunshot noise. Jennings kept rocking between his boot heels and his toes as he looked from the track to the screen, seeing both provided him an ample view of the race as the horses all flew out of the starting gate almost all neck and neck.

The field quickly became a cluster as jockeys moved their horses toward the inside rail to shorten the running distance for their horses. Jennings searched for the horse with the "8" on his blanket, but the crowded field made it impossible to see any numbers. He changed his strategy, trying to decipher the blue and gold uniform Johnny Gomez wore out of the colorful pack as they streaked down the main straightway.

"I can't see him," Margaret's son said, trying to look through binoculars.

"There," Teakon spoke up, finally spotting their horse. "In the middle."

Jennings picked up on the colors about the same time his colleague spoke the words, finding Phantom and Gomez stuck between a few other horses. By the time the first turn came about, a few horses had already dropped off the pace, freeing up some space for the frontrunners. Gomez still didn't have anywhere to maneuver, but he kept Phantom safely in the center of the pack without brushing against any other horses and upsetting his own mount.

"Oh my," Margaret said, cupping her mouth and nose with her hands in nervous anticipation.

Feeling like his head was about to explode from the one-hundred-fifty-thousand voices reverberating around him, Jennings concentrated on locking his eyes onto the gold and blue silks worn by Johnny Gomez. As the pack rounded the first turn it grew difficult to track any individual horse because the group became one brown blur.

Turning his eyes to the screen, Jennings felt disheartened and happy at the same time when he saw Phantom in the middle of the pack when the group rounded the next bend. He noticed Gomez trying to hold the horse back because Phantom wanted to surge forward and the jockey was trying to conserve the horse's energy until the end. Jennings questioned just how much extra the colt might possess in his reserves.

Teakon nudged him in the ribs, apparently reaching the same conclusion.

"Johnny is really struggling with him, Craig."

"I noticed," Jennings replied just above a whisper. "It might be nothing. The horse likes to surge."

Grimacing, Teakon said nothing more as his eyes locked on the screen. He gnashed his teeth noticeably, nervous about the outcome like his undercover partner.

When the horses entered the backstretch, little changed except the third and fourth place horses were jostling for position. Phantom remained in the hunt, and when the horse to his left started to falter, Gomez moved him closer to the rail to shorten their ride to the finish line. He visibly continued to hold the thoroughbred back, even while entering the far turn as mud spat upward from every raised hoof. Jennings glanced at Margaret and her son, who both appeared to be holding their breath in anticipation of the impending photo finish. A few more horses had now dropped off for various reasons, but half of the eighteen starters still remained in contention for a place or showing.

Jennings watched the screen as the field rounded the bend into the final turn with a centralized cluster of horses still leaving little room for maneuvering. He spotted the horse he claimed to own in part on the screen, watching Phantom enter the last turn as Gomez finally turned him loose to use every bit of his energy reserve with half a mile left to run.

"Dear God," Teakon muttered as the jockey guided Phantom through two horses that ran dangerously close to the rail.

By comparison, they looked like their gas tanks had expired and Phantom had used a form of illegal booster fuel to overtake them. He passed them within seconds as he entered the straightaway, closing ground between his position and the five leaders remaining ahead of him. Jennings abandoned the screen as though it might deceive him in some way, wanting to see the finish with his own eyes since it would occur directly in front of him.

Down the final straightaway the horse closed the gap as though he was custom-built to run on muddy tracks. He passed the fifth place horse in seconds, securing the fourth position a few seconds later. Only a few lengths now separated him from the three leaders and Jennings unconsciously grasped Teakon's arm, shaking it just slightly from nervous anticipation.

"Hey!" Teakon said, though not in a scolding manner because the competitive bug had bitten him as well. "He might pull this off!"

Jennings stole a look at Margaret, who appeared on the verge of collapse from the excitement of her adopted colt making a name for itself and her family. She held her shaking hands before her, perhaps in prayer, as Phantom passed the third and second place horses almost in succession, leaving only the leader in front of him with less than two hundred yards to the finish.

Gomez barely used the jockey whip as Phantom naturally pressed forward, pressuring the leader almost immediately. For a few seconds they were neck and neck and Jennings felt his body tense from the excitement of being part of history, even if he wasn't a true contributor. They were seconds away from seeing the winner cross the finish line, and Jennings subconsciously grabbed hold of Teakon's arm once again, jumping up and down briefly like a kid about to receive a birthday present from behind a huge curtain.

Teakon didn't seem to mind, his own eyes locked on the horses as he clapped and whistled before holding clenched fists in front of him, channeling energy for Phantom to pull off the impossible.

Both of them observed the final one-hundred yards with baited breath, watching the other horse suddenly run out of steam while Phantom continued to press forward until the finish line where he finished by two lengths.

All around them the crowd went wild while Jennings and Teakon shared hugs with Margaret, her son, and virtually everyone around them. After receiving some high fives from the remainder of spectators and owners around them, the pretend owner and ranch manager locked eyes, exchanging concerned looks as the reality, or the possibility of a different reality, entered their minds. The only bright spot Jennings considered was that the thoroughbred didn't run away with the race like an illegally enhanced athlete might.

Regardless of what they thought, or how they felt, the two men were committed to trudging forward with the ceremony. Neither wanted to wait for the truth, especially if they were powerless to stop someone from being murdered right under their noses, but no one had called or sent a text message their way as of yet.

Jennings followed Margaret and her son toward the nearest exit as they were expected on the infield for photographs and interviews momentarily. Teakon followed without so much as a word, knowing full well what his uncle sacrificed to save lives, even giving his own in the process to protect others.

He wanted out of this dirty, dangerous business, but only if he knew others wouldn't suffer because of his self-indulgence.

CHAPTER 33

Greene knew from the moment the horses left their stables that his chances of finding Daine were practically nonexistent. He monitored Desert Phantom closely and never saw anyone other than the usual staff approach the horse before Margaret Stough's trainer and stable hands came to retrieve it for the procession leading into the race.

"This is hopeless," he muttered, watching several horses prance by as he and Liz watched from the side of one of the stable buildings.

"There isn't anything more we could have done," Liz said, touching his arm with her gloved hand.

Sometimes he wanted her to touch him with a bare hand, not because he sought intimate contact to advance their working relationship to a personal level, but because he simply felt shunned. Liz claimed she tried to avoid touching all people, but she made it a special point to never have contact with Greene. He couldn't recall any abnormally shameful event from his past, and there were no skeletons in the closet that might embarrass him. During their time together Greene told her about growing up in Tennessee, and passed a few hours talking about some of his more interesting cases with the federal government.

Liz touched the horse at a few different intervals, but nothing triggered her ability. Considering there was no science behind her visions, Greene wondered if maybe her powers simply didn't work, or required a recharging of some sort, but the possibility existed that Lincoln Daine never came to the Kentucky Derby, or he somehow slipped past them.

Or he simply chose a different horse on which to use his cursed object.

Neither of them gave up, even after the horses began the walk to the paddock as Liz set to touching the components of Phantom's stable while Greene followed the horse, monitoring the horse's surroundings like a Secret Service agent. His pass only got him so far, however, until the true security force halted him to let the procession pass through some gates. Since he wasn't part of any team, Greene was forced to wait where he stood, feeling his blood pressure rise. He couldn't move forward, and he couldn't readily get to the stands, so he decided his only option was to have Liz continue making contact with people and objects.

She complied, but it wasn't long before the introductions came over the speakers and Greene knew he was too far away from the action to make a difference in time. With glum expressions he and Liz listened to the race without watching, feeling content their secretive mission was a waste of time until the very end when Desert Phantom suddenly made a push to win the race by two lengths.

"Shit," Greene muttered, turning around to discover a sight that heightened his fears.

He found several state troopers and emergency medical technicians standing over a prone body beside one of the isolated restrooms. Drawing closer, Greene didn't want to interfere or draw their attention because he wanted to know if Daine found a victim prior to the race, or something completely unrelated occurred.

Gaining a better vantage point, Greene noticed the person lying on the ground was dressed in a Kentucky State Trooper uniform. His hands were tied behind his back and a wallet was placed atop his pants around the thigh area. One of the troopers picked it up to examine the contents, and Greene dared step close enough for a look, discovering a Tennessee driver's license with a picture of the man he knew as Lincoln Daine and a completely different name on the identification.

He moved back toward Liz before the authorities noticed him, hoping the troopers would reach the conclusion he easily came to with a mere glance.

One of them hunched over, comparing the name tag on the uniform to the identification in the wallet, shaking his head slowly. He handed the wallet to his fellow trooper and they shifted their stances enough that Greene noticed the man lying on the ground didn't appear to be conscious. In addition to that, his hands were also bound behind his back with plastic disposable restraints like the type police officers often used.

"Didn't one of our guys down south have his house broken into?" one of the troopers asked the other, receiving an affirmative nod in reply.

Greene felt newfound respect for Clay Branson because he never once saw the man on the premises that day, yet he felt certain the cop made good on his promise to assist with finding Daine. Apparently he went above and beyond his promise, apprehending the man without assistance and almost certainly saving a life in the process.

"I think our work is done here," he informed Liz, leading her away from the scene before more gawkers stopped to look.

"Did our invisible member strike?"

"It seems so."

Greene looked around, wondering if any security cameras in the area might have caught the events leading to the imposter state trooper's capture. He didn't immediately spy any equipment, but that didn't mean footage wouldn't be appearing on the evening news. The matter of retrieving the cube from Branson remained, but Greene felt safer knowing the cube was with him rather than Daine.

He led Liz to the ground level of the stands where they arrived just in time to see Jennings and Teakon standing beside the horse with Margaret Stough, her son, and the rest of their staff. The roses were already laid across Desert Phantom and the official photographs were being taken by a staff photographer while freelance and newspaper photographers took the best shots possible from further distances. Jennings and Teakon played their parts well, but Greene decided to let them off the hook by sending Jennings a text message so the pair could finally relax.

After this the winning team was escorted up the stairs of a pagoda where television crews surrounded them and the governor of Kentucky made what sounded like a speech for a television spot before handing Jennings the trophy. Jennings quickly passed off the golden icon to Margaret as the reporters asked him how he felt about joining the ownership team recently and winning the greatest race in the world. Extremely humble, he answered that he felt blessed to have helped Margaret bring her horse to Kentucky and that she deserved all of the credit. Bringing a flushed redness to her cheeks and a tear to her eye, Jennings had completed his job because Clouse would honor the agreement and allow her to buy back full rights to the horse.

Once the reporters asked Margaret and her son a few questions they switched to Jeff Slaton and Johnny Gomez who had made their way up the white ceremonial building as well. Greene watched Jennings read the text message on his phone from afar as a wave of relief crossed his face and he whispered the good news to Teakon.

A night of celebration and parties awaited the winning team and Greene wished he could join them, but his job came first. He needed to get Liz back to Indiana and make contact with Branson. From there he would hide the latest cube or surrender it to Clouse who usually turned any cursed objects over to Julie Knowles in Massachusetts.

He understood she kept watch over some kind of secret vault where all sorts of security measures kept anyone except her and a select few from entering and taking hold of the cursed objects hidden inside. Of course some of the select few were lost at sea when Clouse tried to send one of the cubes to the depths of the Bering Sea. Greene doubted some of his employer's planning, but he still felt confident Clouse meant well with his actions.

At least Greene could return to Indiana with good news for the man who signed his paychecks for a change.

CHAPTER 34

Matt Teakon survived a hellacious night of partying after Margaret Stough's horse won the Kentucky Derby. He barely consumed any spirits, but he awoke with a terrible headache the following morning, intensified by the fact that he only slept a few hours. And though he didn't directly participate in interviews with numerous morning shows and local networks, he stayed with Jennings until his cohort offered to drive them back to Indiana.

Another full day of rest prepared him for the trip to Amherst, Massachusetts where he was to deliver the latest cursed cube to Julie Knowles. Clay Branson handed the cube to Russ Greene rather unceremoniously before the group left Kentucky. He explained briefly how he simply disguised himself as a rather feeble old gentleman who relied on a cane to get around. Once Lincoln Daine revealed his true colors and attempted to murder Branson it was a simple feat for the trained assassin to subdue him and reveal the man's crimes by placing his wallet where authorities could readily retrieve it.

Everyone accustomed to locating the cursed cubes found Branson's demeanor difficult to read. They weren't certain if he was any closer to joining their cause or if he simply wanted to use them until he located Nosagi. Either way, the job was nearing completion. Teakon estimated they possessed all of the cubes except for two or three, not counting the one discarded into the unforgiving Bering Sea, which wasn't likely to see the light of day ever again.

"We're almost there," Julie Knowles said when she saw Teakon walk through the door with the cloth-covered cube.

He treated the cubes as living, breathing entities, never allowing them to see the light of day for fear they might turn men to stone like Medusa or lure them with a siren song to conduct evil deeds. It was the same reasoning his uncle used when he transported the cubes outside of their group's secret vault, placing them in a lead box that shielded them from human eyes and made them difficult to detect.

"A few more hazardous trips and we might lay hands on all of these," Teakon replied, handing the concealed cube to Julie.

She said nothing more, simply turning to head downstairs and place the cube in the vault where its siblings resided. Keeping them in one spot wasn't ideal, but the vault contained nearly a dozen safeguards against intruders that would kill anyone who tripped two of them in succession. Mark Teakon designed and practically built the entire level below the bookstore over the course of a few years before his death. His access to historical documents and people in the know provided him with knowledge about the cursed objects long before Paul Clouse's troubles with two particular cubes ever began.

"I got this letter from one of your uncle's old college contacts yesterday," Julie said upon returning and retrieving the sealed mail from beneath the old cash register.

"Thanks," Teakon replied, tucking the letter into his shirt pocket. "You could have opened this. Uncle Mark didn't have any secrets from you."

Julie simply shrugged, perhaps doing a kindness by letting Teakon feel connected to his uncle once more.

He normally dressed business casual regardless of his daily schedule, so Teakon continued to wear button-up shirts after the horse racing ruse ended. Khakis replaced his black jeans, and leather sandals took the place of cowboy boots the day after Desert Phantom made history. Add a cup of expensive coffee in one hand and he might pass for a campus regular like the professors.

"Have a look at that," he said, clenching his fist and moving it closer to Julie so she could view the new ring on his left hand a bit better.

Much like a Super Bowl championship ring, the large gold band was custom made for the ownership team of the Kentucky Derby almost immediately by a jewelry store in Louisville. Primarily gold with some silver trim and the championship trophy enclosed by a horseshoe in the center, the ring was full of detail, likely costing thousands to create. The current year and the words "Kentucky Derby" were wrapped around the top of the ring in a full circle.

"Very nice," Julie said, examining the ring closely. "About time you got some bling."

Teakon chuckled, fully aware that he didn't spend much money on his appearance after working on ranches in rural areas for so long.

Looking through the huge storefront windows, Teakon noticed a slightly purple hue overtaking the sky as dusk came to the East Coast. He walked toward the front door to flip the open sign over when he noticed a large black SUV stopping suddenly in the closest available parking space to the store. Most of the other shops lining the block closed around five, so he didn't understand why someone risked whiplash to take an unopposed parking spot. When four men, two of them armed with automatic weapons, stepped from the vehicle with unfriendly scowls, he received his answer and turned immediately to Julie.

"We need to get downstairs! Now!"

Julie barely found time enough to return a stunned look before Teakon clasped her by the arm and led her to the secret entrance behind the counter. Unlike the main entrance to the vault, this one took them directly to a lengthy panic room that required a code upon both entrance and exit. Short of military-grade weapons, no unwanted visitor could gain access to the room.

Teakon heard the front door being kicked in while he closed the secret entrance behind him. Sounds of wood splintering and glass shattering entered the store without hesitation, as though the thieves were confident they could simply snatch their objective within seconds and disappear. Following Julie down a dimly lit stairwell, he knew no one would be able to get to them or access the vault without making a major ruckus. With luck the brazen thieves might give up once they realized the difficulty of obtaining their prize.

Knowing robbers didn't knock off bookstores, even major chains, Teakon deduced someone was after the cubes specifically, which sent his mind racing. A very select few people knew about the cursed objects, so either a traitor betrayed their camp or a patient outsider was finally making a move.

When the pair reached the basement an imposing steel door awaited them with an electronic keypad beside it, slanted for easy use upon a slab jutting out from the door at hand level. The clomping of footsteps above them provided Julie with enough sense of urgency to type in her personal code quickly upon the keypad. After she pressed enter on the device the door swung open, granting the pair access to safety. Teakon hesitated only to wipe down the keypad with his shirt, trying to eliminate any material left from human fingers in case their visitors tried determining the code by using chemical means or a thermal detector.

"Who the hell could it be?" Julie asked as the door sealed shut behind them with the sound of hydraulics activating.

"I don't know," Teakon answered, looking to make certain both of the panic room doors were secure.

Aside from the one that took them upstairs, another door existed that opened in the heart of the vault, providing them virtually equal security inside its thick concrete walls. Mark Teakon spared no expense when building the shelter, and he considered every possible contingency, including betrayal from within. A number of failsafe options were installed that both the younger Teakon and Julie knew about, but neither expected anyone else to join them in the bowels of the bookstore. Though a phone seated in the center of the room provided access to 911 and police help, Teakon and Julie knew involving the police might cause trouble that outweighed any potential danger.

A dozen security measures separated the intruders from Teakon and Julie, but a noise caught Teakon's attention and his head snapped upward to look at one of the six monitors that watched and recorded various areas of the store on down to the vault. He saw the two armed men, now wearing masks and dressed in black, along with another masked man who seemed to be directing them. Touching his ear occasionally, the stranger acted as though he was talking to someone through an earpiece on his phone, directing the fourth individual to look ahead to the next trap.

"How do we pass through that?" he asked the fourth individual, who did not wear any disguise.

Feeling his body tense from concern and a sense of dread, Teakon realized the group had already penetrated two of the traps. He sucked in a deep breath, seeing something familiar about the fourth man, whose presence appeared to be against his will. Shaking his head negatively, he refused to say a word, but momentarily the unarmed man shoved his face up to a retinal scanner, letting the laser analyze his right eye.

"Dear God," Julie muttered quietly when she looked up to the same monitor. "It can't be."

"It is," Teakon conceded as the three villains passed the third defense system, dragging his unwilling uncle along with them. "Damn it."

How on earth Mark Teakon survived gunshot wounds, freezing water, and months under the radar, his nephew didn't pretend to have a clue. Either Todd Parish lied about the events aboard the *Shamrock*, or the bastards who nearly caused his demise scooped him from the deadly sea like a wounded sea lion. A completely unwilling participant in their scheme to bypass the security measures, Teakon said nothing and stood numbly beside the unarmed masked man. To his nephew, it almost seemed as though they had already extracted the information from him, but if that were the case, why would they bring him along?

"Oh, no," Teakon muttered nervously, three consecutive times, realizing exactly why his uncle remained alive as he saw the weathered, weary look scrawled across the man's face.

"What is it?" Julie asked, touching his arm.

"Remember that I told you Liz thought someone on the other side was getting into her mind?"

"Yes," Julie answered, though her shaky tone indicated she still didn't understand the problem.

"Whoever that guy is talking to is reading my uncle's mind in real time."

Julie muttered something that went unheard as Teakon contemplated several possible ideas to either save his uncle or rescue the cubes from evil clutches. There simply wasn't a way to disable two armed men to retrieve his uncle, and the elder Teakon would berate him for not putting the work of harboring the cursed objects first. But if he dared enter the vault, the chances of him collecting all of the cubes before the men entered the vault were slim.

Julie's life also rested in his hands, and though she was committed to the cause, he wasn't going to see everything lost to the goons making their way closer to the vault.

"I'm going to grab a few of the cubes," he informed Julie, punching his personal code into the second door before she could stop him.

A beep and a hydraulic "whoosh" later placed him inside the vault where a musty smell hammered his nostrils. His uncle hadn't designed the vault with the idea of making a finished basement someday.

The large vault held several secured areas where the cubes were stored for safe keeping. Each of them required a keypad code for access, but the code was the same for each safe built into the walls of the vault. Figuring he could recover a few of the cubes, not being particularly picky about which ones he grabbed, Teakon left the door to the panic room open as he set to opening the first safe. Without looking, he snatched the cube from an elevated perch and performed exactly the same maneuver with the next closest safe, using up a valuable minute overall.

"Matt!" Julie screamed out the door at him, indicating he needed to return to the safety of the panic room.

Her shouted warning startled him, causing him to bobble both cubes before they eluded his grasp and landed on the floor with their coverings, one tumbling beneath a nearby table. Teakon knelt down to recover them but the immense main door to the vault made a stone-on-stone grinding sound as it slid to one side like some kind of Egyptian crypt from the movies. Suddenly confronted with the three men holding his uncle hostage, Teakon barely found time enough to dive for the door to the panic room before bullets struck the floor behind him.

Julie stepped forward to pull the door shut, sealing them safely inside as the gunmen rushed into the room. Regaining his footing, Teakon stared through the thick glass window into the eyes of the leader with the wireless phone device in his ear. The man said nothing momentarily as his henchmen tried opening the door with every means possible short of shooting at it. Apparently realizing the glass and both doors were virtually impenetrable, the trio turned their attention to Teakon's uncle.

Wasting little time, the three men searched the vault, discovering the safes lining the vault's walls. In the meantime, Teakon looked to the eyes of his uncle, finding them bloodshot, sunken, and defeated as the man stared into the concrete floor. Even while standing still his body seemed to sway slightly, indicating some form of drugs ran through his system. Either his abductors wanted him to speak, or think the truth, or they used a serum to keep him subdued. His skin appeared ashen and his drastic weight loss led his nephew to believe he'd been severely mistreated for months and kept alive simply as a source of information. Teakon's uncle deserved a better fate than this, but he could only stare at him through the security of the only window in the panic room. No matter what, he needed to make certain he survived with Julie to carry out his uncle's wishes.

He berated himself for dropping the two cubes before ducking into the room, but at least the evil group couldn't possess the entire collection, even if they cleaned out the vault.

"I'm sorry, Uncle Mark," he said through the glass, doubting his blood relative could hear him through the layers of protection.

For the first time his uncle looked up, looking to Teakon with the last of a defiant fire in his eyes, silently telling his nephew to stay strong no matter how far these armed bastards took this fight.

"How do I get into this safe?" the man with the phone earpiece asked their captive.

Mark Teakon tried to resist assisting the villainous men in any way, the strain showing on his face, but when his thoughts were plucked from the air like fireflies into a jar, his resistance was futile. Moments later the leader of the group typed in the correct number for the keypad of the safe, retrieving one of the cubes.

"Pick those up," the man ordered one of the henchmen who had been standing watch over the sealed door of the panic room.

Teakon knew it was a matter of time before the masked leader asked his uncle for the code to the panic room, but he already had an idea how to handle that predicament when it arose.

"Give me the code to this safe," the leader ordered the elder Teakon after he walked briskly to the next secure door along the wall. "It's the same, eh? I guess you never figured anyone would beat you at your own game and get down here."

Hanging his head, Teakon barely found strength enough to look at his uncle while the intruders went through the remaining safes and stole all seven of the cubes hidden within the basement of the bookstore. When he raised his head, several tears streamed from one eye as he looked to the man who helped mold him while fighting to keep the world safe from tyranny. No man could ask for a better role model than someone who sacrificed everything to keep others safe. If Mark Teakon possessed a weakness, he simply lacked the ruthlessness necessary to keep the cursed objects safe from greedy mercenaries.

Realizing no cavalry was coming for the two people locked in the panic room, the three men took their time until the leader walked behind Mark Teakon, virtually whispering his next phrase into the man's ears, feigning secrecy.

"I want to know how to get into that panic room so I can clean up this mess."

Knowing his uncle couldn't help but compromise his colleagues, Teakon reached for a lever seated just a foot or so away from the window. Observed by the man standing outside the window, who was likely receiving the information from his outside source, Teakon watched a sinister grin finally cross the man's lips. With Mark Teakon's code available to him, the leader of the trio reached for the keypad on the door, but as he touched the first number Teakon flipped the lever upward, effectively killing the power to the panic room, including the entry doors. The monitors, powered by a different circuit, continued to glow and illuminate the two people safely trapped inside the panic room.

Teakon watched the arrogant smirk twist into an angry scowl on the man's face.

"Open the door or your uncle dies," he threatened.

"You can't!" Julie insisted just above a whisper, gently touching his arm.

Keeping his hand on the lever, Teakon refused to throw it downward.

"I know."

Looking his uncle directly in the eye, he pressed his hand against the glass, and his uncle slowly did the same, overcoming whatever mind-numbing drugs they pumped into his veins at last. Both knew the move effectively signed the elder Teakon's death warrant, so they said a silent goodbye through the glass. Teakon felt tears trickle along his cheeks as the thought of losing his uncle a second time overwhelmed him. He found it difficult to look his uncle in the eyes due to guilt, but he understood the need to survive and carry out the man's lifelong mission.

"Goodbye," his uncle mouthed the word through the glass as a pistol was positioned behind his head.

Already knowing he was doomed, Mark Teakon barely uttered his farewell before his blood and brain matter stained the glass.

Teakon immediately turned away, breaking down as his back slumped against the wall and he slid to the ground, sobbing uncontrollably. He could only wait for his enemies to leave before briefly mourning his uncle and moving forward to pick up the pieces. Regrouping wasn't going to be easy, particularly with most of the cubes now in evil clutches. About the only saving grace was that they hadn't found the book that accompanied the cursed cubes, but if they were able to pluck thoughts like radio waves, Teakon couldn't even trust himself with knowledge.

"Damn it," he said, burying his head in his hands, feeling absolutely helpless.

CHAPTER 35

Despite the major setback, Julie and Teakon traveled to Indiana the next day to meet with Greene and Clouse to share their bad news in detail and hopefully learn something from the video footage shot while the two were trapped in the panic room. Toting a briefcase filled with their evidence and the leather-bound book containing the names of everyone that ever possessed a cube, Teakon crossed the atrium of Clouse's hotel with Julie by his side.

Knowing the police and the coroner's office would take the bookstore hostage, the two removed anything they might need from inside the building before calling for help the previous day. Julie also made copies of the footage from the security system's hard drive for them to keep because the police indeed confiscated the hard drive for their investigation. Talking to authorities wasn't easy, but Teakon kept his composure for the most part and explained that the thieves took valuable gemstones from the basement. He found he was able to provide a factual account of the events, simply leaving out the parts about cursed objects and psychics. When the police inquired about the stolen property, Teakon said custom gems were taken, which wasn't an untruth on his part.

When he thought about it, Teakon understood why the leader didn't ask how the group located the cubes. Any rational person would speculate about letters or diaries, possibly never suspecting a cursed ledger that kept track of the cubes. Regardless, the question was never brought up, but Teakon saw firsthand how effective the methods of his adversaries proved.

"You holding up okay?" Julie asked as they pushed open the door for the stairs descending into the basement.

"As good as could be expected I suppose."

He wasn't looking forward to attending a second funeral for his uncle. The first time emotionally tore him apart, but he hadn't witnessed his uncle's alleged death and there was no body. Now he bore witness to Mark Teakon's execution and wanted to divorce himself completely from the bookstore to avoid recalling the horrific image.

Questions remained about how his uncle survived a fall into freezing waters after being shot in the chest. Choppy water no less, Teakon thought as he remembered being told details of the trip by Clouse. Of course the details came secondhand from one of Clouse's paid henchmen, who happened to be standing outside of the secured conference room down the hallway from the stairs Julie and Teakon used.

"Go ahead," he told Julie. "I'll be right in."

Stopping directly in front of Todd Parish, Teakon drew close to the bodyguard until their noses were separated by only a few inches.

"You said my uncle died in front of you," Teakon virtually growled.

"I said your uncle was shot in the chest, maybe the shoulder, and toppled off the side of the boat," Parish answered evenly. "The chances of someone surviving in freezing water without the appropriate gear for more than a few minutes are thousands to one. So, yes, I assumed he was lost at sea."

"And you couldn't be bothered to check?"

Parish's expression grew outright perturbed.

"Bullets were flying in my general direction. Your uncle himself made it clear that disposing of that cube was the first and foremost priority."

"Dropping it to the bottom of the ocean was *his* job. *Yours* was to tag along and keep him safe at all costs."

"Look, I'm sorry for your loss, really I am, but there's no need to lay this at my doorstep."

"I disagree," Teakon said, feeling his face grow hot because any number of minimal differences on that fishing vessel might have left Mark Teakon alive and the cubes securely locked in the vault.

Frustration, more than anything, caused him to take issue with the bodyguard when he knew full well his uncle's mission meant more than his own existence. He was about to walk away and conduct himself properly when Parish decided to critique the situation further.

"Maybe you're just upset with yourself because you followed his orders and locked yourself inside a fortress instead of saving him."

The words infuriated Teakon to the point that he spun and lurched toward the collar area of the bodyguard's suit.

"You mother fucker!"

Each of them exchanged a few punches around the facial area, neither causing much damage from such close range, until Clouse emerged from the room to break up the skirmish. He pushed Teakon back before restraining Parish with his free arm.

"This is the *last* thing we need right now!" he scolded them both with his tone. "Placing blame isn't going to bring Mark or the cubes back. If we're going to do right by him, we need to work together and find the people behind yesterday's attack."

Parish simply scowled before walking into the conference room without another word. He wasn't about to disobey the man who signed his paychecks, but Teakon still felt he crossed the line by implying he cowered behind concrete walls while his uncle was murdered.

Closing the door so no one else inside the conference room could see them in the hallway, Clouse placed his hands on Teakon's shoulders.

"I know you're hurting, and I appreciate you coming here with everything you have. You have my condolences and prayers, Matt."

"Thanks. I'm not sure what hurts more, losing my uncle again, or failing him."

"We haven't failed yet. They don't have everything, and even if they do plan on bringing the cubes together they need to know the ritual."

"That's what scares me, too. We have a book, but we have no idea what those pricks really know."

"I know," Clouse said, stepping back with understanding and sympathy in his eyes. "But I have some ideas, and if these guys were desperate enough to invade your sanctity and put themselves on camera I have a feeling we can turn the tables on them."

Teakon nodded, suddenly feeling numb as he truly let the events of the past twenty-four hours enter his mind for the first time. Everything felt like one big blur, but dwelling on the invasion would keep him from concentrating on the moment and helping people who shared in his beliefs catch the men responsible. Still, he fully realized how close he came to dying the previous day at the hands of people who thought nothing of taking human life.

"Let's do this," Teakon said with as much resolve as his mind permitted.

***

Harlan Stone suspected his benefactor wanted to continue whatever secretive activities he was conducting without the agent's assistance. Though Alan Stewart claimed he needed to return Stone to his old position temporarily for his own good, the agent suspected otherwise. He considered the possibility that Stewart somehow learned about his field trip to Texas, or perhaps the Deputy Director found someone else to carry out his dirty work.

Being assigned Dom Givens as a partner made the transition a bit less traumatic, but Stone's mind constantly wandered. He questioned why he was relegated to New Mexico when Stewart could have easily assigned him to his home state instead. Something didn't add up, and he feared not reaching the conclusion in time to save some lives, including his own.

By placing Stone in New Mexico, Stewart could easily track his movements by monitoring the local Special Agent in Charge.

"You daydreaming again?" Dom Givens asked from the driver's seat of their assigned sedan.

"Nah," Stone answered, shaking off any lingering thoughts as he stared out the passenger window at the desert passing in a blur. "Explain to me again why Lord Asshole is sending us to a motel in the middle of nowhere again."

Givens chuckled.

"Supposedly an informant has red-hot information about a murder-for-hire and won't meet us anywhere else."

"Murder-for-hire?" Stone questioned. "Sounds a little highbrow for Elliot to entrust to the likes of us."

"He assigned it to *me*, partner, and I'm damn lucky he let me keep it. He still hates your pasty white ass."

"Glad to hear he hasn't smartened up."

Givens continued to drive, casually drooping his hand over the steering wheel as he grinned.

"You two are like oil and water. Why do you hate authority so much?"

"Maybe I've just never had a boss worth liking."

"Maybe you Texans are just as stubborn as the mules you ride."

"Oh?" Stone retorted with a chuckle. "At least we don't take surfboards to work like you California types. That way you save the planet by not using fuel while you're battling the evil known as commercialism."

"It helps us sleep easy at night," Givens said, playing along.

"Roller skating along the beach and chasing tail," Stone said dreamily. "Must be nice out there."

Givens laughed.

"Not nearly as fulfilling as bronc riding and cooking barbeque squirrel on the grill, I reckon."

"I can't believe you'd stereotype us Texans that way."

"Your grammar is proving me right. Besides, you're the most racist partner I've ever had the pleasure of being assigned."

Stone scoffed aloud.

"You call yourself all kinds of names and say I did it. That would make you clinically insane in the eyes of most quacks, my friend."

Stone stared out the window momentarily as the morning sky began to show the infant stages of a blue, cloudless canvas. He questioned how long his exile from specialty work might last, or if Stewart planned to disavow himself completely from the agent.

"So, what was your temporary new assignment all about?" Givens inquired.

Stone shrugged while he cleared his throat uncomfortably. He wasn't entirely proud of the body of work he carried out during his time in Ohio and Kentucky, but an unstated need for secrecy kept him from elaborating.

"Mostly surveillance details."

"They dragged you away on some super-secret assignment just to watch someone? They could have any field agent conduct surveillance."

"You calling me a liar?" Stone kidded with a raised eyebrow.

"I'm just saying that you're holding out on me. There's all kind of crazy talk around the office about you going to work for the big man in

Washington. And the way you left with barely a word made me wonder if that shit was true."

"You're just reading too much into it, Dom. It was business-as-usual kind of stuff, but I'm sworn to secrecy."

"Can't even tell your partner?" Givens goaded him. "That's not right, Stoney."

Stone shifted uneasily in his seat. He felt a need to protect Givens by not telling him anything specific, considering the recent turn of events.

"I'm not trying to bust your balls," Givens finally said, relieving the tension. "It's good to have you back, partner."

"It's good to be back."

Stone looked out the window again, seeing nothing except dry, brown flatlands along the Chihuahuan Desert, sparsely dotted with plants that appeared near death. Now well south of Albuquerque, Stone didn't recognize the land or any recent landmarks. Of course he hadn't worked in the state very long, and neither had his partner, but Givens appeared to know exactly where they were heading without benefit of a navigation device.

"You know where we're going?" Stone questioned, looking over to his partner.

"Of course," Givens said confidently. "Matter of fact, it's dead ahead."

Staring ahead, Stone spotted what appeared to be the ruins of a very tiny town with a gas station and a motel readily visible. He thought a few dilapidated houses might have stood some distance behind the gas station, but it was impossible to tell until they drew closer. The entire scenario looked like one of those areas in a low-budget movie where scummy bad guys ambushed the heroes. He questioned why any informant would want to meet two federal agents in such a distant, isolated location.

Touching the firearm nestled along his side, he grew wary as they neared the strange little settlement.

CHAPTER 36

louse looked around the room once the doors were shut, essentially sealing everyone inside the conference room for a look at the video footage. No blood remained on the carpet, and the body of Chase Dalton's impersonator now resided in a shallow grave along the outskirts of some farmland in Monroe County. He decided to take care of the matter personally to avoid placing his friends and employees at risk.

Matt Teakon stood in a distant corner while Todd Parish sat at the table, closer to the screen, looking rather uneasy. Clouse knew all too well that frustration caused Teakon to lash out at Parish from having lost so many of his own close friends and family to heartless, greedy people he thought were allies.

No idle banter filled the room because the tense situation of losing Mark Teakon a second time, along with knowing all of their hard work had just gone down the drain, deflated a lot of spirits. No one, Clouse included, expected to find any evidence in the video to help them locate the people responsible for stealing the cursed objects.

Greene and Liz sat beside one another on the opposite side of the table, and Jennings attended the meeting in case he noticed anything familiar from his time at the race track. Despite an invitation to the gathering, Clay Branson failed to show, leading Clouse to question the man's devotion to anything except finding his former mentor. The glimmer of hope that stemmed from him retrieving the cube at Churchill Downs dissipated with him turning his back on the group once again.

For the first time in a long time Clouse began to lose hope regarding their mission. As long as men with evil in their hearts knew about the cubes the quest could never end.

Julie Knowles started the video footage, which ran through a projection machine onto the huge white wall it faced. Though painful to watch for everyone, the footage provided more detail than real life had for Julie and Teakon. While Teakon said a painful farewell to his uncle and avoided being killed, Julie worked her magic at the video surveillance controls, zooming in whenever possible on the bookstore assailants.

She started with the leader, confirming he was a Caucasian man somewhere around six feet tall, which they pretty much already knew. The microphones captured his voice, and they learned his eyes were a form of hazel. Aside from those few details, they knew nothing else about the man other than the fact he seemed to relish his authority.

"Anything?" Clouse asked Greene, whose eyes remained glued to the image of the man frozen on the wall.

"It's not much help," Greene admitted, "but I might have some contacts who can run his voice through an analyzer."

"Wouldn't you need a sample database for comparison?" Liz asked.

Her experience assisting with police provided some knowledge of their procedures on her part.

"My one buddy designed a program that can go through a sample database or check every single video that's uploaded online for a match. Unfortunately that can take a *very* long time to complete."

Julie allowed the video to continue, pausing as the screen showed a van outside of the bookstore, providing a full view of a man seated inside the passenger seat of the van. He spoke toward the dashboard every so often, indicating a communications radio was mounted there, or some form of speakerphone perhaps. It quickly became clear he was the man responding to the leader's inquiries from inside the bookstore's basement. All eyes slowly gravitated toward Liz, who understood the gravity of the situation because this unknown man was picking her brain for information. When the video came to a close-up of his face, Julie pushed pause, providing a detailed image of the man who likely caused the entire group so much grief.

Not exactly the face of a monster, the man appeared slightly heavyset and only confident when he spoke into the dashboard. When he sat, his body language indicated a timid, uncertain individual who placed his hands near his chest in a praying position, except that he left his fingers curled. His red hair was thinning atop his round face, and he appeared to still have childhood freckles dotting his face, despite an age Clouse guessed to be early twenties. The man spoke normally and clearly enough that everyone in the room came to realize the man before them likely possessed above average intelligence, but perhaps childhood obesity and incessant teasing made him antisocial.

Liz stared at his face, and though she put on a brave front, she felt intimidated because she knew nothing of this individual and it felt as though he had already violated her in every imaginable way.

"Can we locate that van?" she asked aloud with resolve.

"It's probably a rental," Greene surmised. "I'd imagine that we can."

"Think you might learn something if you lay a hand on it?" Clouse asked her.

"I hope so."

Everyone in the room suspected answers would never come that easily for them. They were at least one step behind the collective robbing all of the cubes, but just one fortunate break might put them back on even playing ground.

"You don't have to do that," Greene assured Liz in a hushed voice.

"I *need* to know. Flushing them out is the only way to stop them."

Once everyone stopped conversing, Julie started the video again, which showed closer, more detailed images of the two henchmen who also wore ski masks to hide their identities. One was a fairly stout, powerful white male who did not appear to have any facial hair beneath his mask because none showed when he adjusted the mask's fit a few times. He wasn't as tall as any of the other men in the room with him, but his rigid posture and confidence with an automatic weapon seemed to indicate he was possibly former military. Some soldiers returned from overseas to work at the postal service, or at some local government position, and some found higher wages as mercenaries.

Clouse stared intently at the second masked man, because he was the one who inevitably pulled a sidearm and ended Mark Teakon's life. Julie had already informed him of this, and he wanted to know the man's identity because anyone who killed such an idealist deserved the same in return.

Like the other henchman, this one never spoke a word, but he didn't stand or act as regimented as the first. He certainly didn't lack confidence, though, and when the time came to eliminate Mark Teakon he did not hesitate or question orders. In fact, it took little more than a word from the leader to prompt the act.

"Who are you?" Clouse questioned under his breath.

About the only two things he knew about the man were that he also had no facial hair, and his skin color was that of a black man.

***

A red light went off in the back of Harlan Stone's mind as his partner pulled past the decrepit gas station with its cracked front window, and a faded realtor sign residing unevenly in one corner. Amazingly the pumps were not removed, or even covered, and the price set on their gauges indicated the gas station hadn't functioned in nearly eight years. Even the plastic sign cover looming over the station barely hung by a screw, swinging with the breeze as though daring someone to saunter carefree beneath it.

While the idea of a motel and gas station in the middle of nowhere likely appealed to a weary traveler, Stone understood why it probably wasn't financially feasible to keep either business open with rising business costs. After a brief glance at the gas station, Stone quickly focused his attention on the motel about a hundred yards ahead of them on the opposite side of the road.

"I don't see anyone," he noted as Givens pulled the sedan closer to the front of the building.

The building consisted of one main stretch containing about ten rooms and a check-in window for the manager on duty. Another four rooms branched off from one corner, giving the motel an "L" shape. Faded to an unsightly olive green, the hotel walls were also trimmed with sand and cobwebs. The roof looked like it might collapse if anything heavier than a house cat dared step foot atop the gray shingles, and Stone couldn't help but suspect they were driving into some sort of trap.

"Let's drive around back and make sure we don't have any extra company," he suggested to Givens.

"You're awful jumpy today, partner."

"And you don't seem the least bit concerned about driving the better part of two hours to meet an informant. Is he thinking about settling down and owning a business here?"

Givens chuckled.

"Hard telling."

A drive around the rear of the motel revealed absolutely no vehicles parked on the property, so Givens checked behind the gas station and around the two small houses. The duo found no vehicles anywhere in the isolated settlement, leading Stone to question if their supervisor sent them on a wild goose chase. It wasn't above Elliot to punish him with nonsensical assignments, but typically Givens was spared the wrath of their egocentric leader. Despite his usual lack of common sense as an FBI supervisor, Elliot knew better than to tinker with Givens, fearful of a discrimination grievance landing atop his desk.

Following the full search of the area, Givens parked in front of the motel, putting the car in park before killing the engine.

"So we're just going to wait?" Stone asked as he raised his voice to ensure his objection was clearly heard.

"Maybe the guy's running late. What's got you so riled up today?"

"My patience with life in general is wearing thin."

"You're just mad because the wizard brought you back from Oz to work in the pits with the rest of us."

Stone grinned, rolling down the window to find the dry air already growing warm. Dressed in a long-sleeve shirt with a tie, as usual, he fully expected to be perspiring within minutes if he remained inside the stuffy car. He opened the door to stretch his legs and survey the area further.

"You thinking about buying some property out here?" Givens kidded.

"Not unless this place gets annexed by Texas."

Opting to stay in the sedan, Givens opened a booklet of some sort, studying its contents.

In the meantime, Stone walked along the front of the motel, his nostrils detecting a musty odor as his boots clopped along the dirty concrete landing. Naturally curious, and looking for anything to occupy his mind, he tried the door of the room closest to him, finding it open as it swung inside with a creak.

"That's not the least bit creepy," he muttered to himself, stepping inside the dark room.

Flipping the light switch provided no further benefit and the smell only intensified with the door open. Stone stood aside, letting natural light fill the room to reveal two beds and a nightstand covered with dust. No television or phone remained within the room, and Stone wasn't daring enough to look inside the bathroom. Instead, he stepped outside to find everything much the same, growing impatient with their directive, especially since Givens seemed so calm and collected.

Stone strolled toward the office area, peering inside the glass surrounding the small sliding door where the money was exchanged for a place to stay. Apparently the departing owners made certain to clean out their belongings before heading to whatever grand horizon awaited them.

Looking to Givens, Stone tapped the watch on his left hand with his two forefingers, indicating he was growing tired of waiting. His partner simply shrugged helplessly, quickly turning his attention to the radio to search for a working music station.

Refusing to stand around, Stone walked from one end of the motel to the other, enjoying the shade that the overhead awning provided. It wasn't until he reached the last room along the lengthy portion of the hotel that a strange sound reached his eardrums. Freezing like a statue, Stone listened intently for what sounded like a whimper, or perhaps a muffled cry for help. He slowly turned his head toward the final room as he reached for the doorknob, clasping the firearm holstered at his side. Deciding not to alarm his partner until he proved his imagination wasn't working overtime, Stone pushed the door open as he drew the Glock 22 from his holster.

Seated in an old wooden chair, and strapped tightly to it with numerous synthetic ropes, Kristina Turpin looked to him with widened, desperate eyes, hoping he was there to rescue her rather than add to her torment. A gag encumbered her mouth, preventing her from elaborating upon the peril of her situation. Stone immediately deduced the events surrounding him, his gun clearing its holster too late to assist him as he heard someone step onto the motel's landing behind him.

"You were on the way up," Givens stated, his firearm trained on Stone's head when the agent dared steal a glance. "The boss had big plans for you until you went snooping around."

Stone let his firearm slide into the holster, though he refused to release it from his grip completely. Options raced through the agent's mind, but none of them provided safety for Kristina. Diving for cover put her in the line of fire and didn't necessarily remove him from harm. Turning around while raising his firearm would assuredly get him shot and killed, and curiosity compelled him to find out why Givens was working with Stewart.

He hated the idea of surrendering his firearm and practically signing his own death warrant. While he worried about his own survival, he felt obligated to protect Kristina because he placed her in this precarious situation.

"Tell me, Dom, will my wife be okay after we're all said and done here?" Stone asked, his hand still seated atop his firearm.

The Glock remained in the holster, but loose of the security mechanism that kept the average person from disarming him.

"Oh, they'll find your body, partner. Eventually. She'll get your pension and wonder why you and another dead agent's wife were having a fling."

Stone gnashed his teeth, incensed that a dishonorable death awaited him. His hopes and aspirations for a greater career blinded him to whatever personal gains Stewart placed ahead of human life.

He remained halfway turned around, considering the possibility of testing his right arm's quickness. Knowing full well Givens wasn't going to let either of them leave the motel alive, Stone preferred going out shooting, rather than being shot like a rabid dog.

Kristina made muffled noises through her gag, but any pleas were lost on Givens. Only now did Stone realize the man played him, acting a role better than some Hollywood stars who took home Oscars. Stone looked into her eyes with a solemn indication that he was going to make the only play that might save them.

"You've got it all planned out, don't you?" Stone asked, trying to survey the area around him, realizing no cover existed, particularly while he stood in the open doorway.

"It'll all be covered at a higher level, but you needn't concern yourself with the details, Stoney."

Stone shook his head negatively, hoping his aim was true to atone for his mistakes the only way he knew how. He sucked in a deep breath, drawing his weapon as he turned to shoot down his own partner.

Before he even turned enough to think about firing a shot, he heard the sound of Givens' gun and felt the impact of a bullet entering his abdomen, followed by another round into his right shoulder. The second shot effectively forced Stone to drop his firearm because his fingers and arm felt a spasm go through them that loosened his grip. As he slumped against the doorway, Givens walked over to retrieve the Glock from the ground.

"You're fast, but even you aren't that fast," Givens commented with a confident laugh. "You see, our boss paired me with you to test you out. When I thought you might be the right material for our little team he gave you some simple tasks to test you out. But your little deviation to Texas let us know you were getting too curious for your own good."

Stone couldn't decide whether to clutch his shoulder or try applying pressure to his stomach wound. The shoulder wasn't going to bleed out, and most of his bleeding from the first bullet was occurring within his vital organs where he couldn't prevent his eventual death. Only a surgeon could save him at this point, but he didn't care about his own life so long as he found a way to stop Givens and Stewart from going further with their plan.

"You won't get away with whatever you're doing," Stone stated between labored breaths. "There are people who know."

"Oh, like Clay Branson, the man you did a piss poor job of watching? We have something special in store for him. And just yesterday we carried out the biggest part of our plan in Massachusetts. I've got a big payday coming my way. You would have, too, if you could've stuck to your orders."

"Stewart's going to fuck you hard in the ass, Dom. You're going to wind up in some roadside ditch once he gets what he wants."

Stone groaned, forced to clutch his stomach as the burning sensation inside began to spread. Kristina continued to sob and plead for mercy through her gag, but the words bounced off Givens like bullets hitting Superman.

"All that loss of blood is going to get to you, partner," Givens said. "We better wrap this up quickly, hadn't we?"

Stone gave him the middle finger in response, prompting a grin from Stewart's henchman before he lifted his gun and fired a bullet squarely into Kristina Turpin's forehead. Blood splattered upward before her head slumped forward and her body grew limp in the chair.

"You bastard!" Stone cried, trying to crawl toward Givens to get one last lick in before the man ended his life.

Instead, Givens forcefully kicked him in the shoulder, flipping him back toward the door and Kristina's body.

"You just killed her, buddy," Givens said. "That's what the report is going to read."

"You don't care about anything, do you?" Stone fired angrily, fighting through the pain.

"I care about cold, hard cash. And I mean it when I say you killed Kristina. If you hadn't gone to visit her, she never would've been the wiser about her husband's death. And she certainly wouldn't have contacted an old friend in the Bureau and asked for a second look into Jack's *accident*. But don't you worry about them finding anything new in Jack's death. When I took care of him I made sure it looked legit."

"You should be proud," Stone said sarcastically.

"Thanks. See, Jack was a bit of a loose cannon like you, so Stewart took a liking to him. He even sent Jack to Ohio to offer Clay Branson a spot in our little club, but Branson turned him down. Jack snapped a guy's neck while he was there, pretty much saving the day while he showed what a badass he was. It wasn't until Jack developed a conscience and started snooping that he became a threat."

Stone clutched his stomach, beginning to feel a little cold from the loss of internal blood.

"Stewart thought you were just the man to replace him. You weren't above bending a few rules, could handle a firearm pretty well, and you were even from Texas, just like Jack. But I guess he was wrong about you."

"You can go to hell, Dom. And take Stewart with you."

Givens simply smirked at his partner's final cliché statement, lifting his gun to fire the bullet that ended Stone's suffering.

A low whistling sound reached Stone's ears at the same instant the point of an arrow pierced Givens' chest, sticking out about three inches when it came to rest just below his sternum. Sucking in several labored breaths, the dying agent slowly looked down to the metal point jutting from his chest. A mixture of confusion and shock showed in his eyes as the firearm dropped from his right hand and his fingers reached up to touch the arrow as though it might be some form of illusion.

No sooner had he touched it than he fell to the ground in a heap, dead so far as Stone could tell. The agent strained to see his unknown savior beyond his dead partner's body, discovering little more than a silhouette because his consciousness faded with each passing second. Despite his best efforts, Stone failed to hold his head up long enough to identify the blurry figure walking his way. He passed out before knowing if the stranger intended to rush him to a hospital or wrap him up like a loose end by snuffing out his life.

CHAPTER 37

louse pulled Julie Knowles aside after the meeting, deciding he wanted to search for a different solution while his team attempted to locate the men responsible for stealing the cursed cubes. Nothing earthshattering came from the video, but at least Greene and Liz provided a glimmer of hope, especially if Greene's contacts located the van used in the heist.

Some of the group lingered in the room, talking amongst themselves, or returned to their duties if they worked at the West Baden Springs Hotel for Clouse. He and Julie stood in the hallway, away from prying eyes and eavesdroppers.

"What can you tell me about the origin of the cubes again?" he inquired.

"Just that they were created shortly after the end of World War I. Of course we know who all of the first thirteen conspirators were because of the book."

"And what's the exact date they were created?"

"December 17th of 1918. Why?"

Julie appeared perplexed that his inquiry was suddenly so important in the scheme of their current plans.

"Didn't you or Mark ever consider it odd that we had two of the cubes hovering around this particular area for years?"

Clouse spoke of the two small towns that housed numerous hotels when gambling was at its pinnacle.

"The thought crossed our minds, but we never had time to investigate it further. And no one ever stepped forward with historical information."

"Probably because everyone who knew about the cubes from the old days is dead. I know a little about where they've been, but I also know the history of this valley. Before Los Angeles, Chicago, and New York were the haunts for celebrities and millionaires, everyone who was anyone came down here for the healing waters or the gambling."

Catching on to what he was implying, Julie looked at Clouse with widening eyes.

"Could it be that simple?"

"It *could* be, but I can't guarantee the things were created right here in little old Orange County."

"Right in one of your hotels, perhaps?"

Clouse shrugged doubtfully.

"While some evidence has shown up here before, I don't think this is the place where they would have done the deed considering all of the foot traffic. I'm going to do some historical research and see about hotels, churches, and any businesses that might have been condemned, torn down, or maybe changed hands around that date or early 1919."

"Be careful," Julie said earnestly. "We don't know who's watching us these days."

"I know. I'm about to take precautions to hide my family, and until we find out more about this psychic helping the bad guys, I don't want to know where they are. I miss them like hell when we have to do this, but it's safer for everyone I know if they can't be kidnapped and used as pawns."

Julie gave him an empathetic look.

"I know you've been through this several times. It doesn't get any easier, does it?"

"No, but you've been through a lot yourself this past year. If we can all get on the same page, maybe we can end this once and for all."

"You're right. There can't be that many people left who know about the cubes if it's taken this long for someone to come after us."

"And I'll bet whoever's in charge of their organization isn't planning to leave any loose ends once he obtains the entire collection."

"Whoever these people are, they would never have gotten as far as they have without that psychic. If he can get inside Liz's mind, any of our minds for that matter, we'll never be safe."

"I know," Clouse said, hanging his head momentarily.

He felt as frustrated as anyone, thinking he was ahead of the game when he recruited Greene and Liz to assist him. Such a gift, almost a superpower of sorts, wasn't meant to be used for such evil purposes. All of his hard work, from hiring people to hunt for the cubes to aligning himself with Mark Teakon and his people, suddenly felt worthless. He found it strange how all of the wealth left to him by one of his former mentors could never make things right. Of course that mentor turned out to be pure evil, which also helped set the horrific events of Clouse's life in motion.

"You can't go back to that bookstore," Clouse stated more than suggested to Julie. "At least not until we're absolutely positive we've eliminated the problem."

"Which might be never. But don't worry, I don't plan on returning anytime soon."

"You're welcome to stay here as long as you want to. I'm going to be keeping more security on the grounds just to keep all of us safe, and I have room in the sixth floor suite."

Julie forced a grin.

"I appreciate it, but I still have work to finish in Massachusetts. Besides, they probably won't be targeting me now that they have what they came for."

"I certainly hope not, but I'll be glad to send some protection back with you."

"No thanks. I'm sure Matt's coming back with me."

Clouse nodded.

"Let me know if you change your mind."

Before their conversation could continue, Matt Teakon emerged from the conference room holding a letter in his right hand with a stunned look crossing his face.

"You two need to hear this right away."

"Is that the letter I handed you last night?" Julie asked.

"Yeah. And it talks about the time travel cube, and exactly how the thing works."

Clouse immediately felt a tingle run through his spine at the thought of knowing how the most important of the cursed objects functioned.

"Who is it from?" Julie asked.

All three of them took a quick look around, not wanting anyone else to hear the findings until they deciphered whether the letter was genuine or some sort of fabrication. Clouse thumbed the opposite direction since the other conference rooms weren't being used at the moment.

"We can duck in one of the other rooms."

Once inside the room, Clouse went to close the door just as Todd Parish walked past. The bodyguard looked inside, seeing his boss with Teakon which brought forth a slightly wounded expression. Parish simply ducked his head and continued walking without a word. Clouse might have offered words of reassurance any other time, but he needed to hear what news the letter brought their group.

"The letter comes from one of the former cube guardians my uncle had gotten in touch with," Teakon began. "Apparently this guy was the one who held the cube before Tom Ervin took over the task. There's a journal entry written by some guy named Gene Lusardi who monitored the cube during the Fifties. The whole package seems legitimate to me, and if so, it explains exactly how that thing works and the danger it poses."

"Can we read it?" Clouse asked politely.

"Sure," Teakon replied, handing it over without delay.

Clouse read the companion letter first, which stated what Teakon had told them in a lengthier format. The letter was addressed to Mark Teakon in regards to an earlier inquiry. Apparently Teakon had convinced them he knew about the cursed cubes and requested any information about the time cube that might complete his archives. It was brief, and written by someone other than Lusardi, to help explain that the journal was found in the man's house after he passed away by the protective group.

Beyond that was a diary entry on a page torn from what Clouse surmised was an old notebook of some kind. The yellowed paper appeared dated enough to have come from the Fifties, and the handwriting wasn't particularly easy to decipher in the modern age where cursive was becoming antiquated. Still, he set it on the table and read the front page as Julie's eyes followed the same lines, equally curious to learn what the entry beheld.

11-20-57

Today I had the cube with me at work because I planned to move it to a safe spot after my shift. I know writing about this goes against the secret code we swore when we were chosen to watch over this thing, but this is the only way to keep myself sane. Since this is the only entry I am making about the cube in detail, anyone reading this will probably think I've lost my mind anyway.

My shift went by without a hitch. Just a few domestic dispute calls and a traffic stop because the guy had let his license plates expire. I let him off with a warning. Nothing to write home about. I was about to take the cube to its new hiding spot when I stopped for some coffee and a sandwich at one of the deli shops on South Clark. Bought a turkey sub, not very Italian of me, I know, but those things are delicious! Had the bag and my thermos in hand as I'm walking out of the deli when I spot this guy running down the street with what looks to be a bank bag in one hand. I might not have thought much about it, but he kept stealing looks behind him and people were looking at me in my uniform expecting me to do something. Because of the cube I didn't really want to act, but didn't feel like I had much choice.

There's too much traffic, so I throw my coffee and sub into my car and start chasing the guy on foot, yelling for him to stop. Of course he doesn't, so here I am chasing him for the better part of three city blocks before he finally ducks between some buildings to shake me. I've been on the force too long for some novice robber to shake me. He decides to run down the alley between these two apartment buildings, which I already knew didn't go very far. To cut down on crime the owner of the buildings put up a fence that isn't particularly easy to scale. Knowing he wasn't going far, I entered the alley a bit more cautiously than usual in case he had a weapon.

Good thing I did, because he took two shots at me when he saw my shoulder poke around the corner. I'd been yelling at him the entire time to stop because I was a police officer, so I didn't see the need to say it again. Now I knew exactly where the shots came from, so I hunkered down and threw some pebbles around the corner to distract him. Maybe I forgot about the precious cargo I was carrying, or the nature of my job just took over, but I came around that corner and shot him twice in the chest. He dropped the gun and the bag of loot right away, and as I approached him I saw the guy take his last few breaths.

I started to think of where I might use a phone to call for backup, but something inside me thought about the cube and how it worked. Here I'd just killed this guy, and self-defense or not, I had a chance to see how this power worked. Looking back, I wished I hadn't done it, but I took the thing out and instinctively I knew what to do. I stared at it a second or two and it was like the damned thing told me what to do.

Feeling a bit ashamed, I started to look up at the apartments to see if anyone was watching. There was snow on the ground, so no one opened their windows, and most people were still at work, so I didn't see no one. At this point I didn't care, because if the cube really worked, I was about to travel back in time and I didn't know if I'd be coming back. I just knew I had to think of the time and place I wanted to travel to and rub the thing on this man's blood. Kind of like a sick version of Dorothy and her ruby shoes.

There was only one thing I wanted to go back in time and see. My father had been shot and killed as a Chicago police officer before I graduated high school. They arrested some black guy for the crime. Gordie Brown was his name, but he always swore innocence. Something about his testimony stuck with me, because he never changed a detail in his story, and no one ever connected him to my pop. It always stuck in my craw, so I decided to see exactly what happened that night and maybe save my old man if I could.

No sooner had I pulled the cube from my work jacket and touched the man's blood with it when my surroundings completely changed. Here I was in the summer of 1934, still wearing my uniform, watching my pop from about a hundred yards away as he pulled up to a building in a patrol car. It was surreal because it looked exactly like I remembered it during the Depression. I could even smell fresh-baked bread somewhere in the distance, which seemed strange because it was nighttime.

The area where my dad was shot was on the outskirts of town and I watched him get out of his patrol car and knock on the door of this little house kind of set apart from the rest of the neighborhood. It's dark out, and he seems impatient about something until a woman answers the door. She's wearing a nightgown and tells him to wait a minute at the door, or something like that. I couldn't hear exactly what they said, but I walked toward him to warn him about the danger, or at least get a closer look. There was this patch of trees and shrubs between me and pop, but I kept pressing onward, not sure what I would do or say when I reached him. What could I say to him that wouldn't sound completely insane in time to save him?

Dad, I'm from the future and I'm here to save you, but I don't know from what?

I only knew he was gunned down, and I wasn't convinced the police caught the right guy. It wasn't until I was older that I realized this was a white neighborhood. People like Gordie Brown didn't waltz into these neighborhoods, and they certainly didn't tote guns into these neighborhoods. They still don't. And Brown had no previous arrests or trouble with the law, and no witnesses ever reported him owning a gun, much less using one.

Something just never added up.

I had about a hundred feet left to walk when I saw this car pull up behind my pop's patrol car. Two men dressed in plain clothes stepped out and my father knew them because they started talking about work, so I knew they were cops. Probably investigators the way they were dressed. I stopped behind a bush, thinking my pop was safe for the moment when one of the guys pulls out a gun while he's talking shop and shoots my father twice in the chest without missing a beat. As my pop lays there bleeding, the two men grab the woman and take off in their car as though they had just made a delivery instead of shooting someone in cold blood.

Before the car was out of sight I ran up to see if Pop was still alive. Part of me wanted to see if I could save him, but I just wanted to touch something physically in the past, just to make sure it wasn't some kind of dream. Call me stupid or greedy, but I didn't want to just see it in my head. I wanted to feel something to make sure it was real, but I didn't want to risk changing the past. The guys warned me about how the cube could be used to change things in the past, even if the person using it didn't realize the smallest little thing could alter the present we know.

It barely makes sense to me, so I'm sure if someone else is reading this you're probably thinking I'm off my rocker.

When I got to Pop he was already gone. I tried to resist, but I touched the blood on his shirt and felt certain I was about to sob after reliving all of the pain again, but in an instant I was back in the present beside the guy I just shot in the alley. It took a minute, but I pulled myself together before some of the guys from my precinct showed up. I'm sure what I experienced in the past was real because I came back with Pop's blood on my fingertips. The cube is now in a new safe place where no one else will use it, but I'm going to make sure no one sees this journal while I'm alive. The guys will think I let them down if they ever find out.

I'm glad I didn't change anything the night Pop died because I might have changed my own future. It ain't perfect, but things have turned out pretty well for this cop's son. Good night.

"Am I the only one who read that with a Chicago accent in my head?" Clouse felt compelled to ask. "I kept thinking he was going to say Da Bears any second."

Julie gave him a shocked look for being so offbeat during such a serious moment, but Teakon shrugged with a mischievous smirk.

"I kind of thought the same thing."

"Seriously, you two," Julie said with exasperation. "We just learned a major piece of information and you're laughing it up?"

"Lighten up," Teakon said. "It's not like we can scramble the military over a diary page. But I do have proof that our man was telling the truth."

Teakon produced a document from his back pocket that he placed atop the conference table for them to peruse.

"That's the police report from the diary date that indicates Lusardi indeed shot one Ronald David Thompson who had just robbed a restaurant for their deposit bag at gunpoint."

"Do you trust its authenticity?" Clouse asked, turning more serious because he wanted to know the power of the one trump card he still held.

"I'm inclined to think so," Teakon replied, looking to Julie who agreed with a nod.

"So we can assume the thing gives the user about a five to ten minute window and brings them back to the present in whatever state the present is after time travel," Clouse deduced. "I can't even believe I'm speaking these words. This is the kind of shit you see in films, not what you picture yourself saving the world from."

All three stared at the paperwork momentarily, better informed, but no closer to resolving their other problems until the rest of the team made some headway. Clouse hoped for a lucky break in the near future or the world was in for a whole heap of trouble.

CHAPTER 38

arlan Stone awoke to a daylight fringe around the room-darkening curtains inside what looked like a hospital room. He looked under the sheets, noticing he was wearing a hospital gown, feeling certain no underwear covered his privates beneath the disposable cloth. His right hand reached for his injured shoulder, followed by his abdomen, discovering both were repaired and covered with fresh dressings. Someone brought him to the hospital because he wouldn't have lasted much longer in the desert without assistance.

Lots of questions entered his mind, from who saved him, who brought him to the hospital, where the hospital was located, and whether or not Stewart sent someone else to finish the job Givens started.

Shifting his weight in the hospital bed, Stone found his two injured spots still tender after being surgically repaired. He wasn't attached to any monitors, though a device located on his right side provided the means to summon a nurse. None of his belongings except his eyeglasses surrounded him, so calling his wife with his cell phone wasn't an immediate option if he even dared try. Placing her in danger was the last thing he wanted because he took the risk of working for Stewart to benefit their marriage and lifestyle, especially if they chose to have children.

Stone was about to make an attempt to stand when the door opened, bringing forth a brunette dressed in a nurse's uniform who looked surprised to see him awake. He swiped his spectacles from atop the stand adjacent to the bed and put them on for a better look.

"Glad to see you finally joined us," she said, sauntering over to the bed.

She gave him a cursory examination, looking over his wounds before taking his pulse and checking his blood pressure.

"How did I get here?" Stone decided to ask, testing the waters to see how much information the staff would provide.

She responded with a suspicious stare as though he should already know the answer.

"Your friend brought you in after the search warrant execution went bad."

Is that how it went? Stone mentally questioned sarcastically, virtually confirming his suspicions that Clay Branson brought him in after sending an arrow through Givens' chest. How or why the dangerous man located him and decided to save him eluded the federal agent, but Stone felt certain Branson wanted information. All of his movements and phone calls away from Ohio stemmed from his search for one man.

Nosagi.

Stone had already witnessed what the trained assassin was capable of when he beheaded an even more mysterious killer in Louisville. After watching the video footage, Stone knew he wasn't a match for someone so capable of using firearms and handheld weapons. That kind of training required dedication and countless hours, above and beyond what any normal person in law enforcement endured after the academy.

"Have you seen my friend?" Stone inquired, not using a name because he wasn't going to blow Branson's cover story just yet.

"Not recently, but he was here this morning."

Stone looked at a clock, realizing a day had passed since the events in the desert.

"Where am I?"

"Roswell Regional," she answered casually. "I'm going to have the doctor come take a look at you, okay?"

"Sure," Stone answered almost absently, his mind already wandering.

A few minutes later the surgeon explained Stone's injuries and the surgery required to repair them. Surprisingly, he didn't probe or ask Stone anything, possibly deciding to let the agent heal before authorities bombarded him with questions about how he suffered his injuries.

"Have any police agencies been here?" Stone inquired.

"Local police were called since you were shot," the doctor replied as he stood to walk toward the door. "Your buddy talked to them and gave them the information. Don't you worry about any of that, Mr. Stone. Just get some rest so we can get you home."

At first Stone felt surprised that Branson used either of their real names, but the man probably used their police credentials to keep it under wraps, possibly spinning a story that someone might track them for retaliation. Strangely, Branson apparently tied their actions together, at least for the cover story, which meant he obviously didn't plan on murdering the agent and burying him in the desert.

At least Stone hoped that held true.

Settling in for a nap wasn't the wisest course of action, but Stone felt exhausted after the previous day's events and the toll the surgery took on his body. His eyelids grew heavy, and when the door opened again it revealed a very unwelcome sight to the practically helpless FBI agent.

Though he couldn't identify the beefy man dressed in the black suit, Stone knew this granite-faced individual couldn't be bargained with because he wasn't some local investigator sent to conduct an interview. No, Stone decided, this man was sent by Stewart to extract information and clean up any loose ends.

Loose ends like nosy agents who'd become expendable the past few days.

Finding it too late to fake sleeping, Stone wanted to see any danger coming his way firsthand anyway. The man walked with a purpose toward the bed, but didn't reach for the firearm bulging from the right side of his sport coat. Stone eyed him cautiously, prepared to defend himself with the limited means surrounding him at a moment's notice. Though he was new to accidentally siding with purely evil entities, Stone knew from his investigations concerning organized crime and old covert government dealings how such things went down.

Without a word, the man reached into his sport coat and produced a needle already filled with a clear fluid and removed the tip. The bag of saline beside his bed that sent an IV drip and pain medication to the needles stemming from his arm suddenly became his worst enemy. Stone's body tensed as he realized the mortal danger placed before him in the form of an undetectable chemical that would likely mask his untimely death as a complication following surgery. Often such deaths were ruled as heart attacks, strokes, or some form of blood clot. Stone didn't want his wife thinking he died as a result of shady activities, passing away in his sleep like some nursing home patient to boot.

He was about to use the last ounce of his strength to defend his life against the silent assassin when two arms emerged from behind the assassin, finding pressure points along the sides of his neck. With the blood flow temporarily cut off through the arteries in his neck, the man in the suit was helpless within two seconds. His eyes rolled back and he dropped to the floor with a thump, revealing his attacker to Stone.

"That was efficient," the agent said to Clay Branson, who had emerged from the closet beside the door.

"I suspect he was scouring every New Mexico hospital until he found you here, *or* the local police put some information out to your agency," Branson replied, pulling a bag with Stone's belongings from inside the closet. "I took the liberty of recovering these a few hours ago."

"Did you whack a security guard to get into their secure lockers?"

"I haven't *whacked* anyone since I saved your life yesterday. We need to get out of here before this guy comes to and calls his boss."

Stone looked to the plastic tubes sticking out of his arms, trying to indicate he wasn't in traveling condition. In response, Branson clasped his arm and yanked the needles from his veins with such precision that virtually no pain accompanied the swift action.

Left with no healing devices and nowhere else to go, Stone painfully scooted his way off the bed, staring at the unconscious man on the floor. He dressed as Branson monitored the door, still uncertain what his immediate or distant future held. Once he put on his shirt and tie, followed by his slacks and cowboy boots, Stone noticed the holster secured to his belt held no sidearm. He cleared his throat, pointing to the empty holster once his recent protector looked his way.

"You're not getting that back," Branson said without falter.

"It'll be hard to defend myself."

"You won't need to. After what you've done, you need to prove your worth, or you're going to have a lot more hospital bills."

Stone swallowed hard, though he put forth a tough front as he followed Branson out of the room, feeling a bit uneasy and lightheaded with each step. A need to right some wrongs plagued his subconscious, but he wanted to make certain this enigma of a man wasn't just another form of evil placed along his path.

He looked around, noticing one particular clothing item wasn't present. His black cowboy hat was nowhere to be found, but he hadn't been wearing it when he was shot by Givens. As a federal agent he didn't wear it during official business anyway, but he couldn't remember if he left it in the backseat of the Bureau's car, or at the New Mexico office. The location of the hat made a world of difference when it came time to explain the events of the past few days and what spin he placed on the story, if any.

When the elevator reached the parking garage a few minutes later, Branson stepped out first, surveying the area cautiously without allowing the injured agent to fall behind. Stone wondered if the hospital was going to accuse him of skipping out on his bills and turn him over to a collection agency. Until he felt safe, financial burdens could wait he decided as the sounds of unseen vehicles echoed through the parking garage. From his vantage point Stone couldn't tell what level they were on, though he remembered seeing a number three beside the elevator doors.

"Where are we going from here?" Stone asked, feeling his wounds flare with searing pain from movement so soon after the surgery.

He grimaced, struggling to keep pace with Branson until the sound of the elevator spun them both around warily to find a woman stepping forward, wearing heels and business attire.

"We're going to pay a visit to whoever told you to follow me," Branson answered once they started walking toward the line of parked vehicles. "Because the guy I killed in the desert was just hired help like you."

"I'm not just hired help," Stone said firmly.

"So you don't just jump at the mention of money or promises of glory? I know how people like you respond to people like that."

"Glad to know your degree in psychology comes in handy," Stone grumbled.

Branson led the way until they reached a gray Ford Mustang that looked like a rental car, particularly with a Virginia license plate above the rear bumper.

"Who was that guy?" Branson inquired.

"I've never seen him before," Stone replied, "but I'm sure my boss sent him."

The elevator made a dinging sound again, and both men saw the incensed face of the assassin emerge before he drew his firearm to take aim at them.

"I guess you *didn't* kill him," Stone commented before ducking for cover behind the rental car.

Apparently understanding that firing bullets would attract attention, the man did not fire, which left Stone uneasy because he wasn't armed and he wasn't sure Branson possessed the means to disable the assassin without the element of surprise. Stone looked to his right to ask the man a question but Branson was nowhere to be found.

"Mother fucker," Stone muttered, not daring to peer over the car for fear the sudden movement might make a nice target.

Hoping Branson was sneaking around to assault the man, rather than leaving Stone for dead, the agent decided to provide a distraction since he wasn't in any condition to flee.

"Hey, is there any chance we can talk this over?" he asked, receiving no reply.

His arm instinctively reached for his side, but the lack of weighty metal quickly dissuaded him from actually touching the holster. Stone fought to remain calm, but as two hands clasping a Glock appeared from over top of the car, his crouched position suddenly felt rather unsafe.

Thoughts of ducking under the car and rolling for cover entered his mind when a virtually identical scenario from the hospital room appeared before his eyes. Two arms appeared around the man's neck again, and though he moved to avoid being forced into unconsciousness again after his initial surprise, the stocky man only gained a second or two before he collapsed to the concrete. Stone stared upward, certain he appeared as dumbfounded as he felt upon seeing Branson take out a trained killer twice within minutes.

In the same exact fashion no less.

"We're bringing him with us since he refuses to leave us alone," Branson said, popping the trunk lid with the key remote.

After recovering the man's Glock and a secondary firearm holstered around his ankle, Branson also plucked a cell phone from the man's sport coat. He picked up the unconscious man's dead weight with relative ease, dumping him into the trunk with a thump a few seconds later.

"Won't he just burst through the backseat eventually?" Stone asked.

"Only if he wants to lose consciousness again. We can bind him later."

"We?" Stone asked, regaining his footing while his wounds continued to plague him. "If you're including me in your evil scheme I guess that makes us partners."

Branson shot him a penetrating stare, which preceded his slamming the truck lid shut.

"What?" Stone asked defensively. "You don't really think I'm stupid enough to go crawling back to my old boss after this, do you?"

"Based on your errors in judgment thus far, I'm not so sure. Get in."

Branson took the driver's seat, which suited Stone just fine because his wounds continued to sting and his energy felt depleted.

"How the hell did you find me anyway?" Stone asked once Branson backed out of the spot and down the parking garage inclines.

"I brought you to the hospital yesterday, trying to keep things under wraps."

"I mean how did you get there yesterday? We were in the middle of nowhere. Literally."

Branson exited the garage and quickly found a busy road that led toward highways and interstates.

"You're not the only one who can follow people, Special Agent Stone. I'd taken notice of your activities as far back as South America, and it wasn't incredibly difficult to learn your identity."

"South America? You have to be kidding. I was in a fucking plane."

"I didn't actually know, but you just confirmed my suspicions. Whoever you're working for really wanted to know my whereabouts."

Stone felt his blood boil at the thought of being duped by Branson, but his thoughts quickly turned to how Stewart used him before trying to dispose of him.

"I don't care what you think of me and what I've done, but I'm not an evil person," Stone said.

"But you're not squeaky clean, either," Branson said without emotion. "Even so, I think you got in over your head. I need to know everything your boss asked you to do these past few months before we pay him a visit."

Stone wouldn't have dared confront Stewart alone, primarily because the man held rank and power, but he somehow felt the man in the driver's seat couldn't be stopped when he put his mind to something.

"You'll want to head west," Stone said. "We'll have plenty of time to get acquainted before we reach Los Angeles."

He thumbed toward the backseat.

"What about the big lug in the trunk?"

"We'll probably keep him around awhile so he can't contact anyone."

Beginning to realize that Branson wasn't a murderous bastard, the agent believed Stewart had spun his web of lies to suit his own purpose. He used his own people and their skill sets to his advantage. The man wanted Stone dead, and probably would have taken out Givens at some point to tie up any loose ends. Either the man in the trunk was a government agent or someone Stewart hired as a mercenary to carry out the dirty work. Some former soldiers lost all traces of a conscience, willing to follow any orders so long as their bank accounts grew.

Stone wasn't looking forward to the long drive, particularly the informal interrogation, but he wanted to see the look on Stewart's face when he showed up unannounced, among the living.

***

By the time Stone and Branson reached Los Angeles the next morning, the two found an understanding of one another after piecing together the fragments of their individual stories. While Branson continued to hold out on some information, Stone knew more than Alan Stewart ever revealed to him. Still, Stone felt nervous about confronting the man who still technically oversaw his activities within the Bureau.

Because of the late start the pair stayed in a motel toward the western border of Arizona, keeping their unwanted visitor subdued with ropes they purchased at a hardware store, along with a gag to keep him quiet. Stone was curious about the man's identity and background, but Branson showed no interest in questioning him. Stone might have given interrogation a shot except that vehicles were parked in the slots adjacent to their room. Any strange noises or cries for help might have jeopardized their plans.

The next morning Branson opted to leave the would-be assassin miles outside of a community along a seldom-traveled road once they entered

California. Without transportation or a phone, the man couldn't possibly make a call for hours, particularly since Branson rendered him unconscious a third time far enough from the road that no passersby would ever spot him. They refused to untie him, buying them more time before he freed himself and began walking. Stone wondered if the man dared show his face to Stewart again because no respectable mercenary got bested three times in one day by the same adversary.

Using the navigation device in the rented car, Stone directed Branson toward the Los Angeles FBI headquarters. Even Stone still got lost in the large, unfamiliar city, but he knew the routine in any government building. He waited until Branson pulled the car into a visitor slot before speaking.

"You can't be bringing sharp, metal objects into this place, you know."

"I have a working knowledge of how municipal buildings operate," Branson replied testily. "Just get me in there however you have to so we can pay Mr. Stewart a surprise visit."

"If he's even here," Stone said, reading his watch.

Seeing it was nearly lunchtime, he imagined Stewart dined with bank presidents and people who dabbled in major stocks, drinking fine wine on their charity. Who wouldn't want one of the highest-ranked government officials on their side in case a sticky situation came their way?

"I'll need my Glock," Stone said, receiving a suspicious look regarding his request. "It'll look strange if a field agent enters the building unarmed."

Branson slapped the firearm into Stone's right hand before opening his car door.

"There are two ways we can do this," Stone surmised once he stood beside the rental car. "I can either register you as a guest, or we can act as though you're a suspect or material witness."

"Do you really think they'd let you bring a suspect to your boss? Just register me as a guest."

Stone shrugged.

"I just wanted to see if you could escape handcuffs, to be honest."

"Guess you'll just have to keep wondering."

Sliding his sidearm into its holster, Stone followed Branson toward the multi-story building, expecting nothing less from his agency's headquarters in one of the nation's largest cities. Once they entered the main lobby and cleared security, Stone inquired where Alan Stewart's office was located.

"Top floor," the secretary answered. "Would you like me to make sure he's in?"

"No, thank you," Stone answered. "He's expecting me."

Stone led the way toward the elevators, wondering how events were going to unfold momentarily when Stewart saw him alive.

"You lie very well," Branson noted once they occupied the first available elevator car. "And how do you *not* know where your boss's office is?"

"I've never actually been here. He wooed me in a neutral location."

Stone had already explained the false promises made by Stewart, and how the man never gave him any further orders than shadowing Clay Branson wherever he went. He also elaborated on how he deviated from the orders, and despite his precautions, Stewart discovered he visited the widow of Jack Turpin. Something within Branson stirred at the mention of the deceased FBI agent, but he said nothing. Stone sensed the man wasn't typically so withdrawn and silent, but this edgy, dark side of a man who stood to marry into a major theme park empire worried him.

"Did you know Turpin?" Stone decided to prod as the elevator car ascended.

"I met him once," Branson replied, his voice and expression devoid of emotion as he focused on the moment. "He offered me a job, probably working for your boss I suspect."

The Bureau didn't typically make it a point to recruit people individually, but Stone supposed the rogue agent program wasn't standard protocol.

"I guess I should feel good about being his second choice," he muttered.

"Don't flatter yourself. He's probably used and abused lots of people since he approached me."

"You have a gift with sentiment. If the theme park thing doesn't work out you might get work in the greeting card business."

Saying nothing, Branson simply glared with a minimal turn of his head.

A few seconds later the doors open, revealing the top floor of the building, which looked as spotless as the ground floor with light walls and shiny floor tiles. On this level there were no government logos imprinted into the tiles to exhibit pride and raise employee morale. Several pictures of ranking government officials, including the president, lined the walls behind the receptionist who basically acted as the first level of defense for the directors who wanted their visitors screened.

Stone scanned the names on a sign behind the young woman, finding Alan Stewart's among them.

"Ma'am," he said in his Texas drawl with a nod, not slowing down one second to allow her to offer assistance.

Branson followed the agent, conducting himself as though he belonged in the building. The pair soon approached Stewart's personal receptionist, a lovely woman with strawberry blonde hair who appeared a few years older than either of them. Stone wondered if his supposedly happily married boss and his receptionist conducted any business after work hours that he kept from his wife. He immediately chastised himself for jumping to conclusions simply because Stewart ordered a hit on him.

"Harlan Stone to see Deputy Director Stewart," Stone said, producing his identification since the personal assistant hadn't laid eyes on him before.

She consulted her appointment book, which looked reasonably blank to the agent as his blue eyes peered over the desk.

"I'm from his rogue agent program and I need to report some findings," Stone decided to add, hoping she at least knew the initiative existed.

A bit of intrigue registered in her eyes, as though she hadn't actually met one of the mythical rogue agents until this moment. Perhaps she liked his accent, or the idea of seeing how the scenario before her played out influenced her decision, but she pressed the intercom button to contact Stewart.

"Deputy Director, you have visitors," she stated, patiently waiting for a reply.

Stone wondered whether cameras were monitoring their movements with Stewart now giving them the silent treatment while reinforcements came to whisk them away from the federal building. Almost a minute passed without reply, which brought a look of concern to the receptionist's face. She tried Stewart a second time, met once again with complete silence for almost another minute. Stone eyed the hallway to either side of him, trying to look natural as he guarded against impending trouble.

Growing outwardly concerned, the woman virtually bolted from her chair while snatching a set of keys from the desk. She walked toward Stewart's door, but the doorknob turned without requiring a key, granting all three of them access to the rather spacious office. As soon as Stone peered over her shoulder, finding Stewart slumped over his desk, the pit of his stomach ached with fear that an even higher power than the Deputy Director was eliminating loose ends. Both of the Deputy Director's hands were laid atop the desk with his palms facing downward, while the right side of his face rested against the desk, his eyes still open as though he died suddenly.

"Oh my God!" the woman stammered, retreating from the room, probably to call for assistance.

Branson wasted less than a second before he moved toward the desk, examining Stewart's body without physically touching it, though his eyes came dangerously close when they scrutinized for the smallest of clues.

"What the hell are you doing?" Stone almost demanded, trying to keep his voice from reaching the hallway. "This is a potential crime scene!"

"It *is* a crime scene," Branson retorted. "And it would seem my former *sensei* was here."

Stone followed the man's eyes to a corner directly behind him where a cleaning cart remained, as though a custodian forgot to take it with him. The agent immediately understood that the cart was left on purpose and the assassin simply used it as a prop to gain entry to the office. He wondered if someone else paid the ultimate price to provide the murderer with a false identity.

Taking a closer look at his former boss's body, Stone found no visible wounds from a bullet, blade, or otherwise. A light purple hue encompassed the bottom of the dead man's palms, indicating the blood had pooled there at least the past several hours. He suspected the killer struck Stewart as soon as the man entered the office, possibly waiting until the assistant outside took a bathroom break to sneak out of the building.

Branson stood suddenly, apparently having found the verification he sought regarding Nosagi. He headed for the door, and Stone didn't immediately realize Branson was leaving because he continued to study the corpse.

"Where are you going?" he finally asked, daring to put some authority in his tone.

"I can't get bogged down in this," Branson answered, barely turning his head. "I've got to start tracking him."

Stone knew exactly who Branson referred to, but he didn't see how tracking a man with several hours head start was much help.

"You can't saddle me with this," Stone complained. "How the hell am I supposed to explain the last two days?"

Branson continued walking without so much as looking back this time.

"Just tell the truth and sort it out."

Stone grunted, thinking that telling the truth was either going to land him in jail or a psychiatric ward. He already felt like a pawn, but revealing what he knew combined with the grand total of facts he never discovered only served to make him look guilty or incompetent. Still, his image and DNA covered New Mexico to California and all parts in between. The truth was due to catch up with him, at least in part, regardless of what he decided to do at this very moment.

He caught a glimpse of Branson walking down the hall as Stewart's receptionist frantically called either building security or 911 for an ambulance. Knowing it was too late for Stewart to make amends, Stone hoped his fate proved kinder. He simply wanted to return home and see his wife, hopefully followed by him returning to his job without penalty.

Stone slowly walked toward the door, prepared to accept his fate and leave the crime scene to other professionals.

CHAPTER 39

A few weeks passed before Greene's buddy Chase Dalton located the van used when three armed men stole the cursed cubes and murdered Mark Teakon in Massachusetts. It turned out the van was stolen from a nearby town and burned soon after the heist, presumably just before the thieves left town. Greene expressed his concerns that one of the criminals knew setting the van ablaze might erase traces of DNA, or worse, keep Liz from locating any contact points that might provide a psychic connection.

Apparently the fire also made the van more difficult to track in general because it bounced between several police lots, the property of an insurance company, and finally a junkyard. Dalton feared it might be crushed or otherwise demolished before anyone from Greene's team could examine it so he contacted the junkyard's manager to put a hold on any destructive processes.

When Liz and Greene met the federal marshal at the junkyard late in the morning, Dalton gave her an appreciative look because he knew she was partially responsible for saving him in Tennessee. Greene and Dalton shook hands before exchanging a quick hug, and Liz understood that the two men maintained a friendship that went beyond their working relationship. She knew Greene struggled with the decision to ask Dalton for assistance on their quests because doing so endangered the marshal. Only Dalton's insistence kept him in the fold, even though it put his life and career at risk sometimes.

"Glad you could meet us in person," Greene commented as the three stood just outside the junkyard gates. "How did you pull it off?"

"I told my boss I wanted to come to Massachusetts for a prisoner transport detail scheduled for tomorrow or I was going to take some time off," Dalton answered with a cagy grin. "He can't afford to lose any more people right now, so he reluctantly let me fly over here."

"He probably thought you were crazy for *volunteering* to do a transport."

"I'm sure of that. I told him I was taking a day off to visit family over here before the transfer. He didn't ask any questions, so I'm in the clear."

Dalton led them through a secondary set of mesh wire fencing that essentially entered the heart of the facility. In one corner, readily visible to Liz, sat the remains of a charred van. Reduced to blackened metal, the vehicle was barely recognizable without tires, glass, or any color on the inside or the exterior. Whoever set the van ablaze made certain it burned hot enough to destroy any trace evidence throughout.

"What do you think?" Greene asked her, looking for any sign of optimism on her part.

Liz didn't want to falsely raise his hopes by saying anything reassuring. Getting a reading from people wasn't difficult, and objects owned and handled by people were typically a fifty-fifty shot, but she had never attempted anything destroyed or burned beyond recognition before. She truly needed to find something the psychic who sat in the van touched, or some part of him, like a hair, to activate her ability. Much of the passenger seat was lost in the fire, which left her little hope of entering his world.

Drawing closer for a more detailed examination, Liz thought everything looked exactly the same. Only morphed shapes inside the vehicle created any sort of variation, and there was absolutely no way to search for fibers or discarded belongings.

There simply weren't any.

Wincing at the smell of charred fiberglass and metal, Liz observed a man watching them from the hut that served as the manager's office within the premises. He probably expected local police detectives wearing guns and badges to casually survey the scene, but instead received two men dressed in business casual without firearms, and Liz who dressed as though fall weather surrounded her, rather than the nearly ninety degree temperatures that accompanied late May.

Almost subconsciously rubbing her hands together, Liz peered inside the vehicle before reaching her right hand toward the seat.

"I've always wanted to see this," Dalton confessed to Greene. "Never thought I'd be working with a psychic in this life."

"It's not much to observe from our end," Greene whispered back, but not quietly enough to evade Liz's hearing. "And it's not a psychic power in the normal sense."

"There's a normal?"

Whatever else the former partners discussed went unheard by Liz as she touched the seat's remains, tapping the hardened surface with her fingers from top to bottom. As expected, nothing happened, even when she reached the front of the seat, and finally underneath. Considering the windows had all blackened and shattered, or been poked through by the fire department, she seriously doubted anything inside the vehicle survived the intense flames. Someone, probably the police, had pried open the remains of the glove box to search it. Liz looked inside, seeing some paperwork, including an owner's manual that looked deformed and darkened, but not directly licked by flames.

"Is there a reason they wouldn't seize these papers as evidence?" she asked Greene, who stood to the side with his arms folded.

He sauntered over for a look, peering through the vacated window area. Standing close enough for Liz to feel the warmth of his body, along with his usual calm, collected breathing, Greene took notice of the papers inside.

"This wasn't considered a major crime by local police, so I'm sure they wouldn't waste resources testing for fingerprints. I'm sure they had a look through everything though."

"Not a major crime?" she questioned.

Greene shrugged.

"They probably figured some teenagers went joyriding in the thing and torched it. I'm not sure they ever put it together that this was the van used on the bookstore raid."

Thinking back to the footage of the raid, and Mark Teakon's senseless murder, Liz wanted to conjure a more productive image in her mind, so she reached inside the glove compartment and pulled out the manual and several loose papers. She carefully held them in one hand, rubbing her fingers slowly over each sheet and every corner, trying to evoke a response from the unknown energies that let her see the past.

"What are you so scared of?" Liz questioned under her breath, wondering what deep, dark secrets her fellow psychic harbored.

Nothing under or around the seat brought about a flashback, and the papers provided no spark, indicating the secretive man hadn't touched them, or the damage proved too great to leave whatever physical trace triggered Liz's visions. Basically grasping at straws, she tried to think of any other ideas that might provide a source of psychic energy.

"Where was the van stolen?" she finally asked, looking between Greene and Dalton.

"Not far from here," Dalton answered.

"Did the thieves throw anything out of the van when they stole it by chance?"

Greene's expression showed that he recognized her line of thinking.

Dalton flipped through the report he'd been holding in case they needed information about any of the cases involving the van.

"Not that the owners reported," Dalton answered after a minute or two of scanning the pertinent report.

"It's worth checking with them," Greene suggested as Liz thought the same exact thing.

Nodding in agreement, Dalton motioned them toward the parked cars.

***

Paul Clouse's research took him from every Orange County library available to the county historian and several people who knew the Springs Valley area exceptionally well. Most of them had family connections to the various hotels, knowing intimate details about what happened during the gambling days when people traveled to the area for spirits, games of chance, and occasionally the cleansing mineral water.

He finally discovered and confirmed that the Woxley Hotel, a two-story hotel built in 1898 contained twenty rooms. It shut down suddenly two weeks before the date the cursed cubes were created and the owner sold the property to an unnamed individual. In those days records weren't scrutinized and questions regarding ownership weren't typically asked if no one was affected negatively. He trusted what the local publications printed in the archives he read, but they weren't published daily back then, so he mentally left some latitude on the dates they stated certain events occurred.

While he continued to work on a few additional details, Clouse looked into purchasing the property where a former secondhand store continued to just barely stand. Faded products that never sold remained visible through the dusty display window and parts of the building's exterior showed major deterioration to the point of crumbling. The store once stood a few blocks behind the main thruway, but the rest of town eventually caught up to it as a few residential buildings were built around the store.

Most of them now stood vacant, or close to it, because business gravitated toward the two largest area hotels over time. The apartments and houses built decades earlier still looked the same, only faded paint and typical deterioration marring their outward appearance.

Despite not having everything finalized, Clouse decided to meet with his old high school friend Tim Niemeyer for lunch to discuss a favor he wanted to ask. His friend lost five years of his life, and in turn much more than that, because of the people who wanted to punish Clouse and make his life miserable. And though he helped Niemeyer make his construction business better than ever, Clouse couldn't get the man his marriage back because Niemeyer's wife had remarried, believing her first husband was lying six feet under a tombstone.

A story most soap operas couldn't pull off, the twists and turns Clouse endured with his numerous enemies left him nearly broken. Getting Niemeyer back after the man was held captive for five years came as a blessing to the millionaire, but the two didn't meet up often enough for Clouse's taste. He walked a fine line between keeping in touch with his friend and keeping Niemeyer safe from unseen enemies. History indicated that those close to Clouse often found themselves in peril when someone sought the cubes.

Walking into a local café, Clouse spied his friend sitting in the corner wearing blue jeans and a black t-shirt with the same Harley-Davidson logo as the large touring bike parked outside. An expensive custom leather jacket sat beside him, and Clouse knew Niemeyer was certainly back on his feet. Left with a fringe of brown hair and a matching full goatee dotted with a few gray hairs, Niemeyer stood to give his friend a bear hug that nearly crushed Clouse's ribs.

"Good to see you too," Clouse said between labored breaths.

Still thick around the waist, and barrel chested, Niemeyer took time to lift weights because he ate so well.

They each took a seat before Clouse thumbed toward the motorcycle sitting just outside one of the large windows.

"I see you still love the open road."

Niemeyer scoffed.

"I don't get far enough to really enjoy it. Business has been booming lately."

"I haven't seen you working any sites lately," Clouse chuckled.

"It takes everything I've got just to keep the business in order. I spend my days in a work truck or talking on the phone. Most nights I don't get home 'til dark."

Clouse used to enjoy the way his friend spoke with a slight drawl, acquired from being raised around his grandfather from Tennessee. It seemed his friend spoke a little more conventionally now, having been back in civilization for the better part of two years. Like most things in life, aspects of their friendship had evolved and changed over the years. Things between them felt tense once Niemeyer regained his freedom, as though he blamed Clouse for him losing five years of his life.

"What's going on with the richest friend I have?" Niemeyer asked once they placed drink orders.

"The usual. People threatening my life and the human population as a whole."

"Sorry I asked."

"It's not as bad as it seems," Clouse said with a nonchalant wave of his hand, regretting that he didn't phrase his answer a little more tactfully.

Niemeyer continued to carry the mental scars of imprisonment, though he put forth a concerned, soft-spoken front whenever he met with Clouse. Loyal to a fault, Niemeyer never refused his good friend, so Clouse felt terrible about asking for a favor, but he needed discretion more than ever.

"How are the kids?" he decided to ask first, not wanting to seem as though he only invited his friend to lunch to ask for help.

In truth, he would never have invited Niemeyer at such a dangerous time if not for the fact he required someone with construction and demolition knowledge. He felt like such a heel for asking anything more of his lifelong friend.

"They're good. I get to see them a few times a week when Vicky has to work. Now that school's almost out I'll see them a lot more."

"You can start training them in the family business," Clouse said with a smile. "Won't be long before they'll be old enough to work."

"And drive," Niemeyer grumbled.

Their conversation halted just long enough for them to place their lunch order. Niemeyer then looked to his friend, concern showing in his blue eyes.

"And how is your family holding up?"

"They're away at the moment," Clouse answered hesitantly. "It's safer that way."

"This has to stop, Paul. You need to distance yourself from this place and the curse around that hotel."

"It's a little more complicated than that."

"Bullshit," Niemeyer said evenly. "It ain't your nature to turn tail and run but you've fought the good fight long enough, my friend. It's time to let someone else watch over those things."

Clouse hung his head momentarily before looking to his friend with a face that expressed the desperation he felt inside.

"I don't have them, Tim. Someone raided the place where we were keeping them and got all of them."

"*All* of them?" Niemeyer asked with disbelief. "How many is that?"

"Seven of the thirteen. But I don't know how many others they might already have."

Shaking his head, Niemeyer uncharacteristically remained speechless for almost half a minute.

"I get the impression you want my help with something," he finally admitted. "I'm not sure I have it in me to help you confront these people again."

"What I need from you is much simpler," Clouse confessed. "I need you to knock over a building and see what's underneath it."

Niemeyer looked skeptical.

"You could pay anyone to do that."

"But I need someone to do the job and keep quiet about it."

Grunting and grumbling aloud, Niemeyer weighed over the decision. His loyalty to Clouse was destined to end at some point when he decided his life meant more than helping his friend keep the world safe. Five years of his life were erased because of his loyalty, and no amount of money could ever bring those back.

"Where is this property?"

"Closer than you think."

Clouse pointed to the aging apartment complex that stood out of habit in front of the property he was purchasing.

"Right behind that building."

Niemeyer drew closer so no one around them heard his words.

"And what do you expect to find in there?"

"The center of this entire mess. I think the cubes might have been created there. And if so, that's probably where they have to come together to do their damage."

It took willpower for Niemeyer not to roll his eyes or immediately blow up and chastise his friend's decision, but he collected himself a few seconds before speaking.

"Why in the hell would you dig that thing up then, Paul?"

"Tactical advantage. If I'm going to confront whoever's behind this, it's going to be there. Better I know the layout so I can plan ahead of time."

"And you're sure that's where the things were created?"

"Not one-hundred percent, no."

Now Niemeyer rolled his eyes.

"Do you own the property outright?"

"I sign the papers tomorrow."

Niemeyer took a few additional seconds to contemplate the offer laid before him. It went unsaid that Clouse would compensate him well.

"What's behind that complex?"

"It's an old store. I need it demolished before you can dig into the ground. A small hotel used to stand there back in the day, and I'm sure it had a basement."

"And what do you expect to find inside?"

Clouse shook his head.

"I have no idea."

Niemeyer rubbed the hair on his chin, obviously contemplating the risk versus the reward.

"I can have one of my employees take down the building," he finally decided aloud. "That way it won't look like I'm doing anything for you, especially if your enemies are watching us right now."

No stranger to hazards that came with befriending Clouse, Niemeyer knew how to evade spying eyes. Whether or not it worked this time remained to be seen, but Clouse felt a sense of relief that his friend was willing to assist him once again.

A thoughtful look crossed Niemeyer's face.

"What if we could access the basement without making a scene?" he finally recommended.

"I've got to assume it was filled in soon after the cubes were created," Clouse replied. "If there's anything to be found down there, they wouldn't have taken a chance."

"I can still take a look and see, can't I?"

"Feel free."

Both friends sat silently a moment until their food was delivered. Clouse forked a bite into his mouth before speaking again.

"I can end this once and for all, Tim."

"What makes you so sure?"

"I still have the one cube they need to pull off their plan."

Niemeyer shook his head.

"I worry about you, Paul. One of these times you ain't gonna be so lucky."

Saying nothing, Clouse knew the risk was one he would take repeatedly until the cubes were all safe from evildoers.

"I don't plan on going anywhere," Clouse confessed. "I didn't start this little war, but no one else is going to end it."

"People shouldn't have to go through what you've been through," Niemeyer said.

"Or what you've gone though. I just wish we still had Ken with us."

Clouse spoke of their mutual friend Ken Kaiser, who wound up a casualty in actions against Clouse some years prior.

"To Ken," Niemeyer said, raising his glass.

"To Ken," Clouse mirrored the toast, tapping his glass with Niemeyer's.

Each of them took a sip before Niemeyer spoke again.

"I hear you're in the horse racing business."

"No longer," Clouse said with a grin. "I kept my promise and let the original owners have full stake in their colt after the Kentucky Derby."

"You wouldn't do something like that unless you had a good motive."

"All the right intentions didn't help me in the end, Tim. Those pricks just waited for me to do the dirty work, then swooped in like hawks. That's why I'm asking for your assistance. These people hold all of the important cards except one."

He took a drink from his glass before speaking again to break the tension that always came with talking about the past and the events surrounding his hotel.

"Besides, the horse came in second at Preakness."

Niemeyer gave a smile, but it appeared forced.

Both of them knew Clouse only made business ventures to protect his assets or keep the world safe from cursed objects. He found no reason to cheer against Desert Phantom or the thoroughbred's owner. In truth, Clouse felt thankful that Margaret Stough trusted him enough to sign the pact with him, which gained Clouse another piece of the puzzle. Unfortunately the acquisition proved short-lived, which disappointed him and forced him to take additional precautions going forward.

Eating much of their lunch in silence, the friends had nearly finished when Clouse spied Clay Branson approaching the front door. He wondered how Branson found him, and why the man was visiting the French Lick area unannounced. Another man trailed slightly behind him, wearing dress clothes and cowboy boots, along with eyeglasses and a black cowboy hat. Clouse guessed him to be a police officer, possibly a Texas Ranger based on his shined boots and perfectly pressed clothing. Considering a firearm clung to the right side of his belt he was either a cop or someone who legally carried a gun through other means.

When the two men drew a bit closer, Clouse thought he recognized the man accompanying Branson. The bushy full goatee didn't look like standard regulation for a federal agency, but some outlying areas in states like Texas and New Mexico sometimes allowed their agents some leeway.

Wiping his mouth with a napkin, Clouse outstretched an arm as a pointer before speaking to Niemeyer.

"Tim, let me introduce Clay Branson and his complete stranger of a friend whom I haven't met."

Niemeyer nodded, though openly unsure whether he should feel honored or threatened by the sudden appearance of two strangers.

"Harlan Stone," the agent introduced himself, shaking hands with Clouse. "I've heard quite a bit about you, sir."

"I wish I could say the same," Clouse said before stealing a displeased glance toward Branson.

"This is important," Branson said, not wavering from his usual serious demeanor.

Clouse felt a bit apprehensive about saying anything more in public, so he set down enough cash to cover the cost of both meals before looking to Niemeyer.

"I'll call you later, Tim."

Clouse led the way outside the café, wondering what might be so important that Branson would visit French Lick unannounced and bring anyone outside of Clouse's group with him. Barely comfortable with the idea of a noncommittal Branson in his fold, Clouse didn't want anyone else knowing about the cursed objects or the mission to hunt them down.

"Let's take a short drive to the French Lick Springs Hotel," Clouse suggested, since he also owned that hotel. "I'm sure we can find an open conference room."

CHAPTER 40

Matt Teakon remained focused, if not obsessed, on a name stuck in his head since the day his uncle was lost to him a second time.

Jacob Savitch.

Considering the man's name appeared in the ledger that accompanied the cubes eleven times now, Teakon considered the man a formidable threat. He felt surprised the men who stole the seven cubes and killed his uncle never asked about the old book, but perhaps they simply did not know of its existence.

Two more cubes, however, and the man would indeed hold a full deck according to the old book.

"Do you want iced-tea or something else?" Julie asked as she stood from her couch to fetch some items from the kitchen.

"Tea is fine."

Julie hadn't visited the bookstore since the incident, and openly contemplated selling the property. In a nice downtown location, the building wouldn't be on the market long before some potential business owner discovered it and fell in love. Teakon didn't particularly like the idea of either one of them returning to Massachusetts, but Julie wanted to gather some of her belongings. Her refusal to be bullied potentially put them in danger, but Teakon used the opportunity to finally view the leather-bound book that clearly identified which people possessed the cubes, leaving the remainder of the mystery for the reader to solve.

What bothered Teakon about the find was that he couldn't find anything out about Jacob Savitch through his usual means. He suspected the man was the mastermind behind the raid on the bookstore, the attack on the fishing boat during the winter, and possibly the assassination of Chase Dalton's imposter at Clouse's grand hotel.

Not feeling entirely trustworthy, even of his own mind at this point, Teakon said nothing to anyone about the find, including Julie. While he felt reasonably safe around Clouse's people, he didn't know what the mysterious psychic working for Savitch knew about the group and their plans. Keeping such a secret felt dangerous for Teakon and everyone around him, but if the book ever fell into the wrong hands, regaining the cubes would prove nearly impossible. The pressure ate at his mind and conscience virtually every waking second, but he wasn't going to see anyone else around him harmed. If anyone knew about the book and wanted to come after it, he planned to sacrifice his own life to save innocent people.

"Liz called me a little bit ago," Julie revealed from the next room. "She and Russ were in the area to check over that van they used to rob the store."

"Oh?"

Julie peeked in, looking apprehensive about talking about the robbery and murder, as though he might fall apart any second. Already committed to telling her story, she continued after ducking into the kitchen.

"They didn't find anything useful in the van, and they spoke with the owners, but that didn't help either."

"Sounds like a wasted trip then," Teakon said, feeling more deflated than before.

"Are you okay?" Julie asked, handing him a full glass of tea when she made her way back from the kitchen.

"I'm fine," he said, putting forth his best reassuring smile.

"When do you want to head back to Indiana?" she asked.

Both felt safer around Clouse, who provided ample living quarters and security in the form of former military personnel and police officers, despite their earlier objections. For some reason Todd Parish was an exception to the normal hiring practice Clouse employed for bodyguards and security, but Teakon wasn't harboring any ill will toward the man. Both said some rather regrettable words the day they exchanged glancing blows in the hallway and Parish made it a point to avoid any conversations since.

Now put back for safekeeping, the book remained in a bank vault that required Teakon to present identification, possess a key, type in a passcode, *and* scan a fingerprint before gaining access to his property. He wanted some assurance that picking his mind or severing his finger weren't simply enough for some imposter to steal the last good tool he possessed for hunting down the cubes.

Teakon looked at the ring on his finger from the Kentucky Derby, suddenly feeling like most of his life was fake. He spent so much time constructing and executing cover stories that hardly any aspect of his existence felt legitimate. Protecting the world as his uncle had provided very little time for a personal life. Up to his uncle's true death, Teakon hadn't thought much of settling down, despite recently entering middle age. Growing up around ranches taught him many life skills, but dating and interacting socially didn't always come naturally to him. Julie taught him quite a few tips, whether she meant to or not, but he always regarded her as a younger sister rather than a love interest.

More so than any other living person on the planet, Teakon was prepared to lay down his life to protect her.

"Are you ready to see what the others have found?" she asked.

Teakon wished they hadn't taken time for lunch, but after the long flight neither was ready for travel again so soon. Still, he wanted to help her pack so they could avoid the danger zone in Amherst and leave before any more hazards came their way.

After visiting the book within the lockbox, he felt especially paranoid, as though someone might already be reading his thoughts or tailing him.

"I have this feeling we're not moving fast enough," Teakon confessed. "As soon as we learn something it's like we're a day late every time."

"Losing the cubes was disheartening," Julie admitted, "but we still have the means to find them again. And if that many are with one person we can get them back all at once."

"But what if he sells them to the highest bidder?" Teakon pondered aloud. "Or worse, decides to put them all together?"

"Matt, there's no one else out there who can stop that from happening besides us."

"But that was a close call at the bookstore, Julie. If my uncle wouldn't have thought ahead with the panic room, we would've been collateral damage."

"I know. But if Mark was willing to lay down his life for his convictions, I'm not backing down."

Julie's words felt somewhat reassuring, but he hated the idea of placing her in further danger. Still, if she was in for the long haul, he planned to stick by her side.

"Do you trust our people in Indiana?" he decided to ask.

"I don't have a reason not to. They've been helpful so far."

Perhaps Teakon still wanted to find fault for the fiasco on the Bering Sea, or the near miss at the Kentucky Derby, but he knew Clouse meant well. And to this point, all of his people seemed legitimately concerned about retrieving the cubes, each of them harboring mental and physical scars from previous dealings with the cursed objects.

Julie took a drink from her own glass of tea before looking him squarely in the eyes with a concerned look. She was reading him, reaching the conclusion that he'd been concealing a secret since stealing a peek at the book.

"You know who took the cubes from the bookstore, don't you?"

Teakon nodded slowly.

"And for the sake of safety I'm not telling you that name, Julie. If anything happens to me, you can always look for yourself. After what happened to my uncle I can barely trust my own thoughts."

Both of them shared the same access to the bank box, and both jumped through the same hoops whenever they wanted to check the book. The days of keeping it at the store, even in the vault, were certainly long gone. Although the bank box was always available to them previously, set up by Mark Teakon a few years prior, they'd used it sparingly before their lives felt threatened by outsiders.

"We have to be proactive, Matt, even if it puts us at risk."

"You're right. Maybe it's time we stop working as individuals and make this hunt a true team effort."

Julie stood.

"I'll get my things. The sooner we get back to Indiana, the sooner we can get everyone together for some answers."

Teakon wasn't sure he believed his own words, but he didn't want to live with regret later when the world came to an end around him, or countless people died to fuel the cubes individually. He just hoped someone in their alliance could find a clue that led them to Savitch before he possessed all of the cubes.

***

When he reached a vacant conference room at the end of a hallway within the French Lick Springs Hotel, Clouse asked to speak with Clay Branson privately inside while Harlan Stone waited in the hallway.

"How much have you told this guy?" Clouse demanded once the doors closed behind the two men.

"He's pieced a lot of it together himself. Some big cheese in the FBI had this agent tailing me for the better part of two months."

"And you thought the best move was bringing him here?"

"There have been some developments. I just wanted you to hear his story in person."

Clouse felt his body temperature continue to rise. He was infuriated with Branson for several reasons, and he decided to air them before speaking with the agent.

"I realize it probably wasn't right of me to ask you to help us retrieve these cursed objects in the first place. Maybe I was hoping you would put aside your personal vendetta long enough to help us with a greater good. That didn't happen, and you just come and go whenever you please around here."

Branson pointed a finger directly at Clouse's chest.

"I have a fucking life! I'm not some dog at your beck and call. You've got your hired goons to do your dirty work, and I've got a regular job and a theme park to oversee."

"I fully realize that, and I've come to learn that the only way I can motivate you is by dangling Nosagi's name in front of you. And as though I didn't have enough trust issues with you, you bring a stranger into the mix and show up on a whim. Hunting down these cursed objects is dangerous enough without you pulling this stunt. And I know you could probably kill me with your pinky finger but I've fought plenty of my own battles."

"I'm aware of that, Mr. Clouse. Part of the reason I've been reluctant to join your cause is because I've spent so much time researching you. Now that I know you're a good person, and your cause is legitimate, I'm onboard. I'll be the first to admit I've been blinded by revenge, and it isn't going to be easy for me to drop everything and run over here whenever you have trouble, but I *will* do my best. And you've got to trust me when I say you'll want to hear what the special agent has to say."

Almost apprehensively the door to the conference room opened before Stone stuck his head inside, still wearing his black hat.

"Well, I just heard everything you two said, so there's no need to repeat. I reckon the entire hotel might have heard it too."

Stone stepped inside, removing his hat to reveal hair cut close to the scalp, probably due to his receding hairline. He shut the door behind him, holding his hat respectfully at his waist while he looked between Clouse and the man who'd saved his life.

"Look, I've made some mistakes," Stone admitted, "and I don't completely understand what the hell is going on with these things you're hunting, but I'll help however I can. Even if that's just telling you what I know."

Clouse waved an arm toward the open seats.

"Let's start with what you know, Agent Stone."

Once the three men chose their seats, both Branson and Stone relayed the tale about Alan Stewart recruiting the agent from his usual duties and the setup that followed Stone visiting the widow of his fellow agent. It took nearly twenty minutes to provide Clouse with all of the details leading up to the most recent turn of events.

Stone had set his hat atop the table, upside-down to avoid bending the brim, but he fingered the black felt as though pondering where to pick up the strange tale. He finally sat back, cleaned his eyeglasses momentarily with his shirt, and looked to Clouse because Branson already knew the latest developments.

"After Clay here left me to the wolves at my job, I explained the past few months and played dumb when it came to certain details. And while I couldn't exactly leave out everything because surveillance video showed us together at the hospital and the Los Angeles branch of the Bureau, I tried to keep out some of the stranger things I'd seen."

"I especially appreciate the way you sent your agents to Mason to question me," Branson commented.

"Yeah, because I call the shots at the FBI," Stone retorted sarcastically. "I thought you ninja types were supposed to be invisible, so you only have yourself to blame."

Clouse noticed the two men were well past any issues they might have shared initially. Being chummy with a virtual outsider to Clouse's inner circle certainly didn't provide adequate qualifications for full disclosure. Still, he wanted to hear the end of the agent's story.

"As a result of my actions I'm on paid leave until my superiors decide whether or not they believe my story. But a coworker leaked a few details to me, including how Alan Stewart's body disappeared from the morgue before it was embalmed."

"Disappeared, eh?" Clouse asked suspiciously.

"That's what I thought," Stone noted. "Luckily the mortuary, located in an affluent Los Angeles suburb, caught some of the incident on video."

Stone produced a small computer flash drive after reaching into his pocket, holding it up for Clouse to see. He then slid it across the table toward Clouse, which allowed the hotel owner to scoop it up and plug it in after retrieving a laptop computer from a nearby cabinet.

"I take it you two have seen this?" he asked once the computer read the device and prepared to play the recorded video clip.

Both men nodded affirmatively.

Clouse started the video, watching as someone entered the mortuary following regular business hours because the person appeared as black as a shadow from head to toe. The low lighting made it impossible to make out details, but the intruder walked through the main hallway and out of view.

"Did the owners just have the one camera?" Clouse asked Stone.

"They had one in each of the visitation areas, but our intruder went straight to the basement. He comes back around the three minute mark."

Indeed the intruder came back around the time Stone stated, but this time someone walked through the hallway with him toward the front door. The second person, also a man based on his stride, walked under his own power just behind the first. Clouse could not determine any features because both of them basically appeared as silhouettes with the dim lighting mainly behind them.

"So what did your organization make of this?" he asked Stone.

"They figured a first accomplice let a second one in through the back and the two stole Stewart's body."

"And your take?"

"If I'm going to waltz in through the front door, I'm certainly not going to make the return trip if I'm letting my buddy in through the back. Based on what I saw Clay battling down in South America, I'm guessing one of those two men at the end of that footage was probably my former boss."

An awkwardly tense moment passed with no one saying a word, and at least on Clouse's end he didn't want to confirm or deny anything regarding the existence of the cubes or their powers. Branson hadn't exactly provided a stellar reference for the agent, and Stone readily admitted to working for the enemy. Exactly how naïve the young agent might have been regarding his apprenticeship with Stewart remained to be seen.

Based on the information provided by Branson and Stone, Clouse assumed Stewart worked for someone else who wanted to eliminate any loose ends. It made little sense, then, to murder the man and bring him back just a day or two later. Perhaps Stewart set some kind of failsafe in place to make certain his services remained a requirement, whether he harbored information or some kind of benefit. Any number of possibilities existed, but it seemed whoever wanted the Deputy Director dead took a great risk by eliminating him where he worked.

"You're sure Stewart's death was at the hands of your mentor?" he asked Branson.

"Positive. A tiny hole in his neck indicated some kind of poison was used. I think he wanted it to look natural, like a heart attack, but for some reason he left the cart in the room. Maybe he had a narrow window of escape."

"It turns out he murdered a janitor and assumed his identity," Stone added. "He's on the security footage, but dressed with a baseball cap so you can't see his face. He entered during the overnight when the building is practically empty and waited in Stewart's office until morning."

"I take it you didn't volunteer any information," Clouse surmised.

"I'm in enough hot water already," Stone answered somewhat testily. "The last thing I need is my agency thinking I'm a key figure in assassinating my boss."

Clouse contemplated some risky moves, because once again he found himself knee-deep in a mystery and two steps behind his adversaries. He hadn't dared ask Liz to touch any of the cursed cubes now that he knew someone was able to penetrate her thoughts. If Niemeyer demolished the old store in French Lick and found nothing, Clouse foresaw little other option than to ask Liz for help.

In a few days he might find that weighty decision placed before him.

"I appreciate you gentlemen bringing this before me," he said, intending to wrap up their impromptu meeting.

"That's it?" Branson asked with a raised eyebrow. "You don't have some plan of action?"

"I have several ideas, but they aren't something I can hop to right this second. After what happened in Massachusetts my options are a bit limited."

"What happened in Massachusetts?" Stone inquired, his tone and expression indicating he might possess some useful information. "My boss recently took a flight out there."

Both men stared at him as though they doubted his ability to obtain Stewart's schedule.

"What? I sometimes peeked at his schedule when his assistant went to the restroom."

"Damn it!" Branson stammered. "We may have just let a vital piece of the puzzle walk away."

"I'm confused," Stone said, still out of the loop because he didn't know the backstory.

"What do you mean?" Clouse asked, talking around the agent as though he wasn't in the room.

"If Stone's partner was on Stewart's payroll and he helped rob the bookstore, then maybe Stewart did the talking and the other muscle was the guy who tried to kill Stone in the hospital."

"What bookstore?" Stone asked no one in particular. "Who robs a bookstore?"

"Where did you leave that guy?" Clouse asked, still ignoring the agent's inquiries.

"In the middle of nowhere, basically."

Clouse thoughtfully cupped his chin.

"You need to find him and find out everything he knows."

"He's hired muscle," Branson stated. "Stewart wouldn't have told him anything valuable."

"But they'll kill him just the same," Stone said, finally replacing his hat. "Maybe I can track him down."

"I'm glad," Branson stated, "because I have to get back to Ohio before my fiancée wonders where the hell I've been."

Clouse wasn't particularly fond of the agent assisting the group just yet, but he wasn't willing to risk sending his own people to accompany a suspended government employee. On the other hand, he wanted to test Stone's loyalty, which seemed difficult to measure if he didn't send someone to monitor the agent.

"I'd like to know if you find the man," he informed Stone. "Especially if he knows anything useful."

"It might help if I knew what sort of questions to ask."

"I'm pretty sure you're resourceful enough to get him to squeal without asking too many questions."

Stone nodded, getting Clouse's notion. And with that the three men gathered up their minimal belongings and parted ways.

CHAPTER 41

A few days later Tim Niemeyer entered Clouse's new property alone around dusk, careful to make sure no vehicles followed him down the short street. He exited his truck, closing the door as quietly as possible before taking a look around. Even at the edge of the town limits no crickets chirped and the traffic sounded extremely distant when Niemeyer finally did hear a passing vehicle.

The surrounding abandoned buildings loomed over him from atop their perch on a nearby hill. Their black, unlit windows stared down like evil faces with hollow expressions, providing no indications about what might be hidden along their abandoned floors.

Gripping the entry key in his right hand, and a flashlight in his left, Niemeyer walked purposefully toward the door, opening it to the kind of musty smell that accompanied a building untouched in years. He found a light switch immediately to his right, but when he flipped it nothing happened.

"Perfect," he muttered, illuminating the main foyer with his industrial-grade flashlight.

Dust mushroomed into the air with every step, but Niemeyer aimed the flashlight toward each wall and floorboard with determination. The entire shop took up about a thousand square feet, taking him little time to sift through. Only a few pieces of furniture required moving for Niemeyer to complete a cursory examination of the defunct store. He saw no indications of doors, conventional or secret, that might lead to any kind of basement. Even the cracks along the floor didn't seem to indicate anything lurked beneath them.

Deciding he wanted to check a hunch, Niemeyer stepped outside to examine the building's foundation. He shined the light, verifying that no small windows lined the old bricks to indicate a basement might exist. Strangely, no vents were present to suggest the building sat atop a slab either. Drawing a perplexed face that no one was present to see, Niemeyer tilted his head in confusion, wondering what kind of contractor erected a building with no ventilation for climate changes.

Thinking he needed to examine the subfloor inside before contemplating his next move, Niemeyer let the flashlight's beam guide him through the front door. He tried some of the floorboards with no success, so he grabbed a pry bar from his truck before making a second attempt. He knew demolishing the little store wouldn't prove much of an undertaking, but a concrete floor beneath it might require extra time or equipment. And when the old wood finally gave way, he stared at the concrete slab beneath it, thinking it wasn't simply poured as a minimal slab to support the weight of foot traffic and heavy items.

Niemeyer tested the thickness of the concrete by dropping one end of the pry bar atop it twice, receiving a hardened thud each time in response. He felt certain the foundation wasn't meant to support a heavy load, or house ventilation and water lines, as no vents existed, but rather it was poured thick to conceal something a very long time ago.

Studying the material, Niemeyer found particles in the mix that might escape a less experienced contractor's eyes. He knew from the history of his craft that coal, wood chips, and whatever else builders could find during the early 1900s often went into concrete mixes to accelerate the curing process. This especially held true during the colder months, like December or January for example.

He felt certain the building's later owners likely didn't see a need to alter the foundation, or realized doing so might cost more than the building was actually worth, so it remained untouched for nearly a hundred years. A best-case scenario meant the concrete was crumbling and easy to break apart, but even that required heavy equipment.

Groaning, Niemeyer formulated a plan for the following morning, knowing when he halfheartedly promised his friend to look at the property that it couldn't possibly go smoothly. Helping Clouse with any aspect of his life these days practically put a target on the volunteer's back. While Niemeyer probably didn't have as much to live for as he once did, the man still valued time with his children and the lucrative life owning a profitable construction business provided. And though Clouse never admitted it, the man brought Niemeyer a *lot* of jobs in the surrounding counties.

When he finally stepped outside, the crickets chirped in the distance, providing him with some comfort that nothing ominous scared them. He hoped his near future held an equally promising outlook, because he didn't feel comfortable helping his old friend when the task at hand was related to the cursed objects that caused them both some dear friends.

He returned to his truck, cautiously looking around because the unusually cool evening and quiet surroundings unnerved him. Either his efforts would help Clouse protect the world one last time, or Niemeyer would leave his children without a father once again.

***

Just before noon, Niemeyer received a phone call from the employee he assigned to demolish the old secondhand store. It turned out the building came down easily as expected, and even the concrete beneath it crumbled into smaller chunks that the backhoe lifted and sorted with ease. The employee called to report in and request permission before digging into the remainder of the concrete slab and the dirt beneath it.

Niemeyer gave permission to carefully dig and sift through the dirt, explaining that there might have been a functional basement beneath the slab at one time. Basically he told the young man not to strike any foundation above or below ground level. He wouldn't have assigned that particular employee to carry out the dig if he didn't trust him, but the kid had grown up working with farm and construction equipment. His precision aim and steady hand allowed him to maneuver large equipment without harming important or fragile items around him.

Immediately phoning Clouse with the news, Niemeyer was a bit surprised when his friend declined to come in person for a look at the property. Niemeyer fully expected to lay eyes on the freshly gutted basement within the hour, but Clouse informed him he didn't want to step foot on the property just yet. He asked his friend to meet Todd Parish at a restaurant for a quick lunch, probably to throw off anyone monitoring their activities, before taking him to the site.

When he stepped into the burger joint, he recognized Parish in the booth farthest from the entrance, looking incredibly out of place with the tourists in their khaki shorts, blue jeans, and light summer wear. Wearing a black suit with a blue and white striped tie, Parish even outclassed most of the local bankers who wore golf shirts with logos, or dressed similarly without the benefit of a sport coat.

"Did you just come from a funeral?" Niemeyer asked as he slid into the booth, knowing Parish just well enough to joke with him.

"Just doing my usual thing."

Niemeyer wasn't sure exactly what duties Parish carried out as of late. Once a bodyguard to Clouse's son and stepdaughter, Parish recently spent more time on special assignments and around the two luxury hotels. Niemeyer took notice because the bodyguard occasionally accompanied Clouse to meetings and lunches as well.

"Well you're a little overdressed for what we're about to do," he informed Parish, who simply shrugged indifferently.

"The boss tells me you're doing a little digging for him."

"More than a little. If you've already ordered, you might want to get your food to go."

Parish indeed took a cup of coffee with him when he followed Niemeyer to the site. When the two pulled their trucks into the lot, Niemeyer noticed his employee had cleared most of the old basement. A mound of dirt sat beside the ruins of the building, and remnants of the old store remained only in large chunks of the four walls in a different pile.

"Do you have a permit, or should we expect the police to raid us any second?" Parish asked half seriously.

Niemeyer didn't appear amused.

"Paul was careful not to purchase this place in his name, and I was equally careful when I applied for the permit. I'm hoping to avoid visitation from anyone this far away from the main parts of town."

A young man approached them and Niemeyer didn't bother with introductions as his young employee, Jake Webster, filled them in about his morning dig. He took them around the foundation, pointing out the walls that once comprised a full basement. Despite using large excavation equipment, the young man had managed to remove most of the dirt right to the edge of the walls without damaging one square inch of the foundation.

"There are stairs over there," Webster said, pointing to the remains of an old wooden stairway that had virtually rotted to splinters after years of burial.

"I think I'll pass on trying them," Niemeyer commented, still looking around the small basement, not seeing any huge secrets looming along the dingy walls.

For the most part gritty dirt coated the walls, but one moist spot appeared where a longstanding leak might have allowed rainwater to seep beneath the floorboards and around the solid barrier below them. Niemeyer felt bad that he hadn't found anything concrete for his friend, but Webster indicated he wasn't finished showing the two men his finds quite yet.

"Have a look at that," he said, pointing to the opposite corner.

Niemeyer only saw a dirty wall at first glance, but when he crouched down and squinted a little, he saw the outline of a door. For the life of him he couldn't imagine why the basement, which equaled the former ground floor in square footage, might have a door. Basements seldom exceeded the size of the constructed overhead space.

"Can we get a ladder down there?" he asked, turning to see his employee was already a step ahead of him.

Looking to Parish, he finally cut loose with a smirk.

"Ready to get that suit of yours dirty?"

Parish's reply came in the form of a grunt while he began peeling off his sport coat as though preparing for a fistfight. Instead of setting it aside, however, Parish draped the sport coat over his right forearm to help conceal the gun holstered at his side in case any nosy people suddenly visited the site. He also didn't want Niemeyer's young employee thinking he was a detective, for fear he might tell some of his friends about the site. Parish figured his white shirt wasn't going to fare any better in the environment that awaited him in the bowels of the old demolished store.

Webster maneuvered the ladder into the hollowed basement a few feet from the sealed doorway below. He asked if Niemeyer wanted him to go down first and check the door, but the construction company owner shook off the notion and descended the ladder himself. He waited beside the door until Parish joined him along the solid bottom of the old basement before looking to the door momentarily. A bit apprehensive, Niemeyer brushed an open palm against the old wooden surface, sending some of the old dirt to the ground and revealing an iron clasp handle, rather than a doorknob. It reminded him of some kind of medieval castle door, rather than any décor from the past century.

"Can you cover me a second?" he asked Parish, receiving an affirmative nod.

Trust didn't come easy for Niemeyer, who literally witnessed people backstabbing his good friend Clouse before trying to kill both of them. He at least trusted Parish enough to have the man keep an eye on things while he entered whatever awaited him behind the cryptic, heavy door.

Putting his weight into the door, Niemeyer used his thick arms to begin moving the object inward, finding it heavier than it looked. He strained a bit until the door finally budged a few inches, revealing a small mound of dirt on the other side that likely squeezed through the cracks when the basement was filled in decades prior. It pooled at the bottom of the door, creating a barricade that refused to give way until the contractor put his shoulder into the effort, busting past the gritty obstruction.

The daylight behind him only provided light about three or four feet inside the opening, but the outline of a tunnel appeared before him, and he knew this was no adjacent storage room. Whatever this tunnel led to wasn't close, and he found no form of illumination to light the way if he dared step inside.

"Hello?" he called, verifying his initial thoughts with a deep echo from within, realizing the tunnel spanned a length further than any flashlight beam was going to span.

He returned to the outside, looking up to Webster.

"I need a flashlight."

Within a minute the young man returned, tossing the flashlight down to Niemeyer, who immediately handed it to Parish as though it were a hot potato. Parish looked to the flashlight, then to the contractor, with mild scrutiny.

"You don't want to see what's in there?"

"I don't," Niemeyer answered sincerely. "The less I know, the better. Besides, you're armed."

Parish shook his head, unable to comprehend why anyone wouldn't want to see one of the greatest potential mysteries left in the state of Indiana, if not the world. If the cubes were indeed designed in this labyrinth, the location might provide some long-awaited answers about how to deal with them once and for all.

Setting down the flashlight momentarily, Parish replaced his sport coat, uncertain what awaited him down the dingy tunnel. He tested the flashlight a few seconds later, ready to discover some answers and hopefully make up for the debacle in the Bering Sea. Parish still blamed himself for not performing better on the boat, but outgunned and outmanned, no one aboard the vessel truly had much of a chance. He was lucky to be alive and walking.

"I'm honestly not sure what Mr. Clouse sees in you," he said, turning to Niemeyer at the doorway entrance.

Niemeyer grinned, apparently thinking Parish was kidding.

"I'm going to tell him you said that."

CHAPTER 42

Not particularly happy with Niemeyer and the man's lack of commitment to his best friend, Parish started down the tunnel, immediately finding parts of the walls reinforced with stone and brick. He wondered if some of the tunnel might have served as additional storage for the old hotel in the beginning, because the wall supports suddenly ended about ten feet inside. Parish believed someone might have added on to the old storage room later on, because the tunnel walls suddenly became hardened dirt instead. Old wooden timbers ran perpendicular overhead, occasionally supported by vertical beams to prevent collapse from the weight above. Based on some of the nearby buildings aboveground, Parish considered the logic for reinforcing the tunnel quite sound.

"See anything?" Niemeyer called from the doorway, refusing to step inside.

"Get your ass in here if you want a play-by-play."

No reply came, though Parish felt certain he heard Niemeyer mumble something.

Parish shined the flashlight around the walls and ahead of him, seeing no immediate end to the tunnel. He did, however, find hangers and some very old lanterns along the walls. Probably built when electricity wasn't a household item, the tunnel certainly wouldn't have been provided with such an amenity, because power lines would have risked giving away the secret.

A closer look indicated the lanterns used some kind of oil for fuel, but all of them were covered with dust and dirt after seeing no visitors for nearly a century. Parish didn't have time, or a need, to light them as he walked. Simply amazed by the craftsmanship of the tunnel, he wondered if the cursed objects that caused Clouse fits were truly born at the end of the mysterious tunnel. If so, that made the destination a true place of evil, one rivaled by some of Hitler's estates, or modern day lairs used by terrorists overseas.

Any landmark where the demise of thousands was planned over the centuries was always considered a heinous place. Parish hurried his pace, wanting to see what awaited him at the end of the tunnel. He also felt some-what claustrophobic walking through a tunnel barely able to support the width of two people standing side by side and the height of an average guard in the NBA. He kept telling himself the walls and ceiling had held for nearly a hundred years, but that didn't stop thoughts of collapse from creeping into his mind.

Cobwebs appeared occasionally, though nowhere near as often, or as thick, as the movies made them look in caves. An odor that came with age accompanied the creepy sights, mostly from the wood that deteriorated at a snail's pace due to the lack of moisture and air entering the tunnel until this day. No breeze followed him inside, and the tunnel felt like a basement kept at perfect temperature and humidity.

Monitoring the ground ahead before he stepped foot on it, Parish found the dirt packed to nearly the texture of solid rock. He tried to avoid thinking about the depth of the tunnel, or the heavy buildings above him, continuing to stare at the ground until the texture changed from blackened dirt to some form of tile in an instant. He switched off the flashlight, discovering the tile was illuminated by something directly ahead.

"Wow," Parish muttered, looking into a room that no person ever expected to find at the end of a dingy tunnel.

A pulsating fiery glow emanated from the opposite side of the room that didn't appear to come from nature or any power source Parish had ever laid eyes upon. The glow provided a low light, though enough to illuminate the entire room when the pulse reached its full brightness. Parish tried to take in the entire chamber as he stood at the open doorway, finding it the size of a moderate conference room with some kind of large centerpiece that looked like a strange piece of permanent furniture. He couldn't identify the fixture, but it looked a little bit like an oversized decorative birdbath.

Ignoring the room's décor momentarily, Parish looked to the floor directly ahead, wondering if some kind of snare awaited him once he stepped inside. There was a time when he never would have considered the prospect of stepping onto a brick only to have poisoned arrows firing at him in unison. And back then he wouldn't have believed thirteen cubes could provide people with benefits in exchange for a human sacrifice but he now knew better.

Kneeling down, Parish looked for any tripwire, or variations along the floor. He noticed for the first time that the floor consisted of thousands of small tiles about one inch square apiece. Though they lacked any distinctive patterns sometimes created by different color combinations, he thought they looked exactly like the tiles in the West Baden Springs Hotel's lobby and atrium areas. Based on the time when this chamber might have been created compared to the first renovations ever done at the hotel, a sinking feeling hit the bodyguard.

Staying low, he finally stepped into the room, expecting each step to be his last. Married, with two children of his own, Parish didn't particularly want to throw his life away, even for the greater good of the world. Clouse paid him well, but even Parish's employer didn't expect him to recklessly charge into the unknown and risk life and limb.

With his heart pounding in his chest, Parish took a few crouched steps inside, finally satisfied he wasn't going to be instantly struck down. He stood, finally able to examine the room, finding every inch of the floor covered in the same marble tile. The walls, not to be outdone, were finished in some kind of cloudy marble, in swirls of white and some other medium color Parish could not decipher due to the pulsating orange glow from the far wall.

Before crossing the room, Parish cautiously walked toward the center where the large ornament with a bowl-shaped top stood. From its center, a dozen or so, perhaps even thirteen, small arms protruded outward along the floor, reaching toward an outer ring. The centerpiece held the appearance of a water wheel from above, looking as though someone had simply laid it down upon the floor. No more than eight feet in diameter, and a little more than four feet tall, the custom ornament appeared to be made from some sort of stone, which seemed impossible given its curvature and decorative trim. Parish approached it, finding the wheel portion stood just below his waistline, which provided easy access to any adult standing in his or her assigned spoke. He circled the strange fixture until his foot bumped into something lying along the floor.

Dropping to one knee, he found the skull of a skeleton staring back at him, its head resting against the closest stone spoke. A chain remained attached to one bony foot, appearing to be the culprit for the man never leaving the chamber. Based on lore, Parish assumed the poor soul was the jeweler the original thirteen conspirators hired to construct the cubes before Satan himself cursed them. The legend also told that the man, knowing his life was forfeit, constructed the leather-bound book to record the names and kept it hidden. Apparently people with incredibly unwavering morals found the book sometime later, considering Julie Knowles and Mark Teakon eventually took possession of it.

Not knowing the whole truth bothered Parish almost as much as it perturbed the clan that Mark Teakon once headed. Receiving occasional information through letters and personal items helped, but such testimonials couldn't always be verified or believed. Somehow a group of Chicago police officers obtained the time cube, or the world might have been a completely different place numerous times over. As bad as things seemed with everyone making personal sacrifices and losing loved ones, Parish imagined it could have been *much* worse if not for some unsung heroes over the past century.

He gave the skeletal remains one last examination, finding clothes still intact, though tattered, on the deceased jeweler. They looked like the same attire he might see someone donning on a sepia postcard from around World War I. It wasn't bad enough the bastards forced him to create instruments of evil, but they made him a captive audience for the proceedings as well. Being locked in such a strange room and seeing the demonic procession probably gave the poor working man a heart attack.

With no flesh present on the body, Parish couldn't tell if the man truly suffered before his untimely death. Parish's own skin crawled because he'd never laid eyes on a corpse with just bones before. Not particularly experienced around bodies in the first place, he felt uneasy about seeing anyone in this state, and regretted accidentally kicking the bony figure.

Standing at last, Parish walked the perfectly laid tiles to the source of the pulsating, eerie glow along the far wall. What he found was the source of the strange glow took up virtually the entire wall in the shape of a clock. He drew close, examining the clock with Roman numerals larger than his hands, finding a strange, square indentation beside each of the numbers. Based on the consistency of the pulsating glow, and the fact that he could find no obvious power source, Parish guessed the clock to be powered by unnatural means. Strangely, the entire face of the clock created the ebb and flow of light, though the surface appeared hardened. Made of marble or some form of crystalline rock, the face shouldn't have been able to emit light in any fashion.

"Jesus," he muttered, uncertain if the clock possessed actual workings when he tried studying the metal rods holding the clock's hands in place.

The face of the clock looked very similar to old Victorian grandfather clocks he spotted in antique stores when his wife dragged him shopping. Everything about the room indeed pointed toward the notion that the cubes were born in the room and set free to cause death and destruction throughout the world. Parish sensed some larger picture still eluded him, mainly because he didn't know the local history exceptionally well like his boss. For the first time in a long time he felt like this new information might place Clouse's group on even ground with the people determined to possess every last cube.

Five minutes later he returned to the entrance doorway where the daylight stung his eyes momentarily. Blinking feverishly, Parish was greeted by Niemeyer, who seemed anxious to hear his finds. Parish pulled the heavy door shut behind him as best he could, though it refused to move the last few inches for a full seal.

"Replace all of the dirt," Parish told him. "Bury the basement again."

"What did you find in there?"

"You can hear it when I report to Mr. Clouse, but for now we don't want anyone finding their way down there."

Niemeyer nodded, having some understanding of the difficulties facing the group because the enemy knew their plans the moment they conceived them. He climbed the ladder out of the pit and walked purposefully toward his employee to order the basement filled in once more. Parish followed a moment later, stealing a final look toward the excavated area that led to a place of unspeakable evil and terror. Images of the ominous clock plagued Parish, who considered himself a simple man and no expert on the occult.

Instinct, however, told him that the clock and that room were the focal points of whatever diabolical plans the people with the cubes had in mind.

Filling in the basement kept spying eyes and evildoers away for the time being, but Parish prayed for the day when the cubes and the glowing clock below were a thing of the past, remembered by no one.

CHAPTER 43

Summer passed without incident, which worried most everyone affiliated with Clouse. After hearing about the find beneath his new property, Clouse started formulating some plans, but he never laid eyes on the basement as though he knew eventually his hand would be forced. He kept to himself, encouraging his staff to do the same and not share information, as though paranoid that their thoughts might be plucked from the air at any given time.

Craig Jennings conducted some rounds throughout the hotel on a late afternoon toward the end of September. Sticky morning air gave way to thunderstorms and cooler winds in the afternoon as a stark reminder that the fall season awaited the Springs Valley. He made his way past the front desk in the lobby, coming to a stop at the stained glass front doors. A row of stained glass doors left from the Jesuit occupancy of the hotel grounds were locked beside the clear main doors. One of the truly beautiful features left from the priests, only a few of the doors remained intact when the hotel was found in ruins after being caught up in legislature for nearly a decade. The construction firm Clouse went to work for a decade prior received the bid to piece the hotel together, which included creating replicas of the stained glass throughout the lobby.

Jennings knew some of his employer's past, partly because he had always lived in the area, as did Clouse, and also because Jennings visited the hotel when it stood out of habit. Faded, chipped paint covered the walls both inside and out, while portions of the roof and skylights broke apart during that time. Still, that didn't stop Jennings and countless other people from sneaking beyond the mesh wire fence surrounding the grounds for a look at the old building before a preservation group eventually stepped in to begin saving the hotel.

After some private donations and a few partnerships, the restoration was underway and the public wasn't able to visit the grounds for the better part of a year. Only when the atrium, the ground floor, and the hotel's grounds were renewed did the preservation group overseeing the hotel allow daily paid tours on the hour.

Staring out the clear lobby doors, Jennings saw rain pounding the brick drive that reached the hotel from the highway. It also tumbled down the concrete front stairwell, much like a raging river heading for lower ground. Sometimes barely a drop of rain fell from the sky during the summer months in Orange County, and occasionally the spring season brought enough water to produce a small lake in front of the dome that lasted for weeks.

On a Wednesday afternoon barely a soul was found inside the hotel. Employees and fewer than a dozen guests could be found on the grounds because conventions and weddings often took place closer to the weekends. This week it seemed Clouse's other major hotel down the road received most of the convention business. Staying at the West Baden Springs Hotel cost more, so during the peak vacation season companies tended to take the cheaper alternative a mile away.

Thunder grumbled in the distance, and the lights inside the lobby waned momentarily as though the power might go out, but they recovered. Jennings turned to find Dan Duncan walking in from the atrium as the employees behind the reception desk snapped to attention. By no means a tyrant, Duncan seemed to have the respect of his employees as though he held something over them aside from the ability to terminate their employment.

"Shouldn't you be tending to our seven guests and their every need?" Jennings kidded the hotel manager.

"I'm busy preparing for the additional ten guests coming in tonight," Duncan answered with a chuckle. "I think this weather is scaring people away."

"Not exactly a dream vacation with that monsoon out there, is it?"

"No."

Customarily Duncan refused to wear a suit around the hotel. He seldom interacted with guests because the manager on duty handled the daily affairs, and for that matter he barely socialized with the employees. He ran an efficient, clean hotel, despite having no real experience in the hotel service. A little bit of management schooling, combined with his business background, transformed Duncan into a solid, albeit rather unsociable manager.

Although he never pushed the issue, Clouse asked Duncan to interact more with the staff and guests to practice for the occasions when he needed to appear completely professional in front of wealthy or influential guests and investors. The owner didn't push the dress code, because Duncan knew when he needed to dust off his suit for special appearances.

When one of the lobby doors opened, the two women behind the reception desk looked up while both Duncan and Jennings directed their attention to a lone man carrying a small suitcase. The man wore a suit that appeared slightly wrinkled and very much soaked from the downpour.

"This is your chance to practice," Jennings said, nudging the manager in the ribs.

Rolling his eyes, Duncan grunted doubtfully before stepping forward, struggling to put forth a halfway genuine smile.

Jennings watched the hotel manager greet the man as warmly as possible for Duncan, even shaking his hand and offering to take his bag.

"Thank you," the man said, reluctantly returning the handshake, soiled from head to toe by the unforgiving weather.

At first Jennings entertained himself by watching Duncan struggle to bring forth his amicable side, but as he replayed the man's entrance in his mind, something bothered him about the stranger's appearance.

Even as the man walked to the desk to check in, Jennings wondered where the hell he parked. The parking lot was all the way around the back of the hotel, which meant he would have accessed one of the other entrances closer to the rear if he parked there. Parking at the bank near the highway didn't sound prudent, because the walk to the hotel was currently a hundred yards in torrential rain. Perhaps someone else dropped him off and went to the parking lot, or down to the casino, but Jennings continued with his train of thought, walking toward his security office where he could monitor lots of square footage within the building on a computer monitor.

He felt bad for leaving Duncan, but the manager could handle himself, or hand the guest off to the women working the reception desk. The handshake on the stranger's end seemed forced, as though the man really had no desire for human contact. Jennings remembered seeing that same trait in Liz, although her reasoning was slightly different. She didn't want to know absolutely everything about the people around her, whereas this man acted as though he might be compromised.

Thinking of that led Jennings to his last interesting clue.

Most people who walked in drenched from the rain gave the appearance of having black hair. Jennings arrived at his office, closing the door behind him as he watched the stranger check in and wait for the nearby elevator to arrive. Something about this man struck him as familiar, but it wasn't until the man took the elevator up three levels to the fourth floor where he used his keycard to enter a balcony room that Jennings felt a tingle run through his spine.

Although the man looked somewhat thinner, Jennings felt almost certain this was the man Clouse's group viewed in unison a few months back. He rewound the footage, trying to determine the man's hair color, even replaying the footage in slow motion for a better look. Freezing the screen on a frame where the hallway light struck the man's hair just right, Jennings felt certain he saw several strands of red hair where the rain hadn't saturated them, or they managed to somehow dry quickly.

"Son-of-a-bitch," Jennings muttered, scooping up the phone to call Greene, hoping his initial curious thoughts hadn't given him away.

It wasn't exactly like *Ghostbusters*, where thinking of the Stay Puft Marshmallow Man would cause utter disaster, but Jennings hoped the psychic didn't pick up on any doubts in his mind during the moment he lingered in the lobby.

While Clouse and Parish had basically disappeared since the start of August, Greene and Liz made occasional appearances when they weren't out checking leads on the man frozen on a computer monitor before Jennings. The pair had yet to find any concrete link to the mysterious man, and now he apparently had the audacity to walk into their home ground.

Two rings crossed the earpiece before Greene picked up.

"Hello?"

"Russ, it's Craig. You're not going to believe what just happened here at the hotel."

Jennings spent a few minutes quickly explaining the situation to Greene, praying the red-headed man wasn't somehow picking up on their conversation and heading to the security office with a gun to silence his latest nuisance. As a precaution, while he talked, Jennings stretched the phone cord to its limit and locked his office door with outstretched fingers.

"Craig, Liz wants to know if he touched anything when he came in. Anything she can handle to maybe read his mind."

"Well, the door of course. And Duncan shook hands with him."

"Grab Dan and bring him here."

"Where *are* you guys?" Jennings asked as he returned his monitor to a live feed, making certain no one was sneaking around the ground floor to surprise him.

"We're in Bedford grabbing a late lunch."

"Why can't you bring Liz down here?"

"Are you brain-dead? I can't take her anywhere near that guy."

"But he's *right* here. We could end *all* of this right now."

A momentary pause indicated Greene was at least entertaining the suggestion.

"No," he finally said. "If this guy works for someone and doesn't cough up the name, we're back to square one."

"Fine. I'll grab Dan and call you once we're heading your way."

Jennings hung up the phone, not sure he liked Greene's decision this time around. Maybe thinking of a destructive marshmallow man wasn't his worst course of action after all.

✳✳✳

Jennings quickly found Duncan in his office and took a route through the hotel that kept them away from prying eyes and hopefully psychic minds. Greene requested they meet in the small town of Mitchell, just south of Bedford but a safe distance away from West Baden. The nearly thirty-minute drive gave Jennings plenty of time to explain the situation to the hotel manager. Duncan didn't completely grasp the concept of being a human conductor for psychic power transference, but he didn't ask many questions.

"Did you wash your hands?" Jennings questioned once they finished passing through the town of Orleans, just minutes away from their rendezvous.

"I don't think so," Duncan answered almost blankly, staring at his hands as though mesmerized by them. "I use hand sanitizer a lot though."

"Did you use it after you shook hands with that guy?"

"I don't know," Duncan answered emphatically, more concerned about being useless to the group than annoyed at the questions hurled his way.

His memory proved less reliable as the years went by. Duncan hated most technology with a passion and considered himself a throwback to when men were rugged individuals. He loved riding motorcycles and enjoyed the occasional expensive cigar, keeping his pleasures simple. Never married, and with no children to complicate his life, Duncan threw himself into business, seldom dating or attending social gatherings unless the job required it. Although he remained very sharp and alert in business, some of the simple things often relating to short-term memory eluded him.

Another concern plagued Jennings because Greene wanted to keep Clouse out of the loop until they knew something more. Despite Greene's wishes, Jennings tried calling his boss. Without so much as one ring the man's phone went straight to voicemail, exactly how others reported it doing so for the past few weeks. Jennings believed his employer was on a mission for the greater good, keeping Parish with him for some unstated reason. Clouse informed Greene, Jennings, and a few others that he wasn't going to be in touch for an undetermined amount of time, and Jennings simply believed the man was protecting his family and possibly investigating a lead.

Another five minutes passed before Jennings reached the town limits of Mitchell, continuing onward until he spotted the Arby's restaurant where Greene asked to meet. Jennings pulled to the back of the parking lot, away from any other vehicles and customers, where Greene and Liz stood waiting beside Greene's pickup truck.

Raindrops still peppered the windshield intermittently as the storm clouds refused to move east. Both men reluctantly stepped from the marked resort car Jennings had commandeered for the trip, which suddenly didn't seem like the wisest mode of transportation since everything about the trip was handled so secretly. In the distance the dark gray clouds began parting, but the smell of rain and a sticky humidity lingered in the air.

"I hope I can help," Duncan said, addressing Liz once they approached the pair.

"It all depends on his skin particles, his DNA, being on your hand," Liz answered. "I think. Hell, I don't know how all of this works. I'm just going by past experience."

Duncan held out his right hand as though he expected to lose it. It trembled ever so slightly as Liz stared at it momentarily and gave him a reassuring smile before finally cupping it gently between her palms.

Jennings watched Liz intently, expecting her to stiffen momentarily as though she read something from Duncan's hand. Nothing happened, which disappointed everyone visibly. He wanted to blame Duncan, a creature of habit, for cleaning his hands, but he faulted his own mind for not identifying the mysterious redheaded stranger sooner.

"Maybe the rain kept his DNA from transferring," Jennings suggested aloud, considering the possibility.

Liz picked up on the idea, beginning to rub her palms over Duncan's hand in a massaging motion in search of the slightest skin particle. Her actions only required a few seconds before her facial expression changed and her entire body shivered in the briefest of moments, stuck between stiffening and relaxing as her mind took in something unseen to the three men around her.

The entire ordeal literally lasted only a few seconds, but it took another minute or so before Liz fully recovered while Greene steadied her by gently clasping her elbow. Everyone anxiously waited for a report of what images entered her mind. Shaking off the effects of a psychic transition, Liz took hold of Greene's forearm to steady herself.

"Did you see anything?" Greene asked first.

"I saw part of his childhood," she stammered, "but then he shut me out."

"Shut you out?" Jennings questioned.

"He knew I got inside his mind and forced me out. His powers, they don't work like mine. His ability only works when he's in proximity of his target and he concentrates on reading their thoughts."

"So he can only target people when he's nearby?" Jennings asked, thinking back to the hotel, hoping he didn't give away any crucial information.

"That's why he had to be nearby when they raided the bookstore," Greene stated. "We now know that FBI guy and his two cronies were the ones who raided the bookstore, but they're all dead or missing."

"We do?" Duncan asked. "I don't recall that information being shared with the rest of us during any meetings."

"That's because we aren't even a collective group anymore," Greene argued, raising his voice. "Hell, the guy who pays us disappeared and Stone said the last henchman he was looking for turned up dead back in June. We were running on empty until the psychic for our arch nemesis waltzed into the hotel an hour ago."

Liz stepped in, trying to maintain the peace.

"Guys, take it down a notch. This guy may be fighting to keep me out of his head, but I have a mental connection to him now. He can't keep me out forever, and he's going to be scared."

"And he's going to run," Jennings surmised. "Should we try and stop him?"

Greene rubbed his chin in thought momentarily.

"I don't want Liz anywhere near him. She's the only person who might provide us with information and I don't want this guy compromising us, or getting to her."

"Dan and I can handle this," Jennings said, tapping Duncan on the arm as they marched toward the company car.

He didn't feel especially confident that the man couldn't pick their thoughts, but if he was still inside their hotel, Jennings thought of no reason they couldn't detain him and wait for someone with interrogation experience to question him.

None of his security staff carried firearms, and none of them were experienced enough to carry out an arrest. They were basically there to keep situations from escalating while calling the local police for assistance. Besides, none of them were informed about the secretive nature of the cube hunt, and Jennings refused to place them in jeopardy without providing full disclosure.

Either way, he planned on confronting the man in half an hour, or chasing down any leads in pursuit of the stranger.

CHAPTER 44

When Jennings and Duncan returned to the hotel, Jennings parked the company car in a lane near the lobby entrance beside a sign that clearly read no parking was allowed. All employees within the hotel listened to either man's orders, so when Jennings inquired about the one man who had checked in within the last hour, they knew exactly which person he meant.

The woman behind the desk typed in the name, still remembering the floor and exact room after Jennings requested any guest information in their system.

"Have you seen him?" Jennings inquired while waiting for a printout of the guest information.

"No," the woman answered.

"What room is he in?" Duncan asked, likely thinking of heading upstairs to pay the man a visit.

Duncan impatiently let himself behind the counter to watch the employee's progress over her shoulder, openly making her a bit nervous.

"Tyler Johnson," Duncan read the guest's name aloud. "Probably an alias."

Jennings thought along the same lines, but neither of them was equipped to handle an abduction and interrogation. While Jennings could deal with the security cameras, he possessed no means of drugging the man, and no firearm to lead him to the basement. Even with a handful of guests and staff milling around, the notion of silently executing such a plan felt nearly impossible.

Any potential setbacks didn't slow Duncan as he drew his master key-card and headed for the elevator after he found the room number on the screen the clerk was using. Jennings sighed internally and followed, not wanting the manager to stir up trouble and expose the fact that they knew the redheaded man's identity. He also wanted to protect the older man from harm in case their guest harbored any surprises within the room.

Jennings wanted to check the security footage first, but Duncan appeared determined to visit this man in person.

"You going to play this cool?" Jennings asked as the elevator ascended.

"I'll just ask if there's anything he needs," Duncan replied without much emotion in his voice. "It's a slow day, so he should buy it."

"Just remember he can read thoughts, so try to concentrate on anything except what we're doing."

Duncan nodded, but Jennings didn't feel especially comfortable hoping the manager grasped the severity of the situation.

When the elevator opened a few seconds later, the duo was greeted by the same decorative carpeting laid upon every upper floor. A mix of brown, gold, and green, the pattern mirrored the tile on the ground floor except that the image of a compass was placed in the center of the carpet about every quarter turn. The various compasses always pointed in the true direction as one navigated the two rings of rooms surrounding the atrium.

Hoping they didn't point toward danger and imminent death, Jennings followed them, reading the numbers on the doors he already knew by heart until he reached the correct room facing toward the atrium.

"This is it," he said unnecessarily as Duncan stopped simultaneously at the door.

Jennings stepped aside as his colleague knocked on the door. Unable to refrain from displaying his impatience, Duncan stared at the ceiling while tapping his foot atop the carpet. Several seconds passed with absolute silence from the other side, prompting Duncan to draw the master keycard from his pocket a second time. Before inserting it, however, he rapped on the door several more times with his knuckles, receiving no answer.

Saying nothing, he inserted the key and flung open the door, finding no one inside, and not so much as one travel bag on the floor. The king-size bed remained untouched, its comforter perfectly straight as though nothing touched it and no items were ever placed upon it. As both men stepped completely inside, they found nothing disturbed on the sink, and as Jennings lifted the toilet lid, he saw no evidence of it being used.

"What the hell did he even come here for?" Duncan questioned aloud.

"Maybe he figured us out."

"How? I didn't even know who the hell he was until you told me."

Jennings shook his head.

"Maybe he just picked up on us somehow."

Feeling guilty, Jennings suspected *he* was the only one who might have provided the thoughts that scared the psychic away from the hotel. Still, it made no sense that the man walked up to his room only to leave without so much as a trace of evidence.

He decided even before they finished combing the remainder of the room that he wanted to review the security footage. Something didn't add up about the man making the trip into enemy territory only to leave almost immediately. Whether the psychic hoped to find Clouse, or extract information from the employees might never be known, but Jennings intended to search for answers.

Once Duncan felt content there was nothing useful in the room, Jennings asked the manager to accompany him to the security office.

"You sure you saw him walk in there?" Duncan asked on the way down.

"He went inside the room. How long he stayed, I have no idea."

A few minutes later they accessed the security office and Jennings retrieved the fourth floor footage of the man stepping into his room just to verify his sanity for Duncan. They stared at the video in real time, waiting for the moment when the redheaded stranger stepped from his room. Only a minute passed before the man calmly and deliberately exited the room, carrying his bag. He walked purposefully as though he understood the need to leave the grounds quickly, but his expression showed very little about his intentions. During the elevator ride the man opened his cell phone to place a call. Jennings wished the phone had faced the camera long enough to pick up any information on the screen, but he didn't live in some television show where the picture zoomed in on command with enhanced quality.

Jennings called up other camera footage, following the man from his room to the elevator, then through the atrium out the back entrance where a car waited to whisk him away. Unfortunately the cameras outside simply covered the parking lot and the valet area from a wide-angle distance view. If someone monitored the live feed the cameras could easily zoom in for more detail, particularly if a crime was being committed or security needed to identify a particular person. Unfortunately when Jennings left his post any chance of identifying the driver left with him.

He reviewed the footage several times as the redheaded man slid into the passenger's seat of the sedan, but the driver simply wasn't readily visible. The camera, mounted on an awning just above the valet area, provided a decent view of the driver's side of the car, but the driver wore sunglasses and knew better than to look in that particular direction.

"This stinks," Jennings muttered. "We were that close and he slips away."

"What if he didn't?" Duncan asked thoughtfully. "Maybe we should call Mark Daniels and give him a heads up, then take a little drive through French Lick."

Daniels headed up the security force at the casino just a mile down the road, which worked independently from the security personnel at the hotels.

Jennings couldn't argue with the logic. If the mystery man and his driver indeed planned a reconnaissance mission, it seemed one minor setback wasn't going to deter them. Grabbing the keys to the company vehicle from his desk, Jennings motioned toward the door, wanting Duncan to stay with him a bit longer. Based on the unusual circumstances, Jennings felt uncomfortable dealing with a psychic and any other minions by himself. The fact that Clouse proved unreachable also bothered him, because a feeling that they were drawing close to a confrontation with their unknown nemesis gnawed at the back of his mind.

He hoped the disappearance of Clouse and Parish meant the two men were preparing for the inevitable, rather than hiding. Based on Clouse's credo, Jennings couldn't picture the man backing down all of the sudden, when the darkest hour concerning the cursed objects drew nearer with each passing minute.

***

It turned out Clouse's friend Mark Daniels wasn't working, which made any potential search for the redheaded mystery man nearly impossible. Jennings drove around French Lick and West Baden searching for the sedan from his footage without success. Even the short dead-end streets revealed nothing to him, indicating the man might have left town, or at least provided the indication he did so.

Jennings decided to make a stop at the French Lick Springs Hotel because the parking garage beside it could easily harbor a car on its numerous levels. He stepped inside the main lobby while Duncan headed toward the casino and the nearby garage to cut their search time. Keeping his expectations low, Jennings walked through the lobby toward the nearby hallway that traveled the length of the long hotel, passing gift shops and curio cabinets filled with vintage items along the way.

Although keycards were required by guests to use certain elevators, Jennings knew someone could slip into an elevator with another guest, or hide in one of the numerous areas meant to distract tourists. The basement area consisted of a buffet, bowling alley, and several specialty eateries, along with a tavern. He didn't particularly feel like sticking his head inside every door for a look, knowing full well the psychic might have already left town. Besides, if the man happened to be nearby, how would Jennings know his thoughts weren't being read, allowing the red-headed man to remain one step ahead?

Passing some hotel employees, Jennings gave a friendly nod, noticing he was being eyeballed as though they couldn't figure out how they knew him. Jennings often wore slacks and a tie, but sometimes went corporate casual like Duncan. Today was one of those days where he wore an embroidered polo shirt and khaki pants. Since he wasn't certified by the state as a police officer, and saw no reason to work as a reserve police officer, Jennings didn't carry a firearm at work. Only security personnel at the casino were armed, and none of the hotel personnel were allowed to carry firearms, even if they possessed a permit or police training. Clouse wanted people to feel safe when they stayed at his resort, but he didn't want armed security walking around his grand hotels like the buildings were in danger of lockdowns on a whim.

Thanks to a desire to stay true to history by Clouse and his team, the French Lick Springs Hotel was redone with gold leaf paint, murals, and lots of natural wood. By no means inexpensive, the details provided just as much of a beautiful view as its former rival down the road. Jennings walked along the thick carpeting, looking up to the walls where two gigantic graphically designed murals done with models in vintage attire and backgrounds depicting the two grand hotels and early cars basically advertised the resort as a whole. Further along his path, large canvas posters dotted the lengthy wall, using pictures of more models and resort employees to show absolutely every amenity available between the two hotels.

Jennings didn't mind. The resort, and Clouse, saved him from the drab life of a high school shop teacher. Although his new occupation wasn't the safest, both in his everyday duties and the occasional dangerous quest for cursed objects, he couldn't complain. He wholeheartedly believed in Clouse's quest, particularly after making friends of colleagues like Dan Duncan along the way.

Suddenly thinking about his buddy, Jennings pulled out his cell phone, trying to call the hotel manager who should have made his way from the casino into the garage already. Jennings heard four rings on his end before the phone went to voicemail. He wanted to believe Duncan was experiencing his usual technology trouble while trying to answer his phone, but Jennings worried because the man wasn't always as sharp and alert as one needed to be when part of Clouse's inner circle.

Reaching the end of the hallway at last, Jennings decided not to turn right and head down an escalator into the casino. He walked straight ahead into the garage as automatic doors opened to welcome him into the darker setting. Breathing in the muggy air that still lingered from the thunderstorm, Jennings stepped forward along the first row of vehicles, able to hear his footsteps whenever he walked. Amazingly he found no one else along the central level of the garage, so he continued, looking between parked vehicles since he didn't see Duncan. Calling out for the man didn't seem professional in a place of business, so he tried calling the manager once more on the phone, reaching voicemail a second time.

Groaning to himself, Jennings walked to the end of the row and turned back, rather than move to another level. He passed the entrance doors, rounding the corner to explore the other side of the barrier that separated the various rows of vehicles. Instead of calling out for Duncan, he decided to try the phone once more, hoping to hear the ring of the manager's phone from somewhere in the garage. For all he knew, Duncan might have gone looking for him along the ground floor, or the basement inside the hotel.

When he immediately heard a phone ringing in the distance, but saw no one standing on the entire level, Jennings grew concerned. He picked up his pace, continuing to listen for the phone as he looked from right to left between the vehicles, hoping he didn't find his friend injured.

Or worse.

Realizing the sound originated further down the concrete path, Jennings darted straight for the ringing phone, rather than conducting a search at a jogger's pace. He made an effort to reach the source of the ringing before it stopped, trying to avoid any distractions like looking at his own phone to place another call. Toward the end of the row of vehicles he rounded a large SUV, finding Duncan lying on his side with his cell phone atop the concrete a few feet away.

Kneeling beside his fallen comrade, Jennings tried shaking him, finding no visible wounds or indication why Duncan appeared to be unconscious.

"Dan, wake up," he said, nervously looking around to make sure no harmful figures lurked nearby.

Duncan finally groaned a few seconds later, slow to regain his senses as though he'd been struck in the head. Jennings sat him up, still wary of their surroundings, not seeing any security cameras in their area. He suspected the person, or people, responsible for harming his friend knew the same information.

"Dan, what happened?" he asked, testing whether or not Duncan could get to his feet.

Duncan struggled to assist Jennings, who grasped him by the elbow, but slumped to his posterior before getting very far off the ground.

"Someone hit me from behind," he muttered through the pain, rubbing the bald spot toward the back of his head.

"How long have you been out?"

"No idea."

Duncan started reaching for his phone.

"Were you calling someone?" Jennings inquired.

"No. I didn't have my phone out."

Jennings intercepted his colleague's reach, picking up the phone first and looking at the screen. Right there in plain sight, as though Duncan's attacker *wanted* them to know it, sat Paul Clouse's direct cell phone number.

Only the employees who knew about the cubes and assisted in Clouse's search for the evil objects possessed his personal cell phone number.

And now his greatest adversaries knew it as well.

CHAPTER 45

Russ Greene grew irritated about staying in hiding with Liz while no positive news reached him through the occasional phone call or secretive e-mail. He played it safe, using no credit cards, avoiding the cell phone except during predetermined talk times, and sticking to rural settings whenever possible.

Even more than him, Liz went stir crazy after living in California for so long where activities were plentiful and human contact wasn't so scarce. Although she seldom interacted with other people, she openly enjoyed being around others and picking up on conversations. She felt a sense of normality, hearing mundane chitchat and seeing how ordinary people acted. Strangely, she gained a similar sense through conversations with Greene, learning about his childhood and career while sharing some of her own past.

All without using her abilities.

Whenever Greene spoke with Craig Jennings or Julie Knowles, he felt as though nothing was putting them closer to recovering the lost cubes. Clouse and Parish were out of contact with everyone, and a sense of disorganization put a stranglehold on the group. Toward the end of October, after months of a frustrating life in hiding, Greene asked Liz if she wanted to try something that might provide answers, but place their lives in jeopardy if they weren't cautious.

"What do you have in mind?" Liz asked in response, a devious smirk crossing her lips.

"Let me make a phone call."

Greene talked with Julie Knowles and Matt Teakon during the next scheduled phone call, finally proposing that they all meet. His suggestion was met with initial hesitation, but when he all but blatantly explained *why* he wanted to meet, it was Julie who won over Teakon. Greene heard most of their discussion over the phone, and credited the courage of both Julie and Liz for taking the necessary steps toward ending their ongoing ordeal.

Now, on the day before Halloween, Greene drove toward a secluded area in central Pennsylvania. Literally a truck stop gas station off the highway, and the only occupied facility for miles, Greene felt the location was perfect. He remembered it from a case he worked several years prior when he needed to stop for fuel and it was the only alternative for miles. A navigation device helped him locate it before he called Teakon and Julie with a specific location. For the time being they were simply driving toward the highway he specified, bringing the leather-bound book with them.

"Did you see anything last night?" Greene asked from the driver's seat as fall foliage blurred past the side of the vehicle.

Occasionally, in her dreams, Liz saw past and present visions of the red-headed stranger, realizing his past consisted of being bullied and ostracized by his peers. Unfortunately he continued to block most of the pertinent information regarding his current plans, but she saw fragments of things he had visited and seen the past few months, including the French Lick area.

"Nothing new," she reported. "It's like he knew enough to put up a mental fence because someone attempted to enter his mind at some point."

Greene understood her frustration, because Liz didn't back down or allow herself to be intimidated by the unknown adversary. If anything, she faulted her own lack of knowledge to grow and expand her ability because she understood that the man psychically linked to her had honed his gift over the years.

When asked why she thought her dreams revealed bits and pieces about his life, Liz replied that she figured when he slept his mental guard was let down somewhat. She admitted no lingering dreams or images had entered her mind previously after touching people or objects, so the open line of sorts likely came from the stranger's end.

Within half an hour the duo met Julie and Teakon at the truck stop, occupying a table near the back of a national pizza chain restaurant. Two other eateries and a convenience store complete with gift shop took up the remainder of the large building. Truckers stopped for fuel, showers, and supplies, and Greene kept a close watch on every stranger who crossed their paths inside the store.

Outside, gray skies changed the atmosphere as the four sat beside a corner window. Julie slowly produced the book from a silk cloth shroud, placing it atop the table as all four looked around, finding no one else in the restaurant, and the crew behind the counter preoccupied with gossip and typical duties. Liz took a deep breath, looking into the anxious eyes of the people she considered comrades, dedicated to the same dangerous endeavor as her. Part of her hoped to see nothing, and perhaps avoid the pressures of being the one person who might provide answers while Clouse and Parish remained missing, their objectives unknown to anyone else. The other half of Liz wanted to know everything, and confront the redheaded stranger now linked to her already active mind.

Liz reluctantly reached for the book, wondering what images, if any, were about to flood her mind.

✳✳✳

Paul Clouse's disappearance was by design, and not because he felt a need to hide and protect himself. Instead he wanted to allow Parish the opportunity to formulate a plan without any knowledge of the details. Clouse considered his mind a fountain of information for the enemy to drink from at any given time. Because he already knew where the final showdown was destined to occur, Clouse didn't want to devise a plan himself, for fear that it might be for nothing. He could think of no one more important for the enemy psychic to stalk simply because he and he alone knew where the time cube was located.

Once he felt reasonably certain Parish had managed to devise a plan, Clouse returned to his summer chalet located on the edge of Lake Monroe outside of Bloomington. Thanks to a message, he now knew the man who possessed the remainder of the cursed cubes also possessed his phone number. With his wife, son, and stepdaughter safely tucked inside the custom-built house with windows aplenty to view the lake from any level, Clouse stepped onto the second story deck when an unfamiliar phone number called his cell phone.

Already harboring a mild dislike for the next day's holiday, Clouse wondered if the call's time was bad luck or by design. Closing the sliding glass door behind him, he pressed a button to take the call as the cold and wind slapped him in the face from the lake. Not a soul dared take a water vessel on the choppy water this day as the smell of freshly mulched fall leaves reached his nostrils.

"Clouse."

"Hello, Mr. Clouse," an unfamiliar voice said. "I take it you've been expecting my call."

"I suppose I have. Just so I know it's really you, why don't you tell me what you're wanting before we discuss terms."

A light chuckle crossed the line.

"Right to the point. I like that."

"I'm just used to dealing with these situations."

"And so far you've been lucky. That could all change this time though. I'm not Martin Smith. I'm *much* more dangerous."

Clouse had bested Smith, his arch nemesis, twice on previous occasions, killing him both times. Unfortunately with the cubes not everything always stayed dead.

"You know I want the last of those beautiful little cubes."

"And what exactly do you plan on doing with it?"

"I want to finish out my collection, of course. I've got a little room picked out where I can display them all at once."

From the man's tone, Clouse suspected he already knew about the strange room and the clock occupying one wall.

"You know I can't just hand that over to you."

"I don't see why not. I've played nice and kept all of your friends and family alive. They can all stay that way if you just do as I ask."

"You're talking about the end of the world."

"How would you know that? You're relying on what Mark Teakon told you? He was a fool who didn't know what he was dealing with."

Clouse felt nothing but respect for Teakon, and contempt for the individual speaking to him. He tried to control his anger, but his face flushed and his muscles tightened as the cool wind slapped him constantly when he leaned on the balcony railing. Attempting to calm himself, Clouse watched several clouds lazily cover the sun momentarily.

"And I suppose you have all of the answers?" Clouse finally asked. "Why would you want all of the cubes unless they brought you some kind of power?"

"I never said they didn't give power. Your friend was misinformed about exactly how they worked, however."

"Care to enlighten me so we're on an even playing field?"

"You'll never be my equal, but I will let you see firsthand what their power can do. Meet me at your new property so we can put them to the test."

"And if I refuse?"

An eerie silence crossed the line before the unseen voice spoke again.

"I said I'd played nice with your friends and family so far. Cross me, and everyone you know will die, one by one, until you've attended all of their funerals. Thanks to the cube your good friend Martin Smith possessed, I have forever to torture you and look for the last cube. If you defy me, I possess the ability to pick your mind of every last thought and make the remainder of your life miserable."

Feeling certain the man referred to the psychic when hinting about the mental fleecing, Clouse knew his thoughts could betray him, and had taken measures to counteract that as well. He knew how to play the game when he and his family were threatened, and on his home ground he wasn't going to simply hand over every shred of power to this bastard.

"Believe me, I'll be there."

"Nine a.m. Bring the last cube. Don't be late."

The line went dead before Clouse could say anything more. He didn't have a witty comeback, or anything else to say anyway. Whether this man on the other end of the line knew it or not, the last cube was by far the most dangerous of the thirteen, even by itself. Letting it fall into the wrong hands wasn't truly an option, even if his family and friends were placed in perilous situations. He decided the wildcard in all of this meeting was the psychic. If that man could be taken out of play, preferably without ending his life, Clouse would certainly feel better about his chances of walking away from the morning meeting alive.

He mentally digested the prospects of the following day before opening the door to return to the more comfortable indoors. Leaving his life in the hands of friends wasn't a sound plan ordinarily, but his mind was currently his worst enemy. He didn't feel right about dragging Matt Teakon or Julie

Knowles into his current predicament. If Clouse didn't survive, someone needed to pick up the pieces if there was still a planet left to protect. For similar reasons he ordered Greene to keep Liz away from Indiana, partly to protect her, but also in the hopes of severing whatever psychic link she shared with the redheaded man.

After facing death so many times before, Clouse truly didn't fear his time when it came. In his previous career as a firefighter he took many medical calls to various residences from all walks of life. Young or old, black or white, it didn't matter, because in the end no dignity truly accompanied death. He'd seen people shot in the streets and slumped over on toilets from cardiac arrest. Short of using a cursed object, everyone experienced death eventually, and even those who profited from using the cubes typically met horrific ends.

"What's wrong?" his wife asked him when he stepped inside.

"Nothing," he answered, giving her a quick kiss on the cheek.

He married Jane almost nine years prior, having lost his first wife to a gruesome murder that strained his relationship with the West Baden Springs Hotel. Now it seemed his tumultuous time in Orange County was coming full circle for better or worse the following day.

"I know when you're lying to me," Jane said, tracing the collar of his dress shirt with her index finger.

He hadn't exactly kept her abreast of the latest events, not because she was in the dark about the cursed objects or his past trouble, because she certainly knew specifics about all of that. She also knew he had sent her and the kids into hiding for their protection, but Clouse never provided detailed reasons. Only a few days ago he had brought them home, somehow knowing the ordeal was reaching a conclusion. Clouse received the unsaid message that Duncan could have easily been slaughtered, so he hoped terms were going to be amicable. And he never left Jane or the kids without some form of protection at home, in this case some familiar bodyguards just outside who knew his friends and family by memory.

"You're about to do something dangerous and stupid, aren't you?" she asked, not raising her voice in the least because the children were playing a videogame nearby.

Even Clouse's son, Zach, and Jane's daughter, Katie, had survived their share of traumatic incidents in the past. All the more reason, Clouse figured, to keep them distanced from the danger coming for him in the morning.

Sometimes surprised she stayed with him, after all of the danger and turbulence, Clouse awoke each morning thankful Jane remained by his side. Money hadn't changed them, partially because it came as a surprise just before they wed. Their relationship seemed almost like a feel-good romantic movie to some, with Clouse the working-class hero firefighter and Jane a young doctor working near her hometown. She remained close to home due to a strong bond with her mother, who also shared a love for the grand hotels in Orange County. That love inevitably brought Jane and Clouse together, on the grounds of the West Baden Springs Hotel where Clouse worked on his days off from the fire department.

Even after a decade of growing older with her, he still considered Jane beautiful with her shoulder-length brown hair. Highlighted with streaks of a coffee creamer brown, her hair always looked good because she took excellent care of her entire body, inside and out. Very much a country girl, she looked as good in a flannel shirt as she did an evening gown.

Clouse didn't immediately answer his wife's inquiry about exactly where his recently strange behavior was leading, which drew a sour look from her.

"It's time you let someone else carry out your work," she said quietly enough that the children didn't hear.

"We've been through this before," he replied. "How can I possibly trust anyone else to find these things, knowing they might abuse the knowledge and keep them for themselves?"

"We aren't going to be around forever, Paul," she said, placing her finger across his lips. "You'll need a successor someday, and these kids need a father."

With Zach's mother deceased, and Katie's father never truly in the picture, Clouse considered both children his own. He missed birthdays and holidays on occasion, but he never felt it was fair to ask others to risk their lives if he wasn't willing to do the same.

"I might be able to end this once and for all," he said, playfully drawing across her lips with his own forefinger, failing to immediately change his wife's expression.

She finally let a smile through, guarded in nature.

"I know nothing I say is going to stop you, but I'm going to remind you that you thought the last time was going to be the end."

"I can't see the future, dear."

"I just want you to be safe," Jane said, wrapping her arms around him. "Just once it would be nice to fall asleep, not worrying about whether someone is coming after us."

Clouse forced a grin.

"Maybe it will be. I've got a little errand to run tomorrow that may change everything."

As though sent from above, Clouse's good friend Mark Daniels appeared at the stairwell landing, greeting the kids briefly to avoid distracting them from their game.

Clouse touched his wife's hand gently before heading toward his friend, wondering if friendship or business prompted the visit. Following their usual routine, the casino security manager led the way downstairs where they could talk in private, away from the children and Jane's open concern.

Wearing a dark gray suit, Daniels hadn't removed the laminated name badge from the breast pocket, indicating he was probably just getting off work. Clouse doubted his friend would schedule himself to work a late afternoon or evening without a solid reason. Though he sometimes grew a seasonal beard, Daniels was still clean shaven, a full head of dirty blond hair grown in for the impending cold weather.

"What brings you out here?" Clouse inquired as they stepped into the downstairs family room.

"Isn't a neighbor welcome in your home?" Daniels asked with a friendly smirk.

He seldom smiled openly.

Daniels referred to the adjacent chalet that Clouse ordered built at the same time his own lakefront property was constructed, specifically for Daniels and his family. Daniels and his wife had recently gotten back together after a marital split, so they lived between their city home and the chalet seasonally.

"I guess I figured you were done with the lake property for the season," Clouse answered. "Hadn't seen you around lately."

"I hear you've been rather busy."

Clouse suspected his friend might have conversed with Dan Duncan and Craig Jennings recently. While none of the three men were loose-lipped, they all knew about the cursed cubes and occasionally spoke about the evil objects within their group. Having such a limited focus group tended to make them talk like old women in a knitting circle when they got together. Clouse didn't mind because it relieved their stress levels, but they often voiced concerns over their boss's plans or actions.

He didn't ignore their opinions, but none of his employees had shared in every one of his horrific experiences, meaning they didn't know all of the facts. While Clouse wasn't arrogant enough to call himself an expert, he figured he knew more than the recent additions to his staff.

"I can't imagine who would fill you in about my plans," Clouse said, sauntering toward the front door where two carved jack-o-lanterns stood on the other side of the glass.

Because the kids took to the Halloween holiday, seeking to live halfway normal lives, Clouse catered to their whims. From the ground level the view of the lake remained stellar, though more of the yard took up the view, rather than the boat dock.

"You can't keep doing this," Daniels warned, speaking generally about the quests to retrieve the cubes.

"Now you sound like Jane."

"Just because this shitty ordeal fell in your lap ten years ago doesn't mean you have to take it to your grave."

"You opted out, Mark, and I've respected that. I haven't asked for your help in any of this."

Daniels shook his head, grinning disagreeably.

"That doesn't mean I don't get dragged into it sometimes."

"And I apologize for that."

"There's no need for sorry. I'm just concerned about you and this obsession of yours."

Clouse felt offended, but refused to display his emotions.

"So saving lives is an obsession?"

"If you're writing a résumé for your ticket to Heaven or something, I think you're already in, buddy."

"I haven't told you everything, Mark. If what I've got planned tomorrow works, this may all be over with forever."

Daniels hung his head, shaking it slowly.

"How many times have we thought this was all over before? I'm just afraid one of these times you're not going to walk away."

"This thing tomorrow," Clouse said slowly, "is an all or nothing proposition. Practically everyone left on the planet who knows about the cubes is probably going to be in French Lick. Might be a good day to call in sick."

"I might just do that."

"I've got to meet this guy tomorrow, and I have to go alone. He'll know otherwise."

"Don't worry. I wasn't going to volunteer."

"I know," Clouse said with a weak smile. "Saving my ass cost you your marriage once, and I don't want you risking your marriage or your life again."

"What's the worst that can happen tomorrow?"

"The guy kills me, takes a cube that can transport him back in time, and life as we know it changes forever. Or he just combines all of the cubes into some kind of demonic device that ends the world."

"Maybe you should call the military for backup," Daniels said, half joking because they both knew the secret of the cursed objects could not be allowed to spread.

Clouse read the sullen expression on his friend's face. Helping him in the past had cost Daniels so much, but his friend didn't want to abandon him either. He decided to try lightening the mood.

"Don't worry. If anything happens to me, I'm sure Jane will make sure you keep your job at the casino."

"I wouldn't count on it. She'd probably blame me, so you better come out of this unscathed."

"If I don't come out of it, you'll probably never know the difference."

"I know you. You have a plan."

"You're right, and I pray it works. But it involves me calling a few key people, so if you'll excuse me."

Clouse plucked the cell phone from his side and held it up for Daniels to see.

"Yeah, well just be careful tomorrow."

His friend walked over to give him a hug, which Clouse considered a very rare showing of affection from the former police detective.

"I'll come check on you tomorrow night," Daniels promised. "Do what you have to do and kick some ass."

"You know I'm not going to let some city slickers come to my neck of the woods and push me around."

"Yeah, I know. Be careful just the same."

Clouse nodded as Daniels let himself out the front door. There indeed remained a few important phone calls to make, which served as the first steps in setting his plan in motion. Clouse was relying upon his knowledge of the area to serve him well, but he also needed a little luck to walk away from the meeting alive.

He needed even more if he hoped to obtain the remainder of the cubes once and for all.

CHAPTER 46

The instant she touched the old book, Liz was transported back in time, at least in the visual sense, while a flood of images came her way. What transpired over a period of months entered her mind in seconds, and the details simply fell into place as though she had the front row seat at a movie.

First, the vision of a man in a derby style hat, well-dressed for the period, conversed with a jeweler about creating thirteen various gemstones in the shapes of cubes, about one inch square. Though he considered it an unusual request, the jeweler agreed for a very fair price as the man looked around his shop, admiring the décor. As they talked about it, the jeweler revealed he built the shop with help from some neighbors, designing the interior himself with a variety of wallpaper, paint schemes, and multi-colored tiles.

"I just purchased a hotel in French Lick," the well-dressed man revealed during their second meeting, soon after the jeweler began ordering the gems necessary to create such cubes. "Could I possibly hire you to design a small room there?"

"In the hotel?" the jeweler inquired, writing some information down in a journal atop his store counter without looking up.

"Actually close to the hotel, rather than inside. My colleagues and I want a place to hold our meetings each month."

"The same friends on the order forms for these cubes?"

The well-dressed man hesitated before answering, crafting his words carefully.

"Yes. The same people."

"A list of which person wants which color would help me complete the invoices more thoroughly."

"I'll get to work on that. About the room?"

The jeweler finally looked up from his ledger.

"I'd like a look at it before I give you an answer. This project here will keep me plenty busy once the raw gems arrive."

"We'll make it worth your while. And you'll have plenty of time because our meetings require some planning."

At the mention of meetings the jeweler perked up, looking for additional information that never came.

Within a week the jeweler saw the already hollowed out path, which led to a room beneath the hotel, reluctantly agreeing to complete the cubes and create a magnificent meeting room, all in secret. Believing they were some kind of secretive group, like the Freemasons, the jeweler could only assume that the cubes provided some sort of symbolic membership.

Already harboring suspicions about the group, the jeweler asked a lawyer friend to check into the identities of the men once he possessed all thirteen names. He carried out his assignment, often working on the room during the daytime with leftover materials he purchased from the Cassini Mosaic Tile Company that put down new flooring in the West Baden Springs Hotel. He placed an order with them for more tiles once he knew the required amount to finish the secretive room beneath the Woxley Hotel. Both exhausting and time consuming, the room took up much of his daytime, leaving only an hour or so each evening for work on the customized gems. With no time for anything except work and sleep, the man used the generous checks he received each week as incentive to continue the arduous labor.

Luckily for him someone had already shored up the walls of the tunnel leading to the underground room. The braces looked like those of a mine shaft based on what the jeweler had seen in book illustrations. Carting tools and materials to the room from the hotel's basement wasn't particularly easy, but he devised a four-wheeled cart that allowed him to push items to and from the room with relative ease. The hard ground provided little resistance to the cart's wheels, and he seldom required more than one trip per day based on the required time to lay the tiles.

When his attorney friend finally got back with him, the jeweler learned that all thirteen of the men were wealthy and influential. Some held political positions, while others owned companies, or received their riches from inheritances. While it wasn't specifically clear how the group met, the lawyer said they were all from the New England area, possibly forming some kind of alliance in a country club. In 1918, many of the rich and famous still traveled to West Baden Springs and French Lick to gamble and partake in the mineral waters. The idea of creating a gentleman's club so close to the grounds certainly wasn't out of the question.

After the first ever break-in at his shop occurred, the jeweler decided he truly couldn't trust anyone, because he hadn't laid eyes on most of the men paying his salary. With the names now transferred to a leather-bound book, the jeweler suspected the men were looking to keep their names away from everyone in town, particularly the jeweler. He kept the book in several hiding spots outside of his shop, but he finally decided to place it in the one spot where none of the thirteen men would think to look for it.

One morning he placed it beneath several items in the heavy cart and wheeled the last of his supplies toward the secret room. Everything was now finished except for a few pieces of trim, and the jeweler had already set up a meeting for his final payment from the man who contracted him. By this time all thirteen cubes were masterfully crafted and sitting inside his shop, but he suspected the wealthy men already knew this because he often found himself being studied or followed by strangers.

He never let on that he knew the men were keeping tabs on him, and as the jeweler reached the underground room for the last time in a contractor capacity, he reveled in the masterpiece of a room he created. Based on the specifications laid out by the man who contracted him, the jeweler began to suspect the room's purpose wasn't simply for meetings, but rather for some kind of ritual. While the specified centerpiece was eerie in its own right, the wall-sized clock along the far wall disturbed him greatly. He created a functional clock, just as the work order specified, though the man wanted no winding device attached to the mechanism. How was a clock ever supposed to work if it couldn't be wound to keep time?

Even stranger were the thirteen small, square indentions the men wanted placed along the clock's face. Twelve of them were centered in the Roman numerals that represented the hourly digits, but one was centrally located directly beneath the hour and minute hands. If he were mentally challenged the jeweler couldn't possibly have missed the connection between the cubes and the specified indentions in the clock. Considering there were thirteen cubes for as many indentions, and the cubes would fit inside the housings perfectly, he began to worry that something sinister was brewing. Thirteen spokes, equally spaced, emerged from the centerpiece along the strange wheel laid upon the floor, as though each man had an assigned spot to stand. He couldn't tell anyone his suspicions because there wasn't any proof, but he knew the wealthy men meant to collaborate on something evil.

Oil lanterns lit the room, providing light enough for him to work by on a daily basis. Although electricity existed in Orange County in 1918, particularly at the hotels, the jeweler didn't particularly care to take a chance on his health by stringing together lights with his limited experience in the recent technology. He also didn't want to leave any more traces of his presence than necessary to people coming and going from the hotel above him.

Once the room was sufficiently lighted, the jeweler removed the book from beneath his materials, carrying it with him to the clock's face. About a foot to the right of the center he'd built a secret compartment when creating the clock's face, which remained perfectly concealed because thin seams ran horizontally and vertically across the entire wall. Creating a small, secret compartment that fit into the natural scheme was simple for a craftsman of gems and interior rooms.

No handles or hinges showed on the outside of the compartment, and the little door only swung out a few inches. Opening somewhat like a modern day public mailbox, requiring help from a screwdriver or a thin, sturdy device, the secret compartment provided just enough room to conceal a narrow item such as a book. Once the jeweler hid the book, he completed the room's trim, completing the last of his contracted work. He packed his tools and all of the excess materials into the cart before wheeling them back to the hotel basement over a hundred yards away. Wiping the dust from his hands, he exited the basement and went directly to his store where he conducted business as usual. His final meeting with the man who contracted him was to take place the following morning at the Woxley Hotel, which he now believed one of the thirteen men owned.

The jeweler would never make it to the meeting, or see the light of day the following morning in French Lick. He knew the fate awaiting him, but he wasn't going to stick around to see it come to fruition. After cashing the checks regularly at the bank, he saved the latest one for both traveling money and proof of evil deeds if necessary. He hadn't dared clear out his savings, or venture into the bank other than to cash the checks because the men were monitoring his activities. Instead, the jeweler cleared out the cash drawer at his shop and took some of the money he'd received from the cashed checks and left town rather hastily after making certain no one followed him into the evening.

Making no obvious moves, the jeweler didn't buy a train ticket, or even remove his horse from the barn. Henry Ford's production lines had made the automobile a luxury not only owned by the rich, but still not owned by everyone. Considering the jeweler basically found all of his needs met within the county, he saw no reason to purchase a Model T in the near future. He figured some kind soul would find his horse and tend to it because he needed his disappearance to remain a complete mystery until he chose to return.

He chose to return a week later, after catching a train a few towns over and staying in Indianapolis where the population alone kept him safely hidden. Just as he left, the jeweler returned in the dead of night when only lanterns and a full moon illuminated the streets of French Lick. Though he considered it dangerous, he decided to check on his shop first.

Strangely, he found everything intact, right down to the newspapers piled up on the front landing. He peered through the window, seeing everything the same inside, except that the area where he kept the thirteen gems appeared slightly disturbed. He kept them locked inside a cabinet behind his counter just above shoulder level. The small door was left open as though someone hastily took what they came for and vacated the shop.

Turning to the stack of newspapers, he tucked them under his arm, realizing no major local news had reached him in Indianapolis. Briskly walking from the shop, he headed toward the Woxley Hotel, opening one of the newspapers simply to cover his face when he noticed a story about a local attorney still missing. Immediately stiffening from the realization of his departure's consequences, the jeweler went on to read that Benjamin Land, his lawyer, was the missing person in question.

"Oh, no," the jeweler mouthed his words in silence, knowing his lawyer possessed a spare key to his shop because they often shared a drink after their workdays concluded.

Picking up his pace, he headed directly to the hotel, unconcerned with his own well-being, figuring his friend was a pawn in this evil scheme, meant to lure him out of hiding. Immediately feeling regret for leaving town and placing Land in peril, he left the shadows and crossed streets when necessary to reach the hotel quickly.

When he arrived at the front door, however, he found it bolted shut with a sign that stated the hotel was closed for business. Positive that financial issues hadn't shut down the business, the jeweler peered into a few windows, seeing most, if not all of the furniture still inside. Nearly two-dozen hotels existed between the towns of West Baden Springs and French Lick, but competition was never a reason why one shut its doors. Gambling ensured that the hotels were typically overrun with guests, and the West Baden Springs Hotel in particular was being leased to the military, meaning none of its seven-hundred plus rooms were available.

No, something other than financial woes closed the Woxley.

Returning to the street for a better vantage point so he could figure out where to break in, the jeweler was surprised to hear a voice behind him.

"I hear it's scheduled for demolition," a man carrying a newspaper stated.

Recognizing the strolling man as a local, the jeweler immediately relaxed instead of fleeing into the streets, which would certainly draw unwanted attention. He decided to prod for a bit more information before attempting to make his way into the hotel.

"Demolition? This building isn't even ten years old."

"The owner closed for business yesterday morning and left town. I hear he slated Rudy Halstead and his boys to tear it down this week."

Now fully believing something was amiss with this building before him, the jeweler bid the pedestrian a good evening before examining the building more closely. He took notice that all of the doors had their handles wrapped with chains to deter any trespassing before demolition began. Normally a move to keep looters from breaking in, the chains likely harbored a secret in this instance.

It took another five minutes, but the jeweler found a window along the ground level that wasn't secured, leading into the kitchen area. Not far from the doorway to the basement, the kitchen provided him with a lantern which he lit with some nearby matches once he safely moved from the view of any nearby windows.

After working extensively for months on the secret room, the jeweler knew the layout of the hotel, particularly the area near the basement entrance. While he carried out his work the basement was partitioned into an area for him and another for the kitchen employees because they needed access to their stored goods below.

He found the basement entrance wide-open, as though someone had made a hasty retreat from the secret passage. Feeling a bit less daring about seeing the rest of his completed project again, the jeweler pressed onward, knowing whatever plans the thirteen men created were carried out within the small chamber.

He soon reached the halfway point through the tunnel with only the lantern to guide him. A strange odor crossed his nose, but he pressed forward, finding an eerie orange glow ahead of him when he drew closer to the secret room. Freezing in his tracks when he realized the light was slowly pulsating, the jeweler wondered if someone remained inside, creating the ebb and flow of the unusual illumination. Now able to see, he set the lantern down a safe distance from the doorway just ahead of him to keep from giving away his presence. He practically tiptoed during the last leg of his walk to the doorway before cautiously peering around the edge.

"Impossible," he muttered when he spied the clock, in essence the entire wall, on the opposite end creating the rhythmic pulsating glow.

Completely fixated on the clock, the jeweler stepped into the room, wondering what on earth transpired between the time he completed the room and the present. It took nearly a minute before he finally panned the room for any further clues, making a grisly discovery on the floor that took his breath.

"Ben," he said under his breath when he found the body of his friend on the floor, chained to the centerpiece by the ankle.

The smell of death accompanied his friend, indicating whatever evil deed took the attorney's life happened a day or two prior. Not wishing to handle a body, even his friend's, any more than necessary the jeweler conducted a cursory examination rather quickly, finding two red marks near the man's heart that appeared to have been inflicted through some form of piercing. Feeling a tear reach his eye, the jeweler gently set Land's body atop the ground, deciding only one way to avenge his friend remained.

Standing, he walked with a purpose toward the hidden compartment, unsure whether he dared touch the unnatural clock to retrieve his log. He timidly tapped it with a few fingers in the same fashion people might test for a live electrical circuit. When no harm came to him, the jeweler pressed one palm against the clock, finding it warm and dry despite its surroundings. It continued to glow and pulsate without pause, powered by some unseen force that the jeweler could only assume was the devil himself.

He managed to undo the trim holding the compartment in place by hand before opening it to retrieve the book inside. Somehow the book felt different, almost sturdier in some way, but the jeweler didn't have time to study it while bathed in the strange orange light. Taking up the lantern, he headed back to the surface, ready to find the men responsible for his friend's death and seek some measure of revenge.

***

"Oh my God!" Liz stammered when she finally broke free of the complete trance.

Her three concerned colleagues cupped her by the elbows to steady her as her mind raced to process so much information.

"What did you see?" Teakon asked first.

"What *didn't* I see?" she countered. "There's *so* much about all of this that we didn't know."

After all four of them ordered drinks, including coffee and soda pop, Liz recounted the events leading up to the jeweler recovering his personal ledger.

"So the jeweler was never the one who got killed?" Teakon asked, obviously recalling his uncle's research indicating that was the case.

"No, he let people believe he was dead or missing," Liz replied. "He eventually learned that his book was part of the curse and used it to track down the men who possessed the cubes. And after he located the time cube he asked a police friend in Chicago to keep it safe for all time."

"No pressure in that," Greene said sarcastically.

"If he was tracking down the cubes," Julie said thoughtfully, "he didn't get very far."

Liz took a relaxing sip of her latte before continuing.

"I don't know what happened to him," she confessed. "But I would dare say he put things in motion that we're still carrying out today."

"And what happened to that room?" Teakon inquired. "And the hotel?"

"They tore down the hotel," Liz commented. "The basement was filled in and a new building was erected. It was like the hotel never existed."

A concerned look crossed Greene's face as a realization struck him.

"That's the place Clouse has been toying with the last few months," he revealed slowly, struggling to remember the details. "He didn't think I knew, but he asked his construction buddy to do some digging around some old shop."

"He shouldn't go in there," Liz said, shuddering at the thought of her employer meeting his end in such an evil place. "Those thirteen men left in a hurry for a reason in 1918. If this collector of the cubes lures Clouse in there with the time cube it could literally be the end of mankind as we know it."

"Did you see what would happen?" Greene asked.

"No, but it's not good. Those men planned to have untold power and wealth with those cubes and meet like some kind of fraternity, but they left in a hurry once the cubes were created. Something terrible happened in that room."

"Other than a man being silenced," Teakon said. "Or sacrificed."

"We need to get back to Indiana before Clouse does something foolish," Liz insisted, looking to Greene. "He doesn't know what he's messing with."

"He isn't stupid," Greene countered. "He knows to keep any potential pawns out of play."

"You don't understand," Liz said vehemently. "I had a dream last night where I saw Clouse in his hotel, and again inside this secret chamber. It didn't mean anything to me at first, but now I think he means to meet these people there *very* soon. And he's walking into a trap."

"Damn it," Greene muttered. He directed his attention to Teakon and Julie, who both appeared gravely concerned that the inevitable confrontation was occurring so soon. "You two take that book and keep it safe. It's the only valuable asset we have left at this point. Don't make contact with anyone."

Both nodded in understanding.

Fifteen minutes later the two duos parted ways, but Greene apparently wasn't content with Liz's visions.

"If Clouse confronts these people he'll have help," he insisted. "He's got bodyguards, and he can always call Clay Branson."

"You don't understand," Liz stated as Greene drove them west, directly to Indiana. "Yes, he can counteract the goons, but my nemesis will know the truth and Clouse won't be able to protect his family, and the last cube, all by himself."

Liz didn't want to say too much, but it was as though the redheaded man had somehow established a link to Clouse as well, even though Clouse was not an admitted psychic. Of course any dealings with the dead, or their spirits, left one more susceptible to interactions with the unseen world.

Short of a disaster, they would make it back to the West Baden Springs Hotel by nightfall. Liz still worried that they lacked time enough to assist Clouse, or prepare for whatever battle he planned to virtually carry out by himself.

Her body felt like a bundle of nerves because the world was going to change drastically the next day, for much better or far worse.

CHAPTER 47

After a virtually sleepless night Clouse made his way out of bed just after dawn. Jane, who hadn't slept very well either, took hold of his hand, but he gently pulled it away, assuring her he would return soon. Without waking the children, Clouse dressed and walked out the front door toward his truck with very little daylight to guide him.

He made the hour-long drive from Bloomington to West Baden, finally stopping at a diner for some coffee and a small breakfast. Basically killing time, Clouse barely touched his eggs and pancakes, occasionally sipping on his coffee and looking to his watch, which barely progressed toward the imposed nine o'clock meeting time.

He continually looked behind him, and outside, wondering if anyone was monitoring his every move. Though nothing obvious appeared, Clouse still felt violated, like some unseen force continued to stalk him. Knowing about the psychic, he tried to direct his thoughts toward anything other than the meeting or the last of the cubes. It came rather naturally for his mind to dwell upon his past, considering he was entering a perilous experience. He thought about his former life on the fire department, occasionally fingering the Maltese cross that still hung on a gold chain around his neck.

Some bonds lingered in part, including the brotherhood of firefighters he worked with in Bloomington. He left a job that he considered far more dangerous than being a billionaire, but that notion was soon disproven. Clouse never asked for trouble, but it came looking for him very close to home. Unfortunately a man he trusted and loved like a grandfather ultimately betrayed him, creating all sorts of controversy that surrounded Clouse and created all sorts of urban legends around Orange County.

After leaving the diner, Clouse drove to his hotel, wanting to take one last walk through the atrium. Still dim because the sun was barely rising at this point in the morning, the atrium was filled with comfortable furniture as usual, but not people. For the first five minutes the atrium was all his until an employee who worked the check-in desk walked through to relieve someone at her post.

Most of the shops opened later in the morning, which left the entire hotel eerily quiet. The silence reminded Clouse of the days during the hotel's renovation after it neared complete ruin. He arrived to work, seeing marked improvement inside the building and along the grounds each morning, greeted by a peaceful silence through all six stories.

Deciding not to linger much longer, Clouse visited several other spots around the two adjoining small towns, constantly monitoring his surroundings. Not one time did he catch anyone spying on him, ducking behind buildings, trees, or shrubs the few times he stole a glance. When he finally parked beside the remains of the torn down shop, Clouse stepped from his truck to find a strong breeze passing through the area. Gray clouds created an overcast sky, and he finally felt his ordeal had come full circle, as though a sign from above.

He figured he needed some spiritual assistance if he was going to survive the impending meeting.

Clouse had asked Niemeyer to dig out only the corner where the old basement door led into the tunnel this last time. Instead of leaving a ladder behind, Niemeyer simply created a sloped surface in which visitors could navigate the dirt surface on foot. Considering he was asked to excavate the corner at dawn, Niemeyer did well to complete the job and leave the area with his heavy equipment. In no capacity did Clouse want his friend lingering at the site with such dangerous people coming to town.

Standing over the descent, Clouse felt a knot form in his stomach as he looked at his watch.

8:56 a.m.

He felt alone, but knew in good conscience Todd Parish wasn't going to let him down. He also placed phone calls to Clay Branson and Special Agent

Harlan Stone, knowing both of them wanted a measure of revenge against their respective enemies who were sure to make an appearance. He simply told them the location of the meet and asked that they remain in the vicinity without following him inside. Between the four of them, not knowing what each of the others planned to do, Clouse hoped they might stand a chance against an unknown amount of assailants and their plan. Having knowledge of the area only helped Clouse so much because he was about to confine himself in a small chamber with unforeseen circumstances.

Something near the slightly ajar door to the tunnel caught his eye, and Clouse squinted to see an orange jack-o-lantern against the light brown background. Knowing full well his friend didn't place the gutted vegetable there, Clouse felt certain the sinister person he was about to meet knew something of his past. He took notice of the tiny flame dancing between the facial openings on the pumpkin before turning hastily to grab a small box from the backseat of his crew-cab truck.

Clouse carefully descended the sloped dirt, keeping both hands beneath the fairly heavy box. By no means stupid enough to walk into an obvious trap in the first place, he knew from experience to always have a form of insurance that made it necessary to keep him alive. While he hoped Parish and the two less familiar men planned to back him, they couldn't provide guarantees on his safety.

He gave the jack-o-lantern a light kick out of spite before stepping through the door and walking into the tunnel. Already several lanterns were lit, hanging at intervals along the manmade walkway as though someone who knew his way around the supposedly secret area awaited him inside.

His eyes didn't truly adjust to the darkness before he made his way to the chamber entrance, stepping inside to see the décor for the first time, along with the pulsating orange glow that guided him the last part of his journey. He purposefully told Parish to tell him nothing about the tunnel or the room, because he didn't want either of them to gain knowledge that the psychic might detect when the inevitable confrontation occurred.

Taking a look around, Clouse sensed he was alone as the wall continued to bask him in its glow, like a neon light from the seedy end of a big city. He observed a centerpiece in the middle of the room that appeared large enough to store items inside. The light made it difficult to tell for certain, but Clouse thought the dozens of wooden slats that comprised the centerpiece appeared recent. If the wood was original, he felt certain all kinds of wildlife and bugs would have contributed to wear and tear, if not complete destruction, over the past century. And, strangely enough, he felt certain an odor of freshly cut wood penetrated the otherwise stale, musty smells of the chamber.

Setting the box atop the centerpiece that reached his waistline, Clouse heard footsteps approaching from the tunnel behind him. He turned, hoping to lay eyes on the man responsible for endangering the world and making his life a living hell recently.

Instead of finding just one person walking through the doorway into the chamber, however, he found a man wearing business casual with two gunmen in suits on either side. They looked thick, like ex-military types who made a paycheck doing unspeakable things to strangers without asking any questions. Neither displayed a firearm, but Clouse knew each harbored a sidearm beneath their black sport coats.

"Mr. Clouse," the man stated, rather than asked, because he appeared confident that he knew his adversary very well.

"And who might you be?" Clouse asked, trying to size up the man with dark hair, wondering if the psychic lingered nearby.

If so, he might make an easy target for Stone or Branson, who knew exactly what the redheaded man looked like. Taking the man out of play made the situation markedly easier for Clouse, who could in turn lie or stall for time. Of course Clouse possessed no means of communication, which meant he placed a great deal of faith in his unofficial team.

"You should probably concern yourself more with completing my collection, rather than identifying me," the stranger said as the two men stood stiffly by his side, still not reaching for their firearms.

"Where is your collection?" Clouse inquired, seeing no containers, and seriously doubting this man was going to chance carrying any of the cubes loosely, or in pockets.

"Close. Now, can we get down to this, or do I need to start murdering your friends and family one at a time?"

Clouse wasn't positive this man's voice was the one he heard over the phone the previous evening. He stepped forward, prompting the two men to reach into their sport coats for their firearms. Clouse never intended to pose a threat, but he wanted to verify that the two men weren't just present for showmanship.

"Not a wise move," the stranger said, a rather arrogant smirk crossing his lips.

"You're right about that," Clouse retorted, "but not in the way you're thinking."

***

When Harlan Stone received a phone call from Paul Clouse asking for help in what sounded like a final confrontation with the men who turned both of their lives upside-down the past few months, he nearly turned down the offer. Not only was he lucky to have a job, but now the very people he worked for kept him under constant scrutiny and watched him closely whenever he worked in the office. While most of their suspicions began when Stone's partner was found dead in a desert, things only grew worse for the agent when Stewart was found dead in his office and the body mysteriously disappeared from the funeral home shortly thereafter.

Stone ultimately decided to make the journey to Indiana for the sake of clearing his name, and hopefully laying eyes on his former boss again. Even before he was provided with hints and details about what Clouse and his employees did during their down time, Stone knew deep down that Stewart wasn't truly dead. All of the partial truths and carefully crafted fibs he told during interviews with more experienced FBI agents might actually pan out and clear his name if he brought them Stewart.

At this point he didn't particularly care if the man came willingly, or zipped inside a body bag.

Being highly unfamiliar with the town of French Lick, Stone wasn't particularly sure what vantage point best provided a good view of the area Clouse indicated through a text message. While visibility played a major role in the agent's strategy, the ability to act quickly also factored into his plan.

He ultimately chose the old apartment building that loomed over the excavation site, claiming his spot in time to watch Clouse navigate the slope and enter the doorway. Stone wasn't concerned until three rather unfriendly, well-dressed men entered the same way a few minutes later. From his spot on the second story, Stone turned to find the nearest stairs to follow them into the tunnel for a closer look.

Instead, he found a gun trained on his chest, held by the very man he worked under for a short period of time.

"Surprised to see me?" Alan Stewart asked, his appearance a bit less fresh and lively these days.

"Not really. Some nice people brought me up to speed on your recent nefarious activities. What I can't understand is why anyone would bring you back from the dead."

"That's a pretty big word for someone from your parts."

"You're no better than my boss in New Mexico if you think my people are just stupid hicks."

Stewart gave a brief laugh, his expression indicating he dared not ever underestimate the agent from Texas.

"To satisfy your curiosity, I had information they still needed on a loose end that needed cleaned up, which is why they brought me back. Having something people want is good leverage, and a good way to stay alive. Too bad you don't have anything of value to share."

Stone knew he meant the last agent that he and Clay Branson left stranded when they first entered California during the summer. Of course the man was located and killed before he could ever speak of his experiences to anyone. Stone wanted to punch Stewart in the face so badly that his right fist instinctively opened and clenched slowly, but repeatedly. Fear for his life and anger at himself for letting Stewart sneak up on him provided some balance for the hatred he wanted to direct at his former boss.

Apparently the short period the man spent amongst the deceased altered his physical state, because his flesh still favored a light purple hue. Stone couldn't immediately place it, but the man's eyes appeared different as well. The eyeballs in general seemed to have sunk into the facial structure a bit, and the whites of the eyes themselves now carried a permanent yellow hue that made Stewart look something like a zombie.

"Boss, you're not looking so good," Stone stated, his fingers within striking distance of his sidearm if Stewart looked away for even a second.

Stewart replied with a cagy stare, not amused by the sarcasm from his former agent

"It would serve you better to keep your remarks to yourself," he suggested. "You were all too willing to rise through the ranks of the FBI until you needed to get your hands dirty."

"In my defense, you weren't very forthcoming with my job description."

"And now you're going to be buried six feet under because you don't have an ace in the hole like I did."

"Did?"

"My boss got his information, but he kept me around to make sure no one like you interfered with his plan."

A question suddenly occurred to the agent.

"Why would you even do his bidding? You could just leave all of this behind and escape before he tries to kill you again."

"Money, first and foremost. I don't exactly work for the Bureau anymore. Besides, if I tried to leave, he'd know where I went and find me. He knows everything about everyone."

"You mean his psychic does."

"No. *He* does."

Stewart stiffened the gun once more, aiming it deliberately toward the agent's heart. Stone didn't have time to process exactly what his former boss meant by his last statement.

"You've already heard too much, Stone. It's time for you to join your predecessor in the afterworld."

"So that's how it has to end when you discover your employees have a conscience?"

"Afraid so."

Refusing to simply stand there and take a bullet like an animal being put down, Stone started to reach for his sidearm, prepared to die instantly by forcing Stewart's hand. At least his murder would allow his wife to collect on his life insurance and pension from the federal government and be set for life.

Instead of a flash of light that meant the end of him, Stone saw the tip of a blade protrude through the front of Stewart's throat. It took him a second to collect himself and realize that a sword had run through the former Deputy Director's neck, severing his head from his body before the man's head fell to the floor with a thumping sound. As the body followed suit, Stone saw Clay Branson running toward the nearest stairwell to continue his ascent.

He was dressed in the traditional ninja garb, neck to toe in black cloth because he wasn't wearing any mask.

"Thank me later," Branson called without turning.

"I had this under control!"

Branson still didn't bother looking back, as though a man possessed to find something, or someone, inside the building.

"Well, that was kind of anticlimactic," Stone complained in a murmur, looking down to Stewart's decapitated body, regretting only that he didn't gain a full measure of revenge against the man.

Still, Stone would be free and clear of scrutiny from his own employers, hopefully regaining his old position in a Texas setting. He lost himself in positive thought momentarily until he looked out the window and spotted an unmarked van pulling up to the site with several armed men seated inside. They waited inside the vehicle, but Stone's instincts told him they were going to enter the tunnel sooner than later to make certain things went smoothly for their mysterious employer.

"I should just leave and call it a day," Stone muttered, instinctively reaching for his firearm instead.

CHAPTER 48

Todd Parish hadn't spent the past few months standing by idly, hoping when the right time came that he happened to be in the right place. Benefitted by the knowledge that it was only a matter of time before their adversaries acquired all of the cubes, Parish spent time examining the tunnel and chamber. From there, he built a box tall and wide enough to accommodate him comfortably, standing upright in the tunnel and perfectly camouflaged by the dim lighting and the surrounding dirt.

One simple text message from his employer the previous day set him in motion. Already knowing where the final meeting was destined to take place, Parish simply used a secret, secondary entrance to the tunnel to gain access without anyone noticing, even before Niemeyer carved out the main entrance through the old basement. Utilizing the old apartment building, Parish created his own small passage that literally dropped into the center of the tunnel, allowing him to slip into the virtually invisible box.

He held nothing but respect for his employer. Though Clouse hardly knew him at the time, he gave Parish a job when the best prospect in his future was working at his father's factory, hoping to someday work his fingers to the bone and inherit a company that barely stayed afloat financially much of the time.

The fact that Parish had worked previously as a bodyguard, coupled with his local ties, inevitably led Clouse to seek him out. And though Parish stayed almost exclusively with the family's two children, Clouse didn't feel right about keeping him in the dark regarding the constant danger around all of them. Little by little Parish learned the truth about the cubes and the motivations for various people to possess them.

Because Clouse trusted him, and because he was brought up to respect the people in his life, Parish remained completely loyal to his employer, even when others lacked the courage to stand by him. In turn, Clouse always provided Parish with the truth and the option of backing out if the situation felt wrong, or it taxed his moral convictions.

Not a trained killer by any means, Parish certainly knew his way around guns, and he felt perfectly willing to fire one at a person to protect his boss. Very well protected by the vertical box he constructed, Parish waited until Clouse passed, followed by the three unfamiliar men a few minutes later. He'd crafted the box from wood, but left a thin steel sheet along the exposed areas of the exterior for his own protection. Able to keep bullets from passing through, he also hoped the metal layer might keep the redheaded psychic from plucking his thoughts.

Carrying his AR-15 assault rifle with him when he left the safety of the protective box, Parish took several quiet steps toward the chamber, listening to the conversation between Clouse and the leader of the three men. He quickly detected that any negotiations weren't going Clouse's way, and when the two henchmen reached for their hidden firearms, Parish was already in position to make certain no harm came to his boss.

Hoping the tunnel muffled any gunfire, rather than amplifying it, he sucked in a breath and held it until he took aim at the left bodyguard's head. Exhaling as he pulled the trigger, he watched the man's head spew a red mist as he immediately trained his weapon on the second threat, hitting him squarely in the chest when he turned around, gun only partially drawn from his sport coat. Just to ensure the leader couldn't pull a firearm, or otherwise threaten Clouse, Parish fired a single round into his kneecap, dropping him to the ground where he immediately clutched the wounded appendage.

Parish sensed the man wasn't very hardened in combat based on the way he moaned and groaned, as though a bullet to the knee was his first major wound. He held the assault rifle in a ready position, walking with purpose toward the fallen man while Clouse walked over to the stranger, still looking very uncertain.

"It can't be this simple," he said, finally standing over the man. "Who are you really?"

Refusing to answer, the man simply continued to clutch his knee and rock back and forth in pain. Parish checked the two henchmen to make certain they were no longer a threat as Clouse kicked at the man's wound, drawing a pained cry.

"Tell me who you really are."

Parish noticed the same thing his boss had a few minutes earlier. There were no cursed cubes anywhere to be found, and he felt certain whoever possessed them wasn't going to let them out of sight so close to acquiring his objective.

Kneeling down, Parish checked the man for any firearms, finding nothing on his side or hidden along his belt. Satisfied the man wasn't carrying a weapon, he nodded to Clouse.

"Get yourself hidden, Todd, in case there are more of them," Clouse ordered.

"Yes, sir," Parish replied without hesitation, returning to the hallway as his employer continued to question the injured man.

Based on the way Clouse's voice barcly carried through the tunnel, Parish didn't expect any police involvement because his gunfire probably went completely unheard. Anyone whose ears picked up the noise would probably mistake it for construction work anyhow, leaving them in the clear.

Parish hated being forced to take a human life, but he wasn't going to let any harm come to Clouse. Think of the greater good, he told himself, trying to soften the idea of going against some of the morals he was taught by his parents and the church during his youth. He decided to ask for forgiveness later, after his colleagues and millions of people were safe from the lunatic who wanted to bring the thirteen cubes together.

Opening the heavy door to his camouflaged box, Parish wondered what kind of madman risked destroying the world as people knew it for power. When the door swung open, he found his answer staring him in the face.

"Hi there," the redheaded man said, thrusting a stun gun into the bodyguard's chest, rendering him physically helpless.

Parish felt incredible pain shoot through his body as his muscles betrayed him, allowing him to slump to the ground in a heap once the trigger was released. For the next five to ten seconds, the man could do whatever he chose to with Clouse's only current form of protection.

***

Clay Branson reached the roof to find a man sitting Indian style with several familiar, sharp weapons placed beside him. The old Japanese man kept his hands close to his chest, obviously meditating and mentally preparing himself for the impending battle. Nosagi certainly hadn't hidden from him, purposely standing on the edge of the roof for Clay to spot from anywhere on the ground. Assisting Stone delayed him only a few seconds, and Clay felt certain Alan Stewart meant to kill the agent, so he provided assistance on his way to the top of the vacated building.

Atop this high roof, far back from the road, no residents or drivers passing by were going to spot the skirmish about to begin.

"My sole purpose," Nosagi said without opening his eyes in reasonably sound English, "is to keep you preoccupied so my employer can carry out his business below."

"You have my undivided attention," Clay growled, taking one step forward.

Completely flat, the rooftop was slightly less than half the size of a soccer field, providing no obstructions other than the air conditioning unit in the far corner. Clay had done battle on rooftops before, and while many of his confrontations threatened his very life, none of them held the personal meaning of this brewing altercation. The man ultimately responsible for three deaths of people directly related to Clay and countess other people he had never met remained seated halfway across the roof.

"Is that what your life is now?" Clay asked. "Being paid to murder people for money?"

"It's what my life was *always* about, dear boy," Nosagi answered, finally opening his eyes with a neutral countenance that served only to infuriate Clay all the more. "You were just too blind to see it."

"I was a teenager when you took me to Japan," Clay said, battling inwardly to control his emotions, realizing his mentor hadn't even mentioned the blonde as though his people were disposable. "You were the reason I straightened out my life, the reason I got married and had a son. And now I find out you were the one who took that all away from me? How could you?"

"Your uncle should have told you sooner."

"My uncle? He's not exactly where I'm placing the blame these days. If you wanted to train me alongside your assassination squad, fine, but I never knew any better. You didn't need to send your people after me and my family."

The thin smirk Nosagi had worn faded away instantly.

"Yes, I did. It was only a matter of time before you discovered the truth, and I couldn't carry out my work while looking over my shoulder constantly. I never thought you were skilled enough to overcome my best warriors."

"I practiced *every* single day," Clay stammered. "You taught me tradition, and that meant something to me. You were my mentor, my *sensei*, and for what? So you could murder my family in hopes that I would abandon those untruths and work for you?"

"More or less. But your development of a strong ethical code sent you packing instead."

"You left me with *nothing*. That country was nothing but a bad memory to me, so of course I returned home."

"And now we come full circle," Nosagi said, shifting his stance so he was kneeling instead of sitting directly on the rooftop.

Clay placed the few weapons in his hands atop the ground and assumed a kneeling position as well. Both men were about to engage in the tradition of *kuji-in*, which various warrior clans from Japan believed invoked powers, both mental and physical, to aid them in combat. Nine primary hand symbols were used by men and women trained like Clay and Nosagi, and Clay fully expected his mentor to use many of the same signs as some of the students who had already died trying to assassinate the police officer.

Kneeling completely, both men stared across the roof to one another, placing their fisted hands in front of them, leaning forward to respectfully bow, regardless of their personal feelings toward one another.

Clay went first, forming his fingers into a shape quite unusual to anyone else. Nothing like a gang sign, his fingers virtually meshed together, forming a symbol he had memorized years before. He held them to the left side of his chest, near the heart, for his adversary to see.

"*Rin*," he said aloud, his blue eyes boring into his mentor.

Rin is used to bring strength to the mind and body.

"*Retsu*," Nosagi countered, forming his fingers into a sword-like symbol.

He wriggled the symbol like a slithering snake, down from above his head before thrusting the imaginary sword forcefully toward Clay.

Retsu enables telekinetic powers in a ninja, allowing him to stun an opponent with a touch or shout.

"*Toh*," Clay stated, which allowed the warrior to reach a balance between liquid and solid states of the body.

He called upon that particular symbol primarily out of habit, especially since he continued to walk among the living after several of these deadly encounters.

"*Hei*," Nosagi said with the command of a battlefield general in his voice.

Considering the symbol was used to psychically mask one's presence to another, the irony wasn't lost on Clay, who formed a final symbol before him with both hands.

"*Zen*," he finished, hoping to bring enlightenment and understanding to himself about his opponent and their tradition before the battle found opportunity to kill him.

Nosagi plucked his sheathed sword from the ground beside him while Clay reached behind him, drawing his sword from the sheath attached to the small pack he wore like a backpack. Both men locked eyes before darting across the roof to engage in true mortal combat.

CHAPTER 49

louse continued questioning the man Parish shot, but no answers came his way. He struck and kicked at the wound, and the man did not even attempt to answer his questions, or even lie. To Clouse it seemed the man literally did not know the answers, as though he was simply another henchman in a long line of paid thugs.

To this point he had put the two nearby dead men out of his mind. Like Parish, he didn't condone murder, but in his defense he never asked to be the guardian of cursed objects either. He kept his focus on the present, trying to figure out where the cubes might be, and the surviving man's identity.

"Where are the cubes?" he asked for what seemed the hundredth time.

"Perhaps you're asking the wrong questions," a voice said from the chamber's doorway. "Or the wrong person."

Clouse looked up to find the redheaded man from the security footage at the bookstore standing in the doorway, pistol in hand. He suddenly wondered if he overlooked such a simple solution, that the man before him was the mastermind *and* the psychic. A bit of smoke and mirrors created the illusion that this man was simply a paid employee, or a reluctant assistant to some secluded villain.

"Jacob Savitch," he spoke the name aloud.

"You're better than I thought," Savitch replied with a cagy grin. "It's no wonder you protected the cubes so well."

He had lost some weight the past few months, possibly attributed to the grinding search for the cursed objects. Clouse still didn't see any of the cursed objects, which made him wonder where they resided, and exactly what Savitch planned to accomplish.

"This man is just another loose end," the redheaded psychic said, aiming the gun toward the fallen mercenary.

"No, please," the man pleaded, ignoring his injuries to put his hands up defensively.

"Too late for that," Savitch said, pulling the trigger and putting a bullet in the man's head to end his life.

"That wasn't necessary," Clouse stated.

"And you've never gotten blood on your hands?"

"Only in self-defense. I don't kill for pleasure."

"Nor do I. This is business, pure and simple. I'm simply eliminating some loose ends."

Clouse looked over the man's shoulder, hoping Parish might take him from behind.

"You're not looking for your bodyguard, are you?" Savitch asked with masked emotion. "I've already dealt with him."

Clouse started to take a step forward until the gun was pointed in his direction.

"He's subdued," Savitch confessed. "I might need him later. Maybe I'll even put him to work for me."

"Unlikely," Clouse grumbled.

"You're right. He's loyal to a fault, which will make him another loose end once I've gotten everything I need here."

"I get the feeling *everyone* is going to be a loose end. I'm no psychic, but I doubt even you know what the hell is going to happen when you put these things together."

"Do you?"

Savitch paused momentarily, and Clouse knew he was trying to read his thoughts. Clouse didn't know the answer, and he wasn't going to waste time putting up mental barriers.

"No, you don't," Savitch said with satisfaction.

Still training the gun loosely on Clouse, the red-headed man stepped in reverse toward the doorway, scooping up a small satchel from just beyond the threshold. Clouse wondered how Parish was holding up, but he wasn't in a position to check on his employee just yet. Instead, he watched Savitch take the pack to the centerpiece and dump all twelve cubes in his possession atop the flat surface. Clouse had never seen so many of the shiny, cursed objects occupy one space before. He never dared bring them together, but he supposed they weren't dangerous when grouped without some kind of ritual.

"I take it you have the last cube," Savitch said casually as he took a handful of the cubes over to the clock embedded in the wall and began inserting them into the slots that were created specifically for them. "We wouldn't want anything to happen to your family."

"Like you care," Clouse replied sharply.

With each cube placed into a slot, something unusual occurred in the center of the room. From the bowl-like middle of the centerpiece a hologram with no specific source appeared, showing a natural disaster of sorts in only the color of the cube. A red cube depicted a ground-shattering earthquake, while a pearl white cube showed pounding rains the likes of which Clouse had experienced only a handful of times in his life. The display all occurred within a neutral gray outline of Earth, like some kind of futuristic sci-fi hologram aboard a starship. Strangely, it even provided authentic sounds that chilled Clouse to the bone because the destructive weather being displayed sounded equally fierce.

He doubted the world was literally falling apart around him, so the cubes were simply showing their hand, indicating what their part in the end of the world would be once they all came together.

"Why would you do this?" Clouse stammered, unwilling to believe anyone could willingly choose to wipe out mankind.

"You really don't remember me, do you?" Savitch asked quite seriously, turning around from his work momentarily to address Clouse personally. "It was *you* who put me in this position and gave me every bit of information I needed."

"No," Clouse muttered, unwilling to believe such a lie. "I would never."

"But you did," Savitch insisted. "You and I go way back, to the time when you first began work on the hotel."

Clouse's head began spinning as he tried to imagine how he and this young man shared any kind of bond. He wasn't sure he particularly cared, because if he didn't find a way out of this situation, the end of the world as he knew it was inevitable.

***

Stone felt like a man with no master and no particular loyalty to either side in this skirmish. Yes, he still worked for the FBI, but his colleagues hadn't exactly been endearing themselves to him lately. Stewart tried to kill him, not once, but twice, and nearly succeeded on both occasions. He didn't really owe Paul Clouse anything, because the man refused to trust him enough to reveal any details about his quest to the agent, even though Stone felt he had proven his worth sufficiently. Perhaps, Stone decided, his own actions hadn't exactly put him in a good light after all, but at this moment he might be able to change some opinions.

Or die trying.

Besides, no world meant no human race, and Stone cared truly and deeply for his family. He wasn't about to let petty squabbles with his agency or the people around him sway him into taking the worst action possible.

Based on the fact that Clay Branson rescued him from almost certain death twice, and Branson allied himself with Clouse, the agent decided to follow suit. As he darted along the windows toward a secondary stairwell, he noticed the sky graying severely outside. He didn't recall any severe weather forecasted, or even thunderstorms for that matter, and he'd made the effort to look when choosing his vantage point.

Even as he descended the stairs, barely hearing his boots hit the carpeted wood because he moved so quickly, Stone's mind raced for an idea to stop four or five armed men. It occurred to him that conventional methods would surely spell the end of him, so he considered ways to keep them from entering the tunnel instead.

Stone didn't consider himself on the level of a double agent or government spy when it came to survival and crafty ideas, but he was brought up to think resourcefully. Splitting time between a rural farm and the urban setting of Houston, Stone found a number of things that fascinated him as a boy. He dabbled in everything from electronics and computers to repairing farm equipment.

Despite his array of knowledge and developed skills, a rather simple solution occurred to him as he reached the bottom step on the ground floor.

He headed to the back of the building, finding his own leased van from the rental company still parked behind the old apartment complex. He wanted a van specifically for potential surveillance purposes, but now he considered a different use for the vehicle that might stall the armed men and buy Clouse and anyone with him some time inside the tunnel.

Scurrying along the parking lot, Stone unlocked the van with the remote control and immediately opened the side door so he could open the middle window on the passenger's side. What he planned required a little bit of luck, and even if he succeeded there wasn't a guarantee he wouldn't be riddled with bullets before escaping the vehicle.

"Hope Clouse will cover the damage deposit," he muttered once the window ajar before jumping into the driver's seat.

He wasn't certain why the henchmen in the other van waited before entering the tunnel, but he suspected some kind of signal was arranged. Stone needed to get into place before that message was received, so he started the van and stomped on the gas. The tires spit up rocks and dirt before engaging the deteriorated parking lot surface, sending the vehicle lurching forward. Stone narrowly missed the apartment building's nearby corner in an effort to steer directly toward the tunnel, which stood about ten feet down a sharp decline in elevation.

Considering the entrance was just barely past the elevation drop, Stone slowed the van at the last possible second, hoping to drop the van down the ten foot drop without destroying it, landing the lengthy passenger side squarely in front of the tunnel. If he landed correctly, the van would block the entrance and provide him with a means of escape. Engaging several individuals with automatic weapons in a gunfight wasn't wise, but he prepared for such an event if his egress was blocked.

He barely shifted his eyes to see the shocked looks of the henchmen as the van flew over the embankment, landing hard, and awkwardly, atop the dirt mound beside the doorway. Stone felt his back jar from the impact, but adrenaline kicked in once he realized he had overshot the intended target.

"Shit," he muttered, throwing the van in reverse so he could better block the doorway.

As it stood, the van was merely an inconvenience to walk around, parked at an incline due to the sloped dirt mound. It immediately shifted, but the wheels didn't respond when he pressed on the gas pedal. They simply spun, unable to grip the dirt in the rear.

Stone yelled out several obscenities as he tried to rock the van from his seat, already feeling several pairs of irritated eyes locking on his position. In a matter of seconds they would draw their weapons and mow him down in a hail of gunfire. He couldn't imagine they possessed any fear of being heard or seen so far from the heart of downtown French Lick.

"Damn it!" he said under his breath as he tried putting the vehicle in forward and reverse.

Although his home state never saw snow accumulation, experience working in the eastern states provided him with knowledge of how to escape a snowdrift. Loose dirt, it seemed, wasn't a far cry from such extreme weather.

He rocked back and forth in his seat, hearing one wheeling spinning in the soil while the other made no sound at all, indicating it might be touching nothing except air. The embankment left by Niemeyer wasn't at all smooth or steady, making it difficult to get all four tires touching solid ground.

Two of the men, dressed in black military style pants and light jackets, stepped from the van with their weapons trained on Stone. Refusing to yield, he threw his weight against the back of the seat one last time while stepping on the gas, finally catching some dirt beneath the back tire that had been spinning in the air. Now the van literally flew backwards toward the entrance, forcing Stone to cut the wheel sharply before the vehicle hit the solid dirt wall in yet another useless position.

He couldn't afford another mistake because now four men were ready to yank him from the van and end his life without fanfare. The van responded to his hard turn of the steering wheel, and he barely applied the brakes in a timely manner, but the passenger side of the vehicle pressed directly against the tunnel entrance, creating a barrier. Though hardly impenetrable, the new wall would make it difficult to enter the tunnel without severe risk of being hit by gunfire from the four mercenaries.

Stone put the van in park, yanked out the keys, and used the remote to lock the entire van within one second. Already expecting bullets to hit the van like rainfall, he couldn't afford to dawdle a split-second in his escape attempt. Realizing the extent of his plan, the four men raised their weapons to fire before one of them spoke up and ordered them to hold their positions. Open gunfire was a greater risk after the commotion with the van, so he ordered them to gain an entry point to the van. Stone heard all of this as he was crawling out the already open side window, scrambling for his life in case the vocal henchman changed his mind.

In too much of a hurry to be concerned with style, Stone fell out of the side window, hitting the ground hard on his right shoulder. He groaned in pain but quickly regained his footing, doggedly running into the tunnel as he clutched his shoulder. Stone decided to see if any assistance awaited him inside, because raising his primary shooting arm wasn't going to be easy with the new injury. He was trained to shoot with his left hand, but against four heavily armed, military-trained men Stone didn't like his chances.

About a minute later he came across a prone body lying face down on the dirt path. Fearing he'd found his second casualty within the last ten minutes, Stone knelt down, reaching to check for signs of life when the person suddenly stirred, startling him. Parish turned to one side to get a look at the agent, unable to move too far because his hands and feet were bound with zip ties. A rag of some sort was stuffed into his mouth to keep him from speaking or calling for help. Stone fished his trusty pocket knife from a pocket and cut the bodyguard loose before pulling the rag loose.

"We need to help Mr. Clouse," Parish insisted immediately, though very quietly so Savitch didn't hear.

"Your boss is on his own," Stone said, immediately glancing toward the chamber easily within walking distance. "We have four armed men about to enter this tunnel and I can't hold them off by myself."

"That son-of-a-bitch used a Taser on me," Parish muttered angrily, looking toward the chamber, obviously wanting some measure of revenge.

"Those pissed off mercenaries up front are going to use live rounds on us if we let them get in this tunnel. I'm thinking that's our priority."

Parish nodded before he stood, looking along the ground for something. With his eyes already adjusted to the light, he found both his Glock and his AR-15 lying nearby where Savitch had discarded them. Scooping up the weapons, he motioned for Stone to lead the way toward the entrance. Though the agent still didn't feel great about his chances against the four men, he felt a little better having some backup with him. He suspected in a few minutes he was going to be pleasantly surprised or dead.

CHAPTER 50

Knowing he needed to overcome Nosagi's experience, Clay exchanged offensive and defensive attacks with his former teacher, realizing that being several decades younger didn't offer him much of a physical advantage. Perhaps it was an illusion, or Clay recalling the days of arduous training in Japan, but Nosagi hadn't appeared to lose a step.

Both men took turns swiping and slashing with their blades, but each countered the other without much issue, leaving their swordplay on equal footing. Clay leapt over a blade aimed at his feet, deciding to distance himself from Nosagi by carrying out a backflip, all while grasping his sword in his left hand.

Instead of giving chase, Nosagi threw a smoke bomb close to where he anticipated Clay landing, trying to disorient his former student. Already wise to the trick, Clay did not land squarely on his feet, choosing to tuck and roll instead, dodging a fatally aimed blow from his adversary's sword that would have pierced his heart. Immediately regaining his footing from the tuck and roll, Clay went for Nosagi's head, feet, and waistline in succession, each of his quick strikes strategically blocked.

Without warning Nosagi began sprinting toward the large air conditioning unit seated along the far corner. Clay gave chase, wondering if the man meant to lead him further away from the action, or simply escape to fight another day. Either way, Clay wasn't having any of it, because his feud with the man ended on this morning one way or another.

He gave chase, expecting his former mentor to cleverly leap over the side of the building with some plan to break his fall, or simply take the higher ground for an advantage. Instead, Nosagi ran to the edge of the unit and jumped to the closest edge of it, springing from the higher surface into a backflip as Clay drew dangerously close. Clay barely reacted to the sudden move in time when Nosagi sailed over him, thrusting his blade toward Clay's heart. Deflecting the potentially fatal blow, Clay turned to confront Nosagi, putting his back to the air conditioning unit as the wind picked up and the clouds turned ominously gray overhead. He sensed the new weather pattern was unnatural, but he was in no position to help Clouse inside the tunnel.

He chastised himself for distracting his mind, because any momentarily lapse in concentration gave Nosagi an advantage. Clay watched his adversary pull off the end of the sword, revealing a small chain from within the handle. Nosagi twirled the chain briefly before tossing the end at Clay's feet in an attempt to wrap his ankle and trip him. Narrowly avoiding the metal, Clay lifted his foot as though skipping rope before lunging at Nosagi with his blade pointed toward the man's chest. Nosagi deflected the blow with his own blade, all the while retrieving the chain with his free hand.

Instead of backing off, or trying a completely different offensive tactic, Nosagi flipped the chain toward Clay, who ducked to one side, realizing too late that the chain was aimed at his sword, and not his body. Like a frog's tongue catching a fly in midair, the chain removed Clay's sword from his grip, sending it well beyond his reach and behind Nosagi.

Clay immediately reached for the two *kama* located in the pack strapped to his back. With the appearance of small sickles, about a foot long with wooden handles, the weapons held short, slightly curved blades that tore into flesh or delivered a killing blow just as easily. Clay twirled both weapons in his hands with the dexterity of a cheerleader using a baton. Showmanship was wasted on a seasoned killer like Nosagi, but he needed the feel of the weapons in his hands to loosen up his fingers.

In the meantime Nosagi wrapped the chain in his left hand while holding the sword in the other. He swung the chain first, which Clay blocked with one *kama* while the other locked against the sword, placing them at a stalemate. Improvising, Clay freed one weapon from the chain, smacking his former *sensei* in the face with the wooden end before kicking him solidly in the gut. As Nosagi reeled, finally proving a tad slower, or more susceptible to fatigue, Clay landed the pointy end of the same *kama* in his forearm.

The weapon struck bone, but Nosagi immediately swung his sword toward Clay's forearm, forcing him to release the weapon altogether. In the closest thing to rage that Clay had ever seen from the man, he stiffly yanked the blade from his arm and threw it on the ground. Still holding the sword, he went on the attack as the winds swirled around them from the unforeseen, impending storm.

Parrying, slashing, and stabbing at one another for close to thirty seconds, neither man landed another blow until Nosagi gained a glancing slice of his sword along the outside of Clay's left leg.

Unlike his last battle, Clay experienced no taunting, because both men held to tradition, letting their actions speak for them. Neither of them had left anything unsaid and each knew the other's position. Their conflict spoke volumes as each went for numerous killing blows.

Left with only one weapon, Clay deflected several strikes, but found himself on the defensive, being backed toward the edge of the roof. When Nosagi used both hands to thrust his sword toward Clay, attempting to push him back even further, Clay caught the blade inside his *kama*, and spun his arm twice in a clockwise motion, dislodging the sword from Nosagi's grip as a commercial pipe behind him tripped him.

As Clay fell to his back, losing the other *kama* in the process, Nosagi found time to assemble two pieces of a wooden rod with a simple snap and stab the dangerous, bladed end toward his former pupil's face. Clay batted the wooden staff away once with an open palm before it could inflict damage. He struck it away a second time with the opposite hand as Nosagi thrust it downward, but his mentor guessed correctly the third time, and Clay found no time to safely bat the weapon aside without risking severe injury. Instead, he caught the blade itself between his palms as it neared the bridge of his nose, threatening to penetrate his brain if he let it go while under Nosagi's full force.

Using his power advantage, Clay pushed the staff back, in turn preventing an eventual tumble off the roof as he regained his footing. Both he and Nosagi grasped part of the staff, vying for control as they twisted and turned it. When they struck simultaneous punches to the face, the staff flew into the air between them. When it came down each of them caught an end and pulled it into its two original components. Much to Clay's dismay, he received a hollow wooden portion that served as a sheath for the short sword that Nosagi pulled, possibly by design.

Nosagi immediately went on the attack, but Clay's sheath deflected the blade until he found an opening to kick his former mentor in the chest without risk of losing a foot. As Nosagi stumbled back a few feet, Clay pulled his own smoke bomb, tossing it to the ground before retrieving his sword and hopping atop the air conditioning unit.

Thunder grumbled in the distance, followed by a lightning strike that returned the illumination stolen by the dark clouds, if only for a split-second. Completely focused on the task at hand, Clay fended off another attack with the short sword from Nosagi when it came. He leaped over the blade at one point, having to sidestep several jabs in between. Unable to accomplish anything, even with the high ground, he dodged another sword jab by flipping to the ground behind Nosagi.

Neither immediately rushed into an attack, so Nosagi, pulled on the handle of his short sword, revealing that a stubby knife occupied the center. Only about three inches in total length, the knife was half blade, and half handle wrapped in black silk. Meant for throwing, rather than close proximity combat, the blade could be potentially deadly in either scenario, but Clay wondered if Nosagi created all of his weapons in the form of nesting barrels. In rather brazen fashion, Nosagi displayed the knife along the flat of his palm before throwing it at his former student.

Knowing the weapon was aimed at his heart, Clay turned sharply to his left to reduce his profile, hoping the blade might sail completely past him. Instead, the sharpened end plunged into his shoulder as an immediate indication of his failure to prevent the injury. He pulled it out, followed by a thin trickle of blood, and used his left hand to return the favor with a sudden throw. Nosagi caught the blade in midair with one hand, turning his hand to display the feat to Clay, who was truly impressed at the man's quickness and instincts. Perhaps a bit too awed by the reaction, Clay reacted too slowly to prevent Nosagi from throwing down another smoke bomb and disappearing from his sight.

Clay looked all around the rooftop, realizing he was completely alone. With the stairwell access behind him, Clay knew Nosagi couldn't have escaped his sight unless he went over the side of the roof. Sucking in a deep breath, he headed toward the air conditioning unit to begin searching for the man who both saved him and murdered his loved ones.

***

"I don't remember you," Clouse said, deciding to stall for time while Savitch continued to savor the moment, slowly placing the cubes in the clock's indentations.

"Of course you wouldn't," Savitch replied, sliding a cube into place. "You were a big shot, walking around the dome like you owned the place."

"Really?" Clouse contested the statement. "I was doing a job, trying to make a living."

"Funny how you actually came to own the place. Isn't it weird how life sometimes throws those little curveballs? They aren't always a bad thing."

Clouse stood and observed while Savitch walked over to retrieve another cube. He seemed rather nonchalant, as though exponentially confident nothing could foil his plan. Clouse didn't know what kind of backup the man brought along, or what knowledge led him to his confidence, but Clouse needed one of his allies to come through for him.

He struggled to remember this young man's identity because ten years had passed since renovation took place at the hotel. Obviously numerous events, many tragic, occupied his mind and put aside many of the older, better memories. His time working at the hotel ended on a particularly sour note after several attempts on his life and a man he thought of as family turned on him.

"I sense that you're struggling to remember me," Savitch said. "For the life of me, I don't understand how you and I are linked, but we are."

"What usually links you to someone?"

"If they have psychic powers of some sort, it's rather easy. But you certainly aren't a psychic, which leads me to think maybe you've had some sort of spiritual experience. Maybe you died at one time? Or someone close to you communicated with you after they passed?"

Clouse thought back to his first wife, who died under violent circumstances, presenting herself to him twice in his bathroom mirror in spectral form. He always thought her appearance was simply a figment of his imagination, but now he questioned its authenticity. Temporary insanity occurred to him as a possibility for Angie's appearance, but the timing on both occasions felt appropriate, and not like something his mind conjured up for reassurance.

"Your wife?" Savitch asked, turning from his work at the giant clock, the gun still clutched in his left hand. "You saw her?"

"Get out of my head," Clouse growled.

"No, not until you remember," Savitch said, walking over to the center-piece with a deliberately slow pace to retrieve another cube.

Clouse believed six were already in place, and that left another six, plus the dark blue cube he had yet to produce. He quickly turned his thoughts to the past, concentrating on his first wife accidentally, before trying to remember his days working at the hotel. He guessed the man before him to be in his middle twenties, but it made no sense that he would have associated with a teenager while advising a construction crew ten years prior.

Also, the last name failed to register with him.

"You're thinking about this all wrong," Savitch said, retrieving the next cube from atop the centerpiece. "I wasn't on the grounds that often, but you should remember a conversation you had with my stepfather."

"I had lots of conversations back then," Clouse spoke before truly thinking.

It then occurred to him that the stepfather probably had a different last name and hadn't adopted this young man.

"Coming to you yet?" Savitch asked, narrowing his eyes like a hawk.

Suddenly an image of the past *did* come to Clouse, and he remembered a red-headed teenage boy who came to work with his father occasionally. Bob Lowery often spoke of how uninterested his stepson seemed about almost everything. He voiced his concerns that the boy was lazy, but also that he acted strangely around certain people as though he needed to learn people skills.

"I think you have it," Savitch said with a satisfied smile that virtually glowed red in the chamber's tinted lighting. "But I wasn't lazy. While most teenagers were busy playing sports, or worrying about getting a driver's license, I picked up on a way to get rich and powerful. I couldn't act on it until later, but you and Martin Smith provided me with all of the informa-tion I needed."

Clouse did battle over two of the cursed cubes with the benefactor who provided his millions on several occasions, considering the matter a local affair that he mostly hid from the press. Only after he ridded the world of Smith and his brand of evil did Clouse learn about all of the cubes and embark upon a worldly conquest to remove them all from evil hands.

"My stepfather dragged me to the hotel grounds occasionally, saying he was going to make a man out of me. I played his game and pretended to observe his work, but I was really spending my time observing you and your problems."

"Me and my problems, huh?" Clouse asked as Savitch inserted yet another cube into the wall, bringing about catastrophic ocean tides in the hologram. "I do remember you now, and how strangely you acted. I just thought you had troubles at home, or maybe you were special needs. I remember Bob Lowery as a gruff worker, and if he was like that at home I'm sure your childhood wasn't the best."

"Don't even play that card," Savitch said bitterly. "You can imply that I was lazy or stupid and I'll let that slide, but bringing up my childhood isn't the opening you're looking for. The only thing that can save you is producing that last cube I need to make all of this happen."

"Why?"

"What do you mean, 'why'?"

"Why do all of this? Even if you basically destroy the planet and you're the only person left to rule over the ruins, then what?"

Savitch lowered the gun slightly, but not from compassion or under-standing. He wanted Clouse to see his face and hear his tone, even in the strange confines of the chamber.

"You can't possibly understand what it was like being me as a child," he said with a sneer. "All of the taunting and teasing simply because I could *see* things, visualize things that they could not."

"So you were picked on and now you want millions of people to pay for the sins of a few? That sounds a bit selfish if you ask me."

"This world as a whole needs to be taught a lesson, but that's not why I'm doing this. It's inevitable that someone is going to put these cubes together one day, and you never had the balls to go through with it, so I will."

"Your power is a gift and you've done nothing but abuse it," Clouse said, shaking his head, feeling he'd experienced a nearly identical confrontation once with Martin Smith.

Appealing to the man's faith was an obvious waste of time, and Savitch didn't appear to have much of a conscience if the lives of millions meant so little to him. Running out of time and options, Clouse felt sickened over the worldly visual display centered in the room. If the cubes truly held the ability to tear apart the planet when combined, it was only a matter of time before Savitch succeeded in wiping out a majority of the human race. Perhaps the prediction of a global event in or around 2012 wasn't so far out of touch after all, but even ancient civilizations could never have anticipated the greed of men creating their own doom.

Clouse's attention remained divided between his new adversary and the strange hologram, but he felt certain the pulsating orange light brightened and subsided at a faster rate with each cube added to the wall.

"You're a man with religion," Savitch stated as though Clouse had wasted his entire life believing in something that didn't exist. "Your good book says not to associate with my kind, yet you went out and hired your own medium."

"The same book also says not to wear clothing of different threads, but I'm pretty sure I've broken that rule a few times. What's your point?"

Savitch walked over to retrieve yet another cube, eyeing the box Clouse had brought with him and set atop the wooden centerpiece. He had yet to inquire about the box, probably having too much fun trying to pluck Clouse's thoughts in the meantime.

"My point is we have one life and one only, so why not make the most of it? You stand atop your pedestal and preach your moral garbage. Your money and influence may have convinced the people who work for you that they're doing right, but you're all just spinning your wheels and wasting your lives away."

"So I should have used my money and power to put these cubes together and kill millions instead?"

"Exactly. But now it's too late for you and everyone you love."

"I don't believe that. Just like I don't believe I surround myself with people who care only about the checks they cash from me. Every one of them is told the entire truth, and every one of them has the right to step away whenever they choose. How can someone like you, who sees the unseen, not have religion?"

"Because I'm above all of that. I choose to live for the moment and make the most of my life after people like you did nothing but shit on my childhood. You're lucky enough to be the one person who witnesses my triumph."

"Funny, I don't feel very lucky."

Savitch took another cube, this one yellow, from the pack atop the wooden centerpiece. He shot Clouse an almost mischievous look as he walked over to place it in yet another empty slot, bringing forth another hologram. Clouse felt tense, and sickened, as only three cubes remained before the strange glowing clock felt sated and began hypothetically tearing apart the world. He wondered if any chance remained for one of his people to save the day, or he needed to take a major risk on his own.

CHAPTER 51

Still not entirely familiar with the FBI agent who freed him from his bonds, Parish found little choice except to trust the man, but exercised caution nonetheless. He rounded each bend of the tunnel with his AR-15 held in a ready position, wondering if someone waited for them in similar fashion.

When the two finally saw daylight near the entrance, Parish carefully positioned himself against the wall, trying to safely assess the situation ahead.

A van blocked the entrance, and he looked questioningly at Stone, who gave a playful shrug. One of the men the agent had mentioned was partway through the vehicle, about to reach the side door with the open window and breach the tunnel. They had apparently broken the front windshield to gain access to the vehicle before unlocking the doors and sliding the side door open.

"Warning shots or wait for them to start coming in?" he asked Stone.

"They didn't seem like the types to be scared of a little gunplay. I say we hit 'em directly."

Parish felt torn between defending his boss against this invading horde and taking his side directly inside the chamber. He had left Clouse an advantage, if only it presented itself in a timely manner and his boss knew how to use it.

Returning his attention to the task at hand, Parish waited until the man presented his full body mass at the van's open door before firing, virtually ensuring his assault rifle wouldn't miss the mark. The man never stood a chance of defending himself, much less pulling his own weapon into position, before the three-round burst peppered his chin, neck, and chest in under a second.

If the bullets didn't stop his heart from beating, the awkward fall where the butt of his chin made contact with the hard soil and contorted his neck certainly finished the job. Parish dared take a step closer, hearing hushed concern among the three remaining mercenaries. By no means panicking, they were instead planning a strategy to enter the tunnel without drawing public attention while wiping out any remaining defenders.

"My kingdom for a grenade," Stone muttered with a sour look.

"I hope that's not what they're thinking," Parish replied, wondering what kinds of toys ex-military types might have at their disposal.

Each of them exchanged concerned looks, realizing they had just put the mercenaries on the defensive, which might have proven a terrible idea. Parish couldn't fathom the three remaining henchmen throwing an explosive device or a gas canister into the tunnel until they were reasonably certain of gaining entry. He could think of nothing outside the entrance that might provide them the means to move the disabled van, and crawling beneath the van with their packs and equipment would slow them down too much and make them easy targets.

Finding his options extremely limited, Parish found his arsenal rather useless unless the mercenaries started trying to break inside. The option of calling local authorities was really no option at all if he wanted to keep Clouse's secrets intact. He considered using the secondary entrance from the old apartment complex, but doing so would require a boost from Stone. Heading back to the area would also leave the front door exposed, and while he doubted the henchmen were going to make their way past the van and try shooting their way inside, he wasn't sure he dared take the risk.

"What are you thinking over there?" Stone asked, obviously seeing his mental wheels churning.

"There *is* another way out of here," Parish admitted, "but I'm not even sure it's a good option."

"Why's that?"

"It leads to the apartment building that overlooks the entrance," Parish said, pointing toward the blocked opening. "Even if one of us got up there, we don't have a sniper rifle, and we'd get mowed down after firing a single shot."

"At least the cops would show up."

"We don't want that either."

Stone rolled his eyes in frustration.

"I know you're trying to keep all of this a big secret, but is it worth dying for?"

Parish nodded slowly and thoughtfully in the affirmative.

"You bet it is."

Stone seemed to accept the situation and Parish's stand.

"Let me have a look at this other entrance."

Parish glanced worriedly toward the tunnel opening, where only a few beams of light pushed past the van.

"They aren't coming, at least not until they regroup. Besides, they can't risk killing the guy who's paying them if he's inside."

Agreeing with the FBI agent's logic, Parish walked him back to the secondary entrance, not far from his protective box. Stone looked up at the hatch which automatically sprung to a closed position after someone dropped down through it.

"There's no way I can lift you up there," Stone chuckled. "You're going to have to let me try it."

"There's no need for fat jokes, you know."

Parish felt reluctant, partly because he didn't fully trust the agent, and also because the man wasn't armed well enough to make much of a difference.

"I can at least make a distraction out there and buy you some time," Stone insisted.

Groaning, Parish set down his rifle and cupped his hands together to try boosting Stone upward toward the hatch. As the agent stepped into the makeshift step, Parish lifted his hands, allowing Stone access to the hatch. It opened with ease, and after a few seconds of struggling to pull himself up with elbow strength, Stone disappeared through the opening. Taking up the AR-15, Parish debated whether to assist Clouse or return to the tunnel entrance. He ultimately decided the three men needed to be stopped or there would be no hope for anyone on his team, so he returned to the blocked opening.

***

Clay exercised caution when descending the stairs to the level just below the rooftop, knowing many of the apartment doors remained wide-open. Nosagi could be lurking around any corner, just waiting for the right moment to ambush him. Keeping his sword before him wherever he walked, Clay stepped from the last stair, finding a hallway full of open doors ahead of him. Any of them might be concealing danger, so he stepped forward, his senses attuned to his surroundings.

Even his sense of smell seemed heightened as various musty smells of mildew and mold entered his nostrils, along with animal urine that felt overwhelmingly toxic to his nose. Unsure of why the building was open to humans or animals in any sense, Clay doubted the old complex housed squatters like vacant houses often did in the larger cities.

He concentrated on other, more useful senses instead, listening for any movement on either side of the hallway. Part of his training with Nosagi was to develop a sixth sense of impending danger that came from an almost spiritual intertwining with the physical body and the elements around it. Whether an unseen sword came at him, or an arrow whistled through the air, Clay often detected such dangers before they struck home.

If not for the sense instilled within him from hours of meditation, practice, and focus, he knew he would long since be rotting away beneath a tombstone. Too many times during his young life death had sought him out, and somehow Clay beat the odds.

After passing the first four doors with the utmost caution, Clay barely found time to react when Nosagi jumped out from the next one, prepared to run a sword through his torso. Clay blocked the stabbing action and slashed his own sword toward his former mentor, lodging it in the wall when it missed the mark. Left with no time to free the weapon, Clay dodged another stab toward his chest with a sidestepping motion, ducked a sweeping blade aimed at his head, and a slice toward his arm as he raised the appendage just in time. Clay kicked Nosagi's hand as the blade sailed upward, helping lodge the tip of it in the deteriorated ceiling.

Both men were temporarily weaponless, leaving them on even ground for the time being as they exchanged kicks and punches, trying to gain an upper hand. If one landed a solid blow, it easily meant broken bones, torn cartilage, or crushed organs for the other. Of course delivering such a forceful strike required more than the split-second each gave the other between offensive moves.

Nosagi went for a punch that Clay blocked with his left hand before throwing a solid fist of his own, striking the older man in the bridge of the nose, stunning him momentarily. For the first time Clay sensed the longer the battle went, the greater his chances for success in spite of Nosagi's excellent conditioning, age took a toll on his body and endurance.

Clay watched the man recover from the blow rather quickly, backpedaling a few feet before throwing down another smoke bomb. Already accustomed, and weary, of the man's tricks, Clay drew a *shuriken* star from a padded pocket within his garb, throwing it directly down the hallway where he felt positive Nosagi would retreat, simply trying to hide and recover before his next round of attacks.

If the four-pointed star struck home, Clay would have a blood trail to follow so Nosagi couldn't keep hiding from him. He didn't particularly relish the idea of stalking the man like a wounded animal, but Nosagi had sent nearly half a dozen assassins to murder him *before* the incident at the island, so Clay's sympathy only traveled so far.

Brushing the artificial smoke aside with his hands, Clay found his weapon had indeed caught Nosagi in the right shoulder blade before the man ducked into a room three doors ahead of him. Not allowing his mind to trick him into thinking he was close to securing a kill, Clay dislodged his blade from the wall before darting to the side of the open door. He exercised caution by holding the sword before him, knowing Nosagi still possessed several weapons hidden within his gear.

A glance toward the ground revealed blood droplets, so Clay backed up to the opposite wall for a better look inside. Seeing nothing except an open window, he wondered if Nosagi might have tried escape once again, but left his mind open to the possibility of a trap. Instead of rushing headfirst into the room, he shot forward, but ducked and slid into the room like a baseball player stealing a base. Like a slow-motion movie shot, Clay's view of the ceiling above him as his back slid along the linoleum floor revealed Nosagi bracing his entire body with his arms and legs like a spider just waiting for his prey to appear beneath him.

He clutched a *sai* in his right hand, which surely would have forcefully entered Clay's skull had the former apprentice entered the room conventionally. The weapon, barely over a foot in length, looked a bit like a pitchfork with three prongs, the two exterior of which were almost twice as short as the sharpened center blade.

Holding out his hand, Clay stopped his own momentum near the center of the old apartment, quickly regaining his feet as Nosagi dropped from the ceiling, using the *sai* with precision skill. Clay deflected the attacks from the single weapon, backing off slightly, which allowed Nosagi to pull another *sai* from inside his black clothing. Seldom did one use the weapons in singular form, and two of them used by a master were absolutely deadly.

During the next few seconds it was every bit of focus and skill Clay could muster to fend off the furious assault from the pair of weapons using just his sword. Forced to go on the defensive, he backed up toward the only window in the room, quickly running out of room in the process. He received cuts in the left shoulder and the right side of his abdomen from the weapons, though both were grazing wounds and he ignored the pain. It wasn't until Nosagi lunged with one of the *sai* and Clay deflected it with his sword that the other *sai* came down in a stabbing motion from above. Turning his attention to the second weapon, Clay made certain his sword kept the first *sai* at bay while he grabbed Nosagi's wrist, turning both of their bodies toward the window like two dancers in an awkward stride.

His momentum carried him into the structurally weakened glass and he wasn't about to fall three stories without taking Nosagi along for the ride. Using his sword arm he locked Nosagi's arm with the inside of his elbow, continuing to clasp the man's wrist with his other hand while their momentum took them tumbling out of the window.

Falling three stories took only a few seconds, but Clay couldn't let his guard down one instant. Not enough time existed for either of them to jockey for a safer landing position because they were too busy keeping the other's weapons at bay. Both men knew better than to land with tense, stiffened muscles that came with fear of impact because their bones and tendons would certainly snap, possibly leading to serious injury or death. They had overcome any fear of death and injury years ago because of their training, but they still had to wait until the last possible fraction of a second to relax their bodies.

To Clay, the impact still felt like getting struck by a bus as his chest and neck hit first, followed by the whiplash of his legs and feet bouncing off the unforgiving ground. It took him a second to figure out if he was going to lose consciousness or not, and once his body refused to pass out, he tried to assess the physical damage.

His mind contemplated the immediate danger before getting too analytical and he scrambled to separate his body from Nosagi's. Only once he backed away from his former mentor's injured form did he realize how fortunate he was to land atop the older man. Clay discovered several aches and pains throughout his muscles, figuring the adrenaline kept his body from feeling the full extent of his injuries. On his knees, still grasping his sword about two feet removed from Nosagi, he took a moment to assess the damage his former mentor endured.

Nosagi's arms extended to his sides, and one appeared broken based on the hump only a few inches from his right elbow. His weapons lay beyond fingertip reach, but the fact that he was visibly and audibly coughing up blood informed Clay that their skirmish was indeed over. Glass had rained down upon the ground with the two men, and based on the pool of blood emerging from beneath Nosagi's back, the man had landed on something sharp enough to penetrate his flesh and internal organs.

Clay's ribs ached from landing so hard atop another human being. Extremely fortunate he hadn't suffered any serious injuries, he realized Nosagi was mortally wounded without immediate medical assistance or the use of one of the techniques used by their clan to self-heal over a period of time. Both men knew Clay wasn't going to allow any benefit to come Nosagi's way, so they simply stared at one another, breathing rather heavily even by their own standards.

Despite his injuries, Nosagi remained a dangerous individual, but Clay recognized something from the few precious seconds it required to recover from the fall.

"You could have killed me," he stated thoughtfully, realizing his mentor wasn't evil through and through.

"I have nothing left to offer in this life except yours."

"You were like a father to me, Ryo," Clay said, calling his *sensei* by his first name for the first time in a long time. "But everything you and my real father taught me was built on lies."

"Not everything," Nosagi said, his breaths becoming a bit more labored. "You must let go of the past and be the man you were meant to be."

"But you both robbed me of everything," Clay said, shaking his head.

"You'll be married again," Nosagi said before coughing up some blood. "Make peace with your father, and be a better father than he was for you."

Realizing for the first time that his enemies were no more, Clay saw a figurative light at the end of the tunnel. He *could* wed Casey, he *could* work and retire as a police officer, and he *could* make his fiancée's family business stronger. Clay loved his career, and for the first time since the untimely death of his first wife, Casey made him happy. Only one task remained before he returned to Ohio to finally enjoy his new life.

As he watched Nosagi's body shudder while the man gasped his last few breaths, Clay gripped his sword and stood to see if he might be of assistance to Clouse and his colleagues.

CHAPTER 52

"I realize you followed me and my people around to steal all of the cubes, but I have to know how you retrieved one from the ocean," Clouse said, drawing a rather sly smile from his latest nemesis.

"Over the years I've learned to use my talents for financial gain," Savitch answered. "Sometimes I use blackmail, sometimes I gather sensitive information for cash. Let's just say I had someone who owed me a big favor and got me the use of a Russian boat and its research team. We already had the location where your lackey dumped the cube, so it was easy to find once we found it lodged in an old crab trap."

"How fortunate," Clouse said, adding a layer of sarcasm.

"You really shouldn't be upset. After you put your faith in regular people, you should expect no less. I work with predators."

"And you throw them away like common trash once they've done your bidding."

Clouse had taken notice of the orange light from the wall pulsating at a faster rate with each added cube, as though the wall grew excited with anticipation. He didn't know how architecture could possibly comprehend such things, but it likely synced with the cubes since they were created together. On a primal level, the cursed objects likely sensed one another and the destruction they were about to cause. Clouse still didn't know exactly how the wall emitted light in the first place, considering it was covered completely in small tiles.

"You've got some blood on your hands as well," Savitch said. "Your best friend was murdered in a hospital where your beloved Jane worked, you basically let your brother-in-law fall to his death, and twice you killed the man who bestowed you with your millions. Being friends with you, Paul, is a death sentence."

Though the facts were wickedly twisted, the words still stung Clouse because not a day passed that guilt didn't eat away at him. He never asked for any of the terrible things that happened to him, and he certainly never sought riches, but it seemed one cataclysmic event started a chain that carried through the past ten years. Clouse felt his face flush with anger, beginning to lose his cool with the evil stranger before him for the first time.

"Good," Savitch said with eerie satisfaction. "I can *feel* your anger."

Unconcerned with his own health, Clouse began taking a step forward, but Savitch aimed the gun toward his heart.

"I don't want to kill you. I want you to be a part of what you created."

"What I created?" Clouse asked incredulously. "You either haven't been paying attention, or your powers aren't getting the gist of what I'm thinking at all."

With the gun trained on Clouse the entire time, Savitch finished placing the last of the twelve cubes he already possessed within open slots, exciting the wall even further. He then turned his attention to the box Clouse had brought with him, openly disgruntled when he looked inside and saw the box stacked from top to bottom and end to end with cubes of the same navy blue color.

"You knew I wouldn't just hand it over," Clouse said, standing his ground.

"But I've read your thoughts and it's just a matter of time before I find the correct one. My only hope is we'll be able to watch your friends and family die together until you're left with nothing."

Clouse felt his blood boil. He wasn't going to stand around much longer and simply watch this man incidentally murder those he loved while tearing the world to shreds.

"So much for your charitable side," Clouse grumbled.

"My charity ran out when you decided to make things tougher than they needed to be. You're simply stalling, hoping your friends will come through for you one last time. Well not this time. Nosagi will take care of any threats, including his former student, before joining me in here."

Savitch took the box of cubes and unceremoniously dumped every last bit of the contents on the tile floor. Clouse watched with a feeling of dread, knowing the real cube wouldn't simply sit there and let its purpose, its destiny, simply pass it by. He wondered if the cube might have regrets or second thoughts like its creators apparently did, not wanting to join its siblings.

Any such thought was fleeting because the cube barely waited a second before shimmering, making its presence felt even in the dark amongst so many pretenders.

"See?" Savitch asked with a smirk and a raised eyebrow. "A little cooperation goes a long way."

"I hate those things," Clouse muttered.

"I don't. Now kindly take a few steps back so we can witness the end of the world together."

Clouse complied, knowing that getting himself shot and killed wasn't helpful in any sense. He also harbored a suspicion that Savitch was about to be unpleasantly surprised. He put his hands in the air to imply compliance, stepping back from the centerpiece and his latest adversary.

Taking up the cube as though it were a fragile egg instead of an indestructible cursed object, Savitch carried it slowly toward the wall, ready to fulfill the destiny he'd imagined for himself since childhood. He stopped suddenly, just short of the wall, turning to give Clouse a look as though Clouse had just insulted his mother, or whatever Savitch held most dear.

"How do you know about that?" Savitch asked with anger and surprise in his voice.

Clouse's mind scrambled to find the answer, certain he hadn't truly let any thoughts enter his head that might provoke such a reaction.

"How do I know about what?" he finally asked, exasperated.

"You couldn't possibly have known about that," Savitch said slowly, unable to process whatever statement he thought he plucked from the air.

He pointed the gun at Clouse's heart, visibly shaken about whatever he thought someone knew about his past. Taking a step back, Clouse didn't particularly care to be shot for something he didn't initiate. He began to question whether Savitch possessed all of his mental faculties because his powers had read Clouse like a book until the past thirty seconds. Perhaps the man was clinically insane, hearing voices inside his head, or maybe his powers picked up someone else's thoughts. Clouse couldn't imagine what other person the psychic might tune into, considering he was the only person near Savitch. The only good thing about the mysterious distraction was that it kept the man from placing the final cube in the wall.

"No," Savitch finally said, shaking his head. "You aren't going to stop me from fulfilling my destiny."

As though anticipating the insertion of the last cube, the hologram began providing sound effects that accompanied the natural disasters the various colors projected. Clouse fully understood how men in 1918 were shocked and frightened by the prospect of what they'd accidentally created. They should have known that making a deal with the devil didn't mean they were the only ones gaining something from the pact.

Clouse began taking a step forward when the large wooden centerpiece in the room shifted slightly. He stopped as Savitch continued toward the wall, unaware of the movement behind him that soon revealed Greene and Liz once several pieces of the structure came apart. They had remained hidden inside the recently constructed addition to the room the entire time. Greene appeared especially sweaty, already clutching a firearm in his right hand as Liz escaped the confining wood to make her way toward Clouse. Savitch seemed too preoccupied with the voices inside his mind to even notice.

"You had me worried," Clouse confessed in a whisper.

"Me too. We need to leave."

"Why?" Clouse questioned. "Savitch won't get what he wants."

"I know, but your bodyguard gave Russ something rather destructive."

"Oh."

Clouse wanted to stick around to see the look of disappointment on his enemy's face, but getting Liz to safety took precedence above all else. He hoped Greene knew what he was doing as he watched Savitch carefully place the last cube into a slot that was perfectly centered within the mammoth clock face. Backing toward the doorway, Clouse looked to Greene, who gave a reassuring nod that he knew what needed to be done.

"Did you put those thoughts in his head?" Clouse asked Liz quietly.

"Yes. I brought up some rather bad childhood memories for him."

Once he and Liz were safely on the other side of the doorway, looking in, Clouse observed Savitch turned from the clock, expecting to see some grand miracle awaiting him in the centerpiece. Instead, a look of disbelief crossed his face when he saw the wooden part of the centerpiece lying in chunks, and the thirteenth element and color floating within the hologram. Complete with sound and lights, the entire hologram hovering above the centerpiece looked like a laser light show, but nothing more. Clouse wasn't sure if the man expected fireworks, or some sort of sign from above, but the hologram simply continued to circle a pattern within itself.

"Nothing?" Savitch questioned aloud, obviously expecting the ground to tremble, the skies to open, and the seas to part. "This *can't be.*"

"Hold it right there," Greene warned, his firearm already trained on Savitch, who had no chance of outgunning the former marshal after allowing his gun hand to fall limply to his side.

Savitch directed his attention to Liz next.

"Bitch. You were the one inside my head. How did I not detect you?"

Clouse had shielded Liz behind him, but she emerged from the doorway with the danger averted.

"You were too focused on Mr. Clouse to notice anything else," she answered. "And I've learned a few things after dealing with the likes of you, like how to quiet my mind."

Savitch scoffed at the words, unable to believe he was bested by a fellow psychic. A scowl crossed his face when he stared at the hologram as though it and the cubes somehow failed him.

"Why didn't it work?" he finally asked Clouse, certain the hotel owner already knew why his plan fell apart.

"You're missing a key component."

Savitch concentrated on picking up thoughts a moment, and despite his best efforts, Clouse couldn't help but let the answer come to mind.

"Ledger," Savitch said thoughtfully. "Your failure will come full circle after I kill your friends and complete the clock."

"You're not going anywhere," Greene said with a tone of authority obtained from his government days.

Savitch grinned sadistically.

"This isn't over by a longshot."

***

Clay found Harlan Stone standing near the edge of the excavated basement, looking down upon the three mercenaries who were about to execute a hasty plan to yank the van from the entrance with their own vehicle after shifting the van into neutral. With its hind end against a hardened wall of dirt, the van could only move forward or toward the driver's side, the latter of which wasn't a realistic option in this case.

He silently took the agent's side, startling the man who never heard him approach.

"I wish you wouldn't do that," Stone said after collecting himself.

"Just pointing out your weaknesses for you."

Stone sighed as they observed one of the men jumping into the large SUV the mercenaries drove to French Lick, parking it on the opposite bank.

"We going to attack them or just let them spot us?" Stone inquired as the driver got out of the SUV, tossing a thick chain to his colleagues as he wrapped his end around the vehicle's hitch.

"You're okay at hand-to-hand, right?"

Stone shrugged casually, indicating he could take care of himself.

"Follow my lead," Clay said, jumping into the pit before the agent found time to answer the inquiry.

Doubting Stone possessed confidence enough to confront men and their automatic weapons with just fists and feet, Clay made quick work of disarming the two men beside the van. The first, standing beside the van, turned when he heard Clay land behind him, but a quick upward kick knocked the firearm upward with his arms. Following the kick with a punch to the nose, Clay knocked the man off-balance enough that he twisted the automatic weapon, giving the henchman the option of releasing the gun or breaking some bones in his hands. Clay discarded the firearm quite a distance behind him, leaving the henchman for Stone, who had finally joined him in the excavated pit.

By this time the man hooking the chain to the front of the van came around the side to check on the commotion, carrying his weapon in a ready position. Clay smacked the barrel down with an open palm, discovering the henchman didn't have his finger on the trigger because no shot was fired. Knowing the man above them on ground level was going to take aim or jump down, Clay took hold of the automatic weapon with one hand to keep it from being used. He forcefully yanked the man toward him, swiftly drawing the large knife sheathed at the man's side and striking him between the eyes with the handle. Stunning him momentarily, Clay turned the knife around and stabbed him in the shoulder, away from any vital organs, drawing a brief scream before he pinpointed a punch into the carotid artery. The man went limp instantly, collapsing to the ground and allowing Clay to focus on the third hired gun.

Without turning around, Clay heard Stone doing battle with the first mercenary, apparently holding his own. He figured the agent was still armed if things turned sour in unarmed combat.

Deciding not to shoot, the third henchman showed an expression that indicated he wished he could, because he wanted no part of jumping into the pit and being rendered unconscious. Because of his previous orders, he knew not to shoot and compromise whatever plans were occurring inside, so he pulled two large knives from straps along his legs, displaying them for intimidation purposes before jumping down into the excavated basement.

"Uh huh," Clay said under his breath, not impressed.

He immediately discovered the man was well-trained with blades, but Clay managed to dodge several stabs and slashes that came his way with the deadly knives. He figured his adversary was likely trained in the Special Forces based on his quickness and dexterity with handheld weapons. Taking a few steps back, Clay waited until the man used the same attack a second time, catching his wrist when the knife flashed past him as he ducked. Predicting the man would come from the side with the second knife, Clay needed to block the blade before he was able to look.

Guessing a fraction of a second too late, with his arm just slightly off-course, Clay blocked the blade, but at the expense of a laceration. He swung a kick over his arm that still held the man's forearm steadily, landing the blow upside the mercenary's skull. As his adversary staggered, Clay drew a short sword from his pack, better equipped to deal with multiple blades as blood dripped from the fresh cut along his forearm.

Holding the blade in his right hand in reverse, the mercenary took a swing at Clay, trying to catch his neck along the backside. Clay ducked the knife, kicking the man in the knee, which gave way with a snapping sound before he chopped the man in the side of the neck using the flat side of his hand. With the man's other hand out of range, Clay grasped his armed wrist and forced it upward, behind the mercenary's back as he twisted the wrist, finally seeing the knife drop to the ground.

A fighter to the last, the man swung with the other knife once Clay released his compromised arm. Clay blocked the attack easily this time, catching the knife with his sword's blade. The man appeared perplexed by the sight of the sword, which bought Clay enough time to punch him in the gut and elbow him in the nose before thrusting the back of his head against the van, rendering him unconscious.

Hearing nothing behind him, Clay's sense of danger flickered within his mind, so he turned to see how Stone had fared.

Standing erect, with the first thug laid out a few feet behind him, Stone aimed his sidearm where the last thug had been positioned. Clay realized quickly, however, that the agent meant him no harm, particularly once he holstered the Glock. He provided a country grin before speaking to the man who twice saved him from certain peril.

"What took ya so long?"

Clay frowned outwardly, though he felt relieved the agent had suffered no harm.

"Remind me why I keep saving your ass again?"

"It's because I'm so damn charming."

"Definitely *not* that," Clay retorted, looking to the van. "We need to get in there."

Parish poked his head through the open window of the van on the opposite side.

"Have your best buddy there unlock the doors," the bodyguard suggested.

"Oh, yeah," Stone said, indicating he should have thought of doing so much sooner.

He held up the keyless remote, unlocking the entire van with the press of a button, which provided access to the rear hatch. It opened automatically, providing Clay and Stone the opportunity to head inside and assist Parish and Clouse with whatever final stand was unfolding at the end of the tunnel.

CHAPTER 53

Liz couldn't believe the bizarre setting before her might be the end of the hunt for the thirteen cubes, or the beginning of a redefined planet.

Parish provided them with the means to hide within the chamber if they so desired, and ultimately handed Greene a device that served as a game changer. After removing the original metal spokes and outer rim that surrounded the centerpiece, Parish constructed the new wooden portions specifically with the idea of someone hiding inside. Up until the moment she and Greene ducked inside the new addition, Liz questioned whether she endangered their plans.

She succeeded beyond her wildest expectations, quieting her mind and keeping Savitch from violating her thoughts as he had in Illinois and later in Indiana. Granted, he spent a lot of time focused on Clouse for the past decade, and that fact distracted him from searching for her thoughts in this case.

Now, standing in a room that pulsated orange at a greater rate than ever before, Liz took Clouse's side, wondering what Savitch meant with his ominous last statement.

"This isn't over by a longshot."

From left to right, Liz saw Greene standing with his gun drawn, a corpse lying atop the tile floor, chunks of the wooden centerpiece, the original centerpiece with the multicolored hologram floating above it, and Savitch refusing to back down. In fact, the man still held a firearm loosely at his side, despite Greene's orders to drop it.

Liz fought to silence her mind and shield it from Savitch, but he already appeared to be concentrating deeply on something as he assessed the room around him. Clouse tensed, apparently noticing their adversary was up to no good, but unwilling to ask Greene to execute him. At this point, with the floating hologram circling itself ominously, and millions of lives at stake, Liz found no moral dilemmas restraining her. She was about to yell for Greene to pull the trigger when something appeared to materialize from nowhere behind the former federal marshal.

She couldn't imagine where they came from, or how they managed to get behind Greene, but two men wearing suits went unseen by his eyes. They both immediately reached for firearms hidden inside their sport coats.

"Russ!" Liz screamed. "Look out!"

Greene followed her eyes, but looked absolutely befuddled when he looked behind him as though he saw no threat. He turned his attention to her with a confused expression for an explanation as the two men fizzled from Liz's line of sight. She immediately knew Savitch had used her as a distraction, implanting images within her mind, but her guilt only compounded when she saw Savitch raise his firearm against the only threat remaining within the room.

The split-second Greene turned to Liz was enough for Savitch to carry out the second part of his plan and raise his firearm against the former marshal. Greene somehow sensed the danger, turning and firing at the same time as Savitch. Both men reeled from bullets striking their bodies, but Savitch got off a second shot before collapsing to the floor, striking Greene again as his body jolted from the impact. Greene fell to the floor first with a thud that echoed through the small chamber, losing his firearm in the process. Savitch swayed momentarily, shaking his head as though mentally spent after creating the elaborate mental hoax. He collapsed behind the centerpiece and the wooden components a moment later, leaving no evidence about his true injuries.

"No!" Liz screamed, dashing across the floor to take Greene's side and assess the potentially fatal damage she unwittingly helped Savitch cause.

Although she heard scuffling noises from behind the centerpiece, Liz focused her attention on Greene, who immediately displayed signs of labored breathing. One bullet entered in the lower part of his abdomen, but the other was more centralized in his torso, quite possibly striking a lung.

Sweat already poured from his forehead as he reached up to touch her face, gently rubbing a few fingers along her hair and her cheeks.

"Go," he insisted.

"No, I can't leave you. I'm so sorry."

"It wasn't your fault," Greene spoke each word between labored breaths.

The entire time the pair had worked together Greene had presented himself as a gentleman, opening car doors and never letting their relationship escalate above business, even though they both showed subtle signs that they wanted it to. All those times in close proximity, sharing personal stories and their past, coming close to physical contact, never materialized beyond a bond they shared through work.

Greene was too old-fashioned and professional to let their relationship become physical, while Liz dared not touch him for fear of seeing his past. Knowing a person's past, she discovered early in life, tended to distance people from her, rather than create some form of a lasting bond.

"But it was my fault," Liz reiterated. "I'm sorry, Russ."

"It was Savitch. I forgave you the second it happened."

Liz felt a tear come to her eye as her chest heaved and she fought to hold back the river of emotions ready to burst through the floodgate. The tear slowly rolled down her cheek, landing atop Greene's shirt that was already soaked with sweat and blood.

"Go," Greene insisted again. "I've got this."

His words sounded reassuring, and she knew what he meant to do. Liz no longer harbored fears about knowing this man, or his past, because he was genuinely good through and through. She gently placed her lips on upon his, and he reciprocated the kiss at length, with enough emotion that Liz regretted never following through with her earlier instincts. She felt no jolt, followed by a vision of the past, when they finally touched. Liz harbored deep disappointment and sadness, knowing this man might have been the one. For some reason he was immune to her ability, or perhaps his clean slate of a life required no explanation, but either way she was destined to never see him again.

Clouse knelt beside Liz, looking over Greene's wounds with a solemn expression. As a former EMT on the fire department, Clouse knew how to treat wounds, and the chances of survival from a variety of injuries.

"Are you sure about this?" he asked Greene. "We can call an ambulance."

Greene shook his head weakly.

"There isn't time, and I just winged him," Greene answered painstakingly. "Let me end this before that bastard gets up."

Clouse briefly considered grabbing the gun beside Greene and ending the situation himself, but he wasn't certain about the extent of Savitch's injuries. Someone needed to get Liz to safety before the other psychic regained his footing and mowed them all down with gunfire. A quick glance around him didn't reveal the firearm's location because he at least wanted to give Greene ample opportunity to defend himself.

"Don't worry about it," Greene said, sensing his thoughts. "I won't need it."

Clouse hung his head, hating to lose yet another person in his camp to the evil cubes. A noise across the room quickly reminded him of the danger, and he took Liz by the arm.

"We have to go."

Liz already felt the tears streaming down her cheeks as Clouse lifted her away from Greene. She followed his lead toward the door, stealing one look back at Greene who was already focused on his final task.

They ran down the hall for cover, because only certain doom awaited them if they stayed inside the chamber. A few seconds later they encountered Parish, Stone, and Clay Branson. The three men looked like hell, but none of them appeared gravely injured.

"We need to get out of here," Clouse informed them immediately.

"Why?" Stone questioned. "Where's the guy behind all of this?"

"Back there," Liz answered.

Parish understood the urgency, since he was the one who installed the failsafe device and provided Greene and Liz with the trigger mechanism. He motioned for everyone to head the opposite way in a hurry, just in case the explosive devices he planted inside the chamber went off without warning.

Continuing to look behind her, Liz felt warm moisture atop her cheeks and forming below her eyes. She couldn't believe after everything she and Greene had endured that their story was ending like this. Unfortunately theirs was a tale that could never be told to the public, which meant Greene's sacrifice would go without spoils.

But not without virtue.

✳✳✳

Greene placed his palm flat against his upper bullet wound, trying to keep it from sucking in oxygen, which made conventional breathing more difficult and painful. He knew he didn't have very long without true medical assistance, because the pain grew more intense by the second when the lung began to collapse. Still, he felt determined to wait until the arrogant Savitch stood up to confront him once again.

He didn't have to wait long once Clouse ushered Liz from the chamber for the psychic to slowly regain his footing and painfully saunter his way. Greene dared not move too far from his spot because of potential blood loss, so he simply remained reasonably still, even as Savitch loomed over him.

Examining the damage his bullet did to the man's side, near the waist-line, Greene felt a little satisfaction. Had Greene been permitted a split-second longer to aim before firing, the bullet surely would have struck Savitch in the heart, ending the affair much sooner. A year prior, the man working for the federal government wouldn't have believed in fate, but after experiencing a year around cursed objects and psychics, Greene knew he was lying on the tiled floor of this chamber for a reason.

"So, your friends abandoned you?" Savitch taunted.

"Not exactly," Greene answered, feeling the intense burning inside his body from the bullet and the damaged lung.

It was like someone had heated pokers in a fireplace, stuck them inside of him, and left them there.

"I'm going to enjoy killing you and using one of these cubes to heal myself," Savitch said with his usual smugness, as though nothing in the world could touch him.

A bullet wound in his guts said otherwise, but he wasn't about to acknowledge any weakness.

Once Liz left with Clouse, Greene managed to locate the firearm, which one of them had been obscuring in their attempts to assist him.

Greene attempted to reach for the gun just over an arm's length away, but Savitch kicked it toward the opposite side of the chamber. With only one play left, Greene simply tapped the little remote switch located in his pants pocket, finding it still in place. His breathing felt labored, partly because of the lung injury, but also due to what he figured was internal bleeding. The lower bullet passed through his intestines and out the back, but the first bullet struck more susceptible organs and remained inside so far as he could tell.

Giving a malicious smile, Savitch slowly walked toward the mammoth clock embedded within the far wall.

"Nothing is going to stop me now that I've picked your mind clean," Savitch taunted as he walked with what seemed a little jovial skip in his step. "I know about the leather-bound journal, and soon I'll possess it and complete this wall."

Greene said nothing, beginning to wriggle his body toward the main entrance to avoid being shot before he activated the present Parish left for him. He snagged a nearby piece of the dismantled wooden centerpiece that was part of the rounded exterior. It had a handle on the inside, so he was able to hold it like a shield, still inching his way toward the main entrance as Savitch busied himself with trying to figure out which cube was most beneficial to him in the present scenario. None of them were of any assistance unless he killed someone, and Greene didn't plan on being a sacrificial lamb.

Still agonized whenever he took a breath, Greene watched Savitch continue to look over the cubes. Greene tried remaining silent, but dragging his own weight, along with the protective piece of wood, slowed him immensely. The sounds from the hologram centerpiece provided some audible cover, but Greene still needed to move quickly and quietly. He couldn't possibly tell which cube the man was bent on retrieving, because they all looked the same, illuminated by the haunting orange light emitted by the cursed clock.

With no position of comfort, and his body growing weaker by the second from internal bleeding, Greene fought not to scrape the curved wood against the floor. The moment Savitch noticed him moving, the man was certainly going to begin firing at him, because it didn't matter how the victim died to satisfy the cubes.

Although Savitch's activities were mostly blocked by the centerpiece and the scattered wooden pieces, Greene saw him finally pluck a cube from the wall. Deciding he needed to hide from the man's view at any cost, Greene struggled to his knees, still holding the makeshift shield between his body and Savitch. Not hearing any steps along the floor as of yet, Greene fought the burning within his body, trying to regain his footing for a final push toward the tunnel opening. Greene figured he was a goner either way, but he wanted the final word, just to let Savitch know he wasn't as all-powerful as he portrayed himself.

Greene stumbled toward the opening once he stood, clutching the wooden handle with his left hand to cover his exposed side while reaching into his left pants pocket awkwardly with his right hand. He retrieved the detonation device, placing it into his left hand as he slipped the hand through the wooden handle, allowing his wrist to carry the weight of the imperfect shield.

Barely having time, even during his hours inside the newly-created centerpiece with Liz, to study the little black detonator, Greene knew how to operate it. A black and a red trigger, both small in size, needed to be flipped after the protective cover was removed from the front side. Greene reached the doorway, supporting his weight against the side of the opening with his free arm, reaching over just long enough to pluck the small cover from the detonator. He was about to steady himself once more when a push from behind knocked him to the ground.

Greene fell hard atop the solid dirt of the tunnel, turning to find Savitch standing above him, ominously pointing a gun at his chest.

"Did you really think you could escape?"

"No," Greene answered, finding it difficult to utter even a few words.

His wrist kept the wooden makeshift shield in place, but when he struck the ground, Greene accidentally dropped the detonator from his palm onto his lower body. Unsure of exactly where, he searched with his concealed left hand while Savitch basked in his glory momentarily, likely feeling empowered having to carry out his own dirty work.

"You couldn't have made it more simple for me," the possessor of thirteen evil objects bragged. "You've given me the means to heal myself, then I'll take a little trip back in time."

"You can't," Greene muttered weakly, his fingers touching the detonator, trying to gauge its position.

"And why not?" Savitch asked testily, aiming the gun at Greene's upper body to finish the job he started.

"Because you can't time travel when you're dead."

It took a split-second for Savitch to comprehend the words before he grew enraged, pulling the trigger as Greene pulled the wood over his torso and head to protect the most vital areas of his body. A thin metal lining inside the wood, meant to provide protection from being given away inside the chamber, now saved Greene in a different way. The bullets dented the thin metal, one after another, but none of them passed through completely.

While shielding his torso, Greene reared his legs back, taking a chance that they might take damage from some bullets. The sound of repeated gunfire from close range hurt his ears, but it also let him know Savitch wasn't moving from his spot, hoping the bullets passed through the wood and into Greene's already compromised flesh. Pulling his legs back to buck like a mule, he let his feet fly during a moment when the shooting ceased, striking Savitch somewhere along the waistline. His offensive action sent the man flailing backwards into the chamber. Savitch let a few more bullets fly, even as he tumbled awkwardly, his back striking the authentic centerpiece heavily as Greene dared removed the wooden shield for a look. Savitch hit the remainder of the wood surrounding the centerpiece rather hard, which cost him his footing. Without any balance, his back slid downward along the wood while his feet kicked out before him.

Savitch tried to shake the mental cobwebs after landing so hard. After a few seconds he scooped up a nearby firearm, full of ammunition, before looking to Greene with a disgusted look. He looked determined to finish the job, regardless of whatever effort he needed to put forth.

Greene took just a second to glance at the detonation switch in his left hand, flipping it over to see Parish's brief instructions on a tiny sheet of paper taped to the back side.

BOOM!

Greene couldn't help but grin, despite the agony inside his body. He looked over to Savitch, whose eyes seared with anger, staring holes through the former federal marshal. Savitch struggled to regain his footing, striking his head against the curved top of the centerpiece. The blow barely slowed him as he angrily held the gun outward before moving again. Savitch was more careful and deliberate the second time he tried to regain his footing. When he finally stood, Savitch stretched his neck to one side, giving an evil grin that indicated he wasn't going to fail a second time and Greene was going to be just another one of his forgettable victims.

"Goodbye, Jacob," Greene said, flipping the black switch, followed by the red switch, bringing forth an incredible explosion that consumed the chamber before heading for fresher air down the tunnel.

CHAPTER 54

ven before he and Liz were halfway down the tunnel, attempting to reach safety, Clouse pulled his cell phone from his side, calling 911. He hated the risk of police swarming the premises, but he wasn't going to let Russ Greene die if hope remained. Clouse knew most shots to the torso below the heart were typically survivable with prompt medical attention.

He owed Russ Greene a chance at life, even if calling 911 put his entire secret operation at risk. Years of work might be deemed worthless if the authorities asked too many questions and the chamber filled with cubes was discovered. Considering the nearest ambulance service was at least ten minutes away in Paoli, he figured the group had a little bit of time to clean up the mess. He attempted to make the call from inside the tunnel, discovering the phone didn't have a strong enough signal when it beeped repeatedly in his ear.

"Damn," he muttered, continuing to prod Liz toward the entrance.

She continued to look back, worried with good reason about Greene. Both of them knew he intended to blow up the chamber with Savitch, and possibly himself, still inside. Knowing he did no one any good while still inside the tunnel, Clouse hurried along, getting Liz to keep stride. She knew he intended to call for help, so when they saw daylight ahead, she practically tugged Clouse to the opening.

When he finally stepped into the excavated basement, Clouse discovered a complete mess with Stone, Parish, and Clay Branson standing beside a damaged van. The body of a henchman dressed in black lay nearby, his fatal bullet wounds very much visible to Clouse. Three other mercenaries dressed in black were already subdued with plastic zip ties binding their wrists. One had already regained consciousness and began struggling against his restraints, but Clouse didn't have time to deal with everything at once.

"You got a phone?" he asked Liz, his mind already formulating a plan.

"Yes."

"Wait about one minute and call 911, and request an ambulance only because you found someone on the ground," Clouse told her with strong reassurance before turning to Parish. "I need this mess out of here five minutes ago, Todd. The vehicles, these assholes, and the three of you."

"Understood, sir."

Parish turned to begin his task but stopped in his tracks, turning abruptly.

"Oh," he said, as though suddenly remembering something.

He carried a shotgun, which Clouse figured he lifted from one of the subdued mercenaries or brought from his personal arsenal. Parish walked as though on a personal mission toward the rear of the van, so Clouse followed, discovering the lit jack-o-lantern remained on the ground, not far from the tunnel entrance. Its toothy grin continued to flicker visibly in the restrained daylight, the gutted vegetable appearing unscathed by all of the recent violent activity.

Without warning, Parish approached the pumpkin, took aim with the shotgun, and fired downward. The vegetable exploded into dozens of sinewy strands that landed on the old basement wall, the van, and practically everything nearby.

"Was that necessary?" Clouse asked when his hired hand brushed past him.

"Yes," Parish replied without breaking stride, prepared to carry out his employer's orders with his usual rugged demeanor.

Both of them knew the symbolism of the jack-o-lantern in Clouse's life, serving as an omen of impending danger. Clouse really couldn't blame his employee for taking out some frustration on the lingering vegetable, and at least the shotgun blast hadn't carried very far. He doubted the noise even escaped the old basement area with so much surrounding dirt dampening the sound.

"Todd," he called, regaining the man's attention. "Get those three out of here and make them bury their buddy. And make sure they don't have the means or any desire to come back here."

Parish nodded, indicating he understood perfectly. He turned to confer with Stone and Branson, pondering the most efficient method to move two vehicles and three underlings quickly. Clouse was about to make a suggestion when the ground trembled and a muffled boom came from within the tunnel. Everyone turned to look, knowing the explosion had rocked the chamber within, possibly compromising it, but Clouse found Liz already calling 911 for an ambulance. He doubted any residents heard the boom, since the abandoned area wasn't very close to existing homes and businesses.

"Go," he insisted to Parish, who wore a look of concern.

"But-"

"*Go*, Todd," Clouse said with more emphasis. "I'll deal with whatever happened in there."

Parish followed his employer's wishes, openly unhappy about not sticking around to protect Clouse and examine the remains of the chamber with him. He turned from his employer without a word, asking the FBI agent and the Ohio cop for assistance, since they weren't paid by Clouse or obligated to provide any help beyond their personal vendettas.

Clouse wasted little time returning his attention to Liz, who was already speaking with a local dispatcher. He heard enough to know she was requesting an ambulance and he motioned for her to remain outside as he stepped toward the tunnel entrance. Feeling both pressure to hurry and apprehension about what awaited his arrival, Clouse darted toward the tunnel, which remained barely illuminated by the dwindling lanterns hanging along the sides.

When he drew closer to the chamber, however, Clouse found several of the lanterns shattered atop the ground, some of their handles still swaying along the nails where they once hung. He felt somewhat shocked when the eerie orange glow of the chamber remained, guiding him during the last portion of his journey when the lanterns failed to withstand the concussion provided by the explosion.

Clouse expected the room to look like the remains of a town bombed heavily during wartime. His eyes widened when he found several charred lumps across the room's floor. Standing along the right side of the doorway,

Clouse knew not to touch anything around him because the residual heat felt intense on his skin. It reminded him of raging fires from his days on the fire department when he didn't have part of his gear fully donned. Fearing the bottom of his boots might melt and merge with the superheated tile floor, Clouse remained at the doorway, observing the carnage.

He fully expected the room to be compromised, possibly on the verge of total collapse from above, but every tile remained in place without the least little bit of damage. The wall with the clock built into it continued to produce orange light, pulsating rhythmically as a dozen of the cubes remained in place. The thirteenth cube glistened, attempting to gain his attention, beside a charred pile that continued to smolder. Clouse quickly assessed the mass as that of a human body, possibly Savitch or Greene because the shot henchman's body remained where the man was murdered in a charred heap. He still couldn't believe the room remained unscathed, figuring the curse placed on the cubes and the leather-bound book applied to the chamber where they were created. His heart sunk, knowing none of the curse would ever be put to rest, and because Russ Greene apparently sacrificed his life for a cause he believed in wholeheartedly.

Clouse stood on tiptoes, trying to find Greene, determined to give the man proper treatment for his heroic actions, including an appropriate burial. The rest of the organic material burned within the room appeared to be the separated centerpiece components. Their wooden exteriors were charred and black, with tiny splinters sticking up like hair follicles along several edges.

He failed to locate any additional masses that looked anything like charred human remains within the chamber. Growing frustrated, Clouse took half a step inside, hearing a hiss when the bottom of his right foot touched the floor. He retreated immediately, thinking he might have to create an excuse for Liz to tell the medics when they arrived so they didn't enter the tunnel.

"Where the hell are you, Russ?" he questioned under his breath, still looking at the eerie scene before him.

"Down here," a weak voice said from the ground, a few feet to Clouse's left.

What Clouse initially regarded as a chunk of wood thrown to the doorway from the blast proved accurate, but it camouflaged the man lying beneath it. He immediately dropped to one knee, lifting the large rounded piece of charred wood from Greene before checking the man for additional injuries.

The dim lighting made a cursory examination rather difficult, but Greene appeared intact and healthy along his upper body, other than the bullet wounds. Clouse's eyes followed his employee's body below the waistline, finding every part of Greene's legs below the knees suffered burn damage from the explosion.

"Were you thrown?" he asked, suspecting a possible head or neck injury.

"No," Greene answered quietly. "I covered up when I pushed the button."

Clouse took a closer look at the burn damage, finding most of it superficial in nature. Luckily Greene chose to wear blue jeans instead of slacks for hiding inside the new centerpiece, which likely saved him additional damage.

"How do your lower legs feel?" Clouse inquired.

"They're burned, but I think the doorway shielded them pretty well."

Daring to take a closer look, Clouse lifted the cuff along one leg, finding the flesh reddish, and mostly free of blisters. Knowing Greene wasn't plagued by third degree burns made his next request significantly easier.

"Medics are on their way, Russ. I need to carry you to the entrance so no one steps foot near the cubes."

"I understand."

Greene tried to help remove some of the burden from Clouse, but he proved to be practically dead weight. Clouse sat him up before turning him slightly and placing him over his shoulder. Greene groaned, though not from protest, when his injured torso came in direct contact with his boss's back. Clouse took hold of his legs to ensure he didn't drop him before heading into the tunnel. He hurried along, feeling absolute respect for Greene, who was being a complete trooper despite his life-threatening injuries.

It took a little over a minute for Clouse to reach the entrance, but his ears immediately detected sirens in the distance.

The daylight stung his eyes momentarily, but he spotted Liz standing on ground level above him. Both vehicles were gone, along with his colleagues, the three living henchmen, and the body of the last thug. He watched Liz cup her face worriedly with both hands, looking anxiously toward him for answers as he labored to carry Greene up the hill.

"Is he?" she asked, unable to finish her question when Clouse drew closer.

Instead of answering, Clouse gently laid Greene down on the ground, reassessing him after having to carry his already compromised body through the tunnel. Greene's breathing grew more labored as the sirens grew closer, and Clouse worried it might be too late. He watched helplessly as the man's body convulsed when he coughed, as though the internal bleeding had taken a major toll.

Clouse applied pressure to the wounds with his bare hands, even though they weren't really leaking much blood at this point. Liz took Greene's other side, holding his hand as she looked into his eyes.

"Don't quit on me," she insisted.

Greene's face lit up when his eyes finally focused on Liz, but Clouse knew the former federal marshal was fading fast. He heard the ambulance drawing extremely close, so he looked to Liz.

"Go with him to the hospital, Liz. Act like you're too distraught to talk to the police and I'll handle them from here."

Liz nodded before Clouse turned to Greene, also clasping his hand.

"Hang in there, Russ. I can't have our hero leaving us after saving the day."

"I'll try," Greene replied.

He grimaced when he tried providing a weak smile as the ambulance pulled beside them in the otherwise abandoned lot.

Unfortunately for Clouse the local police showed up almost immediately, either because Liz told the dispatcher Greene was shot, or the medics called in additional information when they arrived. It mattered little because Clouse was forced to conjure up a story almost immediately to police officers who always took whatever he reported with a grain of salt. After hearing so many fantastical stories over the years, authorities seemed to always know they weren't getting the full truth from Clouse or his people, but his very charitable donations to the community bought him a lot of leeway.

He put a tight spin on the truth, stating that he and Liz were working on the property when they heard gunshots ring out. They ran from the basement area to level ground, finding Greene lying on the ground from bullet wounds. Clouse did not deny that Greene worked for him, though he reported that he didn't know why Greene was on the grounds or how he traveled to arrive there.

Fortunately the medics surrounded Greene while they worked on him, which prevented the police from getting a close look at his injuries. When they asked about the odd coloration of his blue jeans below the knees, Clouse simply said he didn't know what caused the damage and that they would have to ask Greene when he was able to talk. The last thing Clouse wanted was for the police to ask for permission to search inside the tunnel, so he kept everything about his fabricated story outside of the old basement and the visible doorway.

More concerned about talking to Greene, the police took a brief statement from him before leaving for the hospital. Clouse promised a more thorough statement later, which also provided him an opportunity to strengthen his story. Parish returned to the site near the end of the entire ordeal, waiting until the authorities left before informing his employer that everything else was under control.

"We shouldn't have any more problems from those goons."

"Good," Clouse thought aloud. "It's been one hell of a day already."

"Everything okay, sir?" Parish inquired, a look of concern etched across his face.

"I think so," Clouse answered, realizing he probably appeared numb, because he certainly felt that way. "We still have some cleanup to do."

He started toward the excavated basement, wishing he could check on Greene at the hospital instead of worrying about the thirteen cubes awaiting human contact inside the chamber. Even with Savitch dead nothing about his mission, or his life in general, felt any different. Danger from unknown people was always going to be a threat, because if someone like Savitch could wait ten years to strike, Clouse knew other enemies likely existed.

Parish followed him down the slope, into the partially excavated area after Clouse took a few staggered steps. His knees still felt rubbery after barely surviving the latest attempt on his life. Even worse, more of his own people were hurt because he put them in harm's way. He felt his eyes well with tears, the emotion of the incident, in fact the entire past ten years, catching up with him.

"Sir?" Parish asked hesitantly.

"I'm okay, Todd," Clouse answered, trying to brush back the moisture along his eyes while he inhaled stiffly through his nose to keep the snot at bay.

"I can take care of this, sir."

Clouse dropped to the sloped dirt short of the doorway, patting the ground for Parish to join him.

"This is my burden," he said. "I'll take care of it."

Parish said nothing momentarily, as though wondering exactly how to console his boss. Always respectful and loyal, Parish seldom spoke out of turn, and certainly never interjected his opinion unless Clouse asked for it.

"Sir, you're not alone in this," he finally said, looking straight ahead to avoid viewing his employer in a moment of weakness.

Always loyal, Clouse thought, feeling even worse that he put such good people directly in the path of evil.

"It's my fault Russ Greene might not make it," Clouse said slowly. "Back when all of this started and I lost some friends, that wasn't any of my doing and I knew that, Todd. I *knew* it. But now, with everything I've learned, and the things I feel compelled to do, it *is* me putting all of you in harm's way."

Parish finally looked his way now that Clouse had dried his eyes and composed himself a bit.

"Sir, you laid this out for me early on. You recruited Greene and Liz after you researched them thoroughly and they knew the score. They didn't have to say yes, and I seem to recall you giving me plenty of opportunities to back out. We do this because we *choose* to, sir. You can't do this alone, nor should you have to. Most people in your position would just let the chips fall where they may, but you still personally risk your life."

"How could I not with everything I ask of all of you?"

"And that's why I've gone through hell with you, sir. There's no other job in the world I want after all of this, especially since we might finally be free and clear."

Clouse shook his head negatively, certain he could never live comfortably because he was the key to locating the cursed cubes for those rare few who knew about them.

"These things will never go away," Clouse bemoaned. "We're going to be forever defending the world from them."

"Not *forever*," Parish said with a chuckle, drawing a thin smile from his employer.

"No, not forever. I'm sure we'll find suitable replacements down the road. History won't remember our deeds, Todd, and they can never be allowed to."

"I'm pretty sure they'll remember *you*, sir."

Feeling reasonably certain his life would be little more than a footnote, Clouse didn't mind. He needed the spotlight away from him to make the job of protecting the cubes much easier. Looking upward, he noticed the previously ominous gray clouds drifting away while growing lighter in color. He couldn't recall a single drop of rain falling from the sky, which made the strange sight that much more unusual.

Clouse finally set his arms out, using the ground to help him regain his footing when he stood. Taking a deep breath, he decided to clear out the mess inside the chamber before the police returned with more questions or a warrant.

"I can take care of this," Parish offered.

"Thanks, Todd, but I've got to get those things out of there and formulate a new plan for them."

"And Savitch?"

"I think I have a final resting spot for him that's just perfect. It'll give me a chance to make sure my other nemesis is still at rest."

Parish nodded with an understanding smirk. Clouse never revealed exactly where he buried Martin Smith to anyone, with good reason, and so far no one had discovered the man's remains. Logic told him that Savitch wouldn't be highly missed, and even if he became a reported missing person, decades would likely pass before anyone dug up his charred remains.

He turned to Parish at the old basement doorway.

"If you don't mind, just keep an eye on the door while I go fetch what I need from inside."

"You got it, sir."

Clouse wasn't sure how he wanted to secure the cubes in the short or long term, but he knew they needed to be hidden from all human beings and kept far, far away from the chamber at the end of the tunnel. He slowly made his way down the dark tunnel, plucking one of the functioning lanterns from the wall to carry with him. Once he neared the chamber the eerie glow would illuminate the area for him, but he didn't want to bump into any walls in between. Clouse planned to gather the remains of Savitch, grab the cubes, and never lay eyes on the evil sanctum again.

CHAPTER 55

It took some time for the two adjacent towns in Orange County to return to normal after local news stations reported that a man was shot in the streets of French Lick. Even in a casino town violence was rare, and speculation ran amuck that Paul Clouse was a key figure in the investigation since his employee was shot. Locals considered him both savior and pariah, but what they thought they knew amounted to a fraction of the truth.

A tiny fraction.

Clouse closed the West Baden Springs Hotel for two consecutive weekdays in early December for a private outing with his family and some of his most valued employees. It wasn't uncommon for the hotel to be booked on a weekend, at a hefty price, for a wedding and reception, but a few guests weren't happy their reservations were changed to the French Lick Springs Hotel down the road. Clouse made amends, giving them resort perks, including credit at the casino and a free night's stay at a later date of their choosing at the dome.

Despite the looming shadow the cubes permanently cast over him, Clouse found reason for celebration. Russ Greene survived six hours of surgery, making a speedy recovery over the following weeks with Liz a constant at his side.

Though he harbored reservations about their blossoming relationship, Clouse refused to say anything. He knew all too well that loved ones were sometimes used as pawns by villains who cared little for human life. Clouse also hoped if they were truly in love that nothing came between them because the work environment would surely be poisoned at that point.

He spotted them sitting in one of the oversized plush chairs within the atrium and walked over to them. The chairs were large enough to accommodate couples, lengthy and curved so that people could sit in them with their feet off the floor. Liz and Greene shared the chair, side by side, Greene with his arm comfortably around the psychic until Clouse approached them. He stiffened a bit, even starting to retract his arm, not wanting his boss to think he was being lazy or cohabitating with a coworker. On this day, Clouse didn't mind one bit.

"At ease," Clouse said to Greene, drawing up a smaller chair of his own. "You're still recuperating, remember?"

Greene gave an uneasy smile, still uncertain what Clouse thought of his relationship with Liz. It wasn't as though anyone, even Greene himself, expected his feelings for Liz to escalate beyond a workplace friendship.

"How are you feeling?" Clouse asked.

"Doing well," Greene answered. "The feet are feeling good, and my insides don't feel like churned butter."

Clouse smiled.

"Glad to hear it. I do have one question for Liz that I've been meaning to ask these past few weeks."

"Oh?" Liz asked curiously.

"How did you ever get inside Savitch's head? I thought that was his specialty."

Liz looked to the floor momentarily, as though Clouse had brought up a bad memory for her. Clouse knew it wasn't easy for her to deal with her fellow psychic when the time came, but she overcame a great deal of adversity to better him.

"When he started reading my mind, he created a two-way portal of sorts," Liz explained. "I started seeing every aspect of his life in my dreams, so I finally wondered if I could return the favor and start sending messages his way. It took a little practice, and a ton of concentration to pull it off. I felt like my head was splitting for two days after that, so I just focused on staying with Russ and making sure he got better."

Clouse nodded in understanding.

"I appreciate everything you've both done, and I'm glad you came."

"Truth be told, we didn't really have anywhere else to go," Greene said, only half kidding, since they were still living in the hotel's sixth floor until more permanent residential plans were formed.

"We'll remedy that soon enough," Clouse said, providing a reassuring smile. "You'll just have to let me know what arrangements you have in mind."

By his last statement, he meant to imply they needed to choose one residence, or two, and they both blushed a bit as he stood to give them some privacy. He couldn't help but wonder if their bond was real, or just a reaction from Liz over Greene's recent heroics. Because Jane stood by him unconditionally, Clouse would never dream of interfering in whatever love they thought they shared.

Clouse bid them a temporary farewell before crossing the atrium, finally settling at an open table near the bar that extended from the hotel into the atrium that provided a great view of the vast atrium.

From there, Clouse watched his son and stepdaughter run carefree through the vast space for the first time in months. Decked out with tables, chairs, and lots of activities, the atrium served as a hub for the two days and all of the events Clouse's wife planned for the group. It felt good to see the employees he held dear and their families all around the atrium. Parish, Jennings, and Duncan were all present with their families. Clouse had also invited Niemeyer and Mark Daniels, even though Niemeyer didn't technically work for him. With Thanksgiving still fresh in his mind and Christmas just around the corner, Clouse longed for time with family and friends, glad so many of them accepted a vacation on short notice.

When he looked up to some of the glass from some of the interior rooms, he thought he spied a dark shape darting across one of the hallway lounge doors along the third floor. Clouse didn't give it a second thought, figuring a member of the staff or one of the guests was simply walking by. His days of living in fear of mysterious strangers stalking him or his family were definitely over.

He no longer viewed the hotel as the place where terrible things happened to him and his loved ones. A change in perspective accompanied the notion that the only people left who knew about the cubes he considered allies. He knew a slim chance remained that someone outside of his circle knew about them, but after a few weeks of separation from the events inside the chamber Clouse felt more at ease.

Harlan Stone had left without a word to anyone except Clay Branson, returning to his job at the Bureau. Clouse learned the agent finally received a transfer back to Texas once he was cleared of any wrongdoing, particularly after he helped his agency wrap up the mystery surrounding his former boss. It seemed the FBI tidied up their case without much fanfare, deciding Stewart went rogue like the small band of agents he was supposed to supervise. Clouse felt certain they put some sort of real world spin on the situation instead of opting for a supernatural explanation. Fortunately Stone was able to truthfully say he wasn't there for Stewart's death, or his disappearance from the mortuary, which left the Bureau with little to hold against the agent.

Clouse never told the agent that he was one of his top picks for Russ Greene's current position. The only thing that held the federal agent back was his questionable ethics in some cases, along with the fact that he was married. For all of his flaws, Stone was truly a devoted husband, and because of that, Clouse didn't want to take a chance on the man's wife becoming a pawn in someone's scheme down the road.

Clay Branson had thanked Clouse for helping him settle his vendetta before graciously declining the offer to stay on the payroll. Thanks to Savitch, no cubes remained on the loose, and Branson wanted a normal life in Ohio with the woman he loved. He seemed content to work as a police officer and learn the security director job at his new family's theme park. Branson did not leave on bad terms by any means, considering he left Clouse his contact information and said he might be available if a sticky situation arose in the future.

Clouse also felt relieved because he wasn't alone in his situation. Julie Knowles and Matt Teakon continued to work with him to ensure the cubes were permanently safe from evildoers, and far apart from one another.

Jane finally approached him, far less worried about allowing the children to run unattended than she had in years past. She bent over, planting a kiss on Clouse's lips before taking the seat beside him. He felt blessed because he was surrounded by people with unimaginable devotion to his cause. After misjudging people earlier in life, Clouse knew to weed out the bad apples when looking for people to aid him. The local police may not have trusted him, but his feelings toward them ran parallel. Trust never came easy when wealth and power were easily available to the morally damaged.

"You look happy," his wife commented, taking hold of his hand.

They sat, watching their friends and employees mingle momentarily across the atrium.

"Do you forgive me?" he asked for what seemed the twelfth time since the day everything went down inside the chamber.

"You know I do," Jane answered, "but promise me you'll never keep that kind of secret from me again."

Like Mark Daniels, Jane wanted nothing more to do with the cursed objects, but Clouse believed she shared his optimism that the group finally had a handle on the situation. He loved his wife and children, but Clouse felt like a soldier when it came to their family life. During the figurative peacetime, when he wasn't tracking the cubes, he seldom left his family except for regular hotel and casino business. During wartime, however, he tried to separate himself from them for their own safety, though it tore him apart doing so.

"There are a couple of things you never fully explained to me," Jane said thoughtfully as a hotel waiter delivered a beer for Clouse and a glass of chardonnay for his wife.

"Like what?" Clouse asked before taking a long swig.

"Why did the original thirteen conspirators take off so fast once the curse was completed?"

Liz had experienced further dreams after her encounter with the leatherbound book, which she explained to Clouse. Glad to have an expanded knowledge of the curse, and how it came about, Clouse made certain Julie and Matt Teakon were also informed.

"I guess the thirteen men picked out the colors for their cubes and what benefit they wanted to receive, but they didn't anticipate the devil himself making an appearance. Liz said the whole thing looked surreal, like a movie, with the multi-colored hologram in the middle and Satan in some kind of reddish spectral form looming in front of the clock. She said he spoke in tongues with a deep voice and let out some kind of maniacal laugh afterwards. I guess the thirteen each grabbed their cubes from the wall and scattered."

"What about the skeletal remains Todd found in the chamber?"

"Liz said when the devil manifested inside the chamber the man fell dead to the floor. She thinks the wounds his friend discovered on him were telekinetically inflicted, killing him instantly. He was the sacrificial lamb for their little soiree."

"Poor man," Jane said with genuine sorrow.

"Poor *us*," Clouse added emphatically. "We've been the ones cleaning up this mess for years now."

Clouse didn't want to reveal to his wife exactly what Liz put inside Savitch's mind that almost caused the psychic to shoot him in the chest. It turned out that Savitch's stepfather did more than demean him verbally. Often psychological torment escalated to physical strikes from the construction worker, which made young Jacob's life a living hell. His fear turned to aggression with age, and when he became an adult Savitch took the scattered footnotes of a plan and put them together. He watched Clouse's torment at the hands of numerous enemies over the years, never once intervening, but rather waiting like a patient serpent for the right time to strike.

From what Clouse recalled, Savitch's stepfather died in a mysterious accident where he operated a piece of heavy machinery in his backyard alone and ended up beneath several tons of metal in the form of the excavator. Everyone wondered how such an experienced construction worker was careless enough to operate a machine with no one else present, but what seemed even worse was the fact that Bob Lowery got beneath the machine to inspect something along a hill. The excavator somehow rolled over part of his body, pinning him and eventually suffocating him over a period of hours. What seemed like a tragic accident Clouse now firmly believed was the work of a devious stepson.

"I'm going to mingle for a bit, if you don't mind, dear?" he said as he turned to his wife.

"Go ahead. I'll catch up with you."

Clouse made the rounds, surprised at how many of his friends and employees knew one another. Of course the people invited to his abbreviated vacation were part of an elite group. No, not a specialized military faction, or the wealthy elite, but rather people who risked their lives in a most unusual way to save others and asked for nothing in return. Of course Clouse took care of these people like they were all family, including Russ Greene when his hospital bills began arriving in the mail.

He held brief conversations with a few people until he spied Tim Niemeyer leaving the atrium, presumably toward the lobby area. Clouse excused himself from Craig Jennings and his wife, quickening his pace to follow Niemeyer through the lobby. Clouse hadn't grabbed any outdoor gear, but Niemeyer brought a leather motorcycle jacket that he threw on before stepping outside to the brisk early December temperatures.

Niemeyer walked straight to the railing, leaning down upon the green metal as though fighting off a headache.

"You okay?" Clouse asked, startling his buddy who hadn't seen him trailing behind.

"Not bad. Just not used to drinkin' more than a beer every now and then. Wow, I'm startin' to feel kinda old."

Clouse noticed his friend had taken advantage of the open bar, ordering some spirits stronger than the typical draft beer. He remembered the times when Niemeyer and Ken Kaiser drank beers with him in the fields by the old farmhouse his parents owned, or down by Lake Monroe when they went camping. He didn't feel they were old just yet, but having marriage, children, and responsibilities matured them over the past twenty years.

The odor of wood burning in the distance reached Clouse's nostrils, briefly taking him back to the days when he battled blazes for a living. An unusually still air kept the smell lingering, allowing him to determine that someone was simply burning wood in a stove down the road. Even years removed from his old job Clouse knew the various smoky smells by heart and what caused them.

"I wanted to thank you," Clouse said as he turned around, basically sitting on the rail while he looked to his friend.

"For what?"

"Taking care of things at that site for me."

"You paid me, Paul. It was a job, and I appreciate it. Hell, if it wasn't for you, I would never have gotten back on my feet."

Clouse exhaled through his nose, letting some of his pent up emotion escape as he looked upward toward the veranda's ceiling with its Victorian light fixtures. He appreciated his friend's modesty a great deal, still feeling guilty because Niemeyer essentially lost years of his life while being used as a pawn against Clouse.

"If it wasn't for me, you wouldn't have gone through all of the hell you did for five years."

"You're forgetting the time I got thrown from the second floor inside your hotel," Niemeyer kidded, though the event was quite real and etched inside Clouse's mind.

Finally smiling, Clouse gave his friend a playful punch to the shoulder.

"I haven't forgotten anything you've done for me, Tim. I'm just glad you took care of things over there for me so I didn't have to call an outsider."

Niemeyer had filled in the chamber and the entire tunnel with dirt once Clouse completed the removal of the cubes and Jacob Savitch's body. It wasn't an easy task, requiring several days, even after the dirt was delivered in bulk. Clouse never strayed far from the area until the task was complete, allowing him some level of comfort that no one was going to find the evil altar again for quite some time.

He still owned the property, and planned to take steps for the near and distant future to ensure no one ever found a reason to dig into the ground again.

As for Savitch, Clouse buried him in the same plot where Martin Smith, his other major nemesis, remained six feet deep. Interred within a concrete mix that made certain his body couldn't simply rise again, Smith was visibly decayed when Clouse dug the hole for a look. He unceremoniously dumped Savitch's remains in with those of Smith, hoping they both burned in hell where they belonged.

"That place was creepy," Niemeyer admitted. "I always knew the stuff you were dealing with was evil, but that was downright satanic."

Clouse nodded, positive his friend didn't know the half of it. He patted his old high school chum on the back, thinking at their roots they were still the same country boys who rode tractors and put up hay during the summer. Maybe the values and beliefs instilled within them as kids created the men capable of confronting evil several times over and never wavering. Clouse hoped so, because he needed to draw from the strength of his friends and family going forward. Though he felt confident about the plan he and Julie Knowles were still in the process of finalizing, Clouse needed a little support and a lot of luck.

He leaned against the railing, much like his friend, staring out to the sunken garden on the hotel property that lacked color with winter fast approaching. In the spring it would bounce back as always, displaying colorful blooms from one end to the other, with the centralized fountain spraying water against sunny backdrops. Taking a deep breath, Clouse planned to see plenty more springs at his luxury hotel, hopefully with his friends at his side and lots of fond memories that didn't include cursed objects and unfriendly faces.

"You feeling good enough to head inside?" he asked Niemeyer, who no longer required the railing to steady himself.

"I reckon."

Putting an arm around his friend's shoulder, Clouse led him toward the lobby doors where just inside a skeleton crew waited to serve the private party during the few days.

"Maybe you should stick to pop," Clouse joked as he stepped inside, finally at peace with his grand resort after so much bloodshed occurred on the grounds.

"Maybe I should," Niemeyer grumbled heavily, as though his skull was already hurting from the alcohol.

Assured Niemeyer wasn't going to collapse, Clouse left him in the lobby when he saw Jane in the atrium looking for him. The kids were by her side, and Clouse finally felt at peace in the domed hotel. It wasn't the building's fault that so many terrible things had occurred over the past ten years. Every ounce of trouble was caused by greedy individuals who wanted money and power, but each of them was now dead and buried while Clouse carried on, fighting the good fight.

Although his son thought he was getting too old for affection, Clouse knelt down and gave Zach a tight hug that the boy halfheartedly resisted to no avail. When he stood, he put his arm around Jane, thankful for the gifts in his life and the opportunity to enjoy them a bit longer. He saw the people he cared about talking, eating, and in a few cases, dancing with spouses inside the atrium. Glad they were having fun, Clouse decided to join them, hoping to get some photos with many of them, and a group picture toward the end of the festivities. Soon he would return to his self-appointed job of saving the world, confident no immediate threats awaited him.

After that, he planned to take a well-deserved and long overdue vacation with the family.

**Continue reading for
character biographies and an
exclusive alternate ending**

Craig Jennings — The man in charge of Paul Clouse's security at the two grand hotels, Jennings gave up his old life for better pay, though his current position isn't routine by any means.

Chase Dalton — A United States Federal Marshal who assists the group after a narrow brush with death, Dalton is a close friend and former colleague of Russ Greene.

Matt Teakon — Nephew of Mark Teakon who begrudgingly takes over the daunting task of hunting down the cubes and keeping the world safe from the evildoers who would use them.

Dan Duncan — An already wealthy businessman entrusted to run the daily affairs at the West Baden Springs Hotel. Duncan's great-grandfather helped develop the Springs Valley where the hotel was built by helping bring the railroad to the area in the late 1800s.

Harlan Stone — An FBI agent who is fueled by a desire to do something more thrilling than solve white-collar crimes. Tempted by one of his superiors to carry out questionable deeds, he must choose to grasp the power within his reach or assist a group of seemingly good people he's never met.

Todd Parish — One of Paul Clouse's most loyal employees, Parish is entrusted with watching over the man's family when not assisting on dangerous missions to retrieve or dispose of cursed objects. There is probably no other employee Clouse trusts more than Parish, and because Parish is always highly respectful of his boss, Clouse occasionally seeks his advice in significant matters.

Russ Greene — A former United States Federal Marshal, Greene is recruited by Paul Clouse to take charge of the retrieval and disposal of the cursed cubes that have haunted the man. In essence, Greene is asked to protect the world, a challenge for any one person, but he discovers some useful resources around him.

Paul Clouse — Once a firefighter by trade, Clouse inherited millions from a benefactor and uses his wealth to keep the world safe from cursed objects and the people who would use them. After losing so many close friends, he's determined to see no one else harmed by standing idly by. His gravest challenge stands before him when an unknown entity begins collecting the very cubes he's worked so hard to conceal worldwide.

Jane Clouse — As the wife of Paul, she has stood by his side for years, constantly worried that he puts the family in peril by dealing with cursed objects. She understands, however, why he takes such risks and hopes for a day when she won't have to look over her shoulder. After giving up her medical practice, Jane realizes that even their riches cannot protect them from truly evil individuals.

Tim Niemeyer — The one remaining childhood friend of Paul Clouse, Niemeyer owns his own construction business and has literally lost years of his personal life due to standing up for his friend. When called upon one last time, Niemeyer assists Clouse, understanding the stakes from personal experience.

CHAPTER 55

By the time Clouse finished retrieving the cubes from the chamber he had already phoned Tim Niemeyer and requested his friend order plenty of dirt to fill in the entire tunnel and chamber area. Niemeyer owned some smaller equipment that could basically push the dirt almost as easily as snow. Though the job would require several days to a week, Clouse felt confident his friend would pack the dirt tightly to ensure the chamber wasn't found any time soon. For his part, Clouse planned to tear down the buildings above and create a community center or playground that was basically funded forever through one of his foundations. He didn't want anyone to ever have a reason for unearthing the terrain and discovering the bizarre sights below.

Ever loyal, Parish remained at the doorway and watched for any potential troublemakers or police. The bodyguard informed his employer that Clay Branson had returned for the body of his former mentor, located behind the abandoned apartment building. Clouse supposed that despite their differences, Branson planned some sort of ritualistic burial or cremation for Nosagi, rather than allowing the man's remains to become an unsolved John Doe in the morgue.

While he gathered the cubes, a dark thought entered his mind, and it wasn't the first time he thought about drastic measures when he plucked the time cube from the wall. Turning the dark blue cursed gem between his fingers and thumb, he contemplated what could have been as it glistened in the low light.

Had he never met Martin Smith or known about the cursed objects, Clouse knew his life would now be completely different. His first wife wouldn't be dead, he would be close to drawing a pension from the fire department in Bloomington, and he certainly wouldn't be estimated in the low billions by several financial magazines. While he could have lived with any of that, Clouse wondered about a life without Jane, or the chance to spend more time with his high school friends. He had done a lot of good since coming into millions of dollars, but the notion of changing things in the past didn't stem from his life alone.

Still holding the cube, he pondered how many hundreds, perhaps thousands of people died during the past century because of the cursed objects. He personally knew dozens of people who died because of the cubes, and plenty more who suffered after losing family members. Those people, along with the police, constantly questioned if he orchestrated some kind of evil scheme when their thoughts couldn't be further from the truth.

When he reached the doorway to the old basement after his last trip inside the chamber, Clouse barely noticed Parish because his mind continued to dwell upon an alternative.

"Sir, are you okay?" the bodyguard inquired, a puzzled look crossing his face.

"Just doing some thinking, Todd."

A strange odor crossed his nose, and Clouse remembered that he had set the remains of Jacob Savitch just inside the doorway until he was prepared to leave the site for the last time. A strange mix of charred flesh and the onset of decay, the smell emanated from a large canvas sack that Clouse retrieved from the hotel grounds. A sturdy, stable method of transporting heavy items for the grounds crew, he was able to procure the bag from a maintenance man who knew him by sight.

Clouse turned around to grab the bag before Parish could offer, simply throwing the strap around his shoulder and hoisting the bag out of the tunnel. He felt relieved that the entire thing was cleared and ready for Tim Niemeyer to seal off forever.

"Wish I could say I've never done this before," Clouse commented, looking toward the bag.

Parish forced a knowing grin, since Clouse had personally buried two men, and dealt with any number of dead patients during his fire department days.

Clouse loaded the bag into the back of his truck after trudging up the hill with its weight. He carried a leather satchel with him to transport the cubes. While they were grouped together in this instance, they weren't anywhere near the wall. They could shimmer all they wanted, but no one was going to spot them inside the bag, or after they reached their final destinations.

"Sir, do you need help with any of that?" Parish offered.

"Thanks, Todd, but no. I'll get it handled once I borrow a shovel from our grounds crew at the casino."

Parish nodded, standing by until his employer slid into the driver's seat and drove away from the scene after a brief wave.

***

By the time he finished digging six feet of dirt and replacing it, Clouse found his shirt drenched in sweat. He had borrowed a ladder and a shovel from the grounds, finding the tools adequate to dig the hole and climb out when necessary.

Even in the late morning hours he didn't expect anyone to discover his activities because the small cemetery where he laid Smith to rest was filled with corpses from the Civil War era and a few decades beyond. While it remained mowed and tended, the cemetery only received a handful of visitors each year. The grave markers were old and rigid mixtures of gray and black coloration, some crumbling along their edges to openly indicate their age. Off the beaten path, Clouse didn't expect company, and during the few hours he spent digging and refilling the already marked grave, he received none.

While the grave was indeed marked at the edge of the cemetery, it wasn't Martin Smith's official resting place. Clouse simply benefitted from a cruel trick Smith played on him the last time they met, filling in the plot with Smith's body burned and entombed beneath a concrete slab. Finding the slab in place, and one of Smith's partially deteriorated arms jutting partway above the top of the concrete, Clouse felt relieved when he dumped the bag containing Jacob Savitch's remains atop his other adversary.

"You two were made for one another," he commented before throwing the first scoop of dirt atop their corpses, anxious to finish his task in case someone did happen past the cemetery.

Replacing the dirt went much faster than the loosening and digging had, and when he finished, Clouse wiped his brow, instantly soaking his shirt-sleeve with perspiration. Considering he didn't have professional tools with him, the sod didn't look half bad after he laid it over the overturned dirt. Clouse wasted little time placing the shovel and stepladder in the back of his truck, prepared to leave when his cell phone rang.

He looked at the phone's face, realizing Parish was calling. Considering the bodyguard volunteered to travel to the hospital in Bloomington to provide updates on Greene's surgery, Clouse decided his departure from the cemetery could wait.

"Hello, Todd," he answered.

"Hello, sir," Parish replied, the tone in his voice indicating he wasn't bearing good news.

"What's wrong?"

"They had Russ on the table for almost two hours," Parish said slowly. "He didn't survive the surgery."

Clouse felt his heart sink and his legs rubberize beneath him. He couldn't find any appropriate words to reply, or any questions to ask as his back bumped against the bed of his truck and he slid down to the ground. In the back of his mind he knew Greene's death was a possibility, and a very likely possibility at that. He just couldn't believe after a day of such good fortune that his only casualty was the man who saved the entire world from destruction without one ounce of acknowledgement.

Taking in a few somber, deep breaths, Clouse felt the tremble within his chest each time he breathed.

"Sir?" Parish called across the phone. "Are you okay?"

Clouse numbly raised the phone to his ear while the wheels churned in the back of his mind. Instinctively, his thoughts returned to that dark place they traveled to earlier, contemplating how things might have been without Savitch, without Smith, and without any cursed cubes.

Ever.

He rubbed his head in frustration, on the verge of breaking down, whether he cried out loud or shouted something at the top of his lungs.

"Todd," he said, collecting himself long enough to speak a few words to his employee.

"Yes, sir?"

"I want you to make sure Liz gets home safely. Hail her a cab, or drive her yourself if there isn't anyone there for her."

"Yes, sir."

Looking to the blue sky, Clouse closed his eyes tightly, wishing he didn't always have to make the tough decisions. He had already reached an answer on the most important debate of his life, and though it affected numerous lives, he wanted to make a significant change.

"When you're done, please give me a call, Todd."

"Yes, sir."

***

Parish hadn't been allowed to see Greene after the unsuccessful operation, but the hospital staff bent their rules slightly for Liz, even though she wasn't family. Greene was survived by his parents and a sister who lived in Georgia, but none of them were able to make it to Indiana in time. After going through Greene's phone contact list, Liz made the painful calls to each of them, relaying the news that Greene was entering surgery, followed by what minimal updates she received until the end.

Basically inconsolable after hearing the news, followed by visitation with Greene's body, Liz had no one left to take her side. Her mother was on the other side of the country, having no idea what kind of dangerous work her daughter did on a daily basis. Aside from Greene, no one else in Clouse's stable spent much time with her, so Parish offered his shoulder and a few hugs when she emerged from the room where they placed Greene's body temporarily before transporting it to the morgue.

Considering she was heading back to the dome, not far from where Parish expected to meet his employer, Parish offered to drive her. The thirty minutes it took to drive from Bloomington to West Baden felt torturous to Parish because comforting words simply didn't exist and the silence filling his truck made him feel awkward. Liz seemed okay with no sound except the low volume of the FM radio station. Perhaps she was numbed by the death of her close colleague, because she said nothing except a weak thank you when she exited the truck beside the hotel.

Parish hung his head momentarily, feeling emotionally drained because he had lost a colleague in Greene, but also because he didn't realize the bond the former marshal shared with Liz. He watched her slowly make her way into the back entrance where the valet station was located, hoping Clouse checked on her later.

Realizing he was holding up business at the hotel, Parish drove to the parking lot further up the drive, behind the grand building. Only when he was safely parked did he pull his cell phone from the center console to call his employer.

"Clouse," his employer answered after one ring.

"Sir, I brought Liz back to the hotel."

"Are you still there?"

"Yes, sir."

Silence crossed the line momentarily as though something weighty preoccupied Clouse before he made his next statement.

"I'll be there in ten minutes. Meet me in our usual conference room.

"Yes, sir."

Parish decided to kill some time by walking to the coffee shop along the ground floor to purchase an overpriced latte, figuring he deserved to spoil himself after helping save the day. He didn't really feel like he had contributed as much as he wanted to, but he did save Clouse from legal ramifications once again. Sipping from the large brown cup, Parish walked along the ground floor of the hotel until he reached the steel door leading down to the basement that held nothing except conference rooms.

He walked to the door of the room where Clouse often held meetings for their group, startled to find his boss already seated in a chair, rather despondent with his elbows atop his knees and his hands cupping his face.

"Sir?" Parish asked, closing the door behind him, sensing the meeting was intended to be private between the two of them.

When Clouse finally looked up, his face was puffy and red, as though he might have been overcome by emotions once again. He didn't seem strong or self-assured, which worried Parish that something drastic plagued his employer.

"Have a seat, Todd," Clouse said, his voice full of defeat and deflation despite the overall success the morning brought him.

Parish said nothing, simply sliding into a nearby chair before setting his coffee atop the conference table.

"I've given a lot of thought to how much different the world could be if the cubes never existed."

Immediately, Parish knew which direction the conversation was taking, forcing him to contemplate his own morals versus his loyalty to Clouse. He still said nothing, wanting to hear his boss's take on the situation, knowing the boss had endured a great deal of stress the past year since the Bering Sea incident.

"So many people have died as a result of these cursed objects," Clouse said slowly, almost with a dark, distant tone in his voice. "People I know, people you know. I lost my best friend almost nine years ago when a scythe pierced his chest. I've seen a man doused in gasoline and set on fire, I've lost Mark Teakon twice, and my first wife was butchered in my own house, Todd. And that's just the beginning. So many senseless deaths, all because these *things* were created in my backyard."

Parish said nothing, because he instinctively knew Clouse hadn't made his point quite yet. He already felt certain the man was broken beyond repair, as though Greene's death was the decisive loss that pushed Clouse over the edge.

"It's not fair, Todd."

Parish nodded his head in agreement, still saying nothing.

"I mean what I want to do isn't fair. To you."

Parish stiffened, beginning to wonder if his employer might have lost his mind, intending to bring harm to his most faithful employee.

"Sir?"

Clouse sat momentarily without saying a word, simply breathing in and out through his nostrils with an eerie calm.

"I want to set things right," he finally said without looking at Parish. "And by that I mean I want to change events in the past. Doing so is unfair to you because everything you've done for me would be erased, including the life you've made for yourself."

Parish considered his life one of stability, nobility, and occasionally honor. Ultimately he felt no regret for his actions, even when he found it necessary to take a life. If money had been his primary motivation, Parish wouldn't have been the kind of person Clouse sought to protect his family.

"Sir, *that* I could live with, but I'm worried about you. My life would be pretty dull if you hadn't hired me."

"What I'm talking about is a rather radical plan, Todd, and it's also the other reason I feel like I'm being unfair to you."

Parish swallowed hard, unsure of where the discussion was leading.

"I want you to go back in time and prevent the cubes from ever being cursed in that chamber."

Unsure of how to process such an extreme plan, Parish wasn't prepared for the more unthinkable half of Clouse's master plan.

"Sir, that goes against everything you've ever believed in," he decided to argue, finding Clouse shaking his head because his mind was made up.

"That's not all of it, Todd. Because I don't want anyone else hurt in all of this, I want you to kill me and use the time cube. If you're willing, that is."

Parish couldn't believe the words entering his ears, feeling a slight tremble throughout his body as his mind and muscles betrayed him. Like his employer, Parish maintained religious convictions that included not killing people and certainly not using cursed objects. He sat momentarily, unsure of how to answer the request, hoping deep down his boss was testing him, but already knowing that wasn't the case. Paul Clouse never kidded when talking about business related to the cursed objects.

Abhorred by the thought of harming his boss, much less murdering him, Parish knew he couldn't possibly say yes to this absurd proposition.

"Sir, I couldn't."

"It has to be you, Todd," Clouse said, finally coming out of his mental haze. "I can't trust anyone else."

"I'd even be willing to let you take my life and set it right, sir," Parish volunteered, still not certain he meant the words.

He counted on Clouse to refuse his counterproposal either way.

"I'm not that good with guns, Todd," Clouse replied slowly and truthfully. "And you know how to work with explosives."

"Only because I worked demolition with my uncle for six months, sir. What you're proposing is just immoral on so many levels."

"I've considered that," Clouse said, rubbing the sides of his face a few times with his palms. "And though I'm not sure two wrongs make a right, I feel that carrying out this plan will erase any wrongdoings we commit in the end."

"And what if your opinion isn't shared by a higher power?" Parish asked, finally taking a stand because he vehemently opposed the plan. "What if we've reached the end and all of this is really over? I have to believe we as human beings are meant to play the cards we're dealt."

Clouse gave him an unmoving stare that stated he believed otherwise.

"And what if that deck is stacked against mankind?"

Parish knew what he stood to lose and gain if his life reverted back to the path his destiny was originally meant to follow. So many questions ran through his mind, but he didn't see a way he could be swayed to his employer's line of thinking. He understood how much more the man had lost over his lifetime, but Parish couldn't fathom why Clouse suddenly wanted to carry out such an extreme plan.

"Is this because of Russ?" he dared ask.

"This is because of everything," Clouse replied bitterly.

"If we did this, neither of us would be around to see the results, if anything really did change. For all we know, going back in time could create some alternate universe and none of this would ever change."

Clouse buried his head in his hands momentarily, and Parish hoped he might be reconsidering his logic.

"Todd, take an hour or two to think about it while you get what weaponry and explosives you think you would need to successfully eliminate the problem in 1918. I want you to meet me inside the chamber when you're ready. I'll bring the appropriate cube."

Parish started to say something in protest, but Clouse held up a foreboding finger.

"I can't make you do this, Todd. I'm just asking you to meet me once you've gathered those items."

Feeling as though his hands were tied, Parish felt caught between a rock and a hard place. He didn't want to shoot the man who signed his checks because so many things could go wrong with the promised gift from the time cube. Parish knew about the story of a cop going back in time to see his father's death and how simple the process sounded, but he wasn't sure he believed the journal entry. On the other hand, if he didn't carry out his boss's wishes, Clouse might dismiss him from the payroll and carry out his plan some other way. If that happened, and the man Clouse asked to execute him, and his plan, didn't have a straight moral compass, time could forever be altered for the worse.

"I'll see you in about an hour," Parish decided aloud, grabbing his lukewarm cup of coffee before heading for the door.

***

While gathering some of his firearms at the house, Parish's emotions ranged from mental detachment to anger toward his employer. The most difficult part of his brief trip home was basically ignoring his wife and two children. Still uncertain about whether or not he could carry out Clouse's request, he didn't want to say any final goodbye to them. He remained incredibly skeptical about the cube even working, so killing his employer didn't seem like a wise move from that aspect.

Even on the drive to the property where the chamber still remained blocked off, but not yet filled in by Niemeyer, Parish nearly hit a vehicle from behind. The driver ahead of him suddenly applied his brakes for construction, and Parish, still in a mental fog, barely noticed the brake lights in time to stop.

Parish felt as though his life was flashing before him and he was powerless to stop what came next. He wanted to believe he had a choice in the matter, but the circumstances surrounding him said differently.

He pulled into the parking lot of the old apartment building, still undecided as he removed two large duffel bags from the back of his truck. Clouse's truck was parked closer to the entrance, so Parish decided not to waste time. He made his way down the sloped dirt, hoping to talk his employer out of such a risky move.

On the other hand, Parish had spent a little time contemplating what he would do if he traveled back in time. If that happened, he needed to ensure none of the thirteen men survived, and he questioned whether the lawyer could be allowed to live. He supposed the jeweler knew the men were up to no good, but he never knew the extent of their sinister plan until he saw the aftermath. If that was the case, his lawyer friend surely didn't know what kind of ritual he was about to witness until his untimely death.

Making his way through the dark tunnel, which Clouse didn't bother to light in any way, Parish took a small flashlight from one of the bags to guide him until the orange pulse became visible. Parish stopped short of the chamber entrance, taking a deep breath because he still didn't know if Clouse was using better judgment at this point.

When he finally stepped inside, he found Clouse pacing the floor, staring at the pulsating light along the opposite wall. The irony that a giant clock took up most of the glowing wall wasn't lost on Parish, who didn't particularly want to step back in time.

Upon seeing the bodyguard of his children, Clouse tossed him the navy blue cube, which Parish snatched from the air.

"Guess this means you haven't changed your mind, sir?"

"No. Maybe we should get this over with."

Clouse seemed impatient about the process, especially since he was usually very analytical about such important decisions.

Still, Parish wasn't going to simply execute his own boss without speaking his peace first.

"Sir, I think you're playing God. We aren't meant to alter events in the past or future."

"Then why did God allow these thirteen abominations to be created?"

Parish simply shook his head negatively, seeing that Clouse wasn't going to be swayed easily. He had obviously thought out both sides to his own argument more so than Parish originally believed.

Unzipping the first of the duffel bags, Parish pulled out a few semiautomatic pistols, along with a fully automatic MP5. He still wanted Clouse to change his mind, almost robotically going through the motions of carrying out the plan.

"Sir, you're going off one document," he argued. "*One* document that supposedly says what this cube does."

"We verified it three ways until Sunday, Todd."

Parish unzipped the second bag, pulling out a bomb vest he crudely constructed from leftover explosives and an armored vest. If Parish truly went back in time, he didn't want any trace of anything left in the chamber. He certainly didn't want a second version of himself running around for decades, possibly changing the timeline immeasurably.

"If this doesn't work, sir, you'd be leaving behind a lot of unfinished business," Parish added, continuing to unpack the bags just the same.

Now Clouse gave him a cagy smile, understanding that his employee really didn't want to carry through with the plan.

"It's going to work, Todd. And there's nothing here that couldn't be accomplished if I were to suddenly disappear or die. My wife, son, and step-daughter would mourn me and live fairly good lives after that."

"You'd leave Zach without a mother or a father?"

Now his employer's expression turned much more serious.

"That's not fair, Todd."

"And neither is putting the fate of the world on my shoulders, sir," Parish said, absolutely exasperated. "I don't want my life to change, and I certainly don't want to hurt you."

"You have to, Todd. This, this bullshit we go through on a daily basis won't stop for us. And the best we can hope for is to leave our successors a better scenario. But eventually they'd let their guard down and some asshole would bring all thirteen of those things here again. I want a life where I can kick back and enjoy myself once in a while, Todd. Even if I have to work for a living again, and even if my first marriage ends in divorce, the way it was heading, I don't give a shit. *Anything* is better than looking over my shoulder every day of my life."

Parish worried that he might carry out the deed and be stuck as a casual observer in 1918, unable to make any difference at all. Still, if he did as Clouse asked, and succeeded, all of his sins would be hypothetically erased. Parish had only killed men in self-defense or the defense of others, but even that blood would never spill in the new reality.

Looking at his hands, he realized everything he needed was already out of the duffel bags and ready for action. He slipped on the vest, still unsure of whether he really wanted to give up on his present life.

"If you don't do this, Todd, I'll get someone else I don't trust as much," Clouse admitted.

"No pressure there, sir."

Clouse tried to force a grin, but it just didn't come. Parish looked to the pistol in his right hand, feeling the weight of the world on his shoulders. For the first time since meeting his employer, he wasn't sure he truly liked the man as he ran short of reasons not to pull the trigger.

"Do it, Todd," Clouse said with an even tone, still refusing to be forceful under such dire circumstances.

"Goddamn you, sir," Parish muttered as he raised the gun and pulled the trigger in a flash, seeing blood spatter from his employer's forehead as he turned away immediately.

Fighting back his emotions, Parish holstered the sidearm, pulling the blue cube from a small pouch inside the vest as he tried to avoid looking at the man he just killed. Had it been justified, or some kind of mercy killing, Parish might have felt far less regret, but ordered to or not, he had just murdered the man who signed his paychecks. If he failed in any way, or did nothing at all with the cube, he couldn't possibly face Clouse's widow and two children again.

He approached the body, still unwilling to look at the damage he caused until he had to locate some blood to satisfy the cube. Feeling convulsed after simply seeing a glimpse from the corner of his eye, Parish found his boss's eyes wide-open, blood ebbing slowly from his forehead. He clutched his stomach to keep from vomiting, taking the cube and rubbing it against the fresh pool of blood atop the man's body, knowing what to do as though internally directed.

Knowing the cube wanted him to use it, he doubted it maintained anything above primal instinct, certainly unaware that he meant to end its existence.

Daring not take even an extra second to collect his thoughts and emotions, Parish focused on where he wanted to be and exactly when while clutching the cube.

And suddenly he was there.

Though the cube didn't travel back with him, Parish found himself at the entrance of the chamber, immediately after the last of the thirteen conspirators filed inside. Everything from the lights to the dirt walls appeared fresh, and no musty smell accompanied the tunnel this time. Still armed with everything he carried when he shot his employer, Parish stepped forward, finding all eyes turn his way when he entered the chamber. Thirteen wealthy men and one individual chained to the metal spokes Parish removed when he modified the chamber in the future all looked to him with shock and awe.

Based on the way he was dressed, Parish imagined he looked almost alien to them.

Deciding not to waste any time in case the wealthy men brought backup with them, Parish fired off some shots from the MP5, startling the conspirators who had certainly never seen the likes of such a sleek weapon. Feeling determined to see Clouse's plan through, Parish hoped all of the wrongs he carried out within a five-minute span made one impactful right.

"Everyone get back!" he shouted, drawing an immediate response from the openly nervous men.

As they backed toward the wall, which did not glow an eerie orange with a functional clock, Parish approached the man chained to the metal spoke. One of the men stepped forward with his palms open, as though he wanted to speak and negotiate with the gunman who dared interrupt their ceremony. Parish pointed the MP5 deliberately at the man's chest and fired, drawing a stunned look from the man as numerous bullets entered his chest within a second's time. He slumped to the ground, prompting his fellow conspirators to take a defensive step backwards with panicked utterances.

Redirecting his attention to the man helplessly tethered to the metal centerpiece's extension, Parish aimed the MP5 at the chain, firing the weapon to snap one of the links. He helped the lawyer to his feet, grasping the man's forearm before allowing him to leave.

"Tell no one what you've seen here, or what happened," Parish ordered him sternly. "Even your friend the jeweler."

Saying nothing, the man nodded nervously, sweat already dripping profusely from his forehead. He darted toward the tunnel, taking his leave before the man with all of the unusual weapons changed his mind.

Parish returned his gaze to the dozen surviving conspirators, knowing they wished they'd never entered into such a sinister plan. He wanted to tell them how much pain they were destined to cause, how many lives they ruined, and how their selfishness nearly destroyed mankind. If he were so inclined, Parish might have told them about the man who fought to undo all of the chaos these conspirators caused, and how his spirit was ultimately crushed.

In the end, Parish wasn't a man of many words, so he reached into his vest and pulled out the small detonator that activated the explosives lining the black vest. Knowing what amount worked the first time around, Parish had matched the weight of the plastic explosives, hoping to obliterate every-thing inside the chamber.

He removed the safety cap from the small device, looked to the twelve trembling men before him, and flipped the first of the two switches. Knowing his life in the future was going to take a different course, it was too late now for anything except setting things right and carrying out Clouse's plan.

"Goodbye, gentlemen," he said before hitting the second switch with his thumb.

9 781604 146653